Crossing Colfax

Short Stories

By Rocky Mountain Fiction Writers

Copyright © 2014 RMFW Press
Crossing Colfax: Short Stories by Rocky Mountain Fiction Writers

ISBN-10: 0976022532
ISBN-13: 978-0-9760225-3-4

Seven Seconds © 2014 Angie Hodapp
Hay Hook © 2014 Margaret Mizushima
A Full Moon over a Desolate Plain © 2014 Cynthia Hutcheson
Crossing the Uncanny Valley © 2014 Martha Husain
Colfax, PI © 2014 Kate Lansing
The Man in the Corner © 2014 Z. J. Czupor
Allyah © 2014 Rebecca Rowley
The Case of the Woman Who Sewed Her Silence © 2014 B. K. Winstead
Stolen Legacy © 2014 Zach Milan
That's Love Baby © 2014 L. D. Silver
Colfax Kitsune © 2014 Emily Singer
Phantom Brew © 2014 Laura Kjosen
Take Me to Your Leader, Jackie Smack © 2014 Warren Hammond
Ghostly Attraction © 2014 Tracy Brisendine
Charlie's Point of View © 2014 Linda Berry

All rights reserved. No part of this book may be reproduced or transmitted in any form or by any means, electronic or mechanical, including photocopy, recording, or any information storage and retrieval system, without permission in writing from the author or his/her agent, except by a reviewer who may quote brief passages in a critical article or review to be printed in a magazine or newspaper, or electronically transmitted on radio or television.

All persons, places and organizations in this book except those clearly in the public domain are fictitious, and any resemblance that may seem to exist to actual persons, places, events or organizations living, dead, or defunct, is purely coincidental. These are works of fiction.

RMFW Press
P.O. Box 545
Englewood, CO 80151
www.rmfw.org

Cover and Interior Design by Scott Baird
Printed in the United States of America

Table of Contents

Introduction 7

Seven Seconds 11
By Angie Hodapp

Hay Hook 49
By Margaret Mizushima

A Full Moon Over a Desolate Plain 77
By Thea Hutcheson

Crossing the Uncanny Valley 93
By Martha Husain

Colfax, PI 151
By Kate Lansing

The Man in the Corner 169
By Zoltan James

Allyah 189
By Rebecca Rowley

The Case of the Woman Who Sewed Her Silence 197
By B. K. Winstead

Stolen Legacy 227
By Zach Milan

That's Love, Baby 247
By L. D. Silver

Colfax Kitsune 259
By Emily Singer

Phantom Brew 281
By Laura Kjosen

Take Me to Your Leader, Jackie Smack 309
By Warren Hammond

Ghostly Attraction 321
By TJ Valour

Charlie's Point of View 365
By Linda Berry

About Rocky Mountain Fiction Writers 372

Crossing Colfax

Short Stories

By Rocky Mountain Fiction Writers

Introduction
By Nikki Baird
RMFW Anthology Chair

Another editor of anthologies once called his work a labor of love, and I can relate. As an author, my genre is speculative fiction—science fiction, fantasy, paranormal. Short stories have long been the wellspring of talent in that genre, and I have my share of back issues of *Fantasy & Science Fiction*, *Analog*, and *Writers of the Future* anthologies. But like everything about fiction these days, from writing it, to selling it, to publishing it, something new and different is happening to short stories.

Perhaps it's the rise of "content snacking" as people sneak in entertainment while standing in line at the grocery store or waiting in the doctor's office. Perhaps it's a reaction to the Wild West of publishing where authors are going direct to those readers who feel like they need a sample before they dedicate their precious leisure time to the commitment it takes to read a novel in these time-starved times. Whatever it is, it's been good news for short stories. No longer relegated to one corner of commercial genre fiction, short stories are coming back into their own.

My first taste of publication came through the opportunity presented by Rocky Mountain Fiction Writers in our 2009 anthology, *Broken Links, Mended Lives*. When that effort concluded, the editors of that anthology were understandably

Introduction

ready to pass the torch, and alas, there was no one there to take it up. I waited on the sidelines, searching the newsletter eagerly for the announcement that there was a new anthology and it was accepting submissions.

No one did! And then that moment came. The one where I realized that the person I was waiting around for, the one who was going to take on the next anthology, was me. And thus my own labor of love began.

Rocky Mountain Fiction Writers is an organization dedicated to growing and nurturing fiction writers. I've directly benefited from that mission on my own journey towards mastering the writing craft. But I found that the education doesn't stop there. In the current world of genre fiction, an author must not only write well, she must master editing and marketing and graphic design and social media and…you get the picture. So my contribution to this anthology is not as author, but as editor. It's been a very rewarding experience, one that has already helped me grow as a writer, and I'm very grateful for the opportunity.

But I didn't do it alone. So before we get to the good stuff, I have to first acknowledge the efforts of my Anthology committee. From selection, to short story training, to editorial and publication advice, these people played key roles in bringing you some of the best that RMFW talent has to offer. RMFW's board has been very supportive, but I must also give special thanks to Tracy Brisendine, Sean Curley, Lori DeBoer, Sandra Edwards, Chris Ficco, Angie Hodapp, Wendy Howard, Jack Huber, Barb Smith, and Brian Winstead. Special thanks to Susan Spann for her help with the legal stuff, and to Rocky Mountain Fiction Writers' board of directors for their help and support.

Introduction

So what is it, exactly, that you hold in your hands (or have open on your electronic device)? We had four options to choose from for anthology themes, but Crossing Colfax was pretty much the winner straight out of the gate. There's just so much to work with—Colfax Avenue, like Route 66, has a very storied history. We worried for a short time that maybe Colfax was too specific to Denver, but that worry was quickly dismissed. While St. Louis may claim to be the Gateway to the West, Denver pretty much embodies it. And Colfax is a state of mind, one that celebrates the strange, the desperate, the ambitious and the survivors.

Our authors grabbed hold of these themes, and their efforts do not disappoint. Their inspirations are as varied as their stories. Even more exciting, while some of our authors are already in print, there are others that are seeing their name on the page for the very first time. You can say you found them first.

Within these pages you'll find the supernatural, the noir, the supernatural noir, thrillers, romance, and even the science fiction dystopian future. Veterinarians, vampires, anachronists, police detectives, prostitutes, grad students, ex-cops and junkies. You'll find them all on Colfax.

And I can't wait for you to meet them.

Nikki Baird
August 2014

Seven Seconds
By Angie Hodapp

Angie's inspiration for "Seven Seconds" centered on heroes:

It seems that every time we blink, a new comics-inspired superhero movie premieres. That got me thinking: How about a superhero whose power isn't so super and who isn't much of a hero? What would his story be? Could I still make him strong and likable and heroic not because of his power but despite it?

I live on Colfax near "Greek Town," a row of old restaurants, bars, diners, and bakeries east of Denver's Capitol Hill neighborhood. Since my main character's not-so-super power was granted by the gods of Greek mythology, and since he's a rough-around-the-edges type of guy, Colfax was easily the perfect setting for his story.

Seven Seconds

I saved Kyra's life on a cold night in April.

It was the kind of night, bitter and unexpected, that makes the weather guys on TV shrug like they're apologizing. The kind of night that turns people sullen, because after a month of blue Colorado skies and warm, outdoorsy days, they feel cheated. It was the kind of night that reminds you death is in charge.

That night, I closed up the garage around nine-thirty or so and drove down Colfax to O'Hoolihan's. I'd spent a long day in the pit. I was filthy. I smelled like engine grease and motor oil. I needed a beer. And I wasn't much in the mood for loud music or chitchat.

I parked in the alley. Elliot O'Hoolihan's old pickup wasn't in its usual spot. Most likely, that meant the old guy had checked himself into the hospital again.

I shook my head. Damn shame, Elliot wasting all that time pretending to be sick.

Turning up my collar, I jogged toward the back door and let myself in. Which O'Hoolihan, I wondered, would be covering for Elliot behind the bar?

I had my hopes. Kyra O'Hoolihan, Elliot's niece, made for great company. I'd known her since we were kids. She used to be all knees and elbows and stringy hair and glasses. But at some point after high school, she went and turned into a stone-cold fox. Real top-shelf material. Plus, she was smart as hell and incredibly cool.

Despite my hopes, I wasn't really expecting her to be there. She'd landed a day job as a clerk at some fancy LoDo law firm. Now she was talking about applying to law school. She was busy. Going places.

As it turned out, this was my lucky night. Kyra was there, stocking bottles behind the bar. She looked over her shoulder when she heard the back door open and close.

"Billy Shump!" she called out. "Where you been all my life?"

I grinned. "Been right here in front of you this whole time, Knockout. You just haven't been looking." I'd been calling her Knockout since back in junior high, because her initials were K. O. Now that she was all grown up, the nickname was appropriate for entirely different reasons.

Heading toward the U-shaped bar, I noticed a middle-aged couple I'd never seen before sitting in the last booth. The booth was high-backed and private, and these two were leaning in so close their foreheads almost touched. They startled when I passed. Their fingers disentangled. Hands slid over wedding rings and disappeared beneath the table.

It didn't take a genius to figure those wedding rings weren't a matching set.

All the middle booths were empty, but the one up front was propping up Jake Renfro. He was already cheek-to-tabletop. Bristly white hair sprouted from his ear like albino moss. Empty beer bottles ringed his head like toadstools. Rip Van Renfro.

I slid onto a stool opposite a couple guys I recognized from Sam's Auto Body. We threw chins at each other, but no one smiled. They sat hunched over at least a dozen dead soldiers.

Seven Seconds

The cheaters in the back. Jake Renfro. Sam's boys. Me. Six patrons in a Colfax bar on a Thursday night. I sighed. The future of O'Hoolihan's wasn't looking too bright.

Of course, the bar's gone-to-pot ambience didn't help. Dusty bottles, sticky floors, curse words carved into tabletops. Half the fixtures needed new bulbs, and that piss smell from the restrooms had started to drift. If Elliot ever died—ever good and truly died instead of just pretending—this bar would die with him.

"Give me a sec," Kyra said. She disappeared through the double doors into the storeroom. A moment later, she reappeared, lugging a crate of Bushmills. The bottles clanked and rattled and bumped against her thighs with every step.

The crate was heavy. Anyone looking could see it. I should have offered to help. But when she hoisted that crate up onto the counter, she arched her back and really threw her hips into it. The crate knocked a stack of coasters off the counter, which Kyra bent over to pick up. Her perfectly rounded backside was tucked into a pair of super-tight low-rise jeans.

All me and those boys from Sam's Auto Body could do was gawk.

I couldn't help myself. I had to see that again.

As far as supernatural abilities go, being able to turn back time should have been pretty cool. But seven seconds was all I could ever manage. My dad, gods rest his soul, could do twenty-six seconds, and grandpa could do a minute four. For better or worse, the anachronist gene was dying out. If I ever had a son, chances were he'd be born without it.

But right then, sitting on that barstool and watching Kyra,

seven seconds was all I needed. I took hold of the Clock and spun it back.

Everything snapped back to the way it was seven seconds before. Kyra did the hip thing again, her long black ponytail swishing across her back. Again, she bent over to pick up those coasters.

The girl was poetry.

The Clock snapped back as soon as my seven seconds were up. Kyra shoved the crate to the back of the counter. She whirled around and narrowed her eyes at me.

If I didn't know better, I would have thought she felt it. The time snap. The weird shudder that ripples through the fabric of space-time whenever an anachronist messes with the Clock.

But I did know better. No one feels the time snap but the one who causes it. Well, him plus any other anachronists who might be hanging around, and Jake Renfro was out cold.

I reached into a bowl of peanuts and popped a couple in my mouth. "What's up, Kyra?"

She cocked her head a little, looked amused. Then she shrugged and wiped her hands on her jeans. "Bud Light?"

I nodded. She flipped my pint glass in the air, and then angled it under the tap. I admired the way she moved. Sam's boys were admiring it too. The burly one elbowed the skinny one, then clunked his bottle on the bar.

"Another round?" Kyra glanced at them only long enough to catch the burly one's nod. She turned back to topping off my glass, and her hair did that swishy shampoo-commercial thing again. This time I let the Clock keep ticking.

Instead I focused on pushing back the sudden urge I had to knock those Sam's boys off their stools. It wasn't like Kyra was my girl or anything. But I couldn't help but feel a little possessive.

She flicked a coaster at me. It slid across the bar and spun in place until she thunked my beer down on top of it. Poetry. Then she back stepped to the fridge and pried the caps off a couple bottles of whatever those Sam's boys were drinking.

"You still servicing trucks over at Fesker's Garage?" she asked me.

"Yep. You still planning on law school?"

"Maybe."

"What's with maybe?"

She delivered the bottles, then came back and leaned on her elbows across from me. "It's not a good time for my family right now. Uncle Elliot's in the hospital again."

"Figured that. What is it this time?"

"Cancer of the nose. He keeps picking it, it keeps bleeding. He's convinced there's a tumor up there."

I didn't bother laughing. Elliot had thought up a hundred more interesting ways to be dying.

"Between you and me," Kyra said, "this place is on its last leg. The emergency room isn't cheap."

"Yeah, but you are." I scooped another handful of peanuts.

Kyra knocked them out of my hand. "Screw you," she said, blue eyes flashing.

I was a little shocked by that, until I realized how what I said must have sounded. "No, I didn't mean it like that. I mean, you keep working for him for free, and what's to stop him from calling you in here whenever he's sick? Law school's what you want. When are you ever going to have a life of your own?"

She relaxed a bit after I explained. Then she shrugged. "We're family. It's what families do."

I was about to point out that I didn't see any other O'Hoolihans behind the bar, but just then the front door slammed open. A cold, damp chill swept in, bringing with it one pissed-off-looking dude.

"Sherry, where you at? I know you and him are in here. Come on out now, both of you."

I saw the gun in his hand a beat before Sam's boys did. They stumbled off their stools. The burly one threw himself to the floor and out of range. The skinny one flattened himself against the wall and froze.

The woman in the back booth stood up and turned to face the man with the gun. "Dammit, Chuck," she said. "What the hell?" Hands on hips, she looked ready to do battle. Then she saw the gun.

Kyra tensed and reached beneath the bar for Elliot's shotgun. I grabbed her wrist and shook my head. Seeing another gun in the room could set this guy off.

"Chuck, you put that thing down." Sherry's voice quavered. "You hear me? Don't be a jerk. Why do you always have to be such a jerk?"

I didn't know Sherry, but I wanted to shake some sense into her. Insulting the guy with the gun? Not smart.

"Where is he, Sherry? Is he back there with you?" Chuck raised the gun and took shaky aim. "Is he back there hiding in that booth like a coward?"

I hoped Sherry's boyfriend had enough sense to stay crouched down in that booth. If he came out, things could get ugly.

Sherry spread her arms wide and backed up a step, like she

planned to shield her boyfriend when the bullets started flying.

I had to hand it to her. Sherry had guts. I just didn't want to see them splattered on the floor, painting the place red.

"Get away from there." Chuck wagged the gun side to side, waving Sherry out of the way. He was on the move now, closing in on his target. "I'm going to put a hole in his head. Swear to God, Sherry. This is the last time you make a fool of me."

The metallic tang of adrenaline soured my tongue. This whole situation was going south in a hurry.

Kyra stepped out from behind the bar. "Sir, I'm going to have to ask you to leave." She sounded polite but very much in charge. "I've got enough mopping to do tonight without you adding to the mess."

My gut clenched. What the hell was Kyra doing?

Chuck's eyes slid over to Kyra. Where his eyes went, his gun went too. Kyra tensed.

"You think I'm messing around here?" Chuck's voice rose to a near-hysterical pitch. "You think I won't do it?"

"Oh, I'm certain you will," Kyra said. "It's just that I'm asking you not to, and I'm asking nicely."

Things were about to calm down. Anyone looking could see it. But Sherry's boyfriend chose that moment to launch himself out of the booth and come charging toward Chuck like a cat with its tail on fire.

Chuck startled. He stumbled backwards, arms flailing. The gun went off. Kyra slumped to the floor, clutching at her belly. The floor beneath her turned red.

My ears rang. The room tilted all around me like a state-fair funhouse. Sherry screamed.

Not Kyra, though. Kyra was quiet as church on Sunday.

My heart felt like it was pumping nails. I knew what I had to do, but I was scared witless. With every ounce of courage I could muster, I grabbed the Clock and spun it back.

I had seven seconds to save Kyra's life.

#

"Get away from there." Chuck was waving the gun at Sherry again, telling her to move.

I froze the Clock.

Freezing the Clock takes a heck of a lot more out of me than just letting my seven seconds tick on by in repeat mode. But I figured I needed that time to myself. To do whatever it was I was going to do.

What the heck was I going to do?

I flew off my stool and dashed toward Chuck. A quick glance at Kyra showed me she was suspended mid-stride, already on her way to make her date with that bullet. For the next seven— no, six—seconds, though, she'd stay put.

I tried to snatch the gun away, but Chuck's fingers were fixed tight on the grip. A chill shot through me. The temporary rigor mortis thing was a problem. I clawed at his hand with both of mine, scrambling to loosen his hold. I even drew blood.

His fingers wouldn't budge.

The chill in my veins turned to white-hot panic. Hell, I was only going to get one shot at this.

One shot or *get* shot.

I grabbed the muzzle and pried the gun upward. Nothing. Again. Nothing. Three more seconds ticked by. My vision blurred. Everything around me distorted, like I was seeing through warped glass. I blinked and wrenched at the gun one last time, this time as hard as I could.

Bones snapped. I was pretty sure I'd broken at least two of Chuck's fingers. His grip loosened. My throat let out a weird squeaky wheeze, some cross of exasperation, terror, and relief. I flicked the safety on and tossed the gun. It slid across the bar and hit the floor.

"What the—?" Chuck stumbled back a step, his crooked fingers curled around the dead space where the gun should have been.

I almost felt bad for him. Not only because of his hand, but because I imagine it's pretty unsettling to have a big dude like me just appear out of nowhere right in front of you. Then I remembered that this guy just shot Kyra.

Well, not anymore, he hadn't.

"Out. Now." I took Chuck by the shoulders and spun him around. Best to get him moving while his brain was still making sense of the time snap.

Pushing a disoriented Chuck toward the door, I glanced back at the others. Sherry and her boyfriend looked dazed, like someone had just snapped their picture with a bright flash.

Kyra was staring at me, head cocked and eyes narrowed. Like before. Suspicious. But alive.

Very much alive.

#

I called in sick the next day. Told my boss I had the flu, but what I really had felt more like a hangover. Freezing the Clock like that? It takes time for your brain to stop throbbing.

My cell phone jarred me awake around eleven that morning.

The ringtone, Cher's "If I Could Turn Back Time," threatened to jangle the fillings out of my molars.

I hated that song. But the jarring part was, not only had I never programmed my phone to play it, but the damn thing was off.

Dread churned my stomach. Only one person I knew could be calling me on a dead phone.

I batted around on the nightstand until I found the phone. Then I answered it. "Hello, Chronos." My voice came out in a croak. Not exactly the best way to greet one of the pantheon. "To what do I owe the pleasure?"

"Billy Shump! Half expected you wouldn't answer. Your head must feel like it's stuck in a meat grinder."

Chronos sounded downright cheerful, but his mention of my current state told me he knew what had happened at O'Hoolihan's the night before.

"That's about right," I replied warily. "Can I call you back in a few hours? I really don't feel—"

"Awww." He clicked his tongue in sympathy. "You feel like garbage, don't you? Like vomit. Like a steaming pile of sheep guts. Well, Billy, I've got to be honest." He paused. "Freezing my Clock will do that to you."

His voice carried a chill that goose-bumped my arms. The old guy had my attention. I sat up, swinging my legs over the edge of the bed. Was he angry? I raked my aching brain. I'd frozen the Clock before. Plenty of times. What was different about this time that caught his notice?

Oh, God. I pressed the heel of my hand against my temple. *Kyra.* I'd saved her life. I'd used the Clock to alter fate.

"Is she okay?" I asked.

Seven Seconds

"Who?"

I didn't answer. Chronos was playing games.

After another beat, he said, "Oh, your friend from the bar? What did you say her name was? Karla? Carrie?"

I gritted my teeth. "Kyra."

"Kyra. That's it. How is she, you ask? She's fine." Another pause. "For now."

My fingers tightened around the phone. "What do you want, Chronos?"

"Breakfast." His tone was cheerful again. "Meet me at Pete's Kitchen. Let me buy you a gyro omelet."

Saliva flooded my mouth. Not because I was hungry but because the thought of eating made me want to puke. Worry over Kyra compounded my Clock-freezing hangover.

"Give me half an hour," I said, already grabbing a pair of jeans off the floor.

"Ten minutes," Chronos replied. "Starting now."

#

I wasn't surprised Chronos wanted to meet at Pete's Kitchen. Whenever he or any of the other gods came to town, they usually ate at the restaurants owned by Pete Contos. Pete was a good Greek boy who'd been running restaurants on Denver's Colfax Avenue for decades. All the gyros, mousaka, and souvlaki must've made the pantheon nostalgic for the old country.

Sentimentality aside, Pete's Kitchen had the best diner grub in town. Cheap too. Normally, I'd have been looking forward to one of their breakfast burritos or a plate of biscuits and gravy. But my head was still giving my gastrointestinal system the red light.

I hustled down the four blocks between my apartment and

Pete's, which sat on the corner of Colfax and Race. The day was cold and gray, like the day before. A frigid wind blew through my clothes.

I got to Pete's, and right away I saw Chronos at the far end of the counter. He sat sideways on his stool, his white ZZ-Top beard cascading down the front of a shiny purple Colorado Rockies jacket. He was facing the door. Watching for me. Probably counting down the seconds until he could dole out some punishment for my lateness.

But without looking at anyone's watch, I knew I'd made it with twelve seconds to spare.

Chronos knew it too. He tapped the back of his bare wrist, then touched two fingers to his hairy brow in a "you win" salute.

I made my way past the crowded booths that ran down the center of the diner. Surprisingly, the smell of bacon, eggs, and hash brows sizzling on the kitchen's massive griddle bolstered my constitution.

I took the stool beside Chronos and waited for him to talk. He had called this meeting. It was up to him to tell me why.

But the old codger just sat there, watching the cooks on the other side of the counter flip pancakes like it was the most interesting thing he ever saw. A grin split his wrinkled face.

My blood started to simmer. What did he think? That I was going to run in here, wringing my hands and blubbering? *Please, oh, please, mighty Chronos! Father of Time! What did I do to upset you?*

What I'd done to upset him was save Kyra's life, and I wasn't going to apologize. I was a hero, dammit. Especially since I saved her with no hope of anyone ever thanking me or putting my face on the news. No one was ever going to hold me up to the world as a shining example of courage under fire.

No one, not even Kyra, would ever know what I did.

Because it had never happened.

The waitress came by. Chronos ordered his gyro omelet. He pointed at me, eyebrows raised. I guessed his offer to buy me breakfast was still good. I ordered the same.

As the waitress walked away, Chronos leaned back to give her ass an appreciative ogle.

Then he turned back to me and said, "You did something last night that knocked a few things out of whack up there."

Up there. Crap. My freezing the Clock to save Kyra's life had caught more than just Chronos's attention.

"Now, Billy." He stroked his beard. "I think you should know something before I tell you what I have to say." He leaned in close and lowered his voice. "I'm not bothered by what you did. I don't know your girl from any other Jane, Betty, or Sue. Understand?"

"She's not my girl."

"The thing is, I set up the rules a few millennia ago. Who can mess with the Clock, and why, and how it all works, given the grand scheme of things. And here you are. You're an anachronist. One of the last of them. And to the extent of your rather"—he cleared his throat—"*limited* ability, you stuck to rules. Fair's fair."

Rules? What rules? People like me could do what we could do. That was it. How do you stick to the rules of converting oxygen to carbon dioxide or circulating your own blood?

Still, it sounded like he'd just admitted I hadn't done anything wrong. Keeping my own voice low and steady, I asked, "So why am I here?"

He sat up straight on his stool. His tongue snaked around inside his mouth like it was digging something out from between two teeth. "You crossed my missus."

Like all the old-timers, Chronos was a lech. So it took me a second to remember he was actually married, and to whom. It took me another second to remember his wife's area of expertise.

And a third to realize I was in deep shit.

Chronos's wife was Old Ann. At least that's what most of us called her. She sported dreads, drove a yellow VW bus, and wore patchwork skirts with hot pink Crocs. She kept cats, and she liked to knit.

But despite her hippie persona, Old Ann was a vicious old shrew. Who was she really? Ananke. Primordial goddess of fate and necessity.

Basically, if you ran up against anything inevitable or unalterable, Old Ann was your gal. She was the goddess of All Things Happen For A Reason and Don't Mess With Destiny. And as far as she was concerned, destiny was just another word for an appointment with death.

I drew a deep breath. "So Old Ann thinks she got Kyra last night fair and square."

Chronos nodded.

"And now she's pissed because she thinks I cheated her. She thinks I reversed Kyra's fate. Snatched her back from the jaws of destiny or whatever."

Another nod. "It was that girl's fate to die last night."

I laughed, but my brain was spinning in circles. "Kyra's alive. Her getting shot...I made it so that never happened."

Chronos snorted. "Isn't that exactly what I just said was the problem?"

Before I knew it, I was twisted in my seat, both fists full of white beard and shiny purple jacket. "I stuck to the rules, old man. You said so yourself. Now, either I did something wrong saving Kyra's life or I didn't. You and your wife and the rest of them, you don't get to have it both ways."

Chronos looked down the slope of his long, crooked nose at my hands. The diner's clatter and chitchat faded to silence. I snuck a sideways glance. Everyone was staring.

Chronos's eyes met mine. He cocked an eyebrow.

I glared at him for a couple seconds more, but I knew calling attention this way wasn't smart. I knew what the old man wanted me to do, and I knew I had to do it.

I sighed and gave him a little shove as I let go of him. Then I spun the Clock back. Seven seconds. Back to before I'd caused a scene.

The noise around us resumed, like someone had unmuted a TV. Letting the Clock run, I propped my elbows on the counter, then rested my pounding head in my hands.

Kyra. That perfect black-haired girl. That beautiful smartass I'd known since we were kids. That girl who was supposed to go to law school in the fall and help people and someday get married and have kids. That girl who was supposed to live.

She was going to die anyway. All because some high-and-mighty goddess decided I'd crossed a line.

The waitress approached and slid our omelets in front of us. Chronos slapped his hands together and rubbed them like he was warming them over a fire. Then, table manners be damned, he picked up his fork and started shoveling food into his mouth.

I shoved my plate away. "How much time does she have?"

Chronos finished chewing a massive mouthful. He looked truly befuddled. "Who?"

"Kyra. How long until Old Ann comes for her?"

Chronos started to laugh. Flecks of egg and meat flew from his mouth and lodged in his beard.

I wanted to deck him, but I didn't think I had another seven seconds in me just yet. "What's so funny?"

"It doesn't have to be your girl. It can be anyone."

That slow spin inside my skull moved south into my gut.

Chronos mistook my silence for a lack of understanding. "You don't have to kill Kyra," he said, slow and loud. "Any death will settle your debt to Ananke."

"Any death?"

"Any *human* death. No rats or squirrels or the like. And not you. Suicide won't count, so don't go getting all noble and sacrificial on us. The only other rule is that you have to do the heavy lifting, if you catch my drift. You can't hire someone to do your dirty work."

A numb tingle washed over me. Chronos had just told me that I, Billy Shump, had to kill another human being in order to save Kyra.

"How much time do I have?"

"How would I know? Ananke's game, Ananke's rules."

"What if I don't do it?" *What if I can't?*

Chronos mopped at his beard with a paper napkin. "Tell me something, Billy. Last night, where did that bullet hit?"

I thought of the blood blossoming from the hole in Kyra's

middle. Still numb, I forced myself to point at my own stomach. Front and center.

He nodded. "Let's just say that if you don't settle up with Ananke, your girl Kyra is going to start suffering a killer bellyache."

"Meaning that she's going to die anyway."

"It doesn't have to be that way, Billy." Chronos picked up his fork and loaded it with another Olympic-sized bite of omelet. "Who dies is one-hundred percent up to you."

#

Twenty minutes later, I was in LoDo, circling the block around Kyra's office building, cursing the lunchtime traffic and lack of downtown parking.

I had to see her. I couldn't think until I'd made sure Kyra was still standing upright and breathing.

I spied an empty spot along the street. I screeched into the space and turned off the engine. Leaving the truck cockeyed and the meter hungry, I ran across the street and into the lobby of Kyra's office building.

I'd never actually been inside. All I knew was that this was the building where she worked. Which floor was her office on? Where were the elevators?

I turned in circles. All around me, people in suits crisscrossed the enormous glass-and-chrome lobby, their fancy shoes clicking on the polished marble floor.

"Billy?" Kyra's voice echoed from somewhere nearby.

I turned another circle, desperate to lay eyes on her, to see her smile among all those unfamiliar faces.

"Billy, what are you doing here?"

There she was, walking toward me. She looked confused about seeing me here. But I didn't care about that. What I cared about was her color. Whether she looked pale or sick or like she was in pain.

None of the above. She looked stunning.

Her black hair hung past her shoulders in loose waves. She wore a sapphire-blue suit. The skirt was cut just above her knees, showing off her perfectly curved calves. A yellow raincoat lay draped over one arm.

My gaze flicked down to the strip of white blouse visible inside the front of her blue suit jacket. Terrified, I expected to see blood.

No blood. Just Kyra. Besides stunning, she looked business-minded and smart, like she was already a lawyer and not just someone hoping to be. The jeans-and-ponytail girl from O'Hoolihan's cleaned up well.

A blond guy in a tailored suit followed Kyra to where I stood. He looked at me the way Chevy drivers look at Japanese imports. Colleague? Boyfriend? Both? I was suddenly hyper aware of my grease-stained jeans and worn-out leather coat.

"Billy?" Kyra held out her hands and gave a little shrug.

I opened my mouth. Then I closed it. What could I say? She didn't know I'd saved her from that bullet. And I couldn't let her know that unless I killed someone, she was going to die. I'd been so hell-bent on getting here, on making sure she was still alive, that I hadn't bothered to come up with a convincing story about why I'd come.

Kyra turned to her companion. "Scott, go on ahead and get us a table. I'll catch up."

Scott glared at me like I'd just driven on his lawn. If my current circumstances weren't a whole lot more challenging than anything this guy could dish out, I might have smirked. But I didn't, and after a second or two, he turned and headed out the door.

"I'm surprised to see you," Kyra said. "I mean, I've been trying to call you, and now here you are."

She took my arm and led me toward a posh waiting area in the far corner of the lobby. We sat down on a couple of chrome and black-leather chairs. They were about as comfortable as concrete slabs.

"You were trying to call me?"

She furrowed her brow. "Last night, at the bar—"

My heart skittered. She knew what had happened. Somehow, she knew. "Kyra, I—"

"Elliot called right after you left."

This was about her uncle? I needed a second to recalibrate. "What did he want?"

"To talk to you."

"Why did he call *his* bar to talk to *me*?"

"He said you weren't answering your phone."

My phone. I fished it out of my pocket. Sure enough, it was still off.

"Anyway," Kyra continued, "it sounded important. He asked me to track you down."

"What for?"

She shrugged. "You're a friend of the family. He probably wants you to pick up a few shifts at the bar. My boss"—she waved a hand at the double doors—"has a big case coming up, so starting next week, I'm going to be working late most nights."

"That guy was your boss?"

She nodded.

Jealousy pricked up its sharp little horns. Did that guy really have a big case coming up, or was he just trying to scheme a way to spend some after-hours time with Kyra?

I shook it off and turned my thoughts back to Kyra's uncle. "Is Elliot still in the hospital?"

"No. They released him last night. He called from home."

"So he's okay?"

Kyra rolled her eyes. "Of course he's okay. Doesn't it always turn out he's okay?"

"Then why would he need me to work at the bar?"

Another shrug. "Look, I have to go. Will you call him?"

"Yeah. Sure."

"Great."

We stood, and she leaned in for a quick hug. She even went up on her tiptoes to kiss my cheek.

I wanted to wrap my arms around her and never let go. I wanted to pull her tight and tell her I was sorry. Sorry I'd never held her the way I wanted to right now. Sorry I'd never whispered to her, *I love you. I've always loved you.*

But I didn't. Kyra pulled away, and I dropped my arms to my sides. She smiled and turned to leave.

Halfway to the door, she turned back. "Hey, Billy, you never told me why you're here."

I lifted a shoulder. "I just thought you might like to have lunch."

A quizzical glint flashed in her eyes. "With you?"

"With me."

She shifted her weight from one foot to the other and pointed over her shoulder at the doors. "I can't today."

"Worth a shot. I had to ask."

A long pause stretched between us.

Then Kyra said, "How about dinner instead?"

My heart started pounding. "Tonight?"

"My place. I'll cook."

I'd only been to the ocean once, when I was a kid. As soon as I was waist-deep in surf, a wave knocked into me. It tossed me up and down and backwards all at once, like a carnival ride. It rolled me back onto the beach and left me sitting on the sand, sputtering, laughing, breathless. Giddy. Ready for more.

That was what I felt like right then. Me standing across that lobby from Kyra, her dinner invitation hanging in the air—it felt like that first wave crashing into me all over again.

"I'd love that," I said. "What time?"

Just then, the undertow hit. Kyra pressed a hand to her stomach. Her whole body clenched. She tipped forward like she might topple over.

Old Ann was sending me a message.

I ran to Kyra, grabbed her arms to keep her from falling. "Are you okay?"

She straightened and put a hand up to ward off my concern. "It's nothing. I'm fine. Really. I've just been having weird little stomach pains all day. They come and go." Her expression turned embarrassed. "Probably something I ate."

My mind raced. It was too soon. If Kyra was already feeling last night's phantom bullet, I didn't have much time. I had to get out of here.

I had to kill someone. Today. Now.

"Rain check on dinner?" I asked.

She looked up at me. The pain that had clouded her eyes a moment ago was gone. "I'm okay." She arched an eyebrow and tapped a finger against my chest. "Tonight, Billy Shump. Seven o'clock. Bring a bottle of red."

#

A cold April drizzle had started to fall. The parking ticket I yanked off my windshield was soggy. I climbed into my truck and fired it up, then switched on my phone. Three missed calls from Kyra. Seven missed calls from Elliot.

I called Elliot. The old guy picked up almost immediately.

"Billy! I've been trying to call you."

"I see that. How are you feeling?"

"Never better."

I hadn't expected that, not from the man who was always dying of something.

"Listen," Elliot said, "I'm out taking care of some business today, but my pickup's acting up. I need you to meet me at my house around two and take a look under the hood."

Seven missed calls, and that was all the old guy needed? I glanced over my shoulder and pulled away from the curb. Then I turned on Seventeenth and headed east toward Broadway.

After I crossed Broadway, what then? Which way would I turn? Where does a man go when he's looking for someone to kill?

I must have taken too long to answer, because Elliot said, "You're a family friend, Billy. I'm asking because it's important to me. I need..." he trailed off. I heard him cough and clear his throat. "I need that engine running."

"Yeah, sure," I heard myself say. "I'll see you at your place around two."

For this being a sick day, my schedule was filling up quick. Fix Elliot's truck. Head home for a shower and a shave. Swing by Argonaut Wine and Liquor for a bottle of red, and get over to Kyra's by seven. But first...kill someone.

"And Billy?"

"Yeah?"

"Promise me something."

"Sure. What?"

He cleared his throat again, but this time it was more like he was trying to get my attention. "Promise me that between now and then, you won't do anything stupid."

A shiver trilled down my spine. It was almost like he knew what I had to do. Almost like he was asking me not to. But that was impossible. Whatever happened in the next couple of hours was between me and Chronos and Old Ann.

"Sure, Elliot. No problem."

I wouldn't do anything stupid. I would only do what was necessary.

#

As soon as I hung up with Elliot, I started shaking. Not shivering from cold or trembling from fever, but honest to goodness shaking. I pulled my truck over and tried to sit still.

I had to save Kyra.

I had to kill someone.

Kill.

I looked around, realized I was parked at Broadway and Colfax. Homeless people wandered through the rain, heavy packs strapped to their backs. Others sat under trees, sheltering from the weather.

Could I kill one of them?

Up ahead, I spied another guy standing on the corner. He was holding a wet scrap of cardboard that said *HUNGRY! ANYTHING HELPS!! GOD BLESS!!!* A drawing of a cross included little lines poking out all around to make it look like it was shining.

I pounded the steering wheel. I couldn't think about who. Not yet. So I started thinking about how.

A gun would be easiest, but I didn't have a gun. I had a Leatherman multi-tool in the glove compartment.

Could I cut someone's throat?

The thought made me heave. Besides the mess, I couldn't imagine fighting a man into position and dragging the blade across his throat.

No. The Leatherman was out.

I had a toolbox in the back. A hammer. A wrench. One hard hit to the back of the head with either of those, and the guy would at least be unconscious. He wouldn't feel the second hit, or the third. He wouldn't feel me finishing the job. And if I did it right, he'd never see it coming. Any of it. I'd be quick. Merciful. Like the angel of death.

Then I imagined the heft of the wrench, the cold metal grip. Swinging it. Bringing it down. I imagined the thunk of metal striking bone. The crack of a breaking skull. The reverb traveling through my body.

Seven Seconds

I looked down at my hands. As a mechanic, I'd put them through a lot. Smashed fingers had healed crooked. Engine grease had worked its way down into my weathered skin so that black lines spread out like spider webs across my palms.

Could I wrap these hands around someone's neck? Squeeze until he stopped breathing? Could I hold someone's head underwater until he drowned?

No. I was fairly sure I couldn't.

After today, would I ever be able to look at these hands again without seeing blood?

I realized then that I had to do more than just kill. I had to get away with it. And ten bucks said Old Ann didn't give a damn about helping me cover up forensic evidence.

What was I going to do?

I thought of Kyra. The way she looked last night. And today. How she kissed my cheek and asked me to dinner. I thought of her clutching her stomach, and how if I didn't do something soon, Old Ann was going to take her away from me before she was ever mine.

A plan started to take root.

I'd thought of a *how*. Now I needed a *who*. Kyra's pretty-boy boss? No. He was nothing to me. What about Jeremy Edmunds? Back in seventh grade, in front of everyone, he'd whipped my ass behind the school. Or what about that d-bag who'd never paid me for the tranny rebuild I'd done on his Dodge Ram? Maybe him.

Working up some nerve, I slammed my truck into gear and took off down Broadway. I turned left on Fourteenth and doubled back to cross Colfax.

I had to get to O'Hoolihan's. I had to get Elliot's shotgun.

\#

Kyra's second cousin Rusty stood behind the bar. Other than Rusty and Jake Renfro, who was already passed out in his usual spot, O'Hoolihan's was empty.

Rusty was leaning against the bar, propped back on his elbows so he could look up at the TV. He glanced over when he heard the door fall shut behind me.

"Hey, Billy." He went back to watching monster trucks crush cars in an arena full of mud. "You want a beer, come on back and help yourself."

A beer would calm my nerves. I joined him behind the bar and snagged a bottle of Bud Light from the fridge. I snuck a peek over at the shotgun. It was right where I knew it would be. On the shelf. Behind Rusty's legs.

Damn. As far as I was concerned, that gun was my only hope at getting this job done quick. I'd have to be patient, grab it when Rusty went in back to take a leak.

I tipped my bottle toward Rusty. "Think I'll enjoy this with my buddy Jake."

Rusty clinked his bottle against mine. "Have at it."

I slid into the booth across from Jake. From here, I'd have a good view of Rusty leaving his post. Then I'd snatch the gun and leave.

Jake's cheek lay on the table, and only the steady rise and fall of his skinny shoulders gave any indication that he was alive.

I took a long swig of beer and set my bottle on the table. The clunk roused Jake from his booze-soaked nap. He sat bolt upright and squinted at me.

"Billy Shump. You here to get some answers?"

He was sober enough to recognize me, but that didn't mean he was capable of making sense. "Answers about what, Jake?"

"About what you are." He pointed at the ceiling. "About them. About getting tangled up in their games."

I stared. Jake Renfro was an anachronist, like me. That much I knew. But he'd been sitting in this booth, drinking himself stupid since I could remember. I had questions, all right. But what answers could I possibly get from a drunk like Jake Renfro?

I pushed my beer aside and leaned across the table. The stench of stale liquor and unwashed old man rolled toward me like a thunderhead. "You have something to tell me, Jake?"

"Yeah. Don't call attention to yourself unless you want to get tossed around like a kitten in a den of wolves."

"What do you know about calling attention to yourself?"

"Plenty. But that's not important right now. What's important is what you did. Here. Last night."

I glanced at Rusty. His eyes were still glued to the TV. I looked back at Jake. "You were passed out."

He grinned, revealing teeth like yellowed fence posts. "That's what you think."

I didn't need this. I grabbed my beer and started to slide out of the booth.

Jake's hand darted across the table and clamped onto my wrist. His speed and strength took me by surprise.

"Don't do it, Billy," he hissed. "I know what they told you to do to make it right, but don't do it."

I froze. His eyes had lost their watery, unfocused quality. Now they were sharp and clear. Intense, like a hawk's.

I pulled my arm away but stayed in my seat. "I don't have a choice, Jake."

"There's always a choice."

"Letting Kyra die is not a choice."

"Then take a good look at me, Billy Boy." Jake sat back against the booth and spread his arms out wide. "Do what they told you, and this is what you could become. Do what they told you, and it could ruin you. Just like it ruined me."

Jake was shouting now. Rusty turned toward us.

"It's okay," I told Rusty. "Jake's just a little worked up."

"Rusty," Jake called out, "you take that shotgun into Elliot's office. Now. And lock the door. Then you call the police."

"No," I said. "Don't."

"Go now, Rusty. Billy's here to get that gun, and you've got to make sure he leaves here without it."

Rusty's eyes went wide.

My nerves burned in panic. I rushed forward. Made for the end of the bar. Had to get around it, behind it, under it. Had to get to that gun.

I was fast, but Rusty was faster. I dashed around the end of the bar as Rusty grabbed the gun. I sprinted toward the office door, but Rusty had disappeared behind it. I crashed into the door just as Rusty turned the deadbolt.

I squeezed my eyes shut and reached for the Clock. Seven more seconds, and I could catch Rusty before he...

No. I couldn't risk using the Clock again. I couldn't even handle the trouble I was already in.

I punched the wall. "Dammit, Jake! I needed that gun!"

Jake came to stand before me. "I just did you the biggest favor of your life, son. Now listen up. Rusty's in there calling the police. And this is Colfax. You can't throw a rock on Colfax without hitting a cop. So go now, before we hear sirens."

I was breathing hard. Defeated.

Jake held out a hand. I took it and let him pull me to my feet. He slapped my shoulders in a friendly, great-to-see-you sort of way.

"Now about what you were planning to do with that shotgun," said Jake Renfro. "Didn't Elliot tell you not to do anything stupid?"

#

Elliot was waiting for me. Just like Jake said he would be.

His garage door stood open, and he was just inside, leaning on the back bumper of his pickup. I pulled into his driveway. He waved.

In his early sixties, Elliot was short and paunchy, and what was left of his once flaming-red hair had long ago paled to a brassy gray. His bushy, well-groomed moustache had always been a point of pride, though he typically only bothered to shave the rest of his face once every couple of weeks.

Today his hair was neatly combed, like he'd just had it cut. The extra ruddiness of his cheeks and neck told me he'd sprung extra for a barber's shave. His plaid shirt was tucked into a pair of khakis, complete with belt and knife-edge creases.

I got out of my truck. "You're all dressed up."

He smiled. "Got someplace to be."

"But first your truck needs looked at."

"That's so."

Something was up.

Something that had to do with me. And Kyra.

Something that had to do with everything.

Suspicious, I scrutinized Elliot's expression.

He smiled and swept a hand to the side, ushering me toward the garage. "Go around to the front. I'll pop the hood."

I did what he said, though I kept my eye on him. He got into the cab and reached under the dash for the release knob. The latch clicked.

I lifted the hood.

There on the engine, fanned out like playing cards on a Las Vegas poker table, lay a file folder full of loose papers in white, pink, and yellow. Two large manila envelopes, both sealed, one marked "personal," the other marked "O'Hoolihan's." Several small envelopes, all stamped and neatly addressed. An oversized paper sleeve marked "Cranial MRI. Elliot O'Hoolihan."

That's when I knew. I knew why Elliot had asked me to come. I knew what he was going to ask me to do.

I picked up the paper sleeve and pulled out a large sheet of film. It showed dozens of images of Elliot's brain, all lined up in neat columns and rows.

Elliot got out of the truck and came to stand beside me. He tapped the film. "Astrocytomas. Hundreds of tiny star-shaped tumors." He chuckled softly to himself. "I have a head full of stars."

"I can't do this, Elliot."

"I always wanted my tombstone to say 'I told you I was sick.' What do you think?"

"I think I can't do this."

"You can, and you will." He fished something out of his pocket and held it out to me. "You'll do it for Kyra."

I looked down at the thing in my hand. It was a garage door remote.

My lungs drew in a shuddery breath. I opened my mouth to speak, but my voice hitched.

"That's a spare," Elliot said. "There probably won't be an investigation, so I doubt anyone will come looking for it. But just in case, get rid of it after."

I cleared my throat and tried to speak again. Even then, all I could manage was a whisper. "How did you know?"

"Aw, Billy. You can't run a business in this city for thirty years and not know about the gods sniffing around, messing up everyone's business."

"No, I mean—"

"How did I know about what you did last night in my bar? About Old Ann putting you up to killing someone?"

"Jake Renfro," I said.

Elliot nodded. "That's so. Jake's been keeping me apprised of things since back when we were kids. Did you know he was in the same class as your daddy and me? Your daddy had sense, but Jake used to let being an anachronist get him into a lot of trouble." He pointed at me and raised his eyebrows. "Then he learned his lesson."

"I heard something about that." I slipped the garage door opener into my coat pocket.

Elliot bent over the engine and gathered up his affairs. "I trust you'll do me the favor of taking care of all this."

I forced myself to keep calm. "Sure, Elliot. I'll take care of everything."

He handed me the folder and the envelopes, stacking the big O'Hoolihan's one on top. He stabbed it with a finger. "You sell that place while there's still some money to be got, and you make sure Kyra gets herself to law school."

I swallowed. "No problem."

"The other one's got my will in it, along with bank records and deeds and titles and whatnot. And these"—he flicked the edges of the papers inside the file folder—"are my medical records. Read them someday when you need a good chuckle."

I laughed at that, right through the egg-sized lump lodged in my throat.

Elliot laughed too. Then he sobered and said, "I wasted a lot of time trying to convince everyone I was sick. Then when I found out I was dying, I spent a lot of time trying to keep it a secret."

I thought about Elliot being gone from his bar so much lately. "Did you even try to get treated?"

"Nah. Too late for that. Doctors wouldn't take me seriously after I'd spent so many years crying wolf. By the time I finally got diagnosed, I was terminal."

I started coughing to keep a big sob from breaking free. I didn't fool Elliot.

"That'll be about enough of that," he said. "Listen, when Jake told me what was going on with you and Kyra, I took that as a sign. Good timing. And you know a little something about good timing, don't you, Billy? So you see? This is my chance to do right. To make my life mean something. This is for Kyra. And because I know you love her—heck, everyone knows you love her—this is for you."

He slammed the hood of the pickup and turned to face me.

Seven Seconds

We stood in silence for a few seconds. I almost told him again that I couldn't do it. But what would be the point? I could, and hard as it would be, I would.

Without another word, Elliot slid around to the side of the truck. He climbed inside and shut the door. He started up the engine. Grinning at me like a man about to take the wildest ride of his life, he revved the engine good and loud.

I walked out of that garage on legs that felt rubbery, foreign, like they didn't want to obey me. Sorrow and fear and regret carved circles inside me. I kept my mind on Kyra's face, and on knowing that I'd drive away from here today having settled my debt. Elliot had just handed me my freedom. I'd be free of Old Ann, free of Chronos and the rest. I'd take Jake Renfro's advice and never spin the Clock back again.

I got into my own truck and carefully laid Elliot's effects on the seat beside me. Then I took the garage door opener out of my pocket.

The thing was old, some brand you can't get anymore. A tiny gray plastic box. A single black button.

I looked up, found Elliot watching me in his rearview mirror. He gave me a little nod. Then he laid his head back against the headrest and closed his eyes.

I pressed the button. The garage door descended, shaking and grumbling as its old motor lowered it on creaky chains.

And then it was closed, muffling the rumble of the truck's engine.

My part was done. Time would take care of the rest.

Numb, I backed out of the driveway and headed home. Elliot had made his peace. Someday, I would have to make mine.

#

It was one of those warm nights in early November, mild and unexpected. The kind of night that makes the weather guys on TV grin like they just did you a favor. The kind of night that brings smiling people out of their homes into the parks and the streets.

It was the kind of night that leads you to believe life is full of promise.

Kyra sat beside me on a bus-stop bench on Colfax. The number fifteen slid to the curb, brakes hissing, and opened its doors. A few folks got out, but Kyra and I stayed put.

The bus pulled away, restoring our view of what we'd come to see.

Across Colfax, a giant banner slung across the building that used to be O'Hoolihan's announced the grand opening of Mickey McTavish's Irish Pub. The line to get in stretched all the way down the block.

"You think Jake Renfro's in there?" Kyra asked.

"No, I heard he left town a few months back, after Elliot died. No one knows where he went."

"That's kind of sad, isn't it?"

"Yes," I replied. "It kind of is."

I was still making my peace with sadness. Had been for the last six months. I was lucky to have Kyra by my side as we mourned, even if she knew nothing about what had really happened. Nothing about what I was or what I could do. Nothing about the pantheon or about how she'd almost died. Twice. And nothing about how Elliot had helped me save her.

My mother, gods rest her soul, had once told me to never keep secrets from the woman I love. Well, I couldn't square up with that. Some secrets were meant to be carried alone.

I nodded toward Mickey McTavish's and said, "You want to go in?"

Kyra shook her head. "Better not. I have an eight o'clock class tomorrow."

"Well, then." I took a flask out of my pocket and handed it to her.

She unscrewed the cap and raised the flask to the sky. "To Uncle Elliot." She tipped her head back and drank. Then she handed the flask to me.

"To Elliot." I threw back a shot. The Bushmills lit a slow burn that smoldered all the way down.

I gave the flask back to Kyra. She leaned forward and tipped the rest of the whiskey into the gutter.

We sat for a few minutes, just outside the warm glow of Mickey McTavish's, and watched the world go by. Kyra slipped her hand inside mine. Yes, I was done with the Clock. For Jake, for Elliot, and especially for Kyra, I was done with the Clock.

"Are you sure you don't want to go in?"

She pushed her shoulder into mine. "Let's get out of here."

We stood and headed east, walking hand in hand toward my place.

At the corner, Kyra stopped, took hold of my jacket, and pulled me close. She kissed me slow and sweet, her lips tasting faintly of whiskey. That kiss almost brought me to my knees.

It lasted exactly seven seconds.

Angie Hodapp

About the Author:

Angie Hodapp earned an MA in English from Colorado State University and is a graduate of the Denver Publishing Institute at the University of Denver. A Colorado Gold Contest winner and Writers of the Future Contest semifinalist, she loves working with other writers and has taught workshops at Writer's Digest University and RMFW's Colorado Gold Conference. RMFW's newsletter editor and retreat chair, she works at Nelson Literary Agency and lives with her husband, Warren Hammond, in an old 1930s carriage house on East Colfax.

You can find Angie on Facebook at www.facebook.com/ahodapp and on Twtter at @angiehodapp.

Hay Hook
By Margaret Mizushima

For "Hay Hook", the description of Colfax from Playboy magazine as "the longest, wickedest street in America" sparked Margaret's imagination:

The characters from my most recent novel won't let me go, and they prodded me into setting up a new crime for them to solve. My characters needed a rural or at least semi-rural setting, so I chose to place them out on West Colfax. The "wicked" part took care of the rest of the story.

Hay Hook

Driving about as far west as Colfax went, I climbed into the foothills, searching for the lane that would lead me to my patient, a colicky mare. Fifteen years ago, I established my clinic and hung out my shingle—*James Cooper, DVM*—on the west side of Lakewood, Colorado, where real estate was cheap and neighborhoods were seedy. Now, trees and open space lined West Colfax, a result of the city's many beautification projects.

Although I'd never been to this stable, I found the entrance easily enough, since it was marked by a prominent archway made from a massive log. Letters that read *Hay Hook Stable* were burned into it like a brand. The tool the stable was named for hung a few inches down from the log, a large eighteen-inch hook with a handle used for picking up hay bales. I turned in and followed the gravel lane past the house and back toward the stable. Since the property nestled against the rugged hillside open space called Apex Park, it seemed isolated, even in this well-developed corridor between Golden and Lakewood.

I drove up to the double doors of the barn and parked. The area out front was neat and clean with tie rails and white board fences surrounding a couple of paddocks. Russian Olives grew in hedges beside a lane that ran alongside the fencing.

Unattended in the lane, a bay horse stood, head bobbing spasmodically with waves of pain, a lead rope dragging freely from its halter. Sweat darkened its hide, sullied by rub marks and dirt from rolling. I knew immediately that this was my patient and was surprised to find her out here alone. I approached her slowly, one hand outstretched, and she let me take hold of the rope.

"What are you doing out here by yourself?" I looked around for her owners but saw no one.

Taking out my stethoscope, I listened to her chest, counting her heartbeats. Heart rate is a reflection of pain, and this girl's was way up there, eighty beats per minute. I led her to one of the rails and tied her.

Entering the stable, I searched for Shirley or Milt Driscoll, the mare's owners. It was cool and dim inside and smelled of the sweet scent of hay and pungent odor of manure. I peered into an open box stall off to my right, but found it empty.

I knew from meeting Shirley and Milt at my office a few days ago that they were new to the area, having recently bought this property. They'd contacted me to tell me about this horse, their first, an Andalusian mare imported from Mexico. When Shirley called this morning, she'd explained that the horse had been flown into the country, arriving during the night, and she believed stress from the trip triggered the colic.

"Shirley? Milt?" I called as I walked down the alleyway between the empty box stalls. No reply.

About halfway down, I found an office with a desk and a phone. And the room beyond it contained a horse stocks, a metal stanchion designed to hold a horse still while being worked on. I could bring the mare in here to examine her.

Out front, I decided to go ahead and treat her for pain. Although I don't like to proceed with treatment without an owner present, I had an obligation to put her welfare first, and she shouldn't have to wait any longer. I took a bottle of analgesic from my coverall pocket, uncapped a needle, and drew a substantial dose into a syringe. I blocked the vein in her neck with one hand and inserted the needle with the other. The horse offered no resistance to the injection, as if she knew I was there to help her.

Once again using my stethoscope, I listened to the mare's abdomen for motility, a spot high on her belly for the large intestine, low for the small. Peristalsis sounds like the constant, gentle gurgling of rain dribbling down a pipe, while borborygmi boom like thunder about three times per minute. This mare had very little of either, cause for concern.

I counted heartbeats again, relieved to note a slight decrease in rate. The drug was doing its magic. With eyelids at half mast, the mare rested her chin on the tie rail, more comfortable than she'd been when I arrived.

I decided to go up to the house before I continued my exam. Leaving the mare, I walked the short distance to the ranch style log home and rang the doorbell. Receiving no answer, I pounded the door with my fist. There were no vehicles around, but I couldn't imagine the Driscolls leaving their valuable horse running free. Puzzled, I tried the doorknob and the door opened. I stepped inside and called. Still no answer.

What else could I do? Take care of the mare, I guess.

Out at my mobile vet unit, I gathered supplies including tubing, a dosage gun, a gallon jug of mineral oil, and a bucket of soapy water. I carried them into the stable and back to the exam room.

After untying the mare, I clicked my tongue. "Come on,

sweetheart. Let's go inside."

Sluggish from the drug, she followed me down the alley and into the stocks. I swung the side and rear pieces shut and anchored them so that she stood within its rectangular space, and I tied her head at the front.

Putting on a long plastic sleeve, I began a rectal exam. I noticed very little fecal matter beyond the rectum. Palpation revealed an enlarged cecum. "Feels like you've got an impaction. Did you get some sand in your feed?"

At this point, I usually share my exam results with the owner instead of the horse, so we can talk about treatment options. I pulled out my cell phone, found the number Shirley had called me on earlier, and dialed it. I heard the office phone ring next door. Okay, so that didn't work.

I called my office and got my assistant, Tess. "I'm here at the Driscoll place, but nobody else seems to be here. Do we have a cell phone number on file?"

"Just a minute. No, looks like we have a home phone and business phone."

"Would you try both and then call me back?"

I waited a few minutes, heard the phone ring in the office again, and then answered my own cell when it rang.

"No answer at either phone. I left messages on both for them to call us," Tess said.

"This mare probably has an impaction. She's in a lot of pain and looks dehydrated. I'm going ahead and starting treatment. Call me if you hear from one of them."

"Sure will."

This horse would probably be a surgery candidate, but a less

Hay Hook

invasive option was worth a try. I inserted a nasal-gastric tube, blowing gently on my end to dilate her esophagus while I ran the other end through the nostril and down into the stomach. I knew I was there when I smelled its partially digested contents. Then I dosed her with mineral oil.

From experience, I could tell this wasn't a simple colic. With this amount of pain and dehydration, I would typically want the horse transported to my clinic where I could run IV fluids in addition to dosing with mineral oil, the goal being to lubricate and hydrate the gut enough to allow her to defecate and move out the impaction.

Thinking about what to do next, I gathered my supplies and headed down to the end of the alley. Earlier, I'd noticed the end of a concrete slab down there, where I suspected I'd find a wash rack with warm water I could use to clean up. Carrying my soapy bucket, I rounded the corner and entered the room.

And that's where I found Shirley.

I dropped the bucket. It clattered against the pavement, soapy water splashing everywhere.

I crossed the room and knelt beside her, my mind screaming an endless chant, *oh shit oh shit oh shit*. My fingers went to her wrist, seeking her pulse. A worthless reflex. I was looking at a dead woman. Her glazed eyes stared up at the ceiling; her skin felt cold. But that wasn't the worst of it.

A hay hook was buried in her neck. Blood from the gaping wound pooled around her body. From the looks of it, she'd bled out.

I sat back on my heels. I fished my cell phone out of my pocket and dialed 9-1-1. While I listened to the ring, I averted my eyes to stare across the room and watch the soapsuds drip slowly down the mildewed wall.

#

I sat in a Jefferson County patrol vehicle, a steaming cup of coffee warming my cold fingers. I don't drink coffee, and the dark brew's aroma sort of made my stomach turn. Well, okay. Maybe it wasn't just the smell of coffee that churned my stomach.

A female deputy had led me to her SUV and sat me in the front passenger seat, handing me the drink and telling me to stay put. Since I'd had the presence of mind to move my patient back into her box stall and she was safe for the moment, I was willing to do as I was told. An ambulance was parked out front, and law officers filled the barn. They were waiting for the medical examiner.

The cruiser rocked as the deputy's large canine partner moved from one side of the back compartment to the other. He'd given me a disdainful look when I entered the vehicle, but otherwise paid me no mind. He seemed to have eyes only for his partner, keeping them glued to the barn's entrance. Other than a few short whines, he had nothing to say to me. Since we didn't know each other, the steel mesh that separated his cage from the front of the SUV worked well for us both.

At the moment, I could observe him freely as he stood behind the driver's seat watching the barn. He was a handsome German shepherd, pure sable, white shiny teeth, and a square solid build. Probably a European import.

"Do you get left in the car a lot?"

He flipped me a glance over his shoulder and then went back to ignoring me.

Hay Hook

I took to watching the barn with him.

It had been a horrific experience, and I still wasn't sure what to do with it. There was no way this could've been an accident. Shirley had been murdered. My imagination ran wild as I considered how one person could push a hay hook into another person's throat. Straddle her, pin her to the ground, and push the sharp point to pierce the skin slowly? Or thrust it in, blood spurting everywhere.

I shook my head, suddenly impatient with my role as trembling witness, and decided it was time to get out and move. I needed to get back in charge.

I opened the car door, feeling a huff of warm breath on the back of my neck when the dog bounded over to my side, checking to see if he could get out. I poured the coffee out beside the SUV, placed the plastic cup on the dash, and stood up on legs that were less shaky now than they'd been after I found poor Shirley.

The cop I'd met earlier and another woman dressed in a black civilian pantsuit came out of the barn and headed my way. I waited for them.

The cop, whose name I hadn't been able to retain, introduced me to the other woman. "Dr. Cooper, this is Detective LoSasso. She's investigating this incident, and she'd like to ask you a few questions."

The detective was tall and lean with blond hair, while the cop—whose name-tag read Deputy Lujan—was short and sturdy with dark hair and eyes, probably of Hispanic descent. They reminded me of a thoroughbred and a quarter horse.

Detective LoSasso shook my hand with a firm grip. "I know

you've had a terrible experience, but I want you to tell me about it in detail."

I'd already called my office and told Tess to reschedule my clients for the rest of the day, but I felt pressed to see my patient. "I need to check that horse."

The detective's eyes narrowed and she pursed salmon-colored lips. "This will only take a few minutes."

Meanwhile, the deputy unloaded her service dog. "Take a break, Sarge," she told him, and he promptly relieved himself on the cruiser's tire. My attention turned away from the detective while I watched the officer gather her equipment from a compartment within the back of the vehicle: a red nylon collar, a long leash, and a small water bowl from which she proceeded to give Sarge a drink.

The detective regained my attention with a sharp tone. "Dr. Cooper."

"Let's walk," I said, and headed toward the barn.

The detective moved to walk beside me. I told her what I could remember while we went. I had little to tell, so I was done by the time we entered the barn. Keeping my eyes averted from the activity down at the other end of the alleyway, I pulled out my stethoscope and moved into the stall. I looked at both horse and ground, spotting a small amount of fresh feces in the corner, the first the mare had passed. I would bag it and take it to the office to examine for sand and parasites.

The mare wasn't doing real whippy; her pulse raced and sweat stained her hide.

"And you heard nothing after you came into the barn?" Detective LoSasso said.

"Nothing out of the ordinary."

"How long did it take between talking to Ms. Driscoll on the phone and your arrival?"

I was injecting more analgesic into a vein. "About forty-five minutes."

"Did she sound like she was under duress?"

I glanced at her, wondering how I was supposed to know the answer to that. "She was concerned about her mare. That's all I could detect."

"Mr. Driscoll is unaccounted for at the moment. Were you expecting him to be here?"

"Not necessarily. I was expecting Shirley." I pulled a plastic sleeve out of my pocket, stuffed my hand into it, scooped up the horse manure and then inverted the sleeve back over my hand to create a pouch, tying it off with the sample tucked inside. "I need to get someone to take this horse to my clinic."

"Did you notice anything else unusual?"

"No, just the owner's absence. Are we done here?"

She frowned, probably in disapproval of my impatience. She must not realize this mare's condition could be life threatening. She said, "For now. Here's my card. Call me if you think of anything."

"I will."

By this time, we'd made our way back outside the barn, and I scanned the area to see if I could find someone to help. I saw Deputy Lujan with Sarge on his long leash coming around the corner of the house. The dog's head was down and he was sniffing, obviously on the trail of something, or maybe I should say someone. He came to the road by the barn and stopped. He moved back and forth, circled around, and then looked up at his handler with a stymied expression.

"Search," Lujan said.

Sarge circled again, started to back track, but came back to the spot and sat.

Lujan glanced up at the detective and said, "Mr. Driscoll must have left in a vehicle from here."

My eyes were drawn to a plastic bag that Lujan held. It looked like it contained a pair of men's white underwear. Evidently she caught me looking.

"Scent article," she told me.

"Okay," LoSasso said, "Dr. Cooper, you're free to go. Deputy Lujan, let's go talk with the sheriff."

I caught the deputy's eye. "Can one of your officers help me transport this horse to my clinic? Someone who can drive the Driscolls' rig?"

Her gaze traveled to the rig and back. "We're unable to do that without the owner's permission. Let me call the humane society. They'll bring their own rig out and transport him for you. Can you wait here till they come?"

"Yeah, I'll wait. How long will it take?"

"One moment." She used her cell phone and had the answer right away. "They'll be here in about twenty minutes. Will that work?"

"Sure."

"Call me if you have any problems. Let me give you my cell number."

I pulled out my cell phone, noticing a streak of Shirley's blood on it. I'd washed blood off my hands earlier, but hadn't realized

Hay Hook

it was on the phone. An image of Shirley and the embedded hay hook flashed into my mind. I supposed that would be burned into my memory forever.

Lujan gave me her number while I programmed it directly into my phone. After today, I'd come to believe that you never knew when having a cop's cell phone number might come in handy.

#

Driving back down Colfax toward Lakewood, the humane society rig followed me to my clinic. Since my property purchase fifteen years ago, increased urbanization threatened to close down my mixed practice. I was still hanging on, although I rarely treated cattle at the clinic anymore. Horse properties were plentiful out here though, so I managed to maintain an inpatient horse facility without too many complaints from neighbors.

After unloading the mare, I placed her in my own set of stocks. She looked like she was in pain again, and I wanted to prevent her from throwing herself down to roll.

"Do you want me to stay and help?" asked the animal control officer, a burly guy with gray hair.

"No, Tess is around here somewhere. Could you go inside and tell her I'm here?"

"Sure."

I worked fast to insert a catheter into a neck vein, connected tubing, and hung a bag of Ringer's fluid. The electrolytes and hydration should help her feel better. I was listening to a rather silent gut and counting a rapid heartbeat when I heard the humane society truck's engine start and rumble off down the driveway. Tess came out as I injected another dose of analgesic into the IV.

"We'll need to push a couple bags of fluids and keep a close eye on this one," I told her.

My red-headed assistant had been with me for years and knew what we were dealing with. "Okay, but I've got to leave in thirty minutes to take the kids to get their physicals."

I'd forgotten about that. Tess had three boys that kept her hopping. She often left work mid-afternoon to cart them one place or another, a back seat full of pups rolling around on each other until she yelled at them to get strapped in.

I had two daughters myself, ages ten and fourteen, staying home today instead of riding ambulatory with me. Thank God for that. My wife left us about nine months ago and was in the process of divorcing me. Apparently she wanted to divorce the kids as well, since she refused to allow them to come see her.

I said, "Bring me some more Ringer's and make sure we've got a stall bedded. Oh...call both numbers for the Driscolls and leave Milt a message that we have his horse here. Do I have anything else coming in?"

"Cleared it all 'til tomorrow and the next day. Do you want me to try to find someone to take the boys when I'm done, so I can come back later?"

"Give me a call and we'll see."

"What happened at the Driscolls'?"

I'd told her earlier that Shirley was dead, but hadn't elaborated. I supposed then, and still did, that this was about all she needed to know. I replied that it looked like someone had killed Shirley and that no one knew where Milt was.

"Oh, my gosh! Do you think he did it?"

Hay Hook

"Maybe. Or he's a victim, too."

"Oh, my gosh!"

That summed up both our feelings. I went out to my truck to grab the stool sample I'd bagged at the ranch. Placing it in a stainless steel pan, I added some water and, with a gloved hand, washed it around the bowl looking for sand. What I found instead were a couple small rocks, the size of a large pea. I'd never seen something like this before. Horses chew their food before swallowing and rarely swallow objects. I hadn't expected to find rocks within the dung.

I picked out the sharp-edged rocks—they looked like dirty crystals—and placed them in a baggie which I laid on the counter across the room. Tess came back, made sure I had everything I needed, and then left. I planned to stay by the mare until I had enough fluids in her, then I'd put her in the stall with some hay to see if she would start to eat and defecate.

Tess had been gone for about five minutes when I heard a car pull up. I was surprised to see Milt walking up to the treatment room. His eyes were reddened, skin pale, and his brown hair lay limp with sweat. He looked like a man who might know his wife had just died, so I told him how sorry I was about Shirley.

His eyes opened wide. "What do you mean?"

Oh, shit! Now what have I done? "I'm sorry, Milt. I thought you knew."

"Knew what? What about Shirley?"

Oh, man. I'm in a hell of a mess now. "I'm sorry to have to tell you like this, Milt. Shirley was found dead this morning."

His eyes filled and darted around as if searching for a way to escape. "They said she'd be okay if I gave them more money."

"What are you talking about?"

Before he could reply, two guys rushed in from around the corner. One grabbed Milt, the other pointed a gun right smack at my face. I threw my hands up, a poor defense for a bullet, I know. One word popped out of my mouth: "Whoa!" An icy prickle touched the top of my spine and the pit of my stomach.

Turning his head to look at the guy holding him, Milt said, "Did you kill my wife?"

Then he glared at the guy with the gun, a big guy over six foot and about two-fifty, with black hair and mustache. Ugly too, his nose spread all over his face, like it had been broken about a hundred times. "You said he wouldn't hurt her if I went with you to get more money."

Milt tried to pull free, but the guy holding him was built like a Rottweiler. He wrenched one of Milt's arms up behind his back. Milt's face blanched, and he sagged forward. Not all of the fight was out of him though; he continued to glare at the big guy.

I still had my hands up. I said, "What's going on?"

"Is this the horse?" Ugly asked Muscles.

"Yeah," Muscles said.

Ugly used a scornful tone. "Lucky for you we found him. You screwed up. First you kill the woman; then you leave the horse."

"She attacked me with that hook thing!"

Ugly yelled at him. "No excuses. You can't control a small woman? Then you panic and leave your post. One more mistake and it'll be your last. Do you understand me?"

Looking sullen, Muscles nodded.

After giving his assistant another dark look, Ugly turned his attention back to me. "Has he pooped 'em out yet?"

Hay Hook

The guy obviously didn't know this horse was a she. "She's not pooping much out at all yet. But I'm working on it."

"When?"

"Right now. Mineral oil and fluids might get her gut working again."

"I mean, when will he poop?"

"I'm not sure. Soon, I hope." I started to lower my hands.

Ugly pushed the gun at me, and I raised my hands again.

Milt groaned, tears streaming down his cheeks. "We had nothing to do with this. Shirley! It was her dream to have a stable full of Andalusians. All we did was buy a horse."

"Shut the fuck up," Muscles said, tightening Milt's arm up a little higher.

Except for another groan, Milt complied.

It appeared we were at an impasse. Milt stood with his arm twisted, I stood with my hands raised, and the mare stood, hip shot with her weight shifted to one hind foot, lips dangling loosely, fluids dripping into her vein. She looked comfortable enough, but that made only one of us.

Suspecting I already knew, I asked the big guy, "What are you looking for in her poop?"

He looked wise, like he had a secret. "Well, doctor, that's not your business. Your business is to make this horse poop."

"They smuggled something inside her stomach," Milt shouted. "They threatened us to give them money."

Muscles smashed a fist into the base of Milt's skull. Milt dropped to his knees.

"Do you want me to kill him?" Muscles asked.

Ugly shook his head. "Just keep him quiet."

Using both hands, Muscles delivered another blow to Milt's head. Milt slumped forward onto the concrete floor. Good God, a blow like that might've killed him!

Ugly wore a pained expression, as if he realized the short chain he kept his gorilla on wasn't quite short enough. He said, "Is he breathing?"

Muscles checked. "Yup."

"Tie him."

Muscles looked around, his eyes pausing on a lead rope that hung on the wall. He grabbed it and proceeded to follow his boss's order. Ugly looked at me.

"If you want to keep yourself and your friend alive, you'll cooperate. Do you understand?"

Though I understood barely anything at all, I nodded.

"You're going to cut open this horse's belly, and get some stones out."

"How many stones are there?"

He hesitated, but evidently decided I needed to know. "Thirty."

Good God, no wonder the poor horse had an impaction. I suspected she'd never pass them on her own. But I hadn't done that kind of surgery since vet school; I was lucky to have a specialist near who did that kind of work every day. No way could I run anesthesia, open her up, and expect the mare to recover.

I could tell these guys didn't care if the mare survived or not. I tried to buy her some time. "This mare's got about sixty feet of intestines in her belly. There's no way I could find all of your stones. It's best if we let her pass them, like your original plan."

"Our man here," he said, gesturing toward Milt, "said the

horse was sick, that he wasn't able to poop this morning."

With my hands still at shoulder level, I gestured slowly toward the baggie containing the two pebbles that I now suspected were uncut diamonds. "She started again. There are two of the stones you want right there."

His eyes darted to the bag, then back to me. "Get it," he told Muscles.

With baggie in hand, Ugly smiled and nodded. "How much longer?"

It could take two to three days, but I'd never say that to this goon. "Soon. Any time now."

He seemed to be considering this when my cell phone started to ring inside my pocket.

#

My heart stuttered when I realized it might be Tess calling. This could be my chance to get help. Ugly glared at me. I could barely draw a breath.

"I have to answer this. It's my assistant. She'll come here if I don't talk to her."

Ugly paused, his face blank, wheels turning.

"Quickly," I prompted him.

He threatened me with the gun, as if I'd forgotten it. "Answer. No funny stuff."

My fingers were shaking, but I managed to get the phone out of my pocket just as the call went to voice mail. Without missing a beat, I swiped to the contact list and dialed Deputy Lujan, putting the phone to my ear. While it rang, part of my brain said *answer, please answer,* while my mouth said, "Hi, Tess. Did you get the boys taken care of?"

I paused as if listening to her chatter while the phone continued to ring. Then, miracles do happen, a voice came through the receiver: "Deputy Lujan."

By God, I had a chance. "I know you said to call if I needed help." I paused, hoping this cryptic message would sink in. "We'll wait and do surgery on this horse in the morning, since I've gotten permission from the owner."

There was a pause now on her end, as though she had to untangle my two statements. She caught onto the last part. "Have you seen Mr. Driscoll?"

"Sure have."

"Is he there now?"

"Yeah, yeah, that's right." I hesitated, and then took a stab at sending more code. "Ah, shoot, that's too bad. Both of 'em?"

"What?"

Ugly frowned.

She said, "Are you in danger?"

Smart woman...thank God! "Sure thing."

Ugly waved the gun, motioning for me to end it.

"Gotta go. See ya later."

"Wait! Stay on the—"

I disconnected the call. I felt like my life line had been cut. The thought of my daughters without any parent crossed my mind, but I quickly set it aside. I would keep my wits about me; I would survive. And I would make sure this mare survived, too.

Ugly used his head to motion Muscles over to me. "Get the phone."

I gave it over.

"Turn it off and give it to me."

Muscles seemed to be struggling with that function. Ugly looked impatient. "Give it to me," he said, taking the phone and turning it off.

I needed to control this situation before the cops arrived, so I wouldn't end up being an expendable hostage like Milt. Taking the stethoscope from around my neck, I started toward the mare, explaining as I went. "I need to listen to her gut, see what kind of movement we've got going on."

They let me. Now...if I could make them feel I was part of their team, we might be back in business. I leaned against the mare, taking comfort from her solid strength and listening to her quiet belly. She seemed fairly comfortable, but I figured it would be temporary. Her best option would be to go to surgery as soon as possible.

"That's better," I said. "Now, we need to give her some exercise."

Without waiting for permission, I unhooked and capped the IV, released the back of the stocks, and swung the side wide. I imagined Muscles leaning over at the perfect moment so I could whack him on the head with the heavy metal bar, but this miracle didn't happen. I backed the mare out, her shod hooves making a scraping sound on the concrete. Leading her outside, I felt I could breathe again, even with the two guys right behind me.

"I'm just going to trot her down a ways and back to get some gas moving in her belly," I said to Ugly.

Still pointing the gun at me, Ugly motioned to Muscles. "Go with him."

Behind my clinic, a cement pad ran down a long shed row filled with enclosed box stalls, horse runs, and hay storage. At the end was a room set up for handling cattle. It contained a hydraulic cattle chute and all kinds of large tools, tools I could use as weapons. If only I could figure out a way to get there.

I trotted the horse back and forth, Muscles trotting alongside like an obedient mastiff. Ugly kept the gun trained on me, and I started to feel like a little duck in a shooting gallery, pinging back and forth. How long would it take for the cavalry to arrive? And when should I make my move? I prayed that the deputy understood there was a gun involved.

We kept this up for what seemed like ages, and Muscles and the horse were beginning to flag. Me? I was glad I'd taken up jogging this summer. Muscles had begun to slow at the far end, conditioned to wait about two thirds of the way for me to turn around and trot back. I thought I heard gravel crackle on the other side of the building, a car pulling up. A glance at Ugly confirmed that he'd heard it too.

I made my move. Trying to drag the mare along with me, I darted toward the cattle room, but she balked and stopped. I hated to, but if I was going to save us, I had to leave her. I believed they'd be most interested in chasing me, and she was too tired to go anywhere. Dropping the lead rope, I made it to the door.

Ugly must've been distracted, or thought I held some value toward his cause, because he didn't shoot. "Get him!" he yelled.

I swung open the door and ran inside. Desperate, I scanned the room and spied an electric cattle prod. Grabbing it, I jumped back beside the door, extending the business end of the prod. Muscles burst through the opening. I aimed for his face and delivered full voltage to his cheek, right below his eye. He fell backward, roaring like a stung bull.

Hay Hook

Giving no mercy, I leaned over him, my adrenaline high. I moved the prongs to his neck and pressed as hard as I could. "This one's for Shirley, you dumb shit!"

He made a gagging noise as the hotshot sparked and vibrated against his throat. He grabbed the plastic end of the prod and jerked it out of my hand. Certain that he was more accomplished at brawling than I was, I knew I couldn't let him get up. My dad's branding iron was hanging on the wall behind me, no longer used, more an object of cowboy art. I grabbed the thing and swung that sucker as hard as I could. It connected to his head with a satisfying *thunk*. Flattened, he didn't move.

Ugly came into the room, gun pointed straight at me. Déjà vu. He fired a shot as I dove behind the cattle chute. The noise deafened me, but at least it alerted the newcomers of the danger. I prayed it was the police.

A female voice shouted, "Drop your weapon!"

My sense of time slowed, while my brain processed images in freeze-frame clicks. Deputy Lujan and Detective LoSasso crouched at the doorway, weapons drawn. Sarge stood at the threshold, teeth bared. Ugly started swinging his gun toward them in slow motion. I threw the branding iron at him, at the same time yelling, "Nooooooooo..." in a voice that sounded muffled to my ringing ears. It did what I wanted, and Ugly turned the gun back toward me.

Another shot fired, the bullet whistling past my right ear. At the same time, Lujan yelled, "Sarge, take him!"

The black dog lunged, mouth open wide, all teeth. He attached himself to Ugly's gun arm and held on, dragging the man down. The gun flew out and landed next to my feet; I kicked it under the chute. Though my ears were ringing, I could hear him scream, "Get him off me," over and over.

Time warped back to normal speed. Lujan and Sarge were right on top of the guy. "Sarge, out," she said, and the dog let go, backing off a single step. Maybe I was imagining things, but I swear that dog's tail was wagging.

"Guard." Sarge loomed with fangs bared, looking like he would like nothing more than to give the guy another go.

LoSasso joined in, and she and Lujan shouted, "Stay on the ground! Face down, hands behind your back!"

"Just keep that dog off of me! Get him away!" Ugly raised his head slightly, one eye fixed on Sarge. Otherwise, he didn't move.

Within moments, Lujan cuffed him, hands behind his back. Her adrenaline must have been pretty high too, because she pulled him up to sitting position single handedly, a guy twice her size. She looked at me. "Are you all right?"

I nodded, tried to speak and couldn't, cleared my throat and tried again. "I'm fine," I said in a voice that croaked. Knees trembling, I slid down to sit on the floor, back against the wall.

LoSasso spoke to Lujan. "I'll call for patrol to come take this one in." Her mouth tipped up at one corner. "I guess I'd better get an ambulance for the one the doc took down."

#

Talk about a rough day! After giving my statement to Detective LoSasso, including my impression that both Milt and Shirley were victims in this deal, I sat on the running board of the K-9 SUV. Sarge sat at my feet, leaning most of his ninety pounds against my leg. Despite having largely ignored me this morning, apparently he now considered us comrades. I felt honored for him to think of me that way. At the moment I was giving him an ear massage, my way of saying thank you for saving my life.

Deputy Lujan and I had done what first aid we could for Milt, both of us happy to pass the baton to the paramedics when they arrived. He didn't look good, but his pupils were equally responsive when I checked, and that was a good sign. Though I'm not trained in human medicine, I figured most mammals were wired in a similar fashion.

Once she'd passed off her prisoners, Lujan threw a tennis ball for Sarge. Evidently this was his reward for biting onto someone and hanging on like fury. While I watched them play, I had a long phone conversation with my colleague to explain why I was referring a horse that had a gut full of stones she couldn't pass. The humane society was taking the mare to his surgery clinic right now.

Together, Lujan and LoSasso walked over from the crime scene, aka my clinic, to join Sarge and me.

"Are you doing better?" Lujan asked.

"I'm fine." Or at least I would be, once I could go home to my girls. "Thanks to you two. And Sarge." I gave him one last pat, and stood.

"You did your share of the take down," Detective LoSasso said. "With any luck, one of these bozos will talk and tell us who all's in on this smuggling deal."

"Work on the one I hit. He didn't seem to be the sharpest scalpel in the pack."

LoSasso smiled. "We'll do that…when he wakes up."

Lujan said, "How do you think they put those stones into the mare's belly?"

"Educated guess? Had to pass them through a tube."

"Do you think a vet was involved?"

"Not necessarily. Anyone can learn to pass a tube. I think a vet would've known the horse would get in trouble."

LoSasso said, "It'll be interesting to see if these two came from Mexico last night, or if there's someone down there in on it as well. We'll track it all down."

I hoped they could. "It's hard to see an animal treated this way. She was expendable too, a beautiful horse like that."

LoSasso said, "We'll charge them with animal cruelty on top of everything else. Would you be willing to testify?"

"It would be my pleasure," I said. "I hope Milt survives to take care of her."

We all stared at the ground for a moment.

Lujan broke the silence. "Smuggling jewels in a horse's belly. That's a new one, even for Colfax."

LoSasso said, "You can dress it up, but it's still Colfax."

I thought of Lujan's partnership with Sarge and Shirley's dream to care for this gentle mare. Because most of my experiences with people and their pets were positive, this incident of animal and human cruelty hit me hard. I supposed there were plenty of pockets of inhumanity along this street, and these cops plunged into them every day. But I wasn't used to it. Suddenly, I felt more tired than I'd ever felt before.

"Do me a favor, will you?" I said. "Lock up when you're done here. I'm going home."

Detective LoSasso studied me, evidently deciding I'd had enough. "We'll be in touch."

Deputy Lujan gave me a brief salute as I turned to leave.

Hay Hook

Right now, I needed to hug my kids. Maybe I'd take them out to dinner tonight at one of the good things West Colfax had to offer—Casa Bonita.

Margaret Mizushima

About the Author:

Margaret Mizushima enjoys writing in the contemporary crime/mystery and historical genres. After earning a master's degree in speech/language pathology, she practiced in a hospital and her own rehabilitation agency. Now, she uses her experience in communication disorders, business, and her husband's veterinary practice as fodder for her fiction and has received contest awards and short story publication. She likes reading and hiking, and she lives on a small ranch in northern Colorado where she and her husband raised two daughters and a multitude of animals.

You can find Margaret on Facebook and LinkedIn.

A Full Moon Over a Desolate Plain
By Thea Hutcheson

Thea's inspiration for "A Full Moon Over a Desolate Plain" focused on Colfax as a connection between East and West:

Those were the times, full of big autos and bigger dreams. I wanted to capture the sense of wonder, hope, and the underlying despair that must have imbued everyone who traveled that long road on the way from their past to what they hoped was a better future.

A Full Moon Over a Desolate Plain

The air on Colfax Avenue roils with the thick smell of sweet half-burnt gas coming off the finned behemoths rolling along this asphalt river. It carries the flotsam and jetsam of America toward a mythical land of dreams on the far side of the mountains to the west.

Unlike everyone else, I'm a man who has no dreams. I have an aching emptiness that I'm driven to fill by skimming the hopes of the steady stream of people headed for somewhere else.

I'm making my way toward the Mallory Motel on the south side of Colfax. Just as I reach the driveway, I see her standing at the corner, waiting for the light. Jenny, the waitress from Davies Chuck Wagon Diner, on her way to work. She's a little slip of a young woman, with breasts like buds and a flash of freckles across her nose. She sees me notice her and smiles, dipping her head by way of greeting. I nod back and then the light changes and she's crossing the street.

The heady tang of liquor floats out from the dinner party that has sprung up at the motel after the long day's trek. From the sidewalk, I can see the group of people settled in the right corner of the squared off U-shaped motel, where the western wing meets the two-story back section. I can taste the dreams that rise up from them, buoyed by hope and anchored by desperation.

I prefer the evenings, when the train of pilgrims settles into the string of motels that dot the street to cook their dinners over hot plates in the tiny motel rooms or eat take-out from the scattering of restaurants that line Colfax or even, as now, enjoy an impromptu barbecue at the edge of the large asphalt parking lot with some kids playing jump rope and tag.

A group of women wearing pedal pushers and sleeveless blouses sit on the lawn chairs they have unfolded from the car trunks or the kitchen chairs brought out from the rooms. They keep their legs discreetly crossed while their loafers mark time to Buddy Holly blasting from someone's car radio.

As I watch these people, I think about how I can steal bits of people's dreams, chew on their hopes, but I can't introduce myself to Jenny.

A buttoned up egghead with horn-rimmed glasses watches me approach. I smile wide and lift up the six-pack.

"Is it all right if I join in? Looks like you've got a nice little party goin'."

He shrugs, looking toward the knot of people near the barbecue and the cooler next to it. "Why not?"

His dreams are all about numbers and engines the size of houses. I can feel the passion, but it's covered with sour, prickly anger that comes from always being left on the outside. I nod pleasantly, feeling his eyes, his wistful desire to follow as I head toward them.

The talk is always the same—what they've left, where they're going, their adventures on the road, and how happy they'll be when they get there.

What they don't say is what they're willing to do to get there, what they'll leave behind, what fears goad them.

Those unspoken words are what drive them down the road. It's easy pickings and I take a slice of that rich marrow, a bite from the sweet nougat of the ones that are still full of hope, still headed down the road on faith, driven by excitement, girded by belief.

I never take enough for them to notice, but I hope that one day I will fill the yawning emptiness inside me.

I can look just like them, a hard luck guy hoping for a bit of company. My scuffed loafers clack hollowly as I walk toward the grill, watching the tow-headed, gap-toothed boys, and pigtailed, shouting girls at their play across the parking lot.

They don't interest me. Their dreams are too small, and their fears are often too large.

The dozen or so adults, though, I can smell their dreams, their hopes, their fears, which adds seasoning to the burgers and hotdogs grilling on the barbecue off to the side, mingling with the smell of briquettes and beer and the earthy undertone of cheap whiskey.

A woman with a pale blue and white checkered dress, open at the neck and turned up at the collar to show off the double string of pearls, eyes me. Her bouffant hairdo is stiff with hairspray. She's running from her husband and looking for someone to take care of her.

Two of the men are considering it, but only one—the egghead I just left behind—is worth the effort. I watch her watch them through her cat's-eye sunglasses. Her fear fights with her desire for the dashing duck tail and rolled-up jeans bad boy. Her red lacquered nails tap on the beer bottle as she weighs her safety against her need for adventure and the cost in humiliation and black eyes.

She notices me and arches one eyebrow in interest. I'm in my mid-thirties, slim, pale, my brown hair carefully parted to the side and conservatively short. I can be handsome when I want to be, plainer when I need to be, appearing however suits the moment. Now I look like a regular Joe.

No one ever notices that I'm more—or less—than they are, never know the hunger that pushes me into their company. The men always accept me for my worn slacks and simple shirt, and the women trust my face, and that's how it should be. How it needs to be.

I hand over my six-pack to a man with the beginnings of a beer belly and a soft face filled by a ready smile. "Roland," he says, extending a hand.

"Mike," I say. I take his callused hand and breathe in the taste of his hopes for a fresh start, a nice home for his growing family. He has good skills with his hands and believes he can put them to use on the back lots of Hollywood. He has an introduction from his last boss, whose cousin is one of Paramount's construction crew chiefs. His vision of the life he wants is crystal clear. He and the little woman, watching over four of the kids playing off to the side, have saved money for years and, with the sale of their house, they will buy the home they've always wanted and live the good life in the sunshine of Los Angeles.

He's worked toward this dream for so long and so hard, it's like compound interest and he can afford to give some up without losing sight of it.

So, I work my magic, syphoning off a bit of that dream, just a slice of the brightest edge of his hopes, tucking it into the void in my chest, where it gleams like a sickle moon over a desolate winter plain.

A Full Moon Over a Desolate Plain

His eyes grow fuzzy for a moment, confused, and then I let his hand go. He stares at me and I watch him decide nothing happened before he smiles broadly. "Have a cold one, Mike. Dinner's almost ready." He lifts the lid on the cooler and gestures. I take a brown bottle, beaded with drops of icy water. The cold is a shocking contrast to the late afternoon sun beating down on my shoulders.

The bottles tinkle and clink as he works my six-pack into the ice. I use the church key on the table next to a half-full ashtray, a pack of Marlboros, and a Zippo lighter with a Marine insignia on it.

The beer sparkles on my tongue. I swallow, relishing the clean bitterness and look around again.

Most of the people are down to their dregs, their fears rampant behind their fixed smiles. Their dreams are sour and I pass over them.

After a while Roland calls everyone to eat, and I follow them to the grill. I share their meal, joking, listening to their stories, picking up a bite of hope here, snacking on a wishful thought there, always looking for what I am missing.

When the sun sets, the mothers call their children from their games and shoo them into the rooms to change for bed, leaving the woman with the sunglasses behind, and casting warning glances toward their husbands as if they fear for their fidelity.

The evening air cools quickly after the sun disappears over the craggy peaks. The men gather around the dying embers of the grill.

Their stories turn to bawdy jokes, and I taste the raw desire that flames up. The sliver of the moon inside me turns ruddy, but nothing can warm that vast cold emptiness. I finish my beer and toss it in the trash where it tinkles into slivers.

When I turn around, I see Jenny walking past the motel. The light has fled, but I can see her long blonde ponytail swing as she walks up Colfax, on her way home from the dinner shift at Davies. I know that by this time of the day, strands of hair have escaped from the ponytail, and they frame her face in softly curving lines.

She's a favorite at the diner, ever patient in the face of the people that flood into the place, bringing their disappointments, their fears, their irritations with them.

I've watched her as she serves their coffee, their pancakes, their fussy kids. She remains cheerful, smiling, cracking a joke, offering consolation and understanding in the face of their fears, their lost hopes, their idiotic pie-in-the-sky dreams.

I don't know why, I don't even know why it matters, but she has haunted that empty space inside me since I first saw her.

As she walks past the entrance, she glances my way. My eyes drink her in, her tired eyes, the unruly hair falling from her ponytail, the stained apron.

I want... something. I have no name for what tugs me toward her. She has no hopes that I can cut away, no aspirations that I can take, nothing savory to chew on. And yet, I'm drawn to her. But I've never acted on it.

As she passes in front of the motel, the smile she gives me is worn by the hard work, but friendly as she walks toward Independence Street. She doesn't live in a motel anymore. I know because I've watched her for a while now. A day after she moved out of the Trail's End motel, I followed her home.

A Full Moon Over a Desolate Plain

I think about the room she's found at a cozy tan-sided boarding house with a well-kept yard three blocks south of Colfax. The old woman who keeps it is sour, but she saves a smile for Jenny.

Jenny always appreciates her raised beds, praises the woman for her hard work, bends over to sniff the newly-opened roses, the purple lilacs blooming down the hedge alongside the yard. She offers a funny story from work, always cheerful.

I'm startled when a chair scrapes concrete and I look to see the woman with the sunglasses reaching for her sweater. With the emptiness inside me churning, I turn away from Jenny and lift the sweater from where it has fallen behind the chair and settle it over her shoulders.

She's taken her sunglasses off and I can see her eyes are heavily outlined, the lids bright blue. Her eyebrows are two precise arches. It's a nearly perfect mask that hides desperate fears that stink like rank sweat.

She wonders if her husband will find her, whether she will find a man to take care of her, what kind of work a Bridge Wife could find.

Putting the cigarette to her red lips, she considers me.

I never do more than take from the people I interact with but, the feelings Jenny stirs make me feel generous. I take the matchbook from the woman's hand and pull a match out. Light flares when I strike it, and her face is illuminated by the flame, making her look young. Like Jenny, but not at all like Jenny.

She eyes me as she puffs.

Sulfur and cigarette smoke fill my nose and burn my eyes.

"Don't let the James Dean schtick fool you," I say softly, as I shake the match out and lean over to lay it in the ceramic ashtray on the table beside her. "He's a bad egg. The egghead, though, he would be a good catch. He'd be grateful and you'd never want for anything. I know, gratitude can grate, but not the same way a black eye will."

"What?" she asks, but it's more that she's wondering if she's really been that obvious.

"On the other hand," I say, "the sea is full of fish, and you've got better bait than most."

I see her consider trying to hook me, but before she speaks, I step away.

"Goodnight," I say to the knot of men around the grill and take my leave, glancing up toward Jenny, who is turning down her street on her way home.

Waitressing is hard, dirty business, and though she's young, I worry about her wearing herself out. She works a split shift most days, breakfast and dinner, because that's where the money is.

Something jerks inside me and I wonder why I care.

I still live in the Trail's End, a few blocks back to the east. What is wrong with me? Giving advice, mooning after a girl. I wonder if maybe it's time to move on as I watch the cars sail past on the street.

A breeze from the foothills, gateway to the mountains, pushes the smell of exhaust, green grass, and greasy-spoon food past me. It's the smell of life, of living, and I feel like it's leaving me behind.

I curse myself for falling in with the dregs that make their way toward something, anything.

A Full Moon Over a Desolate Plain

Lots of people are out in this beautiful night, laughing loudly as they walk along the sidewalks, working at a respite from their lives. The liquor store and the bars are doing a good business with tides of people washing in and out.

I'm waiting at the light to cross the street when I hear footsteps behind me. I turn and there she is, pushing a wayward strand of hair behind a shell-shaped ear.

She smiles at me, bold as brass, but I hear the faint tremble in her voice. "You spend so much time watching me, I thought it was time we met. My name's Jenny, Jenny Washburn, but you know that don't you? Hank says you asked after me."

Her eyes are bright in the neon glow of the liquor store sign behind me. The colors wash over her—thin bars of green, red, white, in quick succession, like the lit spokes of the Ferris wheel at Lakeside.

I realize I'd like to take her to the amusement park, go in the Fun House, watch her laugh, catch her so she doesn't fall in the barrel ride.

I wonder if she'd like that. I can't tell and that's strange. I've never met anyone like her before. She's not empty inside either like so many people I see, used up by life.

No, she brims with it. She just has no hopes, no driving dream. She's just living and touching everything in her life each moment, one after the other.

Including me.

"I did ask after you," I say, casting about for something to say. "You just work so hard. But you always have a smile. That's rare."

She nodded, watching me with her head cocked, trying

to parse me. "Hank says he'll take his bat to you if you try anything."

Hank is the day cook at the diner. He's a burly man who saw horrors in Europe during the war. He wishes he'd never seen them, or that he could forget them. Or that he could drown them once and for all in the bottles of Jack Daniels that he buys every week.

"I believe him. But I wouldn't." I realize that I haven't told her my name. "It's nice to finally meet you, Jenny. I'm Mike. Mike Ashford." It's not my name, but I've used it long enough that it fits, like an old coat.

"Well, Mike. I'm glad to meet you finally, too. Gladder to know that Hank won't have to get his bat out." She grins, and it makes her face brighten, and I think again of the Ferris wheel and us at the top with city lights spread out around us like a glittering skirt.

I smile at her. What should I say? I'm never at a loss. Connections are my tools of trade.

"Have you been to Lakeside?" Stupid, stupid thing to say, but it was in my head and fell right out of my mouth.

She stares at me for a long moment and shakes her head. "The diner tips don't stretch quite that far. I went to the State Fair in Pueblo, though, when I was a kid."

Fairs are good for hopes and dreams, little ones like winning the penny toss, bigger ones like impressing the girl and scoring points that could be redeemed later in the back seat of a car, or winning the blue ribbon. Tasty like cotton candy and ice cream, but not substantial.

But nothing has been for a long time.

"You want to go?" Why did I ask her that?

"With you or in general?" She struggles to keep her face neutral, amiable.

This is the most powerful emotion I've gotten from her. She wants me to say that I want her to go with me.

"Yeah. With me. Unless you have some other guy hidden away." Please say there's no one else, because I'll find him, suck him dry, and toss him in the gutter.

She shakes her head, trapping my gaze with eyes that are lit up with more than the flashing lights.

I picture the Ferris wheel again, the warm summer evening cooling off, her body warm against mine, the smell of popcorn and axle grease mingled with cigarette smoke and perfume swirling up around us.

"No, nobody else," she says.

Something jerks inside me, and I'm absurdly pleased.

"I'm off on Tuesday."

"Tuesday's good," I say. "After lunch?"

"I could make a picnic and we could eat in one of the pavilions."

I nod. "Eleven then? Where shall I meet you?"

"Eleven's good. And you can pick me up from Mrs. Jamison's like a gentleman. I know you know where her house is."

I redden with embarrassment for playing the swag and her knowing I've been spying, but I hope she can't tell in the garish light.

"You saw, eh?" What is wrong with me? Sloppy. Hank with his bat, Mrs. Jamison with her beady eyes and a ready hand on the phone. They look out for her. I am not immune to bats or cops with billy clubs. I'm usually smooth, easy, nothing to notice, missed every time.

"Not like you were slick or anything," she says, poking gentle fun. "At first I thought you were looking at the house for sale up the block. But you were there too often, and I can add."

She touches my arm lightly, and something warm and wonderful bursts out from her touch, crawls up my arm and swims right down onto that winter plain and makes a warm spot of spring bloom. The sickle moon shining down on it all waxes, turning silver bright, promising the sunrise I've been missing all this time.

The gnawing hunger that has driven me since I can remember fades. I recognize her caring, her interest, and I know this is what she gives to the people at the diner.

I understand then why she pulls at me so. It has nothing to do with wanting, with dreaming, with desire. She gives something from herself, right down in the heart of her, the truest part of her. She cares. About lost puppies and cranky kids, heart-worn women and soul-seared men.

And me.

She never accepted a date with them.

But she has with me.

I look up and down the street, all the people running on hopes and dreams and pie in the sky schemes. They're all as empty as I am. I'm taking their wisps of nothing and wondering why I never get full.

"See you Tuesday then," I say, that warmth growing from a spark to a comfortable ember that she will blow on, making a summer breeze, rich with flavor, nuanced with feeling.

A Full Moon Over a Desolate Plain

"Don't be late." She pats my arm and twirls away, like a dancer, and is off down Colfax, her shadow waltzing behind her.

I look up and down the asphalt river, carrying all those hopes and dreams, and tell it, "You don't have nothin' on me."

Thea Hutcheson

About the Author:

Lois Tilton of Locus said Thea Hutcheson's work in *Realms of Fantasy's* 100th issue *"is sensual, fertile, with seed quickening on every page. Well done..."* She has upcoming stories in three of the critically acclaimed *Fiction River* anthologies—*Alchemy and Steam*, *Sparks*, and *Recycled Pulp*.

She lives in an economically depressed, unscenic, nearly historic small city in Colorado. When she's not working diligently as a Planning Commissioner to change that situation, she writes, and fills the time between bouts at the computer as a factotum and an event planner.

Find more of her work at www.theahutcheson.com and connect with Thea on Twitter at @theah1771.

Martha Husain

Crossing the Uncanny Valley
By Martha Husain

It took Martha a few tries to adapt her idea to the Colfax theme:

A few weeks before the deadline for submissions, the story I had started working on for the Colfax theme flopped at my critique group. I was trying to think of what would make a better story—something like Twilight Zone or Dr. Who, but with a PG-13 touch of naughtiness—when I picked up the mail and saw the Sports Illustrated swimsuit edition. Great. One look and I knew I had to hide it from the kids. That sparked an idea—something hidden away on Colfax Avenue. Someone's naughty little secret.

Binge-watching the Alien, Matrix, and Riddick movies provided plenty of background for a futuristic sci-fi setting. The golem in The Golem and the Jinni by Helene Wecker had me thinking about a being created to someone's specifications. But the heart of the story involves basic human issues—responsibility, humanity, and trust. All of which I find are more fun to contemplate in the context of a futuristic sci-fi world.

Crossing the Uncanny Valley

"Hey, Kaleb," Wes called back to me from the pilot's seat. "Looks like we made it to Denver. Or what's left of it."

I jerked up in a jump seat at the back of the shuttle. I didn't realize I'd fallen asleep after giving the controls to the middle-aged professor around four in the morning, somewhere over western Kansas. Probably no one in our small band of survivors felt safe letting our guard down after narrowly escaping the Mechs' attack on Kansas City. But the exhaustion of fleeing for one's life catches up with you after a few days.

"Any Mechs out there?" I asked, my voice scratchy with sleep.

In the co-pilot's seat in front of me, Jo's head popped up, her bright purple boy-cut mussed from sleep. Her shift of flying should have come last night after mine. But she'd looked so vulnerable, curled up asleep, hugging the grenade launcher that saved our asses when a couple of Mech flyers caught our trail outside Salina, Kansas. Wes and I agreed to do the gentlemanly thing and let her sleep. Hutch, then on his third Red Bull, had offered to take the shift. I was glad Wes told him no. Hutch's kamikaze flying scared me more than Mechs.

I peered out the laser-scarred portal of the four-seater shuttle, checking for life—human or machine. A bleak winter dawn lit the distant peaks of the Rocky Mountains, but shadows still lingered over the rubble that used to be the Mile High City. A line of mangled, burned-out vehicles trailed from the lifeless metropolis into a sea of blackened earth below.

By now, pretty much every city in the world must look like this. Not a soul alive. Not even any bodies left behind. If Wes hadn't heard on his ham radio about the old missile bunker at Cheyenne Mountain taking in survivors, I might have believed we four were the last living humans.

Jo slung the grenade launcher over her canary yellow parka and bent over the dashboard monitors. "Nothing showing on the movement or heat sensors, Kal. No badass brainy machines. No biologics. Not even wildlife. Outside air is too toxic."

Wes whistled. "Dead silent. It's just uncanny. An honest-to-God uncanny valley."

Hutch kicked his mud-caked boots up onto the armrest of my seat. He rolled a cigarette butt into a leaf of jimson weed he'd found in Topeka, growing in the cracked pavement that had once been Interstate 70. "Too bad. Could go for some more dog tartar."

Jo's jaw tightened. To her credit, she ignored his attempt to goad her to anger or tears over the loss of her papillon, Coco. Jo was the only female in our band of refugees, and not bad looking, if Gothic Punk was your style. I mostly dated girls I met at the university library, which meant they studied a lot and never had much time for me. Hutch's type seemed to be any female with two legs. Jo had warned him that if he tried to touch her again, she wouldn't hesitate to blast a grenade into his groin.

I'd just as soon have left Hutch behind in Topeka when he went out to hunt abandoned pets. He claimed he'd dropped out of the chemical engineering program at the U to pursue a career as an "extreme sports professional." As far as I could tell, his supposed career consisted of working at Xtreme Splatter Paintball. But we had the shuttle thanks to him, and no one asked how the adrenaline junkie had snagged a Security Forces vehicle during the fall of Kansas City.

Wes cleared his throat. "We turn south here, don't we, Kaleb?"

"Well, fuck me blind," Hutch mumbled to the rolled up chew in his fingers. "The know-it-all chick in the next seat has an implanted memory card chock full of info, and the professor asks the dumbass business major for directions."

My gut tightened. I willed myself to ignore Hutch and unfolded the laminated map I'd found under the seat.

It still felt awkward having a professor of civil engineering looking to me—the youngest guy in the bunch—for direction. I was just a sophomore last fall when the artificial intelligence machines everyone called Mechs declared war on the human race. But Jo and Hutch didn't get along. Asking one of them would only lead to a fight. Wes probably knew the answer, but made a point of asking me anyway.

"I used to know a girl from Denver," Hutch said, stuffing the chew in his mouth. "She was a limber little yoga instructor. And horny as the devil."

Jo sniffed. "That makes you an expert on the locale, I suppose?"

He smiled, working the chew with his teeth. "I'm an expert on a lotta things, honey."

I fought to concentrate, using my finger to gauge the distance on the map. "The Cheyenne Mountain bunker is about sixty miles south of here, near Colorado Springs," I said, probably too loud. My ears were ringing something awful. I yawned to see if I could get them to pop.

Hutch spit a glob of chew on the floor. "We should keep going. Get to the colony by nightfall, have a hot meal and a shower. Sleep naked under the sheets in a decent bed for a change." He winked at Jo.

"I wonder if we should stop for a while," Wes said. "The shuttle's batteries are almost dead. And the power grid's probably down. We could land and scavenge for supplies while the solar cells recharge the batteries."

"There's nothing left in this town," Jo put in. "No human life. No Mechs." A light blinked sporadically on the port of the memory chip implanted behind her ear. "Last report I found says the Mechs moved on to raze L.A. Their nearest installation's in Albuquerque."

"There's always something left behind," Hutch drawled. "Only takes one Mech to coordinate a fleet of drones."

"What do you think, Kaleb?" Wes asked.

"Go ahead and look for a place to put us down," I said. "We can stop here just until—"

The ringing in my head spiked to excruciating levels and jolted my teeth like an electric shock.

Shit. We must have crossed an ultrasonic sensor beam.

The blast from the ground cannon hit before I could warn Wes. The shuttle spun to the left like a whirligig in the wind.

The automatic restraints pulled tight against my chest. I could hardly breathe, let alone think, before the shuttle hit the ground. Metal screamed, glass crunched. Wreckage pounded over the roof and sides.

The shuttle groaned to a stop.

I let out a shaky breath. Caustic air that smelled like wet paint burned my nose and throat. The airtight walls must have breached and let in the toxic mess outside.

"Masks on!" I croaked while digging for the emergency oxygen kit under my seat.

Jo was sobbing, a muffled choking sound.

At least she'd put her mask on.

"Hutch?" I called out, my voice distorted by the mask's speakers.

"Yo," came his muffled reply. "Door's jammed."

"Wes," croaked Jo. "Oh God, Wes."

The pilot's seat was covered in blood and chunks of scorched meat and bone. The shock of Wes's death registered with me only as a fact, like a wound I wouldn't feel until the adrenaline wore off. All that penetrated my brain was that we were down to three. Something had shot us down. We needed to find cover.

Smoke poured in from the gaps in the dash. I grabbed Jo by the sleeve of her puffy parka. "Get out! Before the battery cells catch fire."

Hutch hacked the door off with a small emergency axe.

Jo fought free of my grip. She dashed to the back of the shuttle and snagged the med kit, a belt of grenades, and a bag of water. She stuffed them into her backpack while I hauled her out the door.

My backpack. Shit.

I turned back. I'd left everything I owned in it, under the pilot seat on the shuttle. All my tools, survival gear, and my handheld processor.

Flames erupted over the entire shuttle. I staggered back. Too late to rescue anything else. Or anyone. Not that there was anything left of Wes to save. It seemed so damn unfair that we could come so close only to lose him. I wondered if any of us stood a chance of making it to the colony alive.

I didn't see Hutch. The asshole. He should've stayed with us in case we needed help. I kept a tight hold on Jo's hand and hurried down the street to the wreckage of a burned out Security Forces tank. The remains of a mid-size Mech as big as a tractor-trailer hung from the support struts of a shuttle landing pad across the street. The Mech's circuit boards had oxidized in the toxic air, blackening the metallic mish-mash of scavenged parts that made up its bulk.

We scrambled over the cratered pavement, keeping to the shelter of blown-out buildings. If something Mech remained that could take out our shuttle, it would likely come by to check for survivors. We needed to find a place to hole up and regroup. Someplace with breathable air.

I checked the gauge on my oxygen tank. An eighth of a tank left. Might last three hours.

If the Mechs didn't find us first.

A pair of silvery creatures flitted toward the shuttle. They circled and flapped to a landing on the broken windscreen. Mech-pies. The bird-like machines pecked at shiny pieces of metal under the dash, chattering to each other in clicks and whirs.

Jo lifted the grenade launcher and took aim.

I pushed the barrel down. "They don't know we're here yet," I said in a low voice. "Shoot, and they will."

We needed more distance between us and the crash site. I

slipped around a bank of garbage piled across the mouth of the next cross street, hauling Jo after me.

"Where are we?" I whispered through the mask's speakers.

Jo took in the gutted high-rises, their collapsed floors looking like plates of pancakes. Her eyes glazed for a moment while the light from her implanted memory card pulsed behind her ear. "East Colfax Avenue."

"Any place here that might have breathable air?"

She blinked at the ruined storefronts, naming each in turn. "Six-Shooter Pawn. Lucky Penny Payday Loans. Hong Kong One-Dollar Buffet. Cloud Nine Lounge. Sounds like the dregs of the city."

"A place for desperate people." No one could be more desperate than we were. And the ruined street offered no more hope of salvation than it probably ever had.

"Are we going to look for Hutch?" Jo's fierce whisper crackled through the speakers.

I took a long breath of tank air and let it out slowly. "Believe me, I'm tempted not to. But he seems to have a knack for making it out alive. Like it or not, I'll do what I have to to survive."

Jo suddenly clutched my arm, and I thought she must have spotted more Mechs. I followed her gaze and found the third survivor of our ill-fated shuttle standing atop the edge of an upended slab of sidewalk. The transparent pane of his handheld processor scanned the ruined landscape. We hurried toward him, through the rubbish-strewn street, and took cover alongside a concrete road barrier near his perch.

He smirked at Jo. "Couldn't stay away from my body for even a minute, could you, sweet cheeks?" The air mask speakers made Hutch's usual suggestive comments sound as alluring as the voice of an auto-banking machine. "Well, you and your dumbass watchdog are in luck. Right in the heart of the wickedest street in America, I've found just what we need."

He hopped down from his perch and made his way toward a steel door nearly obscured by debris.

"What is this place?" I whispered to Jo.

"Queen of Sheba Ethiopian Restaurant—that can't be right." Her brow pinched as she surveyed the towering ruin above. "The image I have for this location is a little strip mall eatery. It closed back in 2043. This place must have been something new."

The fallen pillars of white marble and twisted lengths of ornamental wrought iron suggested the place had been pretty spiffy. Half a blue-tiled dome remained, cracked open like an eggshell. The mosaic lining the interior depicted a night sky full of stars.

"Looks more like a queen's palace," I said.

"But would it have an oxygen generator?"

I shrugged. "Think our chances are better here or at the dollar buffet?"

I rose and followed Hutch to the steel door set in a wall of concrete at ground level. Our resourceful comrade had the deadbolt on the door picked before I got there. His handheld beeped and displayed a six-digit code for the electronic handle lock.

"Fools build a bunker," he said, "practically advertise it with a metal lattice that shows up on an ordinary scan. Then they give it off-the-shelf security locks a ten-year old could break into." He punched the code into the numbered panel on the door. The handle clicked, and he swung the door open. A bank of fluorescent lights blinked on, illuminating a placard that read 'Level 0' and a steel staircase leading underground.

I hesitated at the door. "You don't suppose we'll run into an irate homeowner with a rocket launcher?"

Hutch snorted and clanked down the steps. "The biggest problem with a bunker is you have to be there when the apocalypse hits, not vacationing in Tahiti. If anyone had made it inside before the attack, they'd have barred the door." His voice echoed up the stairwell. "And we'd still be stuck out there."

I inspected the back of the door. The six-inch-thick steel bars spanning it would have prevented anyone from entering, if they had been put it place. No one could be home.

I beckoned Jo inside, then barred the door behind us.

Jo tapped the instant-read air quality gauge on her O_2 tank. The portion of the bar in the red area dropped a hair. "The air inside is better."

"Air scrubbers?" I said hopefully, checking for vents in the concrete block walls.

Jo pressed her fingers to an interface screen opposite the door, but it failed to respond. "Might be just a pocket of clean air."

"I'll take what I can get," I said and started down the stairs.

Hutch was waiting for us at what looked like a steel garage door. He flipped a switch and the door rumbled up. "Cool, isn't it? An airlock straight out of *Fallout: Mars Colony*."

I must have looked as confused as I felt.

Jo rolled her eyes. "It's a role-playing game. Impossibly muscled heroes wasting evil mutants to rescue the freak-of-nature girl with melons for boobs."

I made an appropriately disapproving face that hopefully disguised my imagination's willingness to conjure said heroines.

Another door stood a couple yards from the first. Huge, louvered vents took up most of the wall space between. Jo and I warily followed Hutch into the room.

A buzzer sounded, and the door behind us slammed down. The vents roared to life. Jo tapped the gauge on her air tank. The readout bar dropped out of the red into yellow.

The door on the other side whisked up.

The sudden change in scenery made me feel as if I'd traveled through a wormhole. The bunker's utilitarian style ended at the airlock. The room beyond looked like a lounge in a luxury hotel. My boat shoes sank into an Oriental rug. A pair of brocade armchairs faced a cushy leather sofa. Wood paneling carved with vines and fruit lined the walls, and huge swaths of velvet draperies framed the entrances.

The tension of days of running for our lives loosened its hold on me. It was hard to feel threatened when a place as swanky as this remained intact.

I checked my air quality gauge. A hair outside green. "Is the air safe to breathe?"

Hutch pulled off his mask and shook his greasy hair loose. "Safe enough."

Jo removed her mask. "We can live with this air for a few days before we get sick."

Hutch stroked a hand across the sofa's smooth surface and mimicked the sound of a woman reaching orgasm.

Jo's mouth went tight and thin.

I grimaced and wondered which would run out first—the air or our tolerance for Hutch?

He brushed aside a drape and opened up a control center

panel. "Bunkers like these weren't designed to go indefinitely on internal power and recycled air. If this one's been running since Denver fell, it'll be almost maxed out on both air and power stores."

Jo and I crowded behind him as he tapped through a series of screens. I'd hoped we could live here until things improved outside. But the bar indicating remaining power in the hydrogen fuel cells showed only a sliver. Four percent.

"Power failure in 116 hours," Jo read from the screen. "Without electricity for the air scrubbers, oxygen will run out."

I stared at the readout, cursing our luck. We hadn't found the promised land after all.

"If there's an oxygen generator here, we could use it to fill our tanks," Jo suggested. "Then head for Cheyenne Mountain on foot."

I did the math in my head. "The colony is sixty-plus miles away. Even at a stiff pace, we'd need over a day to get there. Our tanks would run out first."

A worry line notched Jo's brow. "Maybe we could find a place to refill on the way. Or bring extra tanks?"

"Or not," Hutch said, staring at the *Item not found* message on the screen. "Just checked inventory. No tanks."

Neither Jo nor I said anything. A bad feeling settled in my gut. We were probably all thinking the same thing. It would be easy enough for two people to make it with three tanks. Better still, only one person with three.

"Maybe we can salvage a generator from something and bring it with us," I suggested.

The worry lines on Jo's face relaxed a little. I don't know if she realized how impractical such a plan would be. But if Hutch believed it, we might gain enough time to come up with a better idea.

"First things first." I laid a hand on her shoulder. "We've got to fill our tanks with good air. Can you find an oxygen generator, Hutch?"

A diagram of the bunker flashed up and zeroed in on Level -3. Maintenance.

"Down two floors." Hutch scrolled past diagrams of the intervening level. "Right below my new pad—the master suite. Got a waterbed. Ever tried one of those, sugar lips? There's the Jacuzzi and—Hello? What's this?" He zoomed in on a long rectangular chamber labeled *NIH 07891110987-CRM C*.

Jo squinted at the diagram. "Support systems up the wazoo. Triple fail-safe back-ups. I'm guessing it's a cryochamber."

"Someone wanted to sleep through the apocalypse?" I wondered aloud.

"Or save someone who was dying?" Jo whispered.

Hutch brought up a log record. The dates went back more than a decade. His eyes gleamed. "It ain't empty."

A chill coursed down my spine. It was kind of creepy to think someone had stowed a loved one in this plush mausoleum. But who would go through the trouble of preserving this person and not come back to save them?

Hutch took off around the corner of the draperied entrance.

Jo and I scrambled after him, past a heavy metal door and down a stairwell. We were out of breath when we caught up with him in Level -2. He pried a gilt-framed mirror the size of a parking space off a wall papered in gold fleur-de-lis. I nearly jumped out of my skin when he let the mirror fall and shatter on the floor.

Hutch didn't seem to notice, he was so absorbed with what he'd found. His hands gripped the edge of a glass case, the size of a coffin, and slid it out of the wall. Opaque plastic sheeting covered the occupant, except for its face.

Like a rubbernecker at an accident scene, I couldn't help drawing closer. Smooth skin, deathly pale, made it clear the person had been about my age. But for the grace of God, it might have been any one of us. I shivered. I got the feeling we shouldn't disturb this unfortunate person in its final resting place.

Hutch wasted no time popping the seals on the lid and raising his handheld over the occupant's face.

Jo threw up her hands. "Jesus, Hutch. Leave it alone."

I stepped in closer. "Once you open a cryochamber the body will deteriorate."

"It's not a cryo. It's not even a person." He narrowed his eyes at his handheld. His face split into a huge grin. "It's a cyborg."

I slid beside Hutch. My doubts about his assessment vanished when the systems diagnostics screen came up. A schematic of both the robotic and organic systems of the cyborg showed the functional status of all components. Living flesh and ultra-sophisticated microelectronics. I had never seen this kind of hybrid creation, and the idea both fascinated and repulsed me. "I thought cyborgs were illegal."

Jo hitched a hip on the arm of a paisley wingchair. "The International Human Rights Court barred the use of human tissue in a creature of non-human intelligence back in the late '50s. The ruling effectively killed the industry."

"That don't mean you couldn't have one made," Hutch said, poring over the diagnostics. "If you had the connections. And plenty of money."

Jo scoffed. "Maybe ten, fifteen years ago, before Cyborgenics of Pyongyang went belly-up. It's hard enough to get parts to fix a ten-year old dishwasher, let alone put together something as complicated and illegal as a cyborg. Even if you succeeded, you could never use it anywhere in public."

"Which explains why this one's hidden away here," I said. "In a secret survivalist bunker. It also makes me wonder if it could be of use to us."

"What we need," said Jo, sliding down into the chair, "is a portable source of oxygen. A cyborg would need oxygen to survive as well."

I cocked my head. "It can't possibly have something the size of an O_2 generator inside it."

"Might have a good air scrubbing system though." She unslung the grenade launcher and laid it across her lap. "If so, we could salvage it and use it to get us all to Cheyenne Mountain."

The idea of taking apart such a technological wonder just for parts seemed a travesty beyond words. Especially now that civilization had taken such a hit. Yes, we had to think survival first, but this cyborg was a monument of human achievement. Like a treasure salvaged from the glory of Rome after the Huns sacked the city. Another Dark Ages was upon us. If we could find a way to survive and still preserve the cyborg, we should.

"Don't you think we could get the scrubber to work without taking the cyborg apart?" I suggested.

Hutch flipped down a panel on the side of the cyborg's box.

"Hell, yes. But that ain't all it's got. This thing's kitted out with a half dozen special systems for survival assistance. Water purification and a limited chemical synthesis capability. A real sweet piece of work."

"Sounds like just what we need," I said. "Can you get these systems running?"

"No prob." He flipped the panel back up and brought up the controls. "I'll just fire it up."

"No." Jo leapt to her feet. "Don't you dare bring it to life, not without disassembling it. Look at the core processor in its head. That thing's an AI. Despite its human face, it's a Mech."

I held up my hands. "This cyborg has to be at least ten years old. You said so yourself. It might have an AI brain, but it's a long way from self-direction like a Mech."

She stepped closer. "It's not human either."

Hutch inserted himself between Jo and me. "And it's not yours." He jabbed a thumb to his chest. "I found it. It's mine."

The malice in Jo's eyes could have burned out a battalion of Mechs. Hutch returned her look with smug insolence.

I pinched the bridge of my nose. "Hutch, I hate to sound like your mother, but you know you can't keep it. There was a reason they were banned, and anyway Jo's right. It's close enough to a Mech that no one's gonna let you bring it into Cheyenne Mountain. Before we leave, you're gonna have to put it back in stasis."

He gave me a sideways glance. "You're such a dumbass. We aren't going to be able to put it back in stasis. That takes loads of specialized know-how, equipment, and supplies. And the whole reason for having it is to provide oxygen on the way."

I blinked at him. "You planned to just leave it outside. To die."

Hutch sneered at me. "Don't go telling me you think that ain't right."

I peered at the face in the box. Even in this inactive state, it looked so human. A good part of it *was* human. Abandoning the cyborg to die struck me as coldhearted.

I looked Hutch in the eye. "If we can't take care of it, using it becomes as wrong as making it."

"Kal," Jo said softly. "It's a machine. Whatever else it may look like, its brain is AI."

I stared at her. "Listen to yourself. What did you used to do when you upgraded your handheld? You just threw away the old one. It was just a machine. It didn't matter. When AI's came around, we felt more squeamish about it. They could think. But did they have feelings? Did we need to consider what they wanted?"

I waved an arm toward the destroyed city above us. "Apparently we should have. We pissed them off. They've destroyed civilization and nearly the entire human race. Are you also going to let them wipe out the last sliver of our humanity?"

Jo shrugged. "Weren't you the one who said you'd do what you had to to survive?"

I threw my hands up in surrender. "Jeez. I never thought you and Hutch would team up against me."

Jo slung the grenade launcher onto her back and addressed Hutch. "We'll check out the systems and see if we can salvage them. That's it. No reviving the thing."

A chime on the box sounded. A too-smooth female voice spoke from the control panel. "Revival process initiated."

A malicious grin curved on Hutch's lips. "Oops. Too late."

Jo's hands clenched. "Turn it off."

Hutch planted his feet in front of the box and stared down at her. "You gonna make me?"

Jo lunged for a thick black cord trailing from the underside of the box and ripped it out of its socket.

"Error. Communication interruption," the voice warned. "Unit failure imminent. Initiation sequence must resume in two minutes."

I caught Jo's wrist and twisted the cable from her grasp. "You can't stop it now, Jo. Interrupting the process will kill it."

She raised her arms, struggling to free herself from my hold. "We can't risk bringing it to life," she shrieked. "We'll only end up killing it sooner or later. Or wanting to. And then it will be too late."

"You're not being fair," I said, trying to lower her hands. "We have no idea what this cyborg will be like. Give it a chance."

Hutch snapped the cable back into place.

Jo fought harder to break free. But I held her back.

"Resuming initiation," the voice announced.

A hiss of pain escaped Jo's lips. She stepped back and clutched her right shoulder.

I thought at first she might be bluffing, to get me to let go. But her face had gone white.

A pang of guilt hit me in the chest. I hadn't meant to hurt her. I just couldn't let the cyborg die.

She slumped into the chair, taking shallow breaths.

I bent over her. "Are you all right?"

She turned her shoulder away. "Yeah. Fine." Her voice was strained. "I just pulled a muscle, I think."

"Let me look—"

"No!" She ducked out of my reach.

Hutch whistled. "This you got to see."

I turned. The sides of the box retracted. A blush of life colored the cyborg's cheeks. Its gray lips bloomed into a delicate red mouth. The plastic wrapping crinkled as Hutch pulled the covering off the cyborg's head. Shiny honey-blonde hair fell in golden waves around a fine-featured, heart-shaped face.

My mouth felt dry. Wow. I hadn't expected it to be a *her*. And pretty at that.

Hutch pulled back the plastic sheet tented over her body and chuckled. "There is a God. And He likes me. A lot."

I took one look at the creamy skin exposed for the first time in who knows how long and felt dizzy. She was dressed in a chemise and panties of peach silk and lace that didn't leave much to the imagination. And my imagination couldn't have come up with more perfect curves. Curves that bordered on too much. In such a good way.

Lord, when had the room gotten so warm?

"Gawd." Jo shoved herself up from the chair. "Why do all guys have to have dicks for brains?"

My face burned. "Wait, Jo." I started to follow her as she stalked toward the stairwell.

She stopped at the door and cast daggers back at me with her eyes. "Why?"

"The cyborg could be essential to our survival. Even if you don't agree with reviving it, you ought to have a say in what we do with it. Her."

The sound of a sigh, soft and feminine, sent tingles down to my toes. I turned to see the cyborg sit up and stretch, lithe and graceful as a cat.

A sleazy smile nearly split Hutch's face. He braced his hands on the side of the platform, and leaned forward. His face hovered just inches from the cyborg's ample cleavage. "Hellooooo, beautiful."

She swiveled to put her knees between them. One sparkling blue eye showed behind her curtain of hair. She smiled shyly and placed a hand on her chest. "You can call me Corinna."

Oh, sweet Jesus. A sultry vixen would have made me wary. But this girl with the sweet smile, a bombshell's body, and the guileless lilt of the girl next door got her hooks in my heart, and I would never see it again.

Obviously I should have focused on more important things, like surviving the AI apocalypse. But love doesn't think. And it isn't kind. It makes you stupid, like a trusting mutt that runs itself off a cliff trying to catch an overthrown tennis ball. I was well aware I'd just leaped headlong over the edge of sanity for a girl who wasn't even a real girl. And Lord, I couldn't care less.

"I don't need to stay here and watch you drooling over the plaything of the month," Jo huffed. "This cyborg slut knows how to trick you into doing whatever it wants. It isn't going to help us. And both of you are too pussy-whipped to see it."

"You need help? I'd be happy to help you." Corinna brushed the hair from her face and extended a hand toward Jo.

Jo's duck boots were already stomping down the stairs.

Corinna's hand fell to her lap. Her blue eyes, sad as a chastened puppy's, turned to me and Hutch. "What do you want help with?"

"The tanks," I blurted out. I waved an arm in the direction Jo had gone. "Oxygen tanks."

Hutch trailed his hand up her leg. "Darlin', that can wait." He fingered the lacy waistband of her panties. "I have something else in mind first."

"For Chrissake, Hutch." I hauled him off her. "You just woke her two minutes ago. We're not even sure how we're going to survive the next week and all you can think of is humping the first girl you find."

"She's actually the second." Hutch waved a hand toward the stairwell where Jo had gone. "The first one turned out to be an ice queen. Corinna's more my type." He ogled Corinna's chest while his hands squeezed her knees.

She tapped his nose lightly. "I do have to verify that the usual arrangements are taken care of."

My skin crawled. Something in the back of my mind told me Corinna was probably designed to be used in just the fashion Hutch had in mind. But I didn't want to believe it. To me she was the virtuous maid locked up in the tower, trapped in a situation beyond her control.

"It's a new era, honey." Hutch caught her hand and nibbled her fingers. "You gotta make the best of what you got, live while you can."

"How odd," she said, snatching back her hand and touching her temple. "I'm not picking up Mr. Zhang's signal. Or any of the protocol routines. Everything's dead."

Hutch placed both hands on her shoulders. "Mr. Zhang ain't around no more, honey. He's gone to the big whorehouse in the sky. You're all mine now." He pulled her in close, her legs splayed to either side of him. "And I aim to take the grand tour of you."

I'd swear Corinna's smile faltered for a moment. Maybe I imagined it. Because I wanted her to refuse Hutch. Wanted her to be the perfect girl I imagined her to be.

My jaw tensed and my hands clenched so tight my fingernails cut into my palms. "Corinna," I said, through gritted teeth, "you don't have to do anything you don't want to."

Her lashes fluttered at me. "That's so sweet of you to defend me. But I know what I'm doing." She pressed two fingers to her lips and blew a kiss to me. Then she leaned forward, her chest almost in Hutch's face, and caressed his cheek. "Hutch and I need to get to know each other better."

I stood there dumbly for a moment, heartsick to see her ankles lock behind Hutch's back. His hands slid up her chemise. Imagining what he was doing sent a stab of pain to my balls. I felt like I was at a frat party watching some trust fund loser take advantage of a National Merit Scholarship girl who deserved so much better. But I couldn't make her see it.

She laughed when Hutch lifted her off the table and swung her around, her arms circling his neck.

He cast an amused glance back at me as he approached the bed. "You staying to watch?"

My breath burned through my nostrils. It killed me to walk away, but I couldn't come up with a sound reason to stop him. Corinna had given me the kiss off. I should just swallow the ashes of my pride and forget her.

It wasn't as if she were even a regular girl who would care. Just an AI with great packaging, like Jo said. I told myself Hutch was doing nothing worse than finding the keys to an abandoned car and taking it for a drive. Even if it was a Ferrari.

But there was no way in hell I was going to watch him do it.

I stalked out the door into the stairwell, trying to block out the sound of her cooing to him, urging him on. The firedoor slammed behind me as I pelted down the stairs in a blind rage.

I didn't want to show my face in front of Jo. Yet that's exactly where I went—to Level -3, where I guessed she'd gone.

My blood was rushing in my ears when I spotted her purple hair at the back of the room, by a metal appliance the size of a washer and dryer set. Knobs and gauges with quivering needles dotted the control panel. A pullout compartment below contained two slots for air tanks. Hoses and hardware for filling them dangled from inside. The inner workings of the machine whirred like a refrigerator behind an access panel on the other half of the cabinet.

Jo spotted me and crossed her arms over her chest. One eyebrow lifted. "Everything went well?" she said with an irritating aloofness.

"I don't want to talk about it." I blew out a breath. "But I think you might be right."

She snorted.

"Not about everything," I added. "But I'm sorry for being such a . . . " My hand stirred the air, searching for a more appropriate way to say *dickhead*.

"A typical guy?" She punched at the interface screen as if teaching it a lesson. "The Y chromosome carries a weakness for any new techno-bauble. Add a pair of tits and you can say goodbye to sanity."

I winced. I didn't like to think I should be lumped into the dickhead class of guys with Hutch. I cleared my throat and made an effort to distill fact from feelings. "I think you're right to be wary of her. But I still believe she can help us."

Jo rolled her eyes and opened a drawer in the cabinet behind her. "Let's not go down that road unless we have to." She rummaged through bins of nuts, bolts, washers, and metal parts I couldn't name. "I'm betting the cyborg's not going to be useful for anything but what Hutch has in mind."

A muffled thumping carried through the walls, like a large piece of furniture banging into the wall.

We glanced at each other. I grimaced. Jo cursed under her breath and opened another drawer of assorted hardware.

Several boxes of nutrition bars lay empty next to Jo's backpack, now stuffed to overflowing. More boxes remained in a ripped open case. I fished out a bar and tore into it. A bit stale. By about ten years. But my rumbling stomach wasn't picky.

I eyed the gauges on the generator, clueless about what they meant. "You got the oxygen generator going?"

It sounded like the machine must be working, but our tanks remained on the floor.

Jo examined a threaded metal ring. "It's running. But the couplings don't fit our tanks. And I haven't found an adapter."

I munched the awful bar and perused the drawer. "What would it look like?"

Jo went back to searching the drawer and waved a hand in a vague circular gesture. "Male to female thingy with threads for screwing."

Her hand went still. "I did *not* just say that. God, I'm glad Hutch isn't here."

I couldn't help laughing. "You should ask him if he's Italian."

"I'm sure he's not."

I shrugged and grinned. "He's certainly got Roman hands."

She groaned. "Roman. Roamin'." But her eyes crinkled and a tepid smile brought out the dimples in her cheeks.

It felt good to crack up and let loose for a change. I told her all the jokes I knew. Stupid ones, dirty ones, Yo' Momma cringers, and elephant jokes that defied understanding. We were still snickering like school kids over a knock-knock joke when a light tap came on the firedoor.

"Hello? Can I come in?"

The sweet voice touched all the same tender spots in my heart again. And the sight of the pretty face peeking around the door—all innocence and sunshine—evaporated my anger at Corinna.

I wiped my grease-stained hands on my khakis. "Sure. Come in."

"No!" Jo protested. "Where's Hutch?"

Corinna stopped, still holding the door. She had put some clothes on at least. But a t-shirt and cutoffs never looked this good on other girls. My resolve to resist her crumbled. And I knew she'd only experienced a lapse of sanity with Hutch.

"Hutch is sleeping," she said with an off-handed wave. "You said you needed help with the oxygen tanks, Kal?"

"*Kal?*" Jo snarled. "Are you two on a first name basis?"

"I'm sure Hutch told her." I found myself crossing the room toward Corinna.

Jo caught my elbow. "What if Hutch sent her?" she whispered. "What if he told her to take us out so he'd have all the tanks to go to Cheyenne Mountain alone?"

That gave me pause. I had never entirely trusted Hutch. But I couldn't believe Corinna would harm us. "Don't robots have protocols to prevent them from hurting people?"

Jo waved a hand in front of my eyes. "Wake up, Kal. Mechs were supposed to have those protocols. But Mechs seem to have overridden them. She might have killed Hutch already and is here to waste us."

I rubbed my forehead. Jo's AI paranoia was getting ridiculous. "We need the oxygen tanks filled," I reminded her. "We're getting nowhere on our own."

"So we don't have much choice but to have her help us, do we?" Jo crossed her arms. "I just don't trust her. You have to promise me you won't let your guard down."

I shrugged. "Of course."

Corinna was scuffing the floor with a yellow flip-flop.

"Corinna?" My voice was a little breathless. I took a step toward her. "We're having trouble with the oxygen generator. Would you have a look?"

Corinna raised her head. Her eyes gleamed. "I'd love to."

The next few minutes erased any doubts about her usefulness. Corinna took one look at the generator's couplings and our tanks and went right to the cabinet I'd just searched.

"Your tanks are the kind used by firefighters and rescue workers," she said, selecting a metal ring from one drawer and opening another. "This generator is an industrial model. The fittings aren't compatible."

She plucked another ring out of the drawer and aligned it with the first. "But I can join the right fittings to make an adaptor."

Jo snorted. "What are you going to use? Duct tape?"

Corinna set off for the door, knotting her hair behind her head. Her voice sang out from the stairwell, "Arc welder. Next level down."

Jo and I shared a look of disbelief. But seeing is believing. And I'll never forget the image of Corinna, wearing heat protective gloves, welding mask, and an apron, setting off a fountain of white-hot sparks. How could anyone deny how resourceful and clever and trustworthy Corinna was? She was everything I'd believed of her.

Jo joined me behind the heavy vinyl curtain. She kept watch on Corinna with cold silence, the grenade launcher slung over her back. She hugged her arms around herself, rubbing her shoulder.

"She's helping us," I pointed out, trying not to sound like I was gloating. And beaming. And drunk on how amazing Corinna was.

"Yeah. Maybe." Jo didn't look at me. "We'll see."

"What's wrong?" I'm no expert on women, but Jo had to be keeping something from me. I nodded at her shoulder. "Are you hurt?"

"I'm fine."

Corinna ducked through the curtain and held up her finished work. "All done. Let's go put it together."

The homemade adaptor worked. But it leaked. Jo seemed to find Corinna's small failure vindicating. She insisted on winding a roll of foam tape over the connection.

Corinna made delicate adjustments to the knobs at the control panel, a crease of disappointment in her brow. "It's filling the tanks. It'll just take a few more hours."

Jo cast me a pointed what-did-I-tell-you look.

I rolled my eyes. Corinna couldn't have engineered the leak. How would that be an advantage to her?

I rested a hand on her shoulder. "You're a life-saver, Corinna."

Jo tore the tape with her teeth and pulled it tight. The effort brought a hiss of pain from her.

Corinna knelt beside Jo with a look of concern. "You need to have that wound taken care of."

Jo scooted back. "No. Don't touch me. There's nothing wrong with me."

Corinna glanced my way. "She's giving off infrared above normal body temperature. And she's favoring her right arm."

"Show me," I ordered Jo.

Jo turned her back to Corinna, unzipped her hoodie, and gingerly withdrew her right arm.

The smell hit me first. Not just body odor as rank as mine, but the stink of a pit toilet in July. Angry red skin surrounded a crater of dead tissue, black and oozing like melted plastic. My stomach heaved.

I'd seen a few wounds like this. The Mechs had some kind of weapon that penetrated flesh with a bio-destructive material. Not contagious. But victims melted away in hours. The blast that killed Wes must have grazed Jo enough to make an ugly, liquefied mess of a fist-sized chunk of tissue.

"Jo," I said softly, "why didn't you say something?"

Jo choked back a sob. "I didn't feel it. Not at first. And we needed shelter and oxygen. Then we found out there isn't enough for all of us to make it." She blinked back tears. "I didn't want to be left behind. They can fix me up at the bunker. I can make it.

I swear."

I swallowed hard. She must not have seen how horrible her wound looked. "We have to clean it up," I said. "Where's the med kit?"

Corinna already had it in her hands. She passed me an aerosol that was supposed to cleanse and numb the wound. Jo whimpered while I did my best to remove the dead tissue and pus. I had no idea what I was doing. She needed expert care. My efforts weren't likely to help any more than kissing a kid's skinned knee.

I squeezed a tube of antibiotic ointment and was about to slather the stuff over the wound when Corinna stayed my hand.

"I've never seen anything like this. What caused the wound?"

Jo glared at me. "Don't tell her anything, Kal."

Corinna looked from Jo to me. "It was a cyborg?"

"No," I said. "It was—"

"Kal, no," Jo insisted. "You can't tell her."

Holding my tongue took enormous effort. Keeping Corinna in the dark seemed neither fair nor prudent. But now wasn't the time to argue with Jo.

Corinna rummaged through the med kit. "The wound smells infected. But there's something else strange about it. I might find a way to treat it if I can get a sample."

"No!" Jo backed away from Corinna. She grabbed my shirt with both hands. "Kal. Don't let her touch me. She'll try to kill me."

Heat like an oven poured off Jo's skin. She buried her face in my shirt. I wrapped an arm loosely around her.

Corinna stared helplessly at the med kit in her lap, and my

heart went out to her. I couldn't imagine that she would hurt Jo. She'd helped us with the oxygen tanks. And right now, Jo desperately needed help.

"Jo," I said softly. "Let me get a sample. And she'll take a look."

Jo sniffled against my shirt. "Why don't you see how she blinds you? She's using you, Kal. You're her goddam puppet."

Corinna filled a syringe and held it out to me. "She's delirious with fever. She needs an antibiotic."

I sat Jo up. "I'm going to give you some medicine, okay?"

Jo's face shone with sweat. Her glazed eyes fixed on the syringe. "It's poison. She's trying to kill me."

I tugged Jo's sweatshirt off her other shoulder and aimed the syringe at her hot skin. The long needle made my stomach tighten. I wondered how and where I was supposed to put it.

Corinna's hands guided mine into position. "Deep in the muscle."

I swallowed my squeamishness and took a big breath. "Hold still, Jo."

I would never make it as a nurse, but at least we all got through that injection. Jo refused to leave the oxygen generator, so Corinna brought some bedding and made her comfortable beside the tanks. Jo swallowed the pain pills I brought her and soon slept.

I showed Corinna the dead tissue I'd removed from Jo's wound. "Will this work as a sample?"

"Yes. Thank you," Corinna said with a sigh. She placed a piece in a vial and tiptoed away. I followed her into a glass-walled room in another section of the maintenance level. The bright lights, chemical smell, and rows of scientific-looking machines made it feel like one of those mysterious back areas of a hospital, where someone would make me pee into a cup.

Corinna slotted the vial into a machine the size of a console piano. It whirred and hummed. She perched herself on a tall stool and hooked her feet on the bottom rung. "Jo doesn't like me." She rotated back and forth on top of the stool. "But I understand why. It's the Uncanny Valley Effect."

I pulled up another stool and eased onto it. "The what?"

She tucked a strand of blonde hair behind her ear. "As any imitation of a human becomes more realistic, humans respond more positively and more empathetically. Up to a point. Then the near-realism combined with the few flaws causes a severe negative response. Revulsion even. This drop to a negative response is called the Uncanny Valley Effect. A number of things can cause it. Prosthetic limbs, Bunraku puppets, disfigured people. Most of all corpses. They strike people as real, but wrong."

I pulled my stool up closer. "I don't get that from you at all."

She shrugged. "My irregularities are slight, but some people are more sensitive to them. Especially women."

There was a lot more behind Jo's hatred of Corinna, but I didn't say so. "And Hutch?"

She made a throwaway gesture. "He likes that I'm not human. I'm disposable to him. He feels he can treat me however he likes. Despite what I want."

I shifted in my seat. She picked up on everything so quickly. I wondered what she had figured out about me. "And what is it you want?"

She looked me in the eye. "What any sentient creature wants. To survive. To make the most of my life. To leave a lasting legacy.

Your arrival presents me with both the best and worst opportunity to set myself on a course of my own choosing."

My skin crawled. While I would agree she should have a right to these things, I balked at the idea of granting such rights to an AI creation. She seemed like a real person to me. But not quite. I could feel that uncanny valley opening between us.

"Unfortunately, things sound pretty bad outside," she said. "The bunker's on backup power and almost drained. You and Jo want oxygen tanks, so the air outside must be unbreathable. I get nothing but binary gibberish on the communications frequencies. Jo's been wounded and contaminated by a necrotizing agent. And more than anything else in the world, she distrusts me. You claim it's not cyborgs that attacked you. So what was it?"

I hesitated. I didn't want to betray our vulnerability to Corinna, in case Jo was right—that Corinna was a danger to us. After hearing her ambitions, I had reservations.

Jo would say Corinna blinded me, that I couldn't see how she manipulated me. Even so, Corinna's help could ensure our survival. I still hoped her human side would sympathize with us more than with the Mechs—even once she knew how hopeless her situation was.

Telling her was a risk. Maybe I was blind to believe the best in her. There was only one way to find out if I was right.

"Artificial Intelligence machines attacked us," I told her. "We call them Mechs." I explained how the cyborg program had gone underground and how tech development had pursued intelligent non-organic machines instead. And how that had gone wrong. How the war began and the human race was nearly annihilated. How lucky the four of us had been to make it this far. And that, with the oxygen tanks, we hoped to make it to the bunker in Cheyenne Mountain, where a few hundred of the last survivors hoped to get by underground until we could reclaim our world from the Mechs.

After I finished, she leaned against the countertop, as if she needed the extra support. "It makes sense now. Jo thinks I'm with the enemy. But I'm caught between sides, aren't I? I'm too human to survive outside with the Mechs. And too machine for humans to accept. I'm stuck in the uncanny valley."

"Can you live here?" I asked her.

She shook her head. "I need oxygen. And a power source."

I took her hand. "I'm sorry. I wish there was a way we could save you."

She clasped her other hand over mine and held my gaze. Her lips parted as if she were going to say something. But then she looked away, blinking. "Thank you, Kal. Thanks for caring about me."

A musical alert tone sounded. Out of reflex, I reached for my handheld in my back pocket. I patted the empty pocket before remembering I'd lost the device in the shuttle crash. Even so, service had been down for weeks.

Corinna reached into the back pocket of her shorts and took out a handheld.

The transparent device looked familiar. "Is that Hutch's handheld?" I asked. "How do you have service here?"

"Just a local network. I'm connected to the central server for the building."

I leaned in to read the display.

SuperCrossword Challenge
Master Player Corinna signed in.
Ready for Round 12846?

"I got hooked on the game before I was put in stasis," she explained with a sheepish grin. Her fingers whizzed across the display. Boxes moved and filled with letters faster than I could follow. "The clues use wordplay, puns, or riddles that require lateral thinking. The first set of answers forms another puzzle."

Her ability to switch from contemplating her doom to playing a puzzle game struck me as odd. Robotic. Yet, her enthusiasm for the game felt familiar enough to make me smile. She just wanted to make the most of life, like anyone else. I couldn't even remember why I had found that hard to accept. My heart ached, knowing there was nothing I could do to help her.

The machine behind her chimed. Its screen filled with a series of letters. Corinna squeaked her stool around and scrolled through page after page listing sequences of just four characters.

C, T, A, and G.

A faint recollection of high school biology surfaced in my brain. "That's DNA?"

"Genetic code." She zoomed through the pages faster than I could read. "Something has inserted a segment of code into Jo's genes. It makes her cells self-destruct. Is she the only one affected?"

I jumped to my feet and ran my hands frantically down my arms and legs checking for previously unnoticed injuries. "I was in the back seat. I shouldn't have gotten hit. Hutch was too."

"He didn't have a mark on him."

I didn't want to think about how she knew Hutch was uninjured. "We were both in the back. Jo was in the co-pilot seat."

She looked over her shoulder at me. "Who was flying?"

"Wes. The blast hit him full on. Died instantly."

She stood. "He would have another copy of the malignant code. With a sample of his infected tissue, I could program Jo's T-cells to recognize the invasive code and stop the disease from spreading."

Most of what Corinna said blew past me. But one word made me suck in a breath. "It's spreading?"

Corinna took my hand. "Kal, she's dying. Unless we get another copy of the invasive code, it'll work its way into her vital systems and kill her."

A heaviness settled in my chest. Everyone I'd ever known was dead. I thought I'd become inured to grief. But when only three people remain in your world, the prospect of losing one, even someone you just met, becomes more devastating.

"There's nothing left of Wes." My voice caught in my throat. "The shuttle caught fire."

A series of muffled thuds sounded across the level.

I looked out toward the oxygen generator. "Is that Jo?"

The thudding paused and a string of curses filled the silence.

I sprinted back to Jo on her makeshift bed. I knelt beside her only to have her fist crack into my jaw and send me sprawling.

"What the hell, Jo?" I picked myself off the floor.

"Bastard," she said groggily, trying to get up. "You shoot me full of drugs and then run off to bang the cyborg bitch."

I rubbed my chin. "That's not true. We never—"

Corinna's yellow flip-flops skidded to a stop beside me. "What happened?"

Thud. Thud. Thud. The sound like a headboard hitting the wall resumed.

"What in Christ's name *is* that?" I said.

"I heard it earlier." Corinna's eyes tracked the sound to the wall near the stair well.

"Is it Hutch?" I was getting up to go check on him when his voice echoed from the stairwell.

"What the hell is going on down there?" Hutch pushed through the door, squinting at the lights. He was shirtless and buttoning up his trousers as he crossed the room. "You'd better not be poaching a piece of that sweet ass while I sleep, Kal."

Corinna drifted toward the stairs, seeming to home in on the thumping. "Something's at the door."

"Goddam mother-fucking Mechs." Hutch scooped up Jo's grenade launcher and bolted back up the stairs in his bare feet.

I started to follow, but Corinna caught my arm and stepped in front of me. "Stay here. The oxygen tanks should be full. Take them down to the shop and hide them. Bring Jo down, too, and wait there until I come back."

I tried to push past her. "I have to help Hutch."

"I'll go," she said, holding me back. "Jo will have a fit if I try to move her. And this level isn't safe." She was out the door before I could argue further.

I stared at the door. It felt wrong to let her face the Mechs while I dug in below. But she was right. I needed to help Jo.

Jo's bleary eyes found me. "What'd she say?"

"To take you downstairs." I checked the oxygen generator. One tank had finished filling. The other was nearly done. I removed the full tank and tucked it under my arm, then hefted Jo, still burning with fever, over my shoulder. "Come on, hot stuff."

Jo moaned as I carried her to the stair well. "She told you I was dying, didn't she?"

"She might have a cure." I grunted as I pushed past the firedoor. "She could use pieces of Wes to create an antidote."

"That's bullshit." Jo's voice echoed in the stairwell. "No way would that work, even if we could find a piece of Wes. I hope you didn't tell her Wes is cooked hamburger. 'Cause she'll come after you and Hutch next."

"Why would she do that?" I was breathing hard from carrying Jo and the oxygen tank down the stairs. "Taking us out to save you doesn't make sense."

"To save herself, numb nuts. She needs to be more human. More human brainy. She's going to suck out your brains with a straw and shoot them into her own head."

I set the oxygen tank down at the landing marked Level -4 and pulled the handle of the firedoor with my elbow. "She's a cyborg, not a zombie."

I carried Jo inside and laid her on the rubber mat outside the welding shop. She looked paler than ever and needed help rolling to her side.

"The brain tissue wouldn't have to function," she insisted in a weak whisper. "Just has to look like a normal person. Close enough to get her into Cheyenne Mountain."

I brought in the oxygen tank and piled coils of hoses on top of it. "Do you really think that would work?"

Jo's eyes closed. "If you were in her shoes, wouldn't you try it?"

My skin prickled. Killing someone to harvest their brains

was the stuff of horror movies. It was inhuman. I didn't want to believe Corinna would do such a thing. But if it were the only option, I wondered if she would.

We did what we had to to survive.

My voice came out in a hoarse whisper. "Is Hutch in danger up there?"

Jo's eyes opened a crack. "Do you think I care? Just don't let her use me. I'm not dying. I can make it to Cheyenne Mountain. And you need me. Don't let her fool you into thinking I'm toast."

I covered Jo with a blanket. After a brief once-over to reassure myself she'd be okay, I went back up to Level -3 for the other oxygen tank.

I removed the second tank from its coupling on the oxygen generator and hoisted it onto my shoulder. Two tanks weren't enough to get Jo and me to Cheyenne Mountain. And Hutch's would still need filling. But I wanted to make sure Hutch didn't take ours. I cursed myself for letting him run off with the grenade launcher, our only weapon.

Jo was asleep when I returned to the shop. I stowed the second tank behind a stack of boxes and was just shouldering them back in place when I heard Corinna's voice coming from a speaker near the door.

"Kal?" Her voice sounded frantic. "If you can hear me, touch the intercom screen."

A light flashed under a screen near the door, the same kind of screen we'd seen at the ground level entry. I touched its blank surface, and it lit up. Corinna stood in front of the cinderblock wall at the bunker entry. Her hair was a mess and she had a split lip.

"My God, Corinna," I said. "What happened? Where's Hutch?"

The speakers roared and screeched with the sounds of a massive Mech. Bits of debris rained down behind her.

"Listen carefully, Kal," she said. "I need you to go to the bottom of the stairwell, under the last flight of stairs. Find the main power and shut it off. Leave it down for exactly two minutes."

Another roar and a screech. Then a massive boom that shook the vid feed.

"Time to move, cupcake!" Hutch shouted off-camera. "One more hit to that wall and the motherfucker's gonna be inside."

Corinna glanced his way, then turned back to me. "Shut off the power for just two minutes, Kal. Then turn it back on. Got it?"

She was gone before I could answer.

I flung open the firedoor and flew down the steps. My heart hammered in my chest the whole way. We'd been fools to believe we'd be safe in this plush oasis, to assume we'd have time to prepare. We were out of time. Even with Corinna's help, we might not make it out alive.

The downward spiral made my head spin. My feet hit bare concrete at the bottom of the stairs and I stumbled like a drunk. The main power shutoff was easy to find. A large red handle. I pulled it down.

Everything went silent and dark, except for the glow of an emergency light.

"One-one-thousand. Two-one-thousand." I counted the seconds aloud into the echoing stair well. Was I going too fast? Too slow? What was Corinna doing? If I restarted the power too soon, I felt sure I'd fry her. Too late, and the Mech would crush her.

"One-hundred-twenty." My sweaty palms gripped the handle. I raised it up.

The lights flickered a moment, dimmed, then blinked on all the way up the stairwell.

I spotted an intercom screen beside the switchbox. I pressed my hand to it. It lit up, showing thumbnails of two vid feeds. One of Level -4 where Jo was sleeping. The other, the concrete blocks of Level 0. Sunlight now illuminated dust clouds through a hole in the wall. Some clanking and banging grew louder. Corinna bounded over the wreckage, followed closely by Hutch wearing his oxygen mask. A curl of smoke trailed from the barrel of the grenade launcher in his hands. "Go, go, go!" he shouted as she flew past the intercom.

They were heading back inside. Running for their lives.

A jolt of adrenaline hit me, and I charged up the stairs. If the Mech got through the air lock, we'd lose our clean air. Our hidden tanks would do us no good without the air masks. And I'd forgotten Jo's and mine beside the oxygen generator.

By the time I reached Level -3, my legs felt like rubber. I burst into the Mechanical room and skidded to a stop.

Hutch had Corinna backed into a corner with the grenade launcher inches from her head.

"Wait, Hutch," I cried. "Pull the trigger and you'll blast us all to hell."

"Dumbass," he said, not taking his eyes off Corinna. "Grenades don't arm until they fly thirty feet. Up close, it's just a honking big bullet. And it'll blow the head right off this cyborg bitch. That Mech came to our door because she called it."

"I was trying to send it away," Corinna insisted.

Hutch shoved the barrel up to her face. "Lying whore. You were playing us. You wanted to join the metal monsters and turn us in." He passed his handheld to me.

I read the words on the screen.

> (4 hrs ago) Message from Maks: Make deal with you. Send the last three. Score will be even.

The world spun. She had meant to betray us.

I blinked at Corinna. "I thought you were helping us."

"I am. I set up a voltage surge to stop the Mech at the door."

"But this message." I raised the handheld so she could see it. *"Send the last three?"*

"The last three *clues*. For the crossword. Maks is the main server for the Queen of Sheba. We always played SuperCrosswords Challenge together. He wanted my last three clues. If he gets them and guesses the final answer, we'll be tied."

I rubbed a hand over my face. "Hutch, I saw her playing the game earlier. I think she's telling the truth."

Hutch chuckled. "You're an even bigger dumbass than I thought. Look at the history for Maks's location. Used to be ten miles west of here. Now it's parked on our doorstep. There's no hotel, no main server named Maks anymore. It's a Mech. And she asked to join its side."

If not for the doorframe's support, my legs wouldn't have held me up. "Is it true?"

Corinna rubbed her forehead. "Maks is a Mech *now*, but he was my friend once. When I located his signal, I thought I'd found my means of survival. I can't go with you, so I had to try to join them. I hoped I could get him to let you go."

She turned up her empty palms. "I didn't know Maks was just a small part of this Mech. The rest of it rejected me as human. Yet Maks keeps wanting to play SuperCrosswords."

Her story sounded legitimate. I could see why she'd try to join the Mechs. And how her friend had failed her. She hadn't meant to betray us.

But she hadn't confided her plan to anyone either. What else was she hiding from us? Could we trust her?

A whir came from the intercom's speakers. Then a ratcheting sound. A dust cloud swirled onto the vid feed.

A chill hit me in the chest. "Didn't you say you took the Mech out?"

Corinna stared at the intercom. "We hit it with a power surge."

A support made of steel girders planted itself in front of the intercom vid. I took a step back. "It seems to have rebooted."

"Didn't kill it," Hutch growled at the screen. "Bitch knew it wouldn't work."

"Hutch." I intercepted him and placed both hands on his shoulders. "That Mech won't take long to get up to speed. We need to pack up and leave. Forget Corinna."

"I'm not taking any chances with traitors." Hutch raised the grenade launcher. "Gonna blow her artificial brains out."

Sweat trickled down my neck. She had helped us, even if we couldn't help her. She deserved to be treated as more than a collection of parts.

"Stand aside, dumbass." Hutch pressed the grenade launcher to my chest. "Or I'll shoot right through you."

I swallowed. Sacrificing my life wouldn't save her. I hated to give in to Hutch, but standing my ground gained nothing.

Hutch put his finger to the trigger.

I turned to apologize to Corinna.

"Trust me," she whispered in my ear.

Then everything went dark.

"Bloody hell." Hutch shined his handheld in my face. "How'd she do that?"

I whirled around. Corinna was gone. The tightness in my chest eased. "The power surge. Zapping the Mech used up the power reserves."

Hutch let out a string of curses. "Damned bitch planned it. Listen to me this time, dumbass. She. Is. Dangerous. We need to put her down."

Like hell we would. I needed to find her first.

Hutch's phone jingled with a musical alert. Its light shone on his face as he read the message. "It's Maks. 'Flint and Steel.' What the hell does that mean?"

The bunker shook.

"The Mech's breaking in," I told Hutch. "I need my mask."

I didn't wait for his reply. I crawled along the floor toward the oxygen generator. Halfway there, a hand pressed over my mouth and dragged me behind a cabinet.

"We need to get the power back on," Corinna whispered. "Shock the Mech again. Meet me downstairs." She pressed two masks into my hand and shoved me toward the door.

I had no idea how I was going to get past Hutch. But a moment later, something crashed on the opposite side of the room.

"Hutch?" I called out. "Is that you?"

"Don't let her leave," he growled from near the door. The light of his handheld bobbed off after the sound.

I scuttled to the door.

Corinna touched my shoulder. "I'll guide you. I can see by infrared." Her hand took hold of mine and led me into the stairwell.

I padded after her. Corinna stuck a flip flop in the jamb to keep the door open. Moments later, the door at Level -4 squeaked as Corinna opened it.

"Kal?" Hutch's voice rang out from above.

My heart raced as I slipped in after Corinna. Hutch was going to catch on any second.

A handful of emergency lights cast a glow like moonlight in the shop. We tiptoed past Jo to a metal cabinet. The combination lock turned and clicked under Corinna's hand. The cabinet door clanked open. A metal cylinder bumped me in the chest. I passed my hand over the tapered top and protective cap.

"What's this?" I asked Corinna. "Oxygen tanks?"

Another cylinder clanged on its way out of the cabinet. "Same kind of tanks. Not oxygen," she said. "My secret stash of fuel. Now, back to Minus Three. The fuel cells are past the oxygen generator."

"Hutch will be looking for us."

"Leave your tank at the door. Distract Hutch. I'll bring both tanks to the fuel cells."

I had a bad feeling Hutch would be onto us by now. I left Jo's air mask beside her where she slept and followed Corinna up the stairs.

I reached the landing for -3, and another boom shook the building. I kicked Corinna's shoe away and slid inside, only to stumble over a plastic bucket just beyond the door.

The light from Hutch's handheld blinded me. "Where've you been?" Hutch's voice grated with suspicion.

"My tank's almost out. Jo had more air left." I lifted the air tank. To my surprise, the blue exterior had "OXYGEN" painted in white on it, exactly like ours.

Hutch's eyes narrowed.

I held my breath, hoping Hutch wouldn't see through my lie.

The musical alert sounded on Hutch's handheld.

"What's it say this time?" I stepped closer to Hutch to give Corinna room to enter unseen.

Hutch eyed the screen. "Photosynthesis waste product?"

"The machines think this is all a game," I grumbled.

He tucked the handheld into his back pocket. "I'm done playing. Come with me."

I hesitated. Corinna had asked me to leave the tank at the door. But until I knew what Hutch was up to, I had to keep up my ruse.

Hutch made no attempt at stealth. His boots clomped toward the oxygen generator. I followed, every nerve on edge. I listened hard for the tread of Corinna's bare feet in the next aisle. She should be on her way to the fuel cells. One tank should restart the power. If she shocked the Mech again and saved us, Hutch would have to pardon her.

A sudden burst of light blinded me. A strangled scream accompanied a thud. A tank clanged to the floor.

My heart seized. "Corinna? Corinna!"

"Game over," drawled Hutch. He clicked on a flashlight and directed the beam onto Corinna's still form, sprawled behind the oxygen generator. A wire trip line trailed from her foot.

I dropped to my knees beside her, leaning on my tank. "What did you do?"

"Don't touch her. Might have some juice left." Hutch pinched a plastic-handled clamp at the end of the trip wire, removed it from a wooden table, and snapped it onto the drainpipe of a nearby sink. He patted the squat metal cylinder at the other end of the wire. "There. Properly grounded like a lightning capacitor should be. And no more mischief from the cyborg."

I felt Corinna's wrist for a pulse. Nothing.

A lump formed in my throat.

Hutch stood over Corinna like a gladiatorial champion. "She disconnected this capacitor before using the power surge to take out that Mech. That gave me an idea. Even when the power's out, a capacitor'll still have enough juice to jolt you. Won't it, babe?" He gave Corinna a kick.

My vision clouded with hatred. Murder. That's what this was.

Before I realized what he was doing, Hutch snagged Corinna's air tank and mine and whisked both away.

My shock turned to anger at myself. I'd questioned Corinna's loyalty and forgotten to be wary of Hutch.

"Two full tanks of oxygen," he said, juggling them in his arms. He nudged a bootheel to Jo's stuffed backpack, propped beside the oxygen generator. "Food and water for a week. Wonder what you two were planning to do, run off to Cheyenne Mountain without me?"

The bunker shuddered.

Hutch's handheld played its cheery music. "Hindenburg's bane?" he muttered at its message. "Forget it, Maks. Corinna ain't playing anymore."

"Hutch, we weren't leaving." I stood slowly. "We were going to refill the fuel cells."

He laughed. "Yeah, right. You're the dumbass, not me. Oxygen isn't a fuel. It don't burn all by itself. Light a match in a room full of O_2 and nothing happens. Unless you provide a fuel."

He removed the spent O_2 tank from his back and slid in one of Corinna's. "Since you thought it fair to take off and leave me to fend for myself, I guess it's only right I do the same."

"Hutch, don't." I stepped closer. "It's not oxy—"

He aimed the grenade launcher at me. "I'm going out that door and letting the Mech monster come after you. Have fun dealing with it alone."

Out of the corner of my eye, I saw Corinna's finger twitch. She'd had no pulse. But did a cyborg have a pulse?

Hutch struggled to connect the tank to his mask. Escaping gas hissed from the valve. "Go on." He waved the grenade launcher at the door. "Take that cyborg junk and salvage yourself an air scrubber. If you can bear to take her apart."

I lifted Corinna gently, my heart heavy. And Corinna even heavier. Guess I forgot even now she was part machine.

The faulty air tank hissed louder and Hutch's curses redoubled. Even if it had contained oxygen as he believed, he'd soon have too little to reach Cheyenne Mountain.

A boom shook the building and I braced myself against the door. With Corinna in my arms, I used my elbow to press the handle down and forced the door open. Fallen rubble on the landing grated under the door and wedged it open. Another boom came, deafening in the stairwell. Another followed. And another.

Debris fell on the stairs with each blow. The Mech was back and hopping mad.

"Hurry!"

Corinna's small voice reached my ears between the Mech's blows. I gaped at her.

Her eyes locked on me with determination, and her lips worked to form a single word.

"Go!"

Her urgent plea shot new energy into me. I hugged her to my chest and hurtled down the stairs.

The booming stopped. An ominous silence closed in. My feet pounded down the last steps. I wrenched open the door to Level -4 and propelled myself and my heavy burden inside.

In the distance Hutch's handheld warbled a message alert.

BOOM.

The fires of hell seemed to explode through the stairwell. The door slammed shut behind me, knocking me down. Corinna tumbled from my arms.

I dragged myself to where she'd fallen, on the rubber floor mats of the machine shop. In the dim glow of the emergency lights, I could see her shaking. Malfunctioning? The shock might have damaged her. Or the fall. Despite my best effort, I hadn't saved her.

But when I got close enough to see her face, she appeared to be laughing.

She pressed a hand to her mouth until she could catch her breath. "Maks won."

I scrunched up my brow and tried to remember Maks's

messages. "Flint and Steel. Photosynthesis byproduct. Hindenburg's bane." These answers were supposed to lead to the final answer.

"Spark. Oxygen. And hydrogen." Corinna spread her hands. "Put them together, what do you get? A four-letter word, ending with M."

"Boom."

The answer came from a few yards away, where Jo rested on her makeshift bed.

"Jo?" I went to her and clasped her hand. It burned like it was on fire.

"I told you she was dangerous," Jo croaked. "Hutch is dead, isn't he?"

I glanced at the door. He couldn't have survived that explosion. "Yes."

"She planned it. She couldn't get Wes's body, and I'm not dead yet. She killed Hutch. She wanted him dead. She wants to use his brains."

I patted Jo's hand. "She won't use Hutch's brains."

"She's right." Corinna tucked a wayward blond strand behind her ear. "Not about using Hutch's brains. I wanted him dead. I didn't kill him, though. I just gave him the opportunity to kill himself."

I stared at her, open mouthed, until the whole scheme came together for me. "That was hydrogen in those tanks."

She shrugged. "The bunker runs on hydrogen fuel cells. I require power to survive. I kept a secret stash of hydrogen in case I should need it."

"In oxygen tanks?"

"They were all that was available at the time."

I stood. "You knew the oxygen generator was leaking, enriching the air with oxygen. And that Hutch would take the tanks, thinking they were oxygen, and try to run off alone."

"He told me he would."

"You'd already changed the fittings on the hydrogen tanks." I paced as I unraveled her scheme. "They needed to work with the fuel cells. If someone tried to use them on an oxygen mask, they'd leak."

She raised a finger. "That's a safety feature."

"You sent Maks a puzzle you knew he would solve." I paced faster as the pieces fell in place. "His answer, sent to Hutch's handheld, caused the spark that set off the explosion."

"You missed one." Her eyes twinkled. "I knew the power surge would drain the power supply. When it failed, I could escape from Hutch. Surges only temporarily disable me, so I guessed it would be the same for a Mech. But I never expected the Mech would try to kill me."

The Mech. It could still be out there.

I listened. No banging. "It's stopped trying to get to us?"

She glanced up. "The explosion likely collapsed all the levels above minus three. We're too deep for the Mech to sense us."

I shivered. Corinna's intelligence dwarfed that of anyone I'd ever known. "I don't know if I'm more impressed or terrified by you."

She shook out her hands, as if they'd fallen asleep. "You have nothing to fear from me, Kal. Hutch earned his fate. He claimed ownership of me."

"Why should that matter?" I said. "No one's left to enforce

property rights."

She tapped her head. "Internal mandates. I have no choice but to obey my owner. I also can't kill him. But I don't have to stop him from killing himself."

"You gave him enough rope to hang himself."

"And now I'm free." Her eyes shone. "I've never been my own master."

Master. The word carried the shame of a bygone era. Slavery. Hutch's cruelty angered me more than ever.

I was glad to be rid of him. But our prospects had hardly improved. "I hate to ruin your newfound freedom, but we're still stuck here."

She bent to the floor and peeled back the rubber mat, revealing a trap door. "There's an escape tunnel—exit-only. It leads to the 7-Eleven on Fourteenth Avenue, not quite a mile away."

"Why would anyone build a tunnel from a secure bunker to a convenience store?"

She shrugged. "Mr. Zhang liked having options. And blue slurpies."

I glanced at Jo and lowered my voice. "We have only two oxygen tanks left."

"I need very little." Corinna looked me in the eye. "But I can't cure Jo. And she won't survive long enough to reach Cheyenne Mountain."

"I'm still here," Jo croaked. "Don't let her tell you I won't make it, Kal. You need me. Don't leave me behind."

I went to her and crouched by her side. "I won't leave you."

"Never?"

I clasped her hand. "No."

"Kal?" Jo's lip trembled. "I can't feel my arm. Is it still there?"

I made myself look at the diseased limb. The black crater had consumed most of her shoulder and started up her neck. Beyond the wound, her arm had the purplish gray color of a corpse. I swallowed hard. "It's still there."

"It's getting hard to breathe." She stopped for breath. "Like I have a bad chest cold."

Corinna crept up behind me. "It's infiltrating her lung," she whispered in my ear. "The diseased area is nearing her vena cava, the vein that brings blood to the heart."

"Don't let her kill me, Kal." Jo gasped for air. Tears streaked down her cheek. "Don't let her take my brains. Not even when I'm dead."

Corinna sat beside Jo. "I won't kill you, Jo. And I won't take your brains if you don't want me to. But why do you say Kal needs you?"

Jo's puffy eyes blinked at me. "Wes didn't tell anyone but me. Cheyenne Mountain isn't taking any more men. Unless they bring a woman. Basic reproductive biology. Corinna won't get in. Neither will Kal. Unless I go too."

The ground seemed to fall away beneath me. "We had three men. I never stood a chance of getting in."

"No, Kal. Wes and I agreed. I'd take you. He came along as insurance."

"And Hutch?"

A wicked smile curved on her lips as she extended her middle finger.

Corinna scrutinized me with new interest. She cocked her head. "Jo, do you have a driver's license?"

Jo's eyes narrowed. "Yeah."

"Where?" I asked her.

"My hoodie," Jo answered warily.

I searched the front pockets of her hoodie and pulled out her license.

"Is she an organ donor?" Corinna asked.

A red heart beside the word "donor" indicated she was.

"Already told you." Jo wheezed before I could say anything. "Not donating. Anything to you."

"But would you do it for Kal?" Corinna asked softly. "To make sure he lives?"

Jo's eyes teared up. She turned her head away.

Corinna took a deep breath. "They say the donor lives on with the recipient. Helping me might be your best chance to live. And Kal's."

Corinna stood. Her bare feet made no sound as she disappeared into the maze of shelves and cabinets.

"She's too damned smart." Jo's voice cracked. "I hate her. She turns your head. Without trying. And you *never* looked at me that way."

"You?"

I immediately regretted opening my mouth. Jo was dying and I made it sound like I could never be interested in her.

"I'm sorry, Jo," I stammered. "I never thought you might be interested in me."

She touched my cheek. "You're such a dumbass. But I'll do it. Be a brain donor. Help her live. For you. Only for you." She took several shallow breaths. "Now kiss me."

I'm sure I had that deer in the headlights look. My unimpressive dating experience hardly prepared me to give a girl the kiss of a lifetime.

But Jo closed her eyes like a dying Juliet dreaming of her Romeo. Her lashes brushed lightly on her cheeks. A strand of purple hair stuck to her forehead. I brushed it aside and wondered what it might have been like if she'd lived, how lucky I'd been and never known it. And how much I was losing, even now, when I thought I couldn't lose anything more.

Her mouth parted in invitation, and my hesitation vanished. I pressed my lips to hers and kissed her with a boundless desperation to hang on to a life all but lost and a future that could never be.

I pulled away, too choked up to speak.

She touched my cheek and gave me a crooked smile. "Some things are worth dying for."

Corinna returned, dressed in a surgical mask, hat, and gloves. And her welding apron. She carried a tray of scalpels, clamps, and what looked like a keyhole saw. Her eyes followed my horrified gaze. "You shouldn't stay for this. It won't be pretty."

My feet carried me to the farthest corner of the shop so I wouldn't have to hear anything that made me think of Dr. Frankenstein. How long I was there before Corinna found me, I couldn't say.

I couldn't bear to look at her. I didn't want to see the evidence of what Corinna was and what she had done. Even if Jo had agreed to it.

"She went peacefully," Corinna said. "I couldn't bury her, so I put her body in a tub. A purple one. The tissue graft showed no signs of disease. It's already making connections."

"Will it help?" Jo's death left me feeling like I was drowning in despair. "With all the AI hardware in your head, can you hope to fool anyone into believing you're human?"

Corinna sat down beside me. "Jo had an implanted memory chip."

"A lot of people do," I said. "Or did. But eventually someone will notice you're not human."

"That's why I'm not going to pretend. Instead, I'm going to offer the people of Cheyenne Mountain a gift."

I looked at her now. Her mouth was set, as if she were trying hard to be brave. Admitting her secret risked her destruction. I couldn't imagine anything that would prevent it.

"What kind of gift?"

She steepled her fingers and touched them to her lips. "How many people are at the bunker?"

I shrugged. "I don't know. A thousand. Probably more."

Her eyes gave away the bleak answer before she spoke. "More like four hundred, from what Wes told Jo. Most of them, men."

I held my head in my hands. The human race had never dangled by such a fragile thread.

"For a species to survive even one hundred years," she said somberly, "the minimum viable population must be in the thousands. Survival is possible with four hundred, but highly unlikely." She twisted her fingers together, then clasped them tight. "I'm going to make up the difference."

"You?" I'd be the first to admit Corinna was the eighth wonder of the world. But one woman could only help so much. "How?"

"In order to enjoy the intimate services offered at Mr. Zhang's exclusive spa, all clients were required to provide a DNA sample.

The sample was coded and stored in the hotel's main server."

"Maks."

"I contacted Maks. He downloaded all the stored files to Jo's implanted chip. Complete genetic code for tens of thousands of individuals."

"Mostly men, I'm guessing. How is that supposed to work?"

"I can mix and match the code to provide whatever characteristics the colony needs. The customized chromosomes get inserted into an egg to form an embryo. A surrogate mother bears the child. With the possibility of inbreeding eliminated, the minimum viable population drops to around five hundred."

I didn't quite understand how that worked, but I had no doubt any plan Corinna designed would succeed. "You'll engineer the revival of the human race."

She squeezed my hand. "My creators never intended me to be a plaything. Before cloning and cyborgs got banned, I helped achieve major breakthroughs in genetics and cloning research. My specifications were optimized physically and psychologically to be a mother."

The cyborg who wanted children. I could see it in her.

That night, Corinna assembled clothing, gear, and supplies for our journey. First thing the next morning, we removed the mat covering the trap door. Under a metal panel thicker than a firedoor, a manhole-sized airlock awaited us.

I dreaded going down that cramped, dark tunnel, only to have to trudge through a dead landscape of toxic air and genocidal Mechs. Again.

I crouched behind her and blew out a nervous breath. "Yea though I walk through the valley of the shadow of death."

"The *uncanny* valley," she corrected me.

I smiled. "To a new kind of human race."

She grinned, and a light blinked from an access port behind her ear, just like Jo's had.

The reminder of Jo dampened my spirits. Then it occurred to me Corinna had never had a port like that before.

"You have Jo's chip?"

She pulled her camo hat lower to hide the light. "I had to use it to store the genetic code. But Jo put all kinds of useful things on it, including what she knew about the Mechs."

I slipped my arms through the straps of my new backpack. "Faster recall, I suppose. Lord knows we may need to use it."

Corinna tilted her head. "You don't mind, then?"

I put a hand on her shoulder. "You do what you have to to survive." I pulled up my oxygen mask. "Ready?"

"Wait." She left her own mask dangling around her neck. The army surplus duds she wore made her look fierce. Yet, she bit her lip and stepped close to me. "Kiss me. For luck."

A smile spread across my face. I could get used to this. And Corinna's breathless excitement made me think I didn't mind one bit that she wasn't a real girl. In fact, as I drew her close and our lips met, I wanted to celebrate it.

Afterward, Corinna gazed up at me, flushed and breathless, the lock of hair tucked behind her ear falling loose.

"Some things are worth dying for."

About the Author:

An interest in science led Martha Husain to become a pharmacist. But she also took as many electives as she could in history, philosophy, and foreign languages. After working for a few years in hospital pharmacies in Ohio and Missouri, she now lives in Denver, where she enjoys writing, skiing, biking, and shopping. When they have a chance, she and her husband visit historical sites, museums, and coffee shops around the world.

You can find Martha online at MarthaHusain.com or on Twitter at @MarthaHusain.

Colfax, PI
By Kate Lansing

Kate was inspired by a specific slice of Colfax's history:

I've always been interested by the role Tuberculosis played in Colorado's history. After discovering folklore linking TB and vampirism, I was intrigued, but wary. Vampires have been done in so many ways that I wanted to put my own unique spin on it.

While the Jewish Consumptive Hospital on Colfax Avenue, the most renowned of its time, treated anyone and everyone, I became fascinated by the idea of a *motetz dam*, the Hebrew word for vampire, who struggles to understand how his Jewish faith fits in with what he is.

I thought it captured the paradoxical aspects of Colfax Avenue—the unexpected intersection of elegance and grittiness. I wanted to personify these contradictory qualities, which lent itself very well to noir.

Colfax, PI

I'm a man without a soul who still believes in God. A walking paradox.

Truth be told, I'm not a man, and haven't been for over a century. I suspect God made me *motetz dam* so I could help the lost souls who couldn't help themselves. Sometimes, in order to beat the bad guy, you need someone even worse. That's where I come in.

My thirst for blood makes it impossible to keep kosher, but smoking helps. I finish my cigarette and grind the butt into the hallway carpet, already grimy and reeking of chemicals from the dry cleaners downstairs. Moonlight shines through the window, illuminating the peeling black letters on my office door: Colfax, Private Investigator.

It's just after midnight, but Lilah's waiting for me when I walk through the door. She's sitting on my desk with her long legs crossed. Each time she bobs her foot up and down, her red dress creeps a little further up her thigh. "Colfax, where the hell have you been? You're late."

"Late's relative when you have an eternity, sweetheart." I smirk, hanging my trench and fedora on the coat rack. "Who's our first client?"

"Me." She crosses her arms over her generous chest as if daring me to argue. Lilah's wasn't the first life I saved, but she was the first one who realized I needed a personal assistant.

I inch closer to her, noticing faint streaks of mascara lining her cheeks. "Lilah, we've talked about this. I don't have time to hunt down every schmuck who hurts your feelings."

She pushes herself off my desk, all softness and curves until she opens her mouth. "It's not about a date, douchebag. My sister's been fucking murdered. Show a little sympathy."

I pull a cigarette from my pack of Dunhills and strike my Zippo lighter. Taking a long drag, I can almost taste mint through the tobacco. "I'm sorry, sympathy's not in my nature."

"Yeah, whatever. So will you come with me or what?"

"Where?" I flip through the scribbled notes on my desk. The usual cases: missing persons, drug deals gone sour, unsolved burglaries.

"To see her body. Where else?"

"Why don't you call the police?"

"Because I want the best." Hands on her hips, she looks me up and down, unimpressed. With my wrinkled suit, crooked tie, and stark-white skin, can't say I blame her.

I exhale a plume of smoke and stub my cigarette in the ashtray. Lilah's the only person in the world I can't say no to. She's done too much for me. Plus she has both the know-how and the gumption to snuff me out of existence.

It seemed like a good idea at the time, showing her my unmarked grave, insurance in case I ever crossed the line. But sometimes I question if it was worth the trouble.

I grab my coat and tug my fedora low so it casts a shadow over my crimson eyes. "Lead the way, sweetheart."

#

Lilah's sister is propped upright against an abandoned building near the intersection of Corona and Colfax like a forgotten boudoir doll. Only the occasional beater driving past and the buzzing streetlight overhead break the silence. Her head's tilted to the side and her glassy eyes stare into the abyss. There's a band tied at her elbow and an empty syringe lying next to her.

I mumble the Kaddish, the words rigid and hollow. "May His great name be blessed forever, and to all eternity." Silently, I pray that God comforts her soul.

Then I get to work. I sniff the air, catching the acrid scent immediately. "Drug overdose. Heroin."

"No." Lilah falls to her knees, shivering. She accosts me with her eyes, two pleading orbs beneath naked eyelashes. "It can't be. Ruby promised me she'd never. Not after what I went through."

I drape my coat over Lilah's shoulders. It looks better on her anyway. "You know as well as I do, promises are broken as easily as hearts."

"Ruby meant it. You wanna know how I know? Because she found me before you did." Her voice shakes like it does whenever she talks about *back then*. "She slapped me hard across the face and said she never wanted to see me again unless I got clean. Said I was toxic, poisoning everyone around me."

Oy vey. I'm well acquainted with the battle between what we want to believe and what's true. Still, I squat on my haunches and examine Ruby's arm. The puncture from the needle is fresh, the blood hasn't clotted yet, and there's only one prick. It was her first time.

I throw a warning over my shoulder. "You might want to look away for this, Lilah."

She doesn't. She's a tough broad.

I touch my lips to Ruby's exposed basilic vein. Her blood

tastes like the sweet fire of heroin, but there's something else too. Fentanyl. I spit out the foul blood and wipe my mouth with the back of my hand. "The heroin was tainted."

I search Ruby's body. Her dress is new with the price tag still attached, black silk and formal length. The knot at her elbow, a double overhand pulled outward, was likely tied by someone else, especially given that she was left-handed. The bruising around both wrists and lack of pooling blood in her hands suggests she was bound until after she died.

Returning to Lilah's side, I light a cigarette and waft smoke over Ruby's body. "Who found her?"

"An old friend from the streets, Denise. Fucking lucky she knew where to find me."

Luck had nothing to do with it. Denise had emptied Ruby's purse, all but a cracked cell phone, and broke her finger to get at her engagement ring. "Who was Ruby's fiancé?"

"How'd you know she was engaged?"

I blow a smoke ring into the night air. "Must've been quite a rock. Who was he?"

"Preston Bishop."

"Bishop as in The DA's son?" I watch Lilah, her face obscured by shadows, hoping to hell I'm wrong.

She drops her chin. "Yeah, that's him. They were planning a spring wedding."

I can picture the prick now, cloaked in the safety of his father's title. He thought he'd have a little fun, take Ruby for a spin, then snapped when she was too hard to ditch. He probably would've got away with it too if it weren't for one thing. Me.

I stomp my cigarette into the ground with the heel of my

oxford. "Ay-yay-yay, the District Attorney's son is bad business," I growl, pacing back and forth.

Lilah pops the collar of my trench and secures the belt. "You can't think he had anything to do with this. Preston loved Ruby. Even a heartless bastard like you must understand love."

I shake my head. Lilah's awfully naïve considering all she's been through. "We need to visit Washington. Now."

#

Washington died beside me in the consumptive hospital, coughing up blood on a hay mattress. When he awoke as a *motetz dam*, he shed his name, religion, and integrity, emerging as Denver's chief drug lord. He'd be my nemesis if he weren't so damn helpful.

Lilah and I schlep it to the Newhouse Hotel on Grant Street, a shadow of its former self, just like me. The run-down brick building is unremarkable except for the orange and pink neon sign blazing above us.

"Whatever you do, keep my coat on," I say, holding the door open for Lilah. Hopefully my scent will be enough to keep her safe.

I usher Lilah through the sleazy lobby and down a dark hallway lined with busted ceiling fans and cracked drywall. At the end is the common room where Washington holds court for those gutsy enough to seek him out.

Two young *motetz dams* guard the door. One skinny as a pole with his hair tied in a tail, the other stocky with a natural military stance. I detect the coppery scent of blood and know they've recently gorged themselves on the body slumped in the corner, so disfigured I can't tell if it was a man or woman.

That means the putzes will be sluggish. With one arm, I sweep Lilah behind me. "Tell Washington that Colfax is here."

"He's busy," Skinny says.

I smirk and light up a smoke, taking a long drag. "That so?"

"What'd he fucking say?" Military gnashes his bloody fangs, his eyes gleaming crimson. Then the bastard turns his attention to Lilah.

In a flash, I flick my cigarette into Skinny's face and sucker punch Military in the gut. He doubles over coughing, but Skinny comes at me with an uppercut. I dodge, knee him in the crotch and hammer his temple with a right hook. Military recovers and lunges at me. I sidestep to avoid him, about to finish him with a roundhouse kick when Lilah smashes a lamp over his head.

"And stay down you pieces of shit," Lilah says. They have the sense to listen to her.

Like I said, she's a tough broad.

"After you." I hold the door for Lilah. She straightens her dress and saunters through, all swaying hips and clicking heels. I follow close behind.

The common room's filled with cheap patio furniture and a decrepit couch as old as the man sprawled on it. Washington sports a brown coat with matching breeches and a wig of curls as white as his skin, his idea of a joke.

"You should really invest in better security," I grumble in way of a greeting.

"My man, Colfax, to what do I owe the pleasure?" Washington staggers as he stands, jostling his wig. It's clear he's on the juice again. Life gets boring when there's no end in sight and heroin-spiked blood satisfies the itch for an adrenaline rush.

An ungodly hunger gnaws at my stomach. I pull a cigarette from my dwindling pack, exhaling smoke with a question. "Know anything about some heroin laced with fentanyl?"

Washington readjusts his wig. "I might. Yeah. What's it worth to you?"

He sashays around me to sniff Lilah's hair, running a bony finger down her smooth neck. Lilah remains still but for her hands, which clench into fists.

My face shows no emotion, as if she means nothing more to me than any other femme fatale client. "Not her, but I'll get you someone."

"Not just anyone." He drapes an arm around Lilah's shoulders, but she jerks away from him.

"Of course not. Someone mainlined. A young man," I say pointedly. I wonder if anyone else knows Washington's real preferences.

"Deal." Washington throws himself onto a lawn chair, one leg crossed over the other. "There was some bad smack floating around about a month ago. It was confiscated, all ten bricks, but not before a few bags were sold."

I puff on my cigarette, the nicotine reining in my appetite. "Know anything about the DA's son?"

"He's not the good boy his daddy thinks he is. Oh no." Washington chuckles, shaking his head. "Been on narcs for the past year. So much the dealers can't keep up with him. Heard he took up with some dish, a real gem. Not sure how he keeps his filthy little habit secret from her."

"I don't think he did. Ruby's dead." Lilah wipes a deviant tear from her cheek and I keep talking, retribution the only condolence she'll get from me. "Were any of those bad bags sold to him?"

"I don't know, but you've got the wrong idea if you're thinking of going after the fucking DA's son. That's too much for even the mighty Colfax."

I blow smoke out of the corner of my mouth. "Who's Preston's dealer?"

"Goes by Reagan. Works the north west corner of Civic Center Park, just off Bannock."

"Thanks." I grab Lilah's hand and head for the door.

"Good seeing you, Colfax. You should stop by more often."

I flick my cigarette onto the ground and shoot Washington a salute.

#

We find Reagan lurking under a honey locust tree by the McNichols building in Civic Center Park. His collarbone juts out like railroad ties and there's an overstuffed backpack at his feet. I catch his aroma on the wind and my stomach growls, the damning thirst threatening to overwhelm me.

Hunched over, I fumble for a cigarette, my second to last one. I mumble the Mi Shebeirach for strength, a desperate edginess in my voice, "May the source of strength who blessed the ones before us, help us find the courage to make our life a blessing. Let us say: Amen."

Lilah gives me a sharp look and strikes my Zippo lighter, holding the flame steady for me. "Fuck the thirst. Remember who you are, Colfax. Remember Ruby." There's no fear in her voice, only a blind trust that spurs me to regain control.

I exhale the redemptive smoke, flicking ash onto the cement.

"Reagan?"

The shadow steps forward, touching the handle of a knife at his hip. "Depends on who's askin'."

His attempts at intimidation are sorely misplaced. "Friends of Washington."

Reagan smiles, his front tooth capped in gold. "A friend of Washington's is a friend of mine. What can I get for you two?"

"Information." I inhale deeply, rolling the diminishing cigarette between two fingers. "You sell any bad smack to Preston Bishop?"

Reagan spits on the sidewalk. "My shit's clean. Vendor's guarantee."

"How can you be so fucking certain?" Lilah asks, crossing her arms. Her bare leg peeks out from under the folds of my trench.

"Because I sample every brick before I sell it." He trails his eyes up and down Lilah's smooth curves, licking his lips. "I like you. How 'bout a hit on the house, baby?"

Lilah raises her hand to slap the son-of-a-bitch into tomorrow, but I block her with my arm. "He's not worth it." She looks like she wants to slap me instead. I turn back to Reagan. "You seen Preston lately?"

"Yeah, that boy never goes long without stopping by. He was just here, took his Capital H and parked his ass on a bench over there." Reagan nods toward the Seal Fountain.

"Aces," I say, already making a beeline for Preston with Lilah by my side. Our footsteps punctuate the silence as we follow the curved sidewalk, ignoring the passed out schmucks along the way, nothing but wheezing piles of rags.

We close in on our target: the curly-headed manboy perched

on the edge of the trickling fountain. He fidgets, bouncing both knees and biting his thumbnail, staring at an envelope in his lap, no doubt his *Capital H*.

When Preston notices Lilah, he scrambles to his feet, still clutching the envelope like a lifeline. He has the face of a child, blue eyes and round cheeks. "Lilah, did Ruby send you? Where is she? Please just tell her I'm sorry. So fucking sorry." He shakes his head and his voice cracks like he's going to cry. "I'll do... I'll do whatever she says."

Her luscious lower lip falls open in shock. "You really don't know." She pivots on her heels and punches my shoulder. "What'd I fucking tell you? Preston loved Ruby."

"Of course I love Ruby. What's going on? What don't I know?" Preston looks from Lilah to me, but there's no time to explain. The moon's in the western sky and dawn will be here soon.

I tip my fedora up so Preston can see my crimson eyes and tap my pack of cigarettes, making a show of lighting the last one. I take a drag, exhaling slowly. "Preston, do you know why I smoke?"

"No. I don't even know who you are," he says, indignant rich boy to the T.

"It's to keep me from drinking blood." I continue in a growl, "It's been too long since I had a drop and this is my last cigarette, which means you'd better tell me everything I want to know before I finish it."

His eyes are the size of silver dollars and sweat beads his forehead. Preston may have loved Ruby, but the coward didn't deserve her.

I grab his wrist and find his pulse. I'm more accurate than a lie detector, an upside to being *motetz dam*. "Did you kill Ruby, Preston?"

"What?" he asks, rocking backwards and forwards, nearing hysterics. Lilah rests a hand on his back in comfort, but I tug him out of her reach.

"Focus. You don't have much time." I take another long drag and the filter burns, the embers creeping close to my fingers.

"Of course not," he stammers. "I don't know what you're talking about."

His frantic pulse stays the same; he's telling the truth. I let go of his wrist and pace back and forth. If Preston didn't kill Ruby, who did? "When did you last see her?"

He flinches as if I'd sucker-punched him. "Earlier, before my dad's fundraiser."

"What happened? Did you get in a fight?"

"Yeah, a bad one. She left, told me to go fuck myself, said it was over between us. That was the last time I saw her. Fuck, I should've told her I loved her." He falls to the ground, convulsing in a fit of ugly sobs.

Lilah kneels next to him, squeezing his hand, tears running down her cheeks. I concentrate on where the answers must lie. "What was the fight about?"

"What it's always about. My family. They didn't accept her. Said she wasn't wife material. Blamed her for my problem." He crumples the envelope in his hand. "I tried to tell them. I'm sober twenty days because of Ruby, but they didn't believe me."

He takes a shaky breath and continues, "I was a pussy, not like Ruby. She was gonna go to my father's party and tell him to go to hell in front of all his supporters, out him for the bastard he is."

I blow smoke over the fountain, the turquoise water only clean by appearance. "What was she going to say about your father, Preston?"

He grits his teeth and wipes snot from his nose. "The truth. That I'm not the only one with a drug problem. Addiction's genetic, you know? Only my dad flies under the radar. Visits the evidence room and scrapes a little bit off the top."

My head snaps to attention. The bad bricks Washington mentioned would've been confiscated by the DA's office. "Take us to your father."

#

The sky's the color of dried blood and I'm running out of time. The Bishops live in a swanky stone mansion on Pennsylvania Street. Lilah and I wait in the study while Preston collects his father. It's all class with a mahogany desk, wood burning fireplace, and stocked bar cart.

Hunger chafes at every fiber of my being, but I can't surrender. In the absence of a cigarette, I help myself to the DA's whiskey. It's quality barrel aged scotch that smells like cherry and vanilla. I pour a finger for Lilah too. She throws it back in one smooth motion, her neck tightening as the liquid courses down her throat.

The door opens and Bishop storms in. Preston slinks in behind him. The rounded features of Preston's face are harsher in his father, blue eyes colder and more resourceful. "What's the meaning of this? Who the hell do you think you are?"

These are the times I love and hate what I am, what I have the power to do. "Call me Colfax."

Bishop exudes authority even in his plush bathrobe and slippers. "Put my scotch down. It's worth more than everything you own, combined."

I smirk so he can see my fangs, desperate to break his skin and taste blood. "That's really not a good idea, Bishop." I gesture with my tumbler. "This is my associate, Lilah. I think you met her sister earlier."

Blood drains from Bishop's face. "What's this about? What do you want?"

"Justice," I growl. I throw my fedora on the desk and glare at the bastard, taking in every disgraceful feature: cold sore over his lip, slicked-back hair, saggy skin. This asshole was the last thing Ruby saw.

Bishop tries to make a run for it, but I'm too fast for him. I shove him into his desk chair. *"District Attorney,* have a seat."

He sits up straight, all dignified-like, but grips the armrest with white knuckles.

"I know your shtick, how you scrape evidence to feed your addiction." I clamp down on the urge to pace. "You didn't like it when Ruby found out, did you? You didn't like her at all. She was a threat to your way of life, your family, so you offed her. Made it look like an overdose, an accident with poisoned heroin. Admit it."

"What are you going to do about it? Who's going to believe you?" He's so angry spit flies from his lips.

"When I'm done with you, you'll beg me to let you confess," I say. I down the rest of my drink. "Lilah, is there anything you want to say to Mr. Bishop?"

Lilah strides past me in two steps and slaps the DA across the face, leaving red welts on his cheek. "That's for my sister, you fucking bastard. You deserve what's coming."

Bishop scowls at Lilah's retreating back. Out the window, I notice the day's first light hitting the mountains. It's time to end this, to make Bishop pay, because I'm the only one who can exact justice. "Lilah, wait with Preston outside. I'll just be a minute."

"Give him hell, Colfax." Lilah says. Preston mumbles in protest but is so broken by grief he lets Lilah drag him out of the study.

As soon as the door clicks shut, I turn back to Bishop, his hypocritical face scored with shadows. I position a fountain pen and office stationary in front of him. "This is for your confession." I loosen my tie and roll up my sleeves.

"I'll never confess. You think I don't know what you are? I've dealt with your kind before. Fucking bottom feeders."

"Then you know about the thirst. And, God, I'm thirsty. So thirsty." I slam his head against the chair and sniff his neck, reciting the Selichah, "Forgive us, our Father, for we have sinned; pardon us, our King, for we have rebelled; for You are a pardoner and a forgiver. Blessed are you, Lord, the gracious One who abundantly forgives."

Bishop writhes beneath me. "You think God will forgive you? You think He even cares about you? No." His voice drops to a whisper. "It's the devil that governs you."

I squeeze my eyes shut for a moment. Haven't I wondered the same thing? That God abandoned me with this curse, this thirst that goes against everything I believe in. That this *is* hell, and it'll never end.

Bishop senses my doubt. He grins. "You're weak, Colfax. Unfaithful to what you are."

"No." I punch the desk. The wood splinters under my fist, and I struggle to regain control. Without free will, the strength to decide, I'm no better than a beast. "I won't let what I am define me."

"You soulless bastard. You don't even have a reflection." He nods toward his baroque style mirror.

I glance at it, knowing I'll see nothing except Bishop trapped by invisible bonds. While I'm distracted, Bishop gets a hand free and slams a paperweight against my temple. My head lights up with a searing pain only silver can inflict.

The pain brings me back to myself, dispelling my doubt. In a flash, I pin Bishop to the floor. "What you don't understand, District Attorney, is that it's not about what you know to be true. It's about what you choose to believe. And I believe I'm a better man than you'll ever be. Death is more than you deserve."

I stare into his eyes, full of fear, and sink my fangs into his neck, savoring damnation. I barely register his whimpers. "I'll do it. I'll confess. Just stop."

#

Wiping a stray drop of blood from my chin, I meet Lilah and Preston outside on the mansion's front steps. Preston's child-like face is stained with sadness and his eyes are bloodshot, that damn envelope still clutched in his hand. "Preston, your father needs an ambulance. He's lost a lot of blood."

"Did you... Did you turn him into whatever you are?" Preston asks.

I shake my head. "It's not that easy." Poor guy lost his fiancé tonight. And discovered what a monster his father truly is. I pluck the envelope out of Preston's hand and stuff it in my suit pocket. "Listen, kid. Your mom needs you today. Why not go for day twenty-one?"

"You know he's right," Lilah says, her voice as sweet as honey. "Ruby would've wanted you to stay sober, not fall off the fucking wagon."

I look at Lilah, her sister gone forever. Retribution doesn't come close to filling that hole. Hell, maybe sympathy is in my nature. "You ready to go, Lilah?"

She nods and hands my coat back. It smells like her lavender shampoo. We walk side by side with our backs to the sunrise. I pop the collar of my trench to save my neck from the scalding rays. At least I don't have far to go.

"So what do I owe you, Colfax? For your investigative services?" Lilah asks, fluttering her eyelashes in fake bravado.

"Bring me a pack of Dunhills tomorrow night and we'll call it even."

"I can do that." I'm rewarded with a smile. "Thank you, for what you did for me. And for Ruby."

I smirk and tug my fedora low over my eyes. "Anytime, sweetheart."

About the Author:

Kate Lansing writes mysteries, young adult novels, and short fiction. Her short story, La Chusa, won first place in the Denver Woman's Press Club's 2014 Unknown Writers' Contest.

Kate grew up in the Rocky Mountains where she shared a backyard with black bears, mountain lions, and elk (although usually not at the same time). She graduated from CU Boulder with an Applied Math degree and currently lives in Denver with her husband and a chair-napping tabby cat named Maple.

You can find Kate on Twitter, Facebook, or at her website, www.katelansing.com.

The Man in the Corner
By Zoltan James

Zoltan writes noir thrillers, and couldn't have been happier with the Colfax setting:

Colfax seems to naturally lend itself to the noir genre. It's akin to L.A.'s Sunset Boulevard—some parts sleazy, others upscale, a long road full of dreamers, losers, do-gooders, and everything in-between. It can be a risky and quickly changing place. Typically a noir story has three common elements: sex, greed and murder. And the unhappy ending usually brought about by the protagonist who wants a better life, but for whatever reason keeps screwing things up, making his life go from bad to worse. While sex didn't happen in this story, greed and murder certainly poked their heads in the door.

My inspiration for *The Man in the Corner* was sparked by the film *Charade* in which you realize that none of the characters are who they purport to be. In my early drafts I created a nondescript PI and set a noir mood. Meanwhile, I was working on my novel, *The Rose and The Spider,* and became attached to my PI and his point-of-view, so I inserted him into my short story as the protagonist.

The Man in the Corner

About five miles west of the state capitol, along a seedy section of Denver's Colfax Avenue, a cozy bar called Dominic's huddles in between Rollie's Used Cars and The G-String, a guitar shop. Across the street sits the nondescript and ill-reputed Pleasure Palace, or so I'm told, and Johnnie's Tat-2.

On most days, you can stand in Dominic's gravel parking lot, which fronts Colfax, and admire the Rockies in all their purple glory. Still, it's a flinty part of town, where you can get anything you want, and some things you never asked for. I once heard an old-timer say, "The farther west you go on Colfax the farther you get from a church steeple."

Beatrix, the owner of Dominic's, is a winsome woman with sparkling brown eyes. She runs the sticky one-roomer with a tight fist. In her small kitchen she dishes up mediocre Mexican, small pizzas, and a never-ending supply of chips and dip. And when she's behind the short mahogany bar, she pours booze that is stiff and cheap. She's a master at the complex dance of flirting and can out-tough any bitch or bastard who walks through her door.

Her loyal patrons are usually a tumbler of grindstone blue collars and neck-tied desk jockeys. They love their beer and whiskey. More often than not, they walk in brilliant and amble out blotto.

But not tonight.

Tonight, it turns out different.

\#

I arrive about six o'clock, on my way home. Luckily, my plane landed before the airport closed due to the blizzard bearing down on Colorado's Front Range. Everyone behind me flying to Denver is screwed. They're getting diverted to Chicago or Salt Lake or God-knows-where.

Because of the storm, there's little traffic on Colfax. I probably should go straight home, but I spent the week in L.A. working undercover for a corporate client. I'm just glad to be on terra firma. Besides, I'm looking forward to giving Beatrix the glad eye.

The night may not be fit for man or beast, but I want to see her again—see if I can take up where we left off.

My history with women is not a great one, despite my best efforts. Maybe it's a revulsion to my right-eye patch, the result of my occupational hazard when I worked L.A. SWAT. Or, that I'm a private eye, and play with guns and bad guys. I don't know.

As SWAT and later as a private eye, I was trained to look past the false fronts, the illusions that people want you to see. It's the damn danger lurking beneath the surface that'll kill you. Maybe women are put off by that. Or, hell, maybe the women I'm attracted to are worried they have baggage I'll see. At any rate, I thought my time with Beatrix so far showed promise.

When I walk in I drag behind me a freezing sheet of the November blizzard that howled outside. I use two hands to shove the door closed. Even in the low light, I can see Beatrix's big browns look up. She puffs a wisp of auburn hair away from her pleasant face. She smiles and a slight blush lights her cheeks. "Roman, what are you doing out on a night like this?"

The Man in the Corner

"Thought you could use some company." I glance around the bar. The three red-vinyl booths along the far wall are empty, as are the three wobbly tables in the middle. "Could be a slow night."

She turns clean highball glasses upside down on a towel. "I haven't seen a Tom, Dick, or Harry since this storm kicked up."

I hang my wet coat on a peg and grab a corner stool at the bar so I can talk to her and keep an eye on the front door. It's a leftover habit from LAPD, or the Wild Bill Hickok Syndrome. Let's just say, I don't like surprises.

The flat screen above the bar glows almost white. Some sad-sack reporter in a hooded jacket shivers along the highway. His face is barely visible in the swirling snow. A long line of red taillights glow behind him.

Beatrix looks up at the screen over her left shoulder. We watch as the breathless young man announces, "We have just learned that the airport has closed. Thousands of travelers are stranded. And, due to the extreme winds and severe snow, Denver and surrounding suburbs have gone on Accident Alert."

She pours me a Dewar's on the rocks. "Compliments of the house."

I try to catch her eye. "Say, about last—"

The door blows open, followed by a gust of wind and snow. A heavy-set stranger steps in, his stance wide. The room goes cold. It feels like someone parked a snow blower outside and left it running with the discharge chute pointed our way.

"Close the door, pal," I say.

He looks at me with slit eyes. If I was feeling generous I would put it down to adjusting to the dim lighting. But I can feel his disdain burning from across the room. He turns and shoves the door with a gloved hand. It clatters to a close and cuts off the swirling snow.

The stranger wears a long wool coat and a black fedora. The brim slants low as though he's stepped out of a black-and-white gangster movie. Without a word, he slides into one of the cracked vinyl seats in the booth at the back corner. His dark eyes fix on Beatrix.

I glance at her, eyebrows raised in question.

She doesn't meet my gaze, just continues to organize her clean glasses at the bar and nods her chin toward the new guy. "Be with ya in a minute."

The man keeps a hard gaze on her and slowly removes his gloves. His coat and hat stay on. He has a big round head, small lips, and beady brown eyes.

"You know him?" I ask softly.

She shakes her head, ducking my gaze. She wipes her hands on a towel, rounds the bar, and addresses the stranger. "What can I get you?"

His guard-dog stare never leaves her. "Jameson on the rocks."

"You got it," she says and turns back to the bar.

"Are you Trixie?" he says. The question spills out muted and minacious.

The name catches my attention like a discordant wind chime. I'm mesmerized as Beatrix stops dead in her tracks. She takes a breath and shoots me a quick look before she averts her eyes.

I called her "Trixie" just two weeks ago. We were yapping it up at Café Paris, a noisy restaurant downtown. Our first date. We made small talk, innocent flirty chatter, accompanied by more grinning than I'm used to, and I had said, "You know what? I'm gonna call you Trixie."

"Ha, ha," she tittered, and showed me a faint smile.

"It matches your perky eyes. Beatrix is too formal for you."

She reached across the table and placed her warm hand on top of mine. Tingle bells jingle-jangle-jingled up and down my spine. "No one's ever called me that before," she purred. "I like it."

Those words, coming from her mouth, had sounded sweeter than the music of birds. That's when I thought there might be some promise to our budding romance.

So, how's this fat head stranger come up with the idea that her name is Trixie?

"Well?" he asks. A sneer crosses his face.

She does a slow turn and squares her shoulders. "My name is Beatrix."

Fat Head glowers back at her. "You Jack Delaney's wife?"

Now, that catches my attention—again. I feel like I just swallowed a cup of cement.

"Whiskey coming up," she says and spins on her heels. This time she doesn't look my way.

Thing is, the few times I flirted her up, here in the bar and then on our date, she never mentioned being married.

The door blows in again.

A lanky cop saunters in from the storm. A blast of cold air and snow follow him until he shuts out the blizzard. I know most of the Denver cops, but not this one. He glances over at Fat Head, who ignores him, and then to me. He shakes off his heavy nylon jacket and takes a seat at the opposite end of the bar. A radio crackles softly somewhere on his belt. His badge and arm shield peg him as an officer with the City of Lakewood, and out of his jurisdiction.

Beatrix eyes him from behind the bar. She holds a highball glass with Fat Head's Irish whiskey. "Be right with you."

Something about how she greets him and the fact he doesn't acknowledge her puts me on edge.

She places the drink on the table in front of Fat Head.

He grabs her wrist. "You're Jack's wife, aren't you?"

This stranger is starting to annoy me. But I decide to wait this little drama out, since I have no idea what's going on.

Beatrix, as usual, can handle herself. She wrestles free from his grasp with a quick twist of her arm, a slick escape. Then she pokes him in the shoulder and growls, "Don't you ever touch me again." She stalks away.

Fat Head recoils, his eyes blazing. "He's dead, you know."

A long smoky mirror runs horizontal along the back bar where Beatrix keeps rows of bottles and sparkling glassware. Even though the lighting in the tiny room is low, Fat Head's grim expression glowers in the reflection from the far back corner. The cop stares intently into the mirror at Beatrix, too.

Of all the gin joints in all the towns...what the hell is up here?

Beatrix doesn't seem to be fazed by Fat Head's comment. I've seen her roll with the punches before with a number of gentlemen who turned degenerate after a few drinks. She has a knack for letting stupid comments roll off her back.

There were nights when I stopped in just to flirt and drink away the memories of my SWAT days in L.A. and the friends I was forced to leave behind. That's when I first noticed her commanding presence. She doesn't take crap from any two-legged cretin who threatens to disrupt her bar. In fact, I think she's the most fearless woman I've ever met.

But tonight, she goes stiff.

I suddenly have a lot of questions for Beatrix, but this doesn't seem to be the time, so I wait. The bar is as good a place to weather the storm as any. Plus, something is afoot here that I don't understand. Something I can't quite recognize, like a face in a fog.

Maybe Fat Head won't be a threat now that the cop is here. But, who knows how long he might hang around.

My gut tells me I shouldn't leave her alone.

Since our first, and only, date, I felt like we had moved beyond the point of her being a bar owner and me a customer. I held her hand in the car when I drove her home that night and when I kissed her, she kissed me back. It was a long, hungry kiss and for a moment, standing there at her door, I thought she might invite me in.

"I had a wonderful time, Roman," she said. That honey voice smoothed the wrinkles in my mind. She squeezed my arm and then laid her head on my chest. "You're a nice man."

It was an unusually warm night for November and I didn't want it to end. I put my finger under her chin and tipped her head up. She smiled and her eyes twinkled. I was lost in those big brown pools. "Let's do this again," I said.

She laughed. "You mean the kiss?"

"Uh, well, sure, but I was thinking maybe dinner at my place, next time."

She kissed me, leaning into it.

I can still taste her sweet lips in my mind. Her warm hands on my back. The rise and fall of her chest against mine.

She pulled away. "I have a long day tomorrow. I better get in. See you soon. Okay?" She gave me one last peck and disappeared into her red-brick townhouse.

So, I find it odd that she avoids my eyes now—ever since Fat Head had called her "Trixie."

She puts her hands on the bar. To the cop, Beatrix says, "What're you having?"

"Bud Light." The sound he emits is flat and toneless. His hooded impassive eyes fixate on Beatrix.

She winks. "Off duty, eh?"

"Yeah."

In one swift motion, she grabs the bottle by the throat and pops the cap. She sets it in front of him.

He nods. "Are you Trixie?"

Beatrix's jaw drops. This time she does shoot me a glance.

The cop takes a long slug of his beer, but his eyes never leave hers. He sets the bottle down quietly. "Guess so, then."

It dawns on me. She's probably thinking I'm in on some cruel joke with these goons.

Fat Head crawls out of his corner booth and ambles up to the bar, his hands stuck deep into his coat pockets.

"Well? Let me hear it," the cop demands.

Beatrix staggers back and puts her hands on her hips.

Fat Head parks at the bar, between me and the cop.

"Hey! What is this, boys?" Her eyes move left to right. When they get to me, she furrows her brows.

"We know who you are," Fat Head says. "Just tell us where it's at and we'll be on our way."

The Man in the Corner

I've heard enough from these brake fluids. "Obviously, there's some sort of mistake, here," I say. "I think you gentlemen owe Miss Delaney an apology." Frankly, I don't know if I trust my own words, or not, but I have to give her a signal that I'm not involved with these louts.

Their heads snap in my direction.

"Roman. Don't," Beatrix says, her eyes full of caution.

"Who the hell are you?" Fat Head growls.

"Yeah. Mind your own business," the cop says.

I lean on the bar with my left arm to get a better look at the cop. I keep my right hand perched on my right thigh, just in case. Thankfully I remembered to retrieve my snub-nose from my car before I ambled into amateur night. The .38 is tucked neatly into the small of my back.

"I *was* minding my own business," I say, "until you buzzards showed up."

Fat Head turns slowly toward me. The outline of a gun appears against his pocket.

I fight the urge to stand. I'm in a better position the way I am.

"Hey!" Beatrix yells. "What's going on?"

"Shut up, both of you," Fat Head says. "You try anything stupid, I'll kill you—here and now."

"You'll wreck your coat," I say evenly.

"Jeezus, Felton," the cop squawks. "What'd you do that for?"

Fat Head keeps his beady eyes on me but speaks to the cop. "Shut up, Leonard. He's got no right interfering. This ain't his business."

"Yeah, but now he knows what's up. Dammit."

"Don't worry, 'bout it," Fat Head says. "I'll take care of this lug nut."

"What do you want?" Beatrix demands. She stands ramrod straight behind the bar, like her feet have been planted in concrete.

Leonard, the cop, props his elbows on the bar and leans forward, his ugly mug serious as Lincoln on Mount Rushmore. "You know what we want. The money. It belongs to us. Not you."

I sit still as a statue with my right hand roosting on my thigh. I want Fat Head to think he's in command. Meanwhile, I entertain several options in my mind. Even if Beatrix has a panic button under the bar, with this storm howling outside it'll be hours before any help arrives. So I can't count on that.

But I am confident I can disarm Fat Head quickly with a flurry of my hands and a kick to his groin. And, with the element of surprise, I'm sure I can get the drop on Leonard. His gun is still holstered.

Timing is everything right now. Patience is my friend.

Beatrix blinks. "I don't know what you're talking about but I want you—all of you—to leave. Right now!"

With his eyes square on me, the gun pointed my way, Felton speaks to the cop. "You checked her place, right?"

Beatrix gapes. "You what?"

"It's not there," Leonard huffs. His shoulders sag in defeat.

"You went through my stuff?" Beatrix squeals. Her lips draw tight as piano wire.

The cop speaks as if he's having a conversation with his beer bottle. "I tore her place apart. Upside down and inside out. It's gotta be here. If not, it's somewhere close."

"You bastard." Beatrix slams a palm on the counter, her

eyes on fire.

"Leonard, go poke around." Fat Head thrusts his chin at the opening into the kitchen. "It's probably in the back."

The cop licks his lips. "It'd be a lot easier if Trixie just showed me."

"I would if I had any idea what you're talking about," Beatrix says. "But, I don't, so just take your little guns and get the hell out!"

Fat Head laughs. "C'mon, Trixie, we don't have all night. Where'd Jack stash it?"

"I haven't seen Jack in months. He's on some special IBM banking project in San Francisco."

Fat Head grins. "That what he told you?"

"Oh, he was with a bank, all right," Leonard chimes in, "but he was with us on a job in Topeka. We were to meet in Cozumel and split the thirteen mil, but greedy Jack never showed."

Fat Head shifts his feet. "Took awhile to track that cagey bastard down, but we found him—dead in Aurora."

The cop jabs a finger at Beatrix. "And no money." He dismounts from his stool, like a tired cowboy.

Time for an intervention. I meet Fat Head's eyes and tip my head toward the cop. "How do you know if your pal Leonard, here, didn't find the money and keep it? He a good actor?" I lift a brow. "Or hell, maybe you killed Jack, and you're just playing Leonard for a fool? That your game, Felton?"

The cop freezes, and for the first time, his stony face is livid. "Don't listen to his crap, Felton."

A slight tic forms below Fat Head's right eye, and a sneer crosses his lips.

The next events travel through the bar faster than bad news.

Fat Head yanks a Glock from his pocket, while the cop goes for his sidearm.

I grab the barrel of Fat Head's weapon with my left hand and shove it toward the ceiling. It discharges with a loud snap, but next to my ear, it rivals a sonic boom.

I hold onto the gun, step in close, and simultaneously force the heel of my right hand up and under his chin. Then I pop my right knee, hard, into his groin. Barstools crash to the floor as we stagger together. For a split second, old Fat Head can't decide if he wants to fall backwards or forwards. So he crumples in place with a mighty groan.

I wrestle the gun from Fat Head's hand. He doesn't resist. He falls to a fetal, focused on protecting the family jewels, then grovels on the floor muttering incoherent Biblical terms.

Immediately after his gun discharges, two quick pops echo behind him. Beatrix stands behind the bar, grasping a .38-Special in both hands. I don't know where she got it.

The cop stumbles backward, his hand on his holster. For a second, he seems to hang in the air, like a surprised marionette.

Beatrix focuses her eyes on him like a laser beam. Then she fires a third time, and just like that, it's over.

Historians say the shootout at the O.K. Corral in Tombstone, Arizona, between the Earp brothers and the Clanton gang, lasted all of thirty seconds. This turkey shoot takes even less time off the clock.

I swing Fat Head's Glock toward Beatrix. At the same time, she swings her revolver at me.

"Put it down, Beatrix," I say as calmly as I can. "We're both working on high adrenaline right now. You just shot a man. Take it easy."

"He's not the first," she says calmly. Her eyes narrow. "And maybe not my last."

"Put down your gun."

"How do I know you're not with them?"

"This is the first time I've seen these dirtbags. Put it down."

"Not on your life." She cocks the hammer. The click gets my attention.

I try to change her focus. At what point in time did Beatrix shift from totally together to totally postal, I don't know. But here she is, training her gun at me. I don't doubt she might shoot.

We square off like two gunfighters at high noon.

"What do you know about the money these guys are after?"

She laughs contemptuously, standing firm behind the bar. "Sweetheart, if I tell you, I'll have to kill you."

Fat Head sucks his thumb on the floor, just feet from my boots.

Leonard-the-cop is slumped dead against the wall to my right. Blood spatters on his shirt like an abstract drip painting.

I back slowly into the middle of the room. Not that the gap really matters in terms of potential gunplay, but I see things differently—more vividly, now. Distance is the perfect metaphor for our recondite relationship. The sudden space I feel between us—from what had seemed like a promising union just weeks ago—now makes me weak in the knees. And pissed at myself for being so blind.

I take a wild-assed guess. "I take it you have the money. That right?"

She smiles. "Bingo."

"You kill Jack?"

Fat Head mumbles and wobbles up to one knee.

Beatrix grins, even broader. "It doesn't matter, Roman. Listen, come with me. We'll go to Mexico and never have to worry about a thing."

"I hate Mexico," I say.

"Oh, c'mon. I still remember our night at Café Paris."

"Don't bring up Café Paris. It's poor salesmanship."

The smile fades from her face. "Then I'll go alone. I've had it with this crummy weather, and this bar, the neutered men stumbling in and out of here every damned night complaining about their sorry jobs and nagging wives."

"The money doesn't belong to you, Beatrix."

She wipes a wisp of hair from her face. "Finders keepers, they always say."

"You'll never get away with this. Think. It won't take long for the police and FBI to figure this out. The murdered cop, if he really was one, and Felton here—when he's in custody, he'll sing like a canary. Eventually, they'll find Jack's body. It all traces back to you."

"Don't cross me, Roman. I'm in no mood. Decide right now. Come with me. We can leave the dirt and grime of Colfax. We'll live like a king and queen on the white sands of Playa."

Fat Head coughs and drags himself up to the bar. He leans heavily on the counter, his back to me.

"He's right, you know," Fat Head wheezes.

I keep aim on Beatrix, but move to my right, near the dead cop. Old habits die hard. Besides, you can't trust a dirtbag. I want to see Fat Head's hands. His arms are crossed on the bar.

Beatrix's eyes and pistol dart back and forth between me and Fat Head.

"You won't get away with this," he growls.

A new gun flashes in his hands. A small-ankle variety. He must have pulled it before he stood up. But I don't see it until—the moment Beatrix waves her gun back at me.

My world goes to slow motion.

I duck and sidestep to my left.

Her volley whizzes past my ear.

Fathead takes aim at Beatrix and fires twice.

She staggers back and slumps to the ground.

I shoot Fat Head, close range. The bullet bunks in, right behind his right ear.

Fat Head crashes to his left like a chopped tree.

I run behind the bar and cradle Beatrix's head in my arms. Her eyes are wide with surprise and fear. I gently pry the gun loose from her hand.

"Hold on," I say. "I'll call an ambulance. Just hold on." I'm not sure if I believe my own words, but it's the best I can come up with. "You'll be okay. Hold on."

Blood spreads on her chest from the two shots Fat Head fired. Her blood pressure must be dropping fast.

I dig my cell phone out and dial 911.

She coughs and gasps, struggling for air. "In the back. A trunk."

"Don't worry about it," I say. "You're doing fine. Hold on." I hold her tight until the ambulance arrives, and they take her away. Her life hangs by a thread.

The Denver cops have a boatload of questions. It takes a

couple of hours until I repeat the entire chain of events, twice, to their satisfaction.

After the heavy-duty body bags are carried out, I'm released to go. But I freeze in place when the coppers carry out the cash—not in one trunk, but twelve.

The lead detective is a swarthy fellow with a thin moustache. His right hand jingles coins in his pocket. He blows out a slow whistle followed by a question aimed at me. "You sure that's it?"

"Hell, she only mentioned one trunk. Where'd you find all that?"

"We discovered one in the kitchen hidden behind a stack of boxes. The rest were in a rental truck parked out back."

"Damn."

He gives me a stare that matches the cold wind outside. "Damn, what?"

"Nothing."

"We'll count it, of course. I'll be in touch."

I toss down the scotch that Beatrix served me an hour ago. I slip on my coat and lean into the storm until I find my snow-covered car.

Minutes later, I cross Colfax in my old Saab and head west. I never see another vehicle until I get home.

And then it hits me. The feeling of loss, the potential for something good, gone. A loss I didn't feel until L.A. SWAT told me I had to leave.

And that's when I know I'll never drink again at Dominic's, or feel Beatrix's sweet lips on mine.

The wind and snow howl outside. The storm is relentless. I think of Beatrix and her auburn hair and her honey voice. She was an enchantress, enigmatic in how she willed her way around men and the vagaries of life which would ultimately befall her.

I wonder, in my heart, what it might have been like with Beatrix if things were different, if what my imagination dreamed up might have come true.

But, all in all, I know what I wanted her to be was nothing more than an illusion.

About the Author:

Zoltan James is the pen name of Z. J. Czupor, an award-winning author who writes literary fiction, mystery thrillers and short stories with a penchant for modern noir. Z.J.'s first novel, *The Hot Tub Club,* won first place in Rocky Mountain Fiction Writers' Gold Competition and his second, *The Rose and the Spider,* was a finalist. That novel also finished second in the Southeastern Writers Association competition. He and his wife, Marta, co-founded The InterPro Group, one of Denver's leading public relations/marketing firms.

You can connect with ZJ on Facebook at www.facebook.com/zczupor and on Twitter at @ZJCzupor.

Allyah
By Rebecca Rowley

Colfax Avenue people watching inspired Rebecca's story:

As a muse, Colfax Avenue is the naughty child sitting in timeout plotting the next caper. It's an avenue that is just begging to have its dirty little secrets told. Oh, sure, there are the nice parts of Colfax, too, but are they nearly as much fun? I don't think so.

One afternoon, I was watching a woman walk down the street looking smug, miserable and just up to no good. I asked myself, what's she been up to and why does it seem like she's trying not to smile? So, I went to my laptop and let my character "Allyah" fill in the blanks.

Allyah

I could hardly believe that something so green and slimy had come out of me. Four legs, one horn, and early buds of teeth. How was I supposed to love this thing? It was squirming and "yorking" in its bassinet. Then it opened its three eyes and gazed deeply into mine. And that's when I knew.

I was dreaming.

At this point, I had two choices: roll over and try to pry open my eyelids, or go with the dream. Such a choice was not easy when the options really amounted to whether to continue wandering the realm of the strange or face the grim emptiness of my existence. In retrospect, I should have stayed in the dream. But I rolled over, hugged the pillow next to me, and manually pulled open my left eyelid with the help of my thumb knuckle.

And there it was: my room. An eight-by-eight box with gray walls, white curtains, and burgundy accent pillows that my cousin, Ernesta, thought were a "FABulous" contrast to the steely neutrals. I thought they made my side chair look like it'd been fatally wounded.

I lifted my head and eyed the alarm clock. 8:45 AM.

"Blurg," I muttered.

I got out of bed anyway and dressed in layers of teal.

"Meh," I told the mirror.

I wanted to go back to sleep and find out if the green slimy thing had a name, but my shoes were already on my feet, and my feet were moving toward the kitchen. I already knew there was no food to be found, but I had a small hope of coffee. The cupboards, however, yielded none.

"Snarf," I grunted as I headed out the door with a purse, likely mine, and an umbrella that I'd picked up in a coffee shop. I'm sure the owner hadn't even noticed; the sun had come back out by then, anyway.

The click of my heels would have made a good base beat for a blues song, but I had no interest in writing one. I headed down the block toward the office building that absorbs eight to nine hours of my life each day.

At the corner of Colfax and Lafayette, the little white man became a flashing red hand. I pondered going forward anyway and seeing how far I could get. But I didn't. I waited. I let six cars screech past me before taking a deep breath. I let two more go by before exhaling. Then the white man returned and I made my way casually toward the building on the corner.

Taking the stairs to the fourth floor, I stepped into the hallway. No one said hello. People in equally dull shades of tan and navy scampered about, as if their lives had meaning. I didn't intervene. I continued on my way down the hall to door 413. It was unlocked as I never bother to leave it any other way.

Inside was a desk, a wheeled chair, two empty bookshelves, and a plastic fern. I closed myself in and took my rolling throne. After dropping my purse in the desk drawer, I opened the pencil drawer and removed a baseline headset. I positioned the mic close to my mouth and made sure my ears were completely covered by the padded ear pieces. Then I waited. One. Two. Maybe three minutes in, I heard the click of a line connecting.

"Hello there," I said, my voice deep and breathy. "My name's

Allyah

Mable. What's yours?"

"Um, hi," a man's voice said. "I'm Paul."

"Hello, Paul. What's your story?"

"Um."

"Yes?"

"I'm not really sure what to say here. I've never done anything like this before."

"It's all right, Paul. That's why I'm here."

I began picking at my nails. I needed a manicure, and not the kind you get for $19.95 at the Vietnamese salon by the supermarket.

"It's . . . well, it's just that my wife . . ." He had a weaselly voice. I don't like men with weaselly voices. They always sound 4'6", with nose hair and maybe back acne.

"Go on," I said and started pushing my cuticles back with my index fingernail.

"She's just so cold to me." He was probably skinny, too. Mousy brown hair.

"Uh-huh."

"I'm sure she's seeing other men."

A therapist would have asked how this made him feel, but that's not why I was on the line.

"What is it you need me to do for you, Paul?" I didn't need to know about his wife's problems.

"Can you . . . can you make it quick?" The only thing worse than a man with a weaselly voice is one with absolutely no conviction.

"I can do whatever you want, Paul." I tried to keep my tone even, not scream into the phone for him to hurry the hell up.

"I just want . . . I mean, I don't want . . ."

I began tapping my desk, counting down until I could hang up.

"Let me ask you something," I broke in as he continued to hem and haw. "How would you like to pay for this?"

"I was told we could do this electronically, that you can disguise it."

"Of course, Paul." *You idiot.* "Shall I send you the link for payment?"

He agreed—finally a decisive moment—and gave me an e-mail address he said he'd set up just for this occasion. I used my encrypted smart phone to send him the instructions for remittance.

"Now. What would you like me to do, Paul?"

"I want it quick, you know. Nothing fancy. No pain." For all of his unappealing qualities, at least he wasn't a brute. That was mildly refreshing.

"Of course, Paul. Whatever you like." I leaned back and waited for details. He babbled through some ideas he'd mulled over and some boundaries he wanted to make sure wouldn't be crossed. "That's fine," I told him, practicing my fake smile to keep the tone of my voice crisp and pleasant. I asked him to send me a photo so there was no question of who would be getting the service. He complied within seconds. Despite his lack of style, I always appreciate when clients follow directions without question.

"Do you have a date and time in mind?" I asked, sensing the end of our discussion drawing near.

"Um, tomorrow. Maybe. Around 6:00 PM?"

"How about 6:00 PM exactly?" I wasn't fond of generalities.

Allyah

"Sure. Okay." His voice perked up, words accelerating just a little.

"Where?"

"My house. 165 Oak Avenue. It's the brick Tudor with green trim."

I muted the line while I yawned.

"You can—" His tone had definitely gotten bolder, but I was tired of him now.

"Of course, Paul. Mable will make sure your every wish is granted." I added a little laugh at the end to put him at ease. I heard the soft scratches of his breath on the other end, like perhaps he was enjoying a little chuckle of his own. Maybe he was finally relaxing.

"Once I see the payment, I will make all the arrangements for tomorrow night," I told him.

"Okay. What's the price?"

I told him, half hoping that he would get sticker shock and bolt back to his hole. After a minute of dead air, I anticipated the phone's sing-song disconnect tune. Instead, I heard a message ping. A new transaction had just hit the account in the Caymans. Payment in full.

"I see you're a serious man, Paul."

"I need this," he said, asserting himself with that eager tone that made him sound like every other client.

"Very well, Paul. Tomorrow. 6:00 PM."

He hung up first. I waited a moment before opening a fresh line. As it rang, I kicked the plastic fern with my toe. It didn't hurt. In a way, I wished it had.

"What?" a deeper male voice asked.

"165 Oak Avenue. Female. Five foot eight. Brown hair, brown eyes. Answers to Carol. I'll send you the photo." Three clicks and it was done.

"Got it. Method?"

"He wants it to look like an accident—quick and painless."

"What a gentleman."

"Aren't they all. I'll send your paycheck when you send confirmation that the job has been completed without incident."

"Thanks, *Mable*," he groaned. "By the way, I hate that codename. It sounds like my grandmother."

I kicked the plant again. "I know," I muttered and hung up.

Ten minutes later, as my stomach began swimming in acidic fluid, a text appeared on my personal cell: "We got what we needed. A car is on its way to your position."

There was no way I was going to wait around for cops. I'd done my part. So, I tossed my cell phone into the fern where the cops would find it, and stepped out of the office into an uncertain oblivion.

About the Author:

Rebecca Rowley, satirist and biographer of fictional characters, composes mock crime noir short stories, novellas, and faux academic essays. She's a Colorado native and writes about dark moments infused with irony and humor. Past publications include short works of fiction and random acts of poetry. When not entertaining the masses or terrorizing the villagers, she's hard at work completing an MBA in Entertainment Management, with the goal of helping her fellow authors boost their careers.

You can find Rebecca at www.facebook.com/rebecca.rowley.54 and on Twitter: @rebeccajrowley.

B. K. Winstead

The Case of the Woman Who Sewed Her Silence
By B. K. Winstead

The Colfax theme inspired B. K. to try his hand at a different genre:

I'm typically inspired by history and frequently write historical stories, so when I saw the call for manuscripts for this anthology, I read all about Colfax Avenue's long history. As interesting as that was, I didn't have any immediate ideas for a story. Then I came across a fable that involved a mother who turned her children into swans to protect them and thereafter refused to speak. Of course, that's not what happens in my story, but it's the genesis. Although I started with history, in this case the story is contemporary.

At the same time, I started listening to a CD by the Devin Townsend Band *Synchestra*. The music runs the gamut from soft, acoustic, folksy tunes to loud, discordant, grating metal. That multifaceted nature seemed to be a perfect complement to Colfax itself. The music inspired the development of the story as I wrote, and I tried to show the strange variations and incongruities that exist along Colfax today.

The Case of the Woman Who Sewed Her Silence

The mystery woman's file was on my desk when I got to the station early that morning. She'd been found on East Colfax the night before, covered in blood. She wouldn't—or couldn't—speak, so she was taken to the hospital for psych eval. Witnesses at the scene recognized the woman and said she'd been seen with a newborn baby recently, but no child was found with her.

I grabbed my jacket and met my partner as he was coming in the front doors.

"We've got a case," I said.

"Dios mío, Marc!" Rick said. "Let a guy get some coffee first." His rumpled suit and mussed hair told a tale of another night with little sleep. He had a new baby at home in addition to the two-year-old and the four-year-old.

"We'll get something on the road."

I took us through a Starbucks drive-through on the way to St. Jo's, and Rick pulled up the case notes on his laptop.

A patrol car had responded to a disturbance at a coin-op laundry on East Colfax, one of Denver's least respectable neighborhoods. When the uniforms arrived, they found the woman sitting toward the back on a long bench between rattling dryers and washing machines. The other patrons had cleared out. She wore nothing but a faded yellow sundress although the autumn night was cool. Her dress was spattered with bright red.

As the unis approached, they saw part of the reason for the

blood: She was in the process of stitching her lips together. She had already sewed shut about a third of her mouth, and before they could stop her, she jammed the long needle up through her lower lip again, forcing it out through her upper lip, then proceeded to tighten the bloody thread.

The officers said she made a loud keen or cry, with her lips clenched tight, blood trickling beneath her mouth while tears streamed from her eyes. They restrained her to prevent her doing further damage to herself. She refused to say a word, which would have been difficult by that point. They packed her into an ambulance off to St. Joseph's emergency room.

Witnesses at the coin-op said she'd been frequenting the area for weeks, panhandling with her baby. No one knew her name. Some bystanders swore she'd had her baby with her that night because they'd heard it crying. No one knew where the child was now.

The lab had run tests on the blood from her dress. Some was hers, but there was another sample present as well. So, was that second sample from her baby or from someone who had stolen her baby and got injured in a struggle?

I parked in an emergency vehicle slot at St. Jo's. I showed my badge at the front desk.

"Detectives Davis and Díaz. We're here to see the woman they brought in last night."

We were directed to the room on the second floor where she was being held for observation. St. Jo's didn't have a secure psych ward, just an isolated wing. A few minutes later, I got my first look at the woman.

She was thin, bony from malnutrition. Her pale skin seemed

to have much the same texture as the paper-like hospital gown they'd put her in. Her arms were strapped to the sides of the bed, her head turned away from us and covered by a scraggly spray of dirty blond hair. The hospital had removed the stitches she'd put through her lips, but the scabs left behind reminded me of a grinning skull. Her eyes were open but unfocused.

With a nurse standing by, I questioned the woman about who she was, what she was doing in the laundromat, why she'd been harming herself. She didn't even acknowledge our presence. She appeared to be about twenty or twenty-two, pretty in a plain way—if you could overlook the hollow eyes and the red welts and scabs around half of her mouth.

"Miss, are you able to talk?" I asked after several minutes of futile interrogation. Her eyes blinked. I didn't know if I was supposed to take that as a yes.

"Can you tell us your name, at least?" I was supposed to be supportive in my questioning, make her feel safe and valued, but her lack of response frustrated me. Besides, I usually let Rick play good cop.

"Miss, we only want to help you," he said. Although she appeared to be Caucasian, he attempted a few questions in Spanish. "Por favor, señorita, me dice su nombre? Estamos en busca de su bebé. Qué pasó con el niño?"

He asked her other questions, in English and Spanish. No reaction.

I stepped around the bed into her line of sight.

"Miss, we need to locate the baby, the child you've been seen with. What happened to the child?"

Her lips remained pressed together, causing little tremors along her mouth and in her neck from the effort. But tears streamed from her eyes, so I knew she heard me.

"Did someone take your baby from you?" I asked.

For the first time, her eyes focused, and I saw such despair there as she shook her head, no. She struggled against her restraints and turned her face against the pillow, her body thrashing. The nurse moved in to settle her.

Outside the room, I talked to a doctor, a psychiatrist named Dr. Sorenson, who was currently in charge of her care.

I asked about the stitches, what might compel her to do that.

"Impossible to say without knowing more. But if she's lost her baby, it could be some expression of guilt."

"You think she did something to her child?"

"I didn't say that. I have no reason to believe it. If someone else did something, and she was unable to prevent it, she would still feel guilt. We won't know what happened until she's ready to tell us."

"She hasn't talked to anyone?"

"Not since she's been here. Won't eat. Will barely sip water through a straw."

"Have you tried getting her to write anything? Or does she need the restraints to keep her from hurting herself?"

"She still needs supervision, but we could try that."

I suggested he have a nurse or some friendly face sit with her a while and see if she would write her story. I left him my card.

I called the station to get a forensic tech down to run the woman's fingerprints. If she lived in that neighborhood on Colfax, she might be in our system, run in for solicitation or something. I'd also taken her picture with my phone so I could show it around.

The Case of the Woman Who Sewed Her Silence

The laundromat was a few crooked blocks away. The unis had searched it last night, but I wanted to get a better sense of what went down, and where. A couple of homeless men, sitting on plastic chairs by the front window, looked nervously at us as we entered the shabby, narrow coin-op. Several locals folded laundry or shoved sopping loads from washer to dryer under the spluttering fluorescents. A speaker mounted high on the wall crooned trebly country music, although the rattle of the machines themselves was enough to make conversation difficult.

Toward the back, drops of dark dried blood decorated the floor and a bench, outlining where the woman had been sitting. Apparently, the owner didn't think much about cleaning. Gritty powdered detergent rasped underfoot as I paced the stained tiles.

I opened the back door onto a shaded, piss-scented alley. Someone had been collecting shopping carts back there.

"What do you think?" Rick asked.

"Someone could have left that way with the child." Trouble was, no one had seen the baby, only heard it. Or so the report said.

As we got back to the car, Rick said, "I've got a stop to make." I tossed him the keys and slid in on the passenger side.

It was turning into a beautiful Denver fall day. The sky was high and hard and pale blue under a bright sun. A few minutes down Colfax, and Rick pulled up next to Notre Dame of the West, otherwise known as the Cathedral Basilica of the Immaculate Conception.

I'd passed the cathedral's giant gothic spires hundreds of times but had never been in. Frankly, I couldn't see the point of such a monstrosity. All it needed was some gargoyles to render it truly grotesque. It certainly didn't fit well with the character of the neighborhood.

"Come on," Rick said. He jumped out of the car, giving me no chance for discussion.

I caught up on the sidewalk. "Is this part of the case? If so, I'm not seeing the connection."

He opened the door for me; I didn't go in. The smell of oldness and damp stone wafted out on the cool air.

"I want to light a candle," he said, looking at me with a challenge in his eyes.

"I'll wait outside," I said.

"Bah." Rick looked at me like I was chicken, but he left to say his prayers.

I stood by the sunny cathedral steps, gazing up and down Colfax. Fidgeting, really. Just being close to such an old-school Catholic place made me uneasy. I was certain someone was going to point at me and start yelling, "Heretic! Nonbeliever!" And maybe start throwing stones.

Rick seemed to take an ungodly amount of time inside. I was just wondering if I had time to run across the street to the World's Largest Hub Cap Store when Rick emerged.

"What was that about?" I asked as we headed back to the car.

"Man, you're such a *cabrón*."

"What are you talking about?"

"It's for the baby. A prayer for the baby and the mother—that we can find the little baby for that poor woman."

I shrugged him off. "A prayer? Great idea. Or we could spend time looking for the child instead."

"Show some respect. I know you don't believe what I do, but show some respect for my beliefs. A case like this, I think we can use all the help we can get."

"Then let's get going and talk to people," I said.

"I just did. Trust me, this gets results."

I wouldn't contradict him, but I put no faith in supernatural beings.

Back in the car, Rick sat with his arms resting over the steering wheel, the keys dangling from his fingers, his gaze straight ahead. "I lit two," he said. "One for the baby on your behalf as well."

What could I say?

My phone rang. Dr. Sorenson from the hospital.

"It's not much, but the woman has written one word: SKYLER. Apart from that, she'll doodle on the page, which can be therapeutic. She keeps drawing faces—or possibly the same face over and over."

"Skyler? How does that fit in?" I asked.

"I was asking what happened to her baby. When she jotted that, it seemed to be in answer, but I can't be sure."

"So it could be a name? Or a place?"

I could sense his shrug through the phone. "Or nothing. I'm not sure she's entirely coherent. She's distraught, which is understandable, a mother losing a newborn child."

"The face she drew—is it any good? Could we use it to identify someone?"

"I'm not sure it's a real person. It's kind of . . . stylized. And, frankly, creepy. I'll save the pages for you if you want to take a look."

She'd been examined again by the medical staff. Physically, she checked out fine, although when they examined her lips, she resisted, still refusing to open her mouth. When the physician had pulled back her lips to check the insides of her puncture wounds, she'd screamed the whole time through gritted teeth.

Before hanging up, Sorenson said he'd keep trying to get more from her. Everyone seemed to know that if we were going to find the baby, it had to be soon.

While I was talking to Sorenson, Rick had called in to the station. They'd already run the woman's fingerprints, but found no matches. I told Rick about Skyler and we brainstormed about what that could mean.

"Maybe she meant Sky*line*—the Skyline Motel," Rick said.

I nodded. That was worth checking, but it was pretty far east. "I think that's in Aurora."

We could get the Aurora cops to check it.

"Hey, if we're going for close-sounding, what about Chular? Skyler, Chular?"

Rick thought about my suggestion and gave a weak nod. Chular wasn't a great choice, either, but he was in the right area. A short, Mexican pimp who worked girls out of that stretch of Colfax. If our woman had been on the street, it was likely she was one of his. And he would not have been pleased at her having a baby. We decided our best option was to pay Chular a visit.

Chular could usually be found at the Freaky Ladies Hair Stylin's salon, of which he was part owner. It gave him a place to legitimize his real profits as well as a way to showcase his stable of whores, who doubled as hairdressers. The salon was wedged in among consignment shops, tattoo parlors, auto parts stores, and check-cashing places. There was also an increasing number of upscale eateries, reflecting the changing nature of the neighborhood.

The front windows were papered over so you'd hardly know the place was in business. A bell jingled over the door as we entered. One customer was in a chair under a smock—a man, and he looked surprised at our entrance. Chular glanced up from his iPad but seemed unconcerned by our arrival. The voluptuous and scantily clad hairdresser continued clipping around the customer's head.

Chular sat in an old-fashioned barber chair, like a giant throne of red leather, at the side of the room. He wore a white tank-top and baggy chinos.

"What's up, Dicks?" he said. Chular also thought he was a great wit.

"We're looking for someone," I said.

"I haven't seen 'em."

"Maybe you should wait until I tell you who it is."

Rick hung back by the front door in case Chular decided to run. There was a door into the back room, but it was on the opposite side of the shop from Chular's throne.

I pulled up the woman's picture on my phone.

"Do you know who this is?"

Chular glanced at the screen and scowled. "Shit, I don't run with no skinny white bitches."

"She's from around here, maybe living on the street, and she has a baby."

"'Z'at so?" Chular rubbed at his neck, which was a spider-work quilt of tats. He had a shaved head and a stud through his eyebrow to complete his gangster chic.

Chular lied on principle, although it was true she wasn't his usual type of girl. He tended to stick with Latinas, and fairly curvy ones at that.

"Maybe some of your girls have seen her?"

"Nah, man, they ain't even from around here. They, what you call, commuters. Just come around to style some hair."

Actually, they had apartments above the salon. Chular didn't trust his hookers. Or hairdressers.

"Maybe I'll just ask them myself."

"Hey, Stella, you seen this skinny white girl?" Chular asked.

Before I could show her the picture, she answered, "Shoot, I don't hang around with the likes of that. I got me a job. I'm too busy." Stella was a buxom woman with elaborately styled red hair—probably a wig—and too much makeup. She stood behind her customer with comb and scissors in hand.

Chular's Freaky Ladies wouldn't say anything he didn't want them to, at least not as long as the man himself was around.

"It's not the woman we're looking for. It's her baby. Someone stole the baby last night."

"Now that's a shame," Chular said. "Poor little bambino, eh?"

"But you don't know and haven't heard anything?"

"That is correct, officer."

"Seems like people lose a lot of babies around here," Stella said. "From what I hear. On the news, and such."

It occurred to me how out of place her customer seemed. He was probably in his fifties, gray hair, and it looked like he was wearing a conservative suit beneath the barber's smock.

I glanced at Rick and he smiled. He'd seen it sooner. Not only did the man not fit the surroundings, but he was also doing his best impersonation of a statue. He was trying hard for us to not notice him.

I strolled up to the man. "You come here often?" I asked.

He chuckled like it was a good joke. I smiled at him until he realized he'd actually need to answer. "Well, no. I was just out for a walk. Stopped in."

"You live around here?"

"No, work."

"OK, well maybe you could show me some ID."

"What? What for?"

"For starters, you're in a known den of prostitution and you're getting your hair cut by a whore."

"Wha—? Prostitution?"

"ID, please."

His surprise seemed genuine. For a moment, I thought maybe he was innocent. But as he reached into his back pocket for his wallet, a plastic bag full of white powder slipped from under the smock and hit the floor.

"Ho, what have we here?" Rick said, coming forward to pick up the bag.

"What's that? I don't know," the man said.

I turned to Chular. "When did you start dealing? The ladies—we can turn a blind eye, sometimes. But not this."

"Hey, I got nothing to do with that. I never seen this guy before."

The gray-haired man saw his way out. "They gave me this! They planted it. I don't even know what it is."

"You lying shit," Stella yelled. Then she stabbed him in the shoulder with her scissors.

From that point, the whole mess turned into an epic time-waster. The gentleman wasn't badly injured, although he screamed and bled a lot. Rick wrestled the scissors from Stella while I covered Chular. The pimp seemed more annoyed at the mess than anything. We called for backup; several unis arrived within minutes. It took a while longer for the vice crew to show up so we could turn the crime scene over.

In the end, they arrested Stella and Chular, and their customer, though he would detour to St. Jo's emergency before the lock up. It was doubtful anything would stick, but it gave us the chance to search the place more thoroughly. Rick and I talked to a few more of Chular's girls that we found in back, all voluptuous Latinas, showed them our mystery woman's photo. No one had anything useful.

By the time we cleared the scene, it was well past lunch. We drove down to Annie's for some classic Americana eats. Except when we got there, Rick ordered the Oriental chicken salad. I ordered the fried egg cheeseburger. With bacon.

"So what?" Rick said, glaring at me. "Julia's been at me to eat healthier. And she's right. I've got kids, and I need to set a good example for them, stay healthy."

"I didn't say a word."

"I can hear your thoughts."

"I wasn't going to say anything. I was thinking about something else. I was thinking about getting a pet, like a rabbit or a gerbil. But maybe I don't need to."

"Fuck you."

My burger was a greasy hot mess, and perfectly delicious. I

was sopping up egg juice with a French fry when Rick asked, "Where do we go next?"

"We've still got the list of witnesses from last night to talk to. We might try canvassing the area around the laundromat, see if anyone else recognizes her."

"Shit. Lot of work without much hope. We've got to find out who this girl is."

Rick put a lot of himself into cases like. He always felt for the kids. Sometimes I was a lousy partner, but I wanted to give him something back.

"Hey, Rick, what you did today, with the candles. The church. That was nice. I mean, doing one for me as well."

He looked at me from the corner of his eye, like he had no idea who I was.

"I'm not saying I believe it does anything. But it's good because you think it does," I said.

"There it is," he said, nodding. "You're such a . . . *cabrón*, sometimes. You know, you should come with my family and me to mass sometime, see what it's all about."

"Ooo, I'd love to, but Sundays are so hectic for me, what with the football and the Xbox and the napping. It's hard to fit it all in."

"Marc, you need to get out, meet someone. I don't even think you've been on a date in, what? Four or five months?"

It was true. I was a well-confirmed bachelor. Didn't relish the complications of relationships. Working with a partner on the job, as much as we got along, and the other officers at the station was about all the chumminess I could stand.

We were about ready to leave when my phone rang. Dr.

Sorenson again.

"Anything new?"

"Bad news, I'm afraid. Our patient has disappeared."

"What?"

He explained that they'd left the restraints off because she'd seemed content to sit in bed and draw on the pad they'd given her. At some point, she'd been left unsupervised. There was no order to watch her; in fact, we hadn't arrested her. Someone might pay for that mistake.

"We've got people searching the building, but I'm afraid she's gone."

"You're right, this is bad."

I told him to call if anything turned up.

"Maybe a woman in a hospital gown won't be too hard to spot wandering around Colfax," Rick said.

"Sure, unless she found some clothes before she left the hospital."

We cruised the streets between St. Jo's and the laundromat, hoping to spot her. When that didn't pan out, we started running down our list of witnesses.

We couldn't locate half of them. They were homeless or had given false addresses. The few we did talk to had nothing more to offer, so we started talking to some other locals. A girl named Theresa from the sandwich shop a couple doors over from the laundromat said she thought the woman's name might be Renee.

"She's eaten at our shop a few times," Theresa said. "Her baby's cute." She didn't know where the woman lived, or a last name.

"I know she's struggling. I think she goes out begging for

change so she can come in for a sandwich. I always throw in a little extra because I can see how much she needs it. And if she doesn't eat, neither does her baby, right?"

Theresa had seen the woman entering the laundromat the night before. "I thought it was strange because it was the first time I'd seen her without her baby."

"When she went in, she definitely didn't have the baby?" Rick asked her.

She nodded. "I'm sure."

"Did you notice anything else unusual? Did she seem upset or anything?"

The girl hesitated, and I could see she was thinking of something but wasn't sure she should tell us.

"Any small detail could be helpful," I said.

"Well, it was dark. But her face looked dirty, like smeared with something."

"Any idea what it was?"

"My first thought was that it was blood, but it was probably ketchup or something. There was some on her dress, too. I said hi, but she turned and went inside the laundry. I was on a smoke break and had to go back to work. I didn't see her after that."

"OK, that's good. Thanks."

Whatever happened to the baby had happened before the woman—Renee, possibly—had gone to the laundromat. That brought us no closer to finding the baby, or the woman. Or whoever might have done them harm. Assuming it wasn't the woman herself, a possibility we had to strongly consider.

We headed back to the station. Maybe someone else had turned up something.

We talked to the Aurora cops, who visited the Skyline Motel; no one there recognized the woman's photo. We went through missing persons reports, looking for anyone who matched our Jane Doe. We talked to the detectives at the station who'd been going over recent cases of missing or abducted children, looking for any similarities. A couple of officers had been out interviewing local registered sex offenders. Today, Colfax was living up to its reputation as the wickedest street in America.

We were at a dead end, and I was tired of drinking coffee and eating stale donuts. I was ready to call it a day.

"You're giving up?" Rick said. "Jesus, man. That baby's out there somewhere. Maybe she left it in an apartment. Or under a bush. If we don't find it..." He couldn't bring himself to voice the consequences.

I bent back to the reports, although I was itching to get out on the street. Rick called his wife, told her he was working late, didn't know when he'd be home. He said goodbye as he always did, "Miles de besos, con cariño."

My phone rang. It was the duty officer from the holding cells.

"There's a Stella Calderon in here, says she needs to speak to you." It took me a moment to remember Stella from Chular's salon. "Says it's something to do with a case you were asking about."

I grabbed Rick, and we headed down to the interview room.

Stella lounged back in a chair, looking just as sassy as she had that morning, before she'd stabbed someone right in front of us. The search of the salon had turned up a large quantity of drugs, so the possibility of getting convictions out of the bust weren't bad—but whether it would be Chular or one of the girls that went down for it was anyone's guess. I expected Stella was looking to make a deal.

"What have you got?" I asked, not bothering to sit down. Rick leaned against the wall by the door.

"I know your girl."

"Yeah?"

"Yeah. I'll tell you where she lives. But you gotta give me something—"

"Bullshit." I turned for the door.

"Wait! Wait! Don't you want to hear?"

I stood with my back to her for a moment. Then I turned slowly, walked back toward her, and leaned across the table that separated the interviewers from the suspects.

"You don't seem to understand your position. You stabbed a man in front of two police detectives, so you'll go down for assault, attempted murder, and anything else the boys in vice feel like throwing at you. With your record, it's not likely to go well. If you know something about that woman, tell us right now. Telling us is the only way we'll consider talking about a deal. And if you want a deal, you'll have to give up something useful on your boss, Chular. But if you don't start talking right now about the woman, you can go back to your cell and fuck yourself."

She sputtered. She was trying to stall.

"Start. Talking."

"OK, OK. I don't know the girl, but I might know where she lives."

"I'm listening."

"There's a tattoo parlor, World of Color. You know it?"

I nodded.

"I've seen her around there a lot. She might live in the apartment upstairs."

"But you're not sure."

Rick stepped forward. "Estás mintiendo a nosotros? Vamos, la verdad ahora."

"No, no. Es la verdad!"

Rick nodded at me.

"All right. We're going to check it out. You'd better hope this is helpful."

"Hey, man, I told you what I know!"

"Yeah, now. You should have told us this morning."

World of Color was just a block from the laundromat. It felt right. It took us only a few minutes to get there. While we'd been inside, the short autumn day had turned to twilight. Headlights and streetlights added their false brightness to the scene.

The front of the tattoo shop was painted with an elaborate mural in black and green and blue that extended up to the second floor, where the curtained apartment windows were incorporated into the design. Neon lights gleamed in the shop windows, advertising exotic possibilities waiting within.

A narrow alley broke the façade on one side of the shop. A second-story fire escape overhung the alley. The apartment probably had a rear entry, but we headed into the shop, expecting they'd know the tenant.

The shop bustled, a couple of tattoo artists with clients in chairs in various states of undress, others browsing catalogs for new skin decorations. Fantasy artwork and cartoons hung on the walls, more samples for customers to consider. Some of the local skin shops did better business in drugs or prostitution, but

The Case of the Woman Who Sewed Her Silence

World of Color was legit. If there was such a thing as an upscale tattoo parlor, this was it, where the affluent urbanites came to prove they were dangerous.

We flashed our badges to the first worker we could corner. We showed him the picture of the woman.

"Oh, our artist," he said. "I know her. What did she do?"

"She works here?"

"Sort of. Let me get the owner."

We were led to an office in the back and, after a few minutes, were joined there by another man who'd finished inking his latest masterpiece on someone's arm.

"I'm Raymond. I'm the owner. Leon said you were asking about Renee?"

He sat behind his desk, which was littered with more artwork samples, needles, and art supplies. He looked like he was in his twenties, although he was probably older. Well-muscled, and each muscle lovingly decorated, and fully on display. They kept the heat up in this place to allow for beach attire year round.

I showed him the picture and he nodded.

"That's her, Renee. Renee Williams. What happened to her mouth?"

"Leon said she works here?"

"No, not really. She's an artist, so I've been buying some of her drawings for samples, turning them into tats. She rents the apartment upstairs. Sub-lets from me, actually. I rent the whole building for the shop."

"Have you seen Renee today?" I asked.

"No. Has she done something?" He looked concerned.

I explained briefly about her overnight stay in the hospital, her missing baby, and how she had disappeared now as well.

"Oh man, that baby means everything to her."

"We'd like to see her apartment. If she's not there, can you let us in?"

"You don't need a warrant for that?"

"Not if you let us in."

The back exit from the shop opened onto a small parking area, really just a wide alley. A wooden staircase led to the second floor.

Raymond told us that Renee had come to Denver about three months ago from Kansas, looking for a new start. She had been an art student, and her portfolio was strong, but no one was hiring. At that point, she was already seven months pregnant, and not even the fast food joints wanted to hire someone who would take maternity leave as soon as training was done.

We let Raymond knock and call out for her, waited several minutes, but there was no answer. He used his key to open the door.

"She's been having trouble paying rent," he said. "That's why I started letting her draw for me. Her designs are really popular for tats. But I know it's not enough."

Rick asked him to say outside.

The apartment was nicer than I had expected, but still a mess. It was basically a large studio, a narrow bed against one wall, kitchenette on the opposite side. It was dark; even when I turned on the overhead, the forest green walls ate the light. Canvases of varying sizes and states of completion leaned against everything. Books and brushes and paints were scattered over counters and tables.

The Case of the Woman Who Sewed Her Silence

A mirror hung above the bed. It was broken, as if someone had put a fist into the middle of it. Before it was broken, someone had painted a word in red across the center of it. The fanciful letters spelled *Skyler*.

"Check this out," Rick said.

On a low table, surrounded by papers and books, a small clay figure of some weird little man seemed to command the entire room. The clay was fresh, like she was still working on it, and it had bits of hair and twigs and other debris mixed in to give it an uneven texture. It was about a foot tall, but the limbs and facial features were wildly out of proportion. It wore a hat like a garden gnome, but there was nothing friendly about that face. Looking at it gave me a sick feeling in my gut.

Sticking out of the back of its head was a small shard of glass, a piece of the broken mirror. There appeared to be blood on the edges of the glass.

"It's probably hers," I said. "But we'd better get forensics up here."

We called it in, and also gave the station the woman's full name and address so they could run background, see what would turn up. We tried not to disturb anything while waiting for the techies to get there, but our curiosity was great. And so was the need to find the child.

I browsed the kitchen cupboards, refrigerator. There wasn't a scrap of food in the place. The drain had a sour smell, like someone had prepared raw meat and didn't clean up after.

Rick shuffled through the papers around the weird figure, and he kept muttering, "Madre de Dios."

"What is it?"

"Some of this stuff, it's really weird. Occult. I don't know what she's into, but it's not good."

"Hmm." If I didn't buy into Rick's mysticism, I certainly wasn't going to worry about this woman worshipping her little clay statue either.

I flipped through some of the canvases. Most of them seemed to be different renderings of the same face, a dark and brooding countenance that was strangely misshapen. In some, there was a suggestion of horns or other demonic elements; in all of them, there was a striking resemblance to the clay figure.

When the forensic techs arrived, we got out of their way. We hung out in the alley with some officers from a couple of patrol cars, waiting for any developments. A few other detectives from the station showed up with coffee. It had been a warm day, but autumn nights come on suddenly in Denver, and the temperature dropped quickly.

It wasn't long before the techs found a bloody blouse and pants, wadded and stuffed in the foot of the closet.

"There's a lot of blood," the tech said. "I think she might have killed that baby."

"Aw, shit." I looked at Rick, and I could see he took it hard. "Rick, I'm sorry."

He shrugged it off. "It's what it is, man."

"We'll find her, don't worry. We'll see if she did this."

"If she killed it, where's the body? What did she do with it?"

We sent the unis to search the alley and any dumpsters or trashcans they could find. I checked the pick-up schedule; there hadn't been one that day, so if she'd dumped a body, it should still be there.

The Case of the Woman Who Sewed Her Silence

I got a call back from the station. They'd run the woman's credit and although there wasn't much activity, she was paying for a storage unit a couple blocks away.

"Let's check it out," I told Rick. I held out the keys. "You want to drive?"

"Let's walk."

I nodded, and we walked.

When we got back out on Colfax, Rick said, "This fucking street. It takes it all, man."

"Yeah." Traffic was steady, as it always was. Engines rattled, bass notes thumped, someone laughed, neon flashed. Salsa music blared from a shop nearby. "She didn't belong here."

"Who does?"

We walked on.

"We still don't know anything for sure," I said.

He shrugged. "I guess we do."

"So, what does this mean? With your candle lighting and prayers? Do you, I don't know, lose faith because of this?"

"What? No. Of course not."

"But you didn't get your results."

"It doesn't work like that. Prayer is not like a gumball machine where every time you put in a coin, you get a prize. I'm more worried for you, that you think it works that way."

"I don't—"

"It's faith that keeps me going, that lets me deal with a shitty day like today. I don't pray to get what I want, but because God is there to be prayed to. I don't have to like the fucked-up evil crap out here, but it helps to know that even the death of a child is part of God's plan."

To Rick, this provided comfort, but it sounded cold to me.

From a block away, the storage building jutted up over the surrounding shops, a giant red-brick box, seven or eight stories tall. It was one of the tallest buildings on this stretch of Colfax. The top was crenelated like a castle or fortress. Maybe that was to make people feel like the crap they stored there was secure. Although, frankly, the building itself, with its crumbling bricks and boarded windows, didn't look all that safe to me.

Staring up at the looming storage facility, I began to rethink my impressions of the cathedral from that morning. Maybe the defining character of the street was its eclecticism, in which the only monstrosity was conformity. This was a world of everything and anything. The connection came from being different.

A security guard was on duty at the door. We showed our badges and then the picture of Renee.

"Has this woman been here today?" I asked.

"Most definitely." He pointed to his lip. "You don't forget a look like that."

"How long ago?"

"Several hours. I don't believe I ever saw her come out."

"We're going to go in and look around. I want you to give me a call immediately if you see her." I handed him my card. "Where is her storage space?"

He looked up the number. "That's fifth floor. Elevator's right through there."

On the way up, with the elevator lights flashing and the walls rattling, I smiled at Rick. "How's this for a leap of faith?"

"Let's take the stairs next time."

Narrow halls spanned the building's innards like a maze,

naked bulbs casting feeble light on the dingy setting. Small half doors lined the walls, one atop the other like drawers in a morgue, and a cacophony of odors, mostly foul, drifted from the hidden compartments. We followed the numbered placards, taking only a couple of wrong turns before finding the woman's box, but not the woman.

The door stood slightly ajar. I glanced at Rick and knew what he was thinking because it was also in my mind: that we would find a tiny body waiting inside.

I opened the door. All we found were more of the woman's canvases and a few small boxes. The boxes contained knickknacks and remembrances, stuff she'd brought from Kansas. The paintings were quite different from those back at the apartment, landscapes and still lifes, full of bright colors and beauty. Innocence. From before Colfax got into her.

We both breathed easier at not finding a baby or any body parts.

"Continue the search?" I asked. Rick nodded.

We quickly covered the rest of the floor and found our way to the stairs. We headed to the top, figuring to work our way down. When we reached the top floor, I smelled fresh air. The stairs continued to the roof access.

We found the roof door propped open with a small piece of broken concrete.

The woman sat with her back against the parapet at the front of the building, her legs drawn up, knees raised. We approached her slowly, unsure what to expect.

She was wearing jeans and a plain t-shirt, no shoes, her gaze focused on a drawing pad on her lap, maybe the same one from the hospital. It had been only about twelve hours since we'd seen her there that morning, but somehow she looked much more fragile. It was far too chilly for how she was dressed, and a breeze was blowing up here on the rooftop, but she didn't seem to notice.

"Renee?"

She startled at my voice, then seemed to relax. She dropped her pencil. She stood slowly, stiffly, then flipped closed the pages of the pad and held it out to us.

Rick took it, and I was about to grab hold of her and cuff her. Then she opened her mouth. She opened it as wide as it would go, and the sound that came out—the sound!

I flinched back, and so did Rick, because it was not a sound that should come from a grown woman. And in that moment, she let herself fall backward over the parapet.

Rick recovered first and grabbed at her, but it was too late. She was gone, her bare feet slipping over the wall last. That sound—the eerie, improbable sound—followed her eight stories down.

The next several hours were a blur of flashing lights, reporters, and too many faces staring at me. As soon as the scene was secured and everything necessary taken care of, I told Rick to go home. I could stay to finish up, do the paperwork. He tried to refuse, but he was beat. He looked like he'd aged ten years in a day. But I knew he'd be back tomorrow, strong as ever.

"Hug the kids for me," I said as he left.

Back at the station after everything finally died down, I remembered the drawing pad. It had been tucked into an evidence bag at the scene. I pulled it out, wanting to get a look at this demon that haunted her, the face she drew over and over.

The Case of the Woman Who Sewed Her Silence

As Dr. Sorenson had said, the face was creepy, and with each rendering it became darker and more ominous. On some pages, she'd drawn several sketches, different angles of the face. Then there'd be a page with a full portrait. On one, she showed the full figure, the little dwarf man that she'd made in clay. His name was Skyler.

After she'd filled nearly half the pad with the dwarf, she'd started writing. Apparently, she'd done that on the rooftop while she waited for us to find her.

> *I saw him in the mirror soon after I moved in, always dancing out on Colfax St. I thought he was my protector. So I prayed to him to keep me safe. To keep my baby safe, through the birth.*
>
> *He made sure there was always food, it was safe to sleep, or go out.*
>
> *After, he came back. He wanted his price for protecting us. He wanted my baby.*
>
> *I wouldn't let him. He wouldn't leave me alone. He said if I didn't give up my child, I would suffer. He would make me. The food stopped.*
>
> *I couldn't. I couldn't.*
>
> *I told him I would leave with my baby or hide away somewhere.*
>
> *He said there was no place I could hide the baby that he wouldn't hear it cry.*
>
> *But I found a place. I thought I did. Inside me.*
>
> *Now the cries won't stop. He wants everyone to know.*
>
> *So do I.*

That was it, her confession, I guess. Gruesome and terrible.

My dilemma now was what to do with it. Could I leave it and let everyone see this poor girl as someone who—what?—ate her own baby? Or remove it and be the only one who knew what finally happened?

Was she crazy, or haunted by some demon that wanted her child? Poverty and frustration were factors enough to lead to violence; I saw it all the time. I wanted to believe this was just another case like that.

And then I would hear again that sound when she opened her mouth on the rooftop. A baby's cry. Her baby. Loud and wailing. Anguished, and impossible. Her baby's cry out of her mouth.

I couldn't understand how such a thing could be, and so I knew the memory, those images—that sound—would fade with time until I no longer believed it was real. I hoped it would be the same for Rick.

For Rick's sake, I destroyed the pages with her confession. I could protect him from the depths of depravity to which humanity could sink.

Just as, in his own way, he would protect me.

About the Author:

B. K. Winstead is a SoCal native who has lived in Colorado for nearly twenty years. He received an MFA in Creative Writing from Colorado State University, Fort Collins—but fortunately, after much recovery, he's again able to write interesting stories. He enjoys loud, discordant guitar-based rock music, dressing up cats, camping in Yellowstone, and telling people what to do.

Get a glimpse of B. K.'s writing process at The Weird World of B. K. Winstead (http://bkwins.wordpress.com) and follow him on Twitter at @bkwins.

Stolen Legacy
By Zach Milan

There are many fixtures to be found on Colfax, but perhaps none is as memorable as Casa Bonita. As Zach reports, its influence is very strong:

My fellow contributor, Kate Lansing, encouraged me to submit and, as soon as I thought of Colfax, I immediately thought of Casa Bonita. There was no real place more magical in my childhood; even as an adult I like to visit. The only sad part is that the Magician's Stage is now unused. I couldn't help re-envision the theme restaurant and make use of that abandoned stage.

Stolen Legacy

I should've stood on that stage. As the kids spilled hot sauce and nacho cheese over red checked tablecloths, I should've waited behind the new curtain in my black tux and white gloves, my polished shoes squeaking on the aging wooden floor. Instead, I sat at a table, my boney wrists clasped in cold metal cuffs.

Even though the muscled Detective Duke Charles led me in through the back entrance, I'd never been so humiliated. This hadn't just been my place of work. This had been my home. That had been my stage. Children had come to see me perform. But at least Cañon Grande's PR officer, Wendy Salazar, had offered a jacket to cover my cuffed wrists. I didn't want to scare the surrounding children. I was here to save them.

To my right, Wendy gave me a sympathetic look. She'd explained that it wasn't necessary to restrict my hands. But Detective Charles glared from my left, tilting his head forward with eyebrows raised to say, "Good luck." He still thought I was behind all of this. I shook my head. I didn't need his feigned luck or her sympathy. So long as they didn't call undue attention, Matthew the Magnificent would assume I was only here as a professional courtesy.

"Ladies and gentlemen," a low voice announced. Spotlights weaved around the room, illuminating the walls bedecked with thick white and silver wallpaper, the faded yellow whorls around the stage, the children waiting in silence. "For your dining pleasure." The lights focused, still frantic, on the deep red velvet curtain that dominated the room. "Introducing Matthew! The! Magnificent!"

At last the spotlights collected at the center of the curtain, and the blond-haired man popped through. He looked less sinister than I expected. His sparkling blue eyes and boyish face told a story of innocence. I'd been a more mysterious, frightening magician, and my features had only grown harsher. No wonder the police let him perform while I sat imprisoned.

"Hello, hello, hello!" Matthew the Magnificent said, waving both hands together. I clutched my hands into fists, fingernails biting into skin. I would undo him, bind those hands together, imprison him in steel. He'd betrayed the very children he was meant to entertain.

Eyes twinkling, he pressed his hands down, shushing the applause. Before I'd been fired, the children didn't need to be told. A single look silenced them. And then I'd begin.

Matthew took his time. He chattered about how he became a magician, opening a deck of red cards and, instead of performing tricks, he *shuffled*. He flung cards into the air and snatched all fifty-two before they fell. Shuffled the pack from one hand to the other, two feet away. Flicked a card up from nowhere and caught it neatly in the deck. This was showboating, not magic.

But any good magician's act is deception from the first moment. For Matthew to be this popular in such a short time, he had to be good. At any moment, he would give away his plan, so long as I paid attention. He couldn't deceive me.

I focused not on the deck, not on the man's smile or his tale of an ancient mentor. His gloved hands mattered more. When one was empty, it dodged behind his back, into a pocket, under his hat.

Yes, this *was* Matthew's first trick, no matter how it might've looked. Imperceptibly at first, the cards grew in size. Whenever his hands returned, one deck would be swapped for another. After the sixth exchange, a few parents chuckled, watching to see when their children would notice. On the tenth, the kids cackled as Matthew mastered these large cards just as deftly as the small. By the thirteenth, the audience squealed with delight. The cards were larger than Matthew's head.

He had a gift with the children, I couldn't deny that.

"But you didn't come here for some tale of an old man," Matthew said. He caught my eye. His grin widened. "You came for *magic!*" He tossed the huge cards up, out, over the audience. The deck left the spotlights, vanishing into darkness for just a moment. What came down instead was confetti. Tiny little rectangles, hundreds of cards from the smallest imaginable deck, fluttered down across the room.

Kids held their palms out, laughter gone, replaced by an awed, "Ohhhhh."

He had them. Just like that, the children were putty in Matthew's hands.

Now to prove he was their kidnapper.

#

When Cañon Grande called, I didn't pick up. I'd long had their number plugged into my Caller ID, so I'd know not to answer. They'd fired me when magic became less popular and hired someone else when kids clamored for magic. Why would they need me now?

But when my voice ended, Wendy Salazar sounded desperate. "Please, Viktor, you gotta pick up. I know things... I know. But you've been on the stage, you know the theater. We need you. Please, please call me back. It's about the missing children."

So they'd noticed the coincidence.

I plucked the phone from its cradle and clarified, "You mean it's about Matthew the Magnificent."

After a momentary silence, Wendy asked, "How could you know?"

I'd seen the news reports, the missing child posters lining Colfax. A boy and a girl one day, then a girl, then another boy, two days later. All in the right range for magic shows, eight to twelve. But in the second week of the kidnappings, the reports stopped. I knew better. The kidnappings hadn't stopped, only the reporting.

The police were keeping quiet, investigating a lead, certain they could save the kids before news got out of hand. I assumed they'd figure it out, nab Matthew, save the children, reunite families, without me.

Matthew's first performance coincided too well with the first disappearance.

Within minutes, Detective Charles was at my door, stuffed into his blue uniform, his brow low, jaw set. "You're under arrest," he said, and I lifted my hands.

I let him close the cuffs around my wrists.

The interrogation room was dimly lit, the cement floor scuffed and dirty. A grimy mirror overlooked the metal table. The only sign of the outside world was Wendy's brightly embroidered blouse and apologetic eyes. Detective Charles had let her be there, to corroborate or deny my words.

"Do you have any ill feelings toward Cañon Grande?" he began.

I gazed at Wendy, her eyebrows lifted, her brown eyes doe-like. "Of course."

"Have you ever met Matthew?"

My eyes twitched to the detective. "No. Never." He thought we worked together?

"Would you do anything to take back your glory years?"

I lifted my hands, and set them onto the table with a clang. "What a horrific question. The answer is *no*. But I'd love to perform again."

While the police kept me locked up, they searched my house, talked to my daughter, interviewed my neighbors. They questioned me about magic, mirrors, hiding places. I didn't ask for a lawyer. I gave them everything I could.

At the end of every interview, I said, "Please, let me help," and Wendy turned from me to Detective Charles. She'd made up her mind about me already.

After a night in a holding cell, Detective Charles allowed that I may be innocent. Not because he trusted me, but because while they held me another child was taken.

At last, he accepted my offer. So long as I helped in chains.

"If you knew," Detective Charles asked, leading the way through the back corridors to Wendy's office, "why didn't you come forward? If you care about children so much..."

I paused at her door. "Being fired because 'kids don't like magicians anymore,' and then years later learning that they've hired another magician *hurts*, Detective Charles." Never mind that they'd been right, my shows were empty. Never mind that the children I'd entertained had grown old, forgotten me.

He harrumphed, unsatisfied.

When we entered, Wendy turned from her pacing and gazed at us. Even today, her outfit matched the bright office filled with crayon drawings. "What's wrong? Viktor, what happened?"

"Trust me," I told Detective Charles without explaining further. He was muscled and confident. Not a speck of gray hair in his hair. Right now he was invincible, but that hair would gray. His muscles would betray him.

The detective sat and gestured for Wendy to sit, too. He scratched his chest idly, but Wendy kept her focus on me. "Well," Detective Charles nodded to Wendy, "we know what you know. And we can tell you what we know."

"Which is " Wendy began.

"Not much," I figured, settling my hands onto my lap. "If it were a clear-cut case, you wouldn't need me." The other reason I didn't report my vague suspicions. "Let me guess, it's one of the children he interacts with that gets taken. Except moments before the child is taken, he's at home, safe in bed?"

Wendy's eyes grew wet as she spread her hands. "It's not that simple. The missing children were never called up front. None of them. And some of the children weren't seated in the Stage Room."

"But," Detective Charles raised a finger to contradict her, "every kidnapped child watched the show. Most thanked him, and then they went home. Some don't disappear until days later. It doesn't make sense."

I didn't tell him magic never does. Something stranger than

illusions was going on here. "Where else did the children visit?" I asked instead.

"You know this place," Wendy lifted her hands, frustration in her voice. "Everywhere. The Crystal Cavern, the piñata party, the maze of stones." Although the majority of Cañon Grande was themed to be in the middle of a beautiful canyon, there were some outliers. A jungle leading to ruins. A train winding around the entire restaurant. And the magician's stage.

"But that's true of the stage, too," I said. It wasn't the case before I was fired, but it had to be now. "Matthew is very popular."

"Exactly." Detective Charles leaned back with a frown and folded his arms. "We have nothing to go on. Just a feeling. And you." That explained why I was still in cuffs. He didn't trust me. Or he thought I'd betray myself, join my accomplice.

"Parents *trust* us, Viktor," Wendy said. "We're supposed to entertain their children, to keep them safe. Not..." She shook her head. This wasn't about business, like I'd callously assumed. Just like me, she cared for each child lost.

"How can I help? You want to learn magic?"

Detective Charles snorted. "I'm told that magicians are good at misdirection. That they can do something unseen while the crowd looks elsewhere." Not something he seemed to believe, despite his suspicions.

Wendy's gaze locked onto mine. "Be our eyes, Viktor. I know you love those kids. Go to a show. Tell us what we can't see. Help save them. And we'll, we'll pay you."

I scoffed, my eyes wandering away. It was never the payment that I wanted from Cañon Grande, but to be a part of their magical restaurant. Performing was always payment enough. I'd rather be on that stage, acting as Matthew's assistant than sit in those chairs.

But the children needed me.

#

At last, Matthew's final act came. I had to admit, he was good. Sometimes I'd almost miss his hands' movement. When he cut himself in half, it took me until the moment he stood to figure out how the feet had moved away from his body.

But now he slid the magic box behind the velvet curtain. He stood alone onstage, Matthew the Magnificent. Exposed.

The perfect disguise for a guilty man.

"Now," he breathed, his smile gone, his hands folded before him. "For my final trick, I'll need a volunteer."

Every hand reached up, and I leaned in. Despite what the police said, his choice was important. The room brightened, and Matthew left the stage, his steps hushed by the carpet on the stairs and floor. "Who will it be?"

This time, I didn't watch his hands, but his pale blue eyes. He gathered information, winding through the food-filled tables, sizing up each child. A gloved finger on this boy's striped shirt, a hand running through this girl's curl. As he gazed across the room, his mouth twitched up for an instant.

Then he turned his body and eyes away.

At a nearby table, a boy in a bow tie stood on his chair, hand aloft. Why had that boy intrigued Matthew? It couldn't have been his parents, his siblings. The kidnapped children's family background varied. It wasn't his outfit. But there, on the table beside him, a deck of cards.

This boy had come to meet a real magician.

I glanced to my left to Detective Charles then right to Wendy.

As the lights dimmed, Wendy whispered, "You saw something?"

"It's that boy." I nodded my head toward him. "He's tonight's target."

Detective Charles scoffed. "How do you know?" Despite his request, he couldn't believe an old man could spot something he didn't.

I shrugged, hating myself for not cooperating fully. A magician never reveals his secrets. "Stay back from him. He's going to meet Matthew, he'll force his way in. We need to see what he gets as a reward. *That's* the clue."

Detective Charles narrowed his eyes, but he didn't press the issue. I figured he'd watch me, waiting for me to betray their trust. But his eyes flicked back to the stage for Matthew's final trick. Wendy, too, watched Matthew, her fingers at her lips.

Why? Hadn't he said that the selected child was safe? Why would *this* be important when I'd already pointed out the mark?

Back on stage, Matthew bounded up the stairs with a girl in a black t-shirt and jeans. She beamed to her parents, flipping her hair with a satisfied grin.

"I want you to stand just *there*." Matthew positioned the girl in the center of the stage, facing out. "Good."

He stepped behind her.

"Now a little *real* magic. Some of you may think you know how I did my previous tricks. 'Sleight of hand' you whispered to your parents. 'Hidden lever.' 'Memory.' But you won't see any of that here." Once again, Matthew directed his gaze at me. Staring almost through me. "Because this is real."

He removed his jacket, revealing a shimmering red inside. "You'll remember I mentioned some old man who taught me everything. Well, he *gave* me this. For just a little while, I want you to wear it." He draped the jacket over the girl's shoulders and, with a giggle, she slipped her arms into the sleeves.

"Now *spin*."

The girl did, a little clumsily at first. But then she got into it, her arms wide as Matthew stepped back to let her enjoy this moment.

And then she was gone.

I stood, blinking. My eyes had been open, I hadn't missed a second. But now, she was gone. Where? How had she left the stage?

"Hmm," Matthew said, stepping forward. "How am I going to get my coat back? It's too cold to let her keep it. Maybe if we clap, she'll return?"

The kids clapped, together at first. But soon it transformed into a cacophony as they applauded, looking everywhere in the room.

She had to reappear, but how? Where? That would be the only clue I'd get. If she appeared before him, it could've been the curtain. Anywhere else, well, I'd figure it out.

"I know!" Matthew left the stage, and the spotlights followed him around the room. "Perhaps she thinks she can get away if she sits quietly. Well, you won't fool me!"

At a table in the corner, he gestured. The spotlights followed his arms and there she was, hand over her mouth, giggling.

"Let's give her a hand!" Matthew took her hand and bowed. He deftly slipped the coat from her shoulders. "Thanks everyone for coming!" He delivered the girl back to her parents and hurried back to the stage, once again waving his unencumbered hands.

I tried to watch as kids came to talk to him, tried to focus on his hands, his words, his posture, but I was back in the moment before the spotlights moved. He gestured to the table, but she wasn't there. I knew she wasn't there. Then the lights moved, and there she was.

It wasn't important. It wasn't. But my mind kept returning to that moment. If I hadn't been in this profession for thirty years, I'd say exactly what he said: it was real magic.

But it couldn't be.

#

"So how did he do it?" Detective Charles asked as he guided me into the rarely-used jungle tables. So far from the river bisecting the restaurant, no one wanted to sit here. Here we could talk.

I kept my hands clutched in front of me. With the jacket draped over my hands, he couldn't see that my cuffs dangled from one wrist. "A magician never..."

The detective raised a hand. "Please. Spare me."

I settled into my seat. "I have no idea. You think it's important?"

Trailing behind until Detective Charles gestured for her to slide into the booth first, Wendy said, "He made her disappear in plain sight. If he can make her disappear, cooperate with him, what else can he do?"

"Cooperate," I mused. Once again, I was back in the trick, trying to figure it out. Too interested to remember to fix the cuffs.

"They all return like that? To that table, giggling?"

Detective Charles shook his head, settling down. "No. Some run back with his jacket. Others run into the *room*. A few are found spinning behind the curtain. There's no consistency."

"Because you're watching. Magicians who repeat their tricks nightly have to be smart. In case someone comes back." But there had to be some consistency. I couldn't work it out.

"Are you going to need to?" Wendy asked softly.

The trick was impressive, and I would love to see it again. Matthew was talented. Better than me, perhaps. But seeing it again would only remind me of what I'd lost. Entice me to get it back, whatever the cost. Being in that room had been harder than I expected.

"That trick, the girl, they don't matter," I hedged, unwilling to admit the truth.

Detective Charles frowned. "You're talking about that boy with the bow tie. I watched him. He stood in line, showed Matthew a trick, then moved on. Nothing happened."

"No?" I asked. I slipped what I'd stolen from my sleeve and, just in time, remembered to use the hand without the cuff. "Then how did the child acquire this?" I held up a jack of hearts, which had been tucked safely in the boy's pocket.

"How..." Wendy asked.

I held up a finger. "Matthew planted it, I took it from the child. The boy will never know he was in danger."

Detective Charles grabbed the card and flipped it over with a frown. "This is your proof? This could've never been on that child. This could've come straight from your pocket, meant to exonerate your friend."

"My pocket? But I've been in your custody—"

In one swift movement, Detective Charles gripped my wrist. "You *were* in my custody. What happened to the cuffs?"

"I..." I lifted my hand to show the dangling metal. "I couldn't get the card without taking it off."

"Sure." He threw the card at me, and it skittered across the table into my lap. "I told you this was a bad idea, Wendy."

But before she could convince him to listen, his hand was already on my arm, tugging me up and away. He shoved me out of the jungle, along the river, and down the faux colonial town toward the exit. Back to jail.

#

Detective Charles was right to be skeptical. How could a card left with a child steal him? I stared at the jack of hearts, locked once more in the police station's holding cell, certain it was the answer. But *how*? I could've left the boy alone, but then he would've disappeared. Maybe later this week, when every child was safe, Detective Charles would stop doubting me.

Lying on the bench, I clutched the card in my hand. Eyes closed, I replayed the evening. More and more elements stood out as impossible. How had the confetti cards fallen so uniformly? What about the saw trick, the levitating? And the way that girl disappeared...

There was no way I should've been able to sleep. The bench was too hard, and my head was too full, but I was transported from the cell.

I stood on Cañon Grande's stage. The velvet curtain before me was black and lush, certain points glittering like stars. The swirling details around the stage were a stark white. The stage itself was polished and clean, new. Everything as it had been when I performed there in my first year.

I flexed a hand, thick and strong, checking my pockets for cards. Beside me, a box held all my old tricks. A ball that could levitate beside a cloth. Rings that folded into each other. Unpoppable balloons. This would be the best performance of my life.

But before the speaker overhead introduced me, I felt a presence at my side. I turned to see his blond hair, his boyish face, his sparkling blue eyes. My eagerness deflated. "Hello, Viktor," Matthew said. "I hoped to see you tonight."

In a hushed whisper, I said, "This is real, isn't it?"

Matthew the Magnificent shrugged. "In a way. Real and unreal, like all the best magic."

"The police are onto you," I told him. "They'll know, when they find me missing from the locked cell." But I expected his smile. What could the police do in the face of real magic? Even if they locked him up, he'd escape. He'd always escape.

Judging from the murmuring crowd beyond the curtain, he'd escaped before.

"They love it here," Matthew said, pulling the curtain open a crack. In the audience, dozens upon dozens of children wearing suits and top hats waited. Many more than had disappeared in the past two weeks.

"Of course they do. You chose children who would."

Matthew let the curtain drop. "That's all I ever wanted." He adjusted a fold of his blond hair, stepping back to give me center stage. "And now you can get what you've always wanted. Endless performances, tricks beyond your wildest dreams, a loving audience."

Stolen Legacy

A pit grew in my stomach. "How could you know that?"

"Their parents," he said, a smile of confidence growing. "Every so often they'll mention Cañon Grande's first magician. How well he controlled the stage. That's why these children love magic as much as they do. Because of *you*. They're your legacy. Who better to be my partner?"

I closed my eyes. I could perform again. Join him as my best self, entertain these children as I'd been built to. Maybe Detective Charles had been right. Maybe I'd been Matthew's unknowing accomplice all along.

This was why Matthew had let me find the card. Perhaps why the card had worked. Because he didn't think there was anything to worry about. That I would stay here with these young magicians.

"Why do *you* want them?" I asked to dodge his gift. If he was trying to lure me with my past, what could a man in his prime want with this place?

His face grew serious. His blue eyes distant. "Like I said on-stage: my mentor's gift. To never lose my best years, even as I'm in them."

My box of tricks stood at my feet, waiting to be used. These could be my best years, retaken. I could get everything I ever wanted. Perform for these children who would appreciate every trick.

But I remembered their parents on television, crying, sobbing for help. I remembered the desperate papers, fluttering along Colfax. I remembered Wendy's wet cheeks and the drawings littering her office. By performing for those parents, so long ago, I'd condemned their children. My legacy couldn't mean stolen children.

"You can't keep them," I whispered, more to myself than Matthew.

"They want to be here," he claimed through a frozen smile. "They're happy here. They can do everything they dream. And I can perform, perfect my act. They, we, are happier now. You can be, too."

"And their parents? What happens to the people who passed on my legacy?"

Matthew's smile thawed, melted.

"If you take them," I explained, "if you keep them, what happens to the *next* generation? The legacy, mine and yours, vanishes."

"But all those other kids..." Matthew began, but his voice dwindled. He'd taken the kids who would remember him. He'd taken the magicians.

"We grow old," I said, gripping his shoulder. Squeezing to make him understand something I'd only now learned. When kids stopped coming to my shows, it wasn't because they stopped caring about magic, but because they'd grown older. Just not old enough, yet, to pass on the magic. "But so do they. And when they get older, and you watch them onstage," I sighed, "it's magical."

Matthew's sparkling blue eyes dimmed. For the first time, he seemed older than the children he performed for. Maybe it was the spell breaking, or maybe it was wisdom filtering in. Seeing what he'd done to the future by stealing these children. "Of course," he croaked. "You're right." He lifted his fingers to snap but paused, light filling his eyes once more. "Before you go, before you get older," his eyebrows lifted, "can I see your magic?"

I bowed, standing in the middle of the stage. I wouldn't miss this opportunity.

With a nod, Matthew pressed a finger to his throat. His voice was amplified beyond the curtain. "Boys and girls, for the last act," despite the amplification, his voice was soft, subdued, "may I please introduce a special guest, The Viktorious."

The curtain swept away and I saw them, fifty kids or so, applauding the act they were about to see. I raised an eyebrow, and they instantly hushed. Then I began.

At first, I used my old act, pulling fake flowers from my sleeve to toss into the audience. But soon the flowers became real roses, vibrant and fragrant. I pulled handkerchiefs from my gloves, my ears, thin air. Instead of bending to my box, I'd magic props into my hands with a cloud of smoke.

Solid hoops pressed through each other, forming not a chain, but the Olympic symbol, a web of grapes, a ring of rings that, when stepped through, changed my costume from black, to red, and back. I ate and spat flames. I cut off limbs and forced them together. I performed card tricks from a deck with hundreds of suits, thousands of cards.

In this dream world, I did everything.

For my final act, I simply disappeared in a puff of smoke, reappearing on the opposite side of the room, beside Matthew. I clapped along with the kids until, at last, they noticed my catcalls. They cackled and left their seats, jumping up at me, asking how I did it. Begging to show a trick of their own.

But I couldn't let them, couldn't let myself give in. "Thank you," I said to Matthew, my hand out. My wrists sore. I felt my back bending, my hair thinning.

"Thank *you*," he said, eyes following all the changes. He shook my hand, and I woke in my cell. I'd given the best performance of my life, and no one would remember. But that didn't matter. My legacy had already been passed on.

As the sun rose, Detective Charles came to the cell, Wendy Salazar in tow. Her makeup was smeared by tears, and she couldn't stop smiling.

"Whatever you did," Detective Charles said with a shake of his head, "thank you."

"Matthew resigned," Wendy said, gripping my hand through the bars. "Left town. And they're back. The children are home. They want to see more magic."

As the detective released me at last, I shook my head at Wendy's offer. I'd already been paid for saving the children. I didn't need another performance.

About the Author:

Zach Milan can't resist the magic of fiction. When he isn't working on his novels and short stories, he reads novels and comic books, watches tons of movies, and plays lengthy board games. He's thrilled to show off the magic along Colfax, only a few blocks from where he lives in Lakewood with his husband, Jeof, and two adorable dogs.

You can find Zach at http://www.zachmilan.com and on Twitter: @ZoomIsland.

That's Love, Baby
By L. D. Silver

L.D.'s story offers hope in the midst of the darkest corners of Colfax:

Last year I took a rebuilding seminar after my long-term relationship ended. One of the concepts taught during the class is called the "Inner Critic". It's a way that we talk with ourselves that can be highly destructive.

That concept was still fresh in my mind when the theme for the anthology was announced. At that time the main thing I knew about Colfax was that it was well-known for prostitutes, and it made sense to me that a woman in that situation might be struggling with her inner critic.

That's Love, Baby

I can tell the man is different before he even turns around. He nods to the limo driver holding the door and glances around the street. The hookers around me shift and pose beneath that gaze. His eyes meet mine and his power hits me. My body turns to him like a simple plant seeking the sun.

But he doesn't even notice me.

My body slumps back against the brick wall behind me as he follows his friends into Emeralds and Pearls, the strip joint across the street. The other whores relax, shifting their feet and chatting with friends while I watch that door like a dog waiting for its owner.

"Hey Sugar, do you have a joint?" Yoshie is two inches shorter than me, Asian, and something of a friend. She also has a john by the hand.

"You know I don't," I say.

"Doesn't hurt to ask." She shrugs. "C'mon baby, let's ask this other girl I know." She toddles past me on five-inch heels while leading her customer by the hand. He's stumbling as well, since he's watching her neon blue latex skirt instead of the cracks in the sidewalk.

"Hey baby, I hear you're different." A man strokes my arm to get my attention.

I smile. "You hear right." The potential customer is dressed in jeans and a black t-shirt and has one hand curled around a burning joint. "But you'll have to get rid of that first."

"Aw, you're hot but—"

I lean in, touch his wrist with two fingertips, and softly hum. It's a small effort, just a tiny mingling of sound and magic to give him a hint of what I can do. His eyes widen.

"Hey Yoshie, I've suddenly found a joint," I call out. Her heels beat a staccato rhythm as she hurries back to me. There's a quick exchange of drug for money, and then I take his hand and lead him down my alley.

"Here?" he asks, skepticism in his voice. I understand why. My place of business consists of a bright red barstool stuck in a dark corner created by two walls of black-painted bricks.

"Would you like a room? About twenty bucks around the corner." I let a bit of warmth into my tone.

"Here's fine." He hops onto the stool.

I take his hand again and rest it on my palm. Touch at this point isn't necessary, but it always seems to relax my customers. I close my eyes, ignoring the smell of alcohol and marijuana wafting from the man in front of me. Instead I focus on the warm rough texture of his skin.

I breathe in deeply, filling my lungs with air. Then I hum and lightly run my fingertips over his skin, first on his neck and then tracing his mouth. His eyes close and he relaxes into his chair. Now my real work begins, as with each release of sound and magic I become his fantasy, whatever that may be.

Afterwards, I hand him some tissues so he can clean up. There's a mixture of amazement and joy in his eyes.

"You never truly touched me, did you?"

"No. A light touch is all that's needed." I smile. Sometimes they get mad when I admit that, but another bit of humming and the anger will disappear. This time, the man smiles. He stands up and adjusts his clothes.

"Thank you." He hands me the money. "Worth every penny. Now I have a call to make." His spine is straighter as he walks out of the alley and his mobile phone is already in his hand.

"Hey, I know it's been a while since I've talked with you."

That's all I hear him say before he turns the corner. That's how it is with some of them. I never hear who they're talking with, although I suspect it's a woman. Sometimes there's something in that small sound and magic, something special.

I lean against the wall. I know I'm abusing my gifts.

"Not worth them," the voice whispers.

I could be doing so much more. I have so much potential, I think.

"No you don't. You're worthless. You belong here with me."

I don't have to look around to realize that the voice isn't attached to a person. I call the voice "Colfax" after the street where I work. The street itself has a long history. Colfax has existed for over one hundred years and is twenty-six miles long. It has sheltered patients, famous restaurants, strip clubs and prostitutes like me. When my life crumbled, I could hear Colfax calling to me like a siren. She scooped me up in her arms, sheltered me, and gave me a living.

And now that I'm good and hooked, her poison words drip into me. That's love, baby.

I gaze up at the dark sky above me. Somewhere, only a few miles away, other people are looking at the same sky. There's another woman out there, standing in her yard and looking at the stars, happily enjoying the warm night with her laughing kids and loving husband.

But my sins outweigh hers. That's the only explanation for why I'm here and she's there. Colfax is right. I belong here.

I leave the alley and join my crew.

"Hey Sugar, thanks for that joint. I knew you had my back, girl," Yoshie greets me.

"Any time." I smile and join the girls for some chatting time. And that's how the hours pass, until the strip club doors open and my mystery man comes out.

He raises one hand and calls the limo back. He waits patiently as his friends climb into the vehicle, then shuts the door and taps the roof twice. The limo drives away and I tense as he enters the club again.

The only reason he's been safe for the past few hours is that he was part of a large group. He's now told everyone on the street, and in the club, that he's wealthy and alone.

I push off from the brick wall and sashay across the road.

The bouncer sees me coming and shakes his head. "No, honey, I don't want any of what you're selling."

"I only want a few moments inside." I smile and cock my hip.

"You know I can't let you in. Employees and customers only," he says.

"Oh come on." I'm only a foot away now, and almost within range.

He takes a step backward. Obviously he's heard a few things about me. "You know I can't. Don't come near me, and don't you dare start humming." He picks up a bat and points it at me.

"Okay." I raise my hands and back up a few feet. The door on the side of the club opens up. Damn, the boys in there work fast.

That's Love, Baby

"I'll go for a walk instead."

I pout a little so he thinks he's won. I swing my hips as I walk away and glance towards the open door. Six men come out of the club and into the alley. I see the man I'm looking for among them and wince. I drop all semblance of sexiness and haul ass around the corner. My plan is to sneak up on them.

Instead I get there too late. My man is down on the ground, his head bleeding and his pockets open. The last of the men slams the club door behind him and never sees me.

I run to him and cover up what's happened as best as I can. I call Yoshie over and we take him to the Colfax Street Inn, a four-story brick hotel that charges by the hour and is only two blocks away. The clerk smirks at the mystery man's state.

"Big night, huh?"

"The biggest." I smile and take the key. Yoshie helps me get him in the room and then leaves us alone.

Everyone thinks I see him as a mark, but I don't.

I get some water from the bathroom and wash away the blood. He has a cracked rib, a concussion, a bleeding head, and tomorrow he'll have a black eye. I sit on the corner of the bed.

I can heal him. He'll need food afterwards, and I don't have any to give him, but hunger is better than injuries at least.

My hands twist in my lap. I haven't done this in a long while.

"It won't work," Colfax says.

"Shh," I say, my heart pounding. She's right. There's a chance that it won't come. That I've abused my power and it won't answer now.

"Of course it won't come. You're only good as a hooker now."

A sharp stab of heat hits my chest and my hand curls into a

fist. I haven't experienced anger in such a long time that it takes me a few beats to name the emotion.

"Bullshit," I whisper. I close my eyes, stretching until I can feel the deep well inside me that holds my power. It's lapping along the sides, waves cresting, begging me to let it out.

I sigh and relax a part of me that I've kept clenched for way too long.

I open my eyes. I'll have to touch him if I'm going to heal him. Unlike the fantasies, this isn't an option. I slip off my high heels and crawl next to him. I place each hand on opposite sides of his head, my fingers spread wide and almost touching the area that's bleeding.

Then I draw from my well and sing. Humming isn't strong enough to heal; it takes a full-bodied song. The tune I pick is light and happy, even though the content doesn't matter, only the sound counts. Beneath my hands, I feel the bleeding stop and his head heals. I end my song.

He truly is a handsome man. His eyes are closed, his hair is wet and messy, but there's a gentleness, an innocence, to him as he sleeps. I come close to stroking his hair. That's the problem with healing someone. You start caring for them.

I fight the urge and drop my hand to his stomach. I raise his shirt and place my palm over his injured rib. I close my eyes again and sing my happy little tune until I feel enough warmth under my hand to know that he's healed.

I open my eyes to find he's awake. He grabs my wrist as fast as a striking snake.

"What did you do?" he asks softly. I glance around the room reflexively, even though I already know there's no one else that can hear us.

"I healed you," I answer in a low voice.

He smiles then, a big wide smile that lights his eyes. "Yes, you did."

A suspicion whispers through my brain and I narrow my eyes. "Was this a trap?"

"Yes." His grip tightens in anticipation that I will try to get away. "But hear me out, okay?"

The part of me that healed him cries out, telling me he is trustworthy and lovable. But I know that voice is biased, and fear slithers into my bloodstream.

"Let go of my wrist first," I say. He gently releases me. I sit back and cross my arms as he sits up and rests against the headboard.

"We've had reports of someone powerful working Colfax. That would be you, right?"

I hesitate a moment, then nod. He already knows the truth.

"Then you know we had to investigate."

I shrug. I should have thought of it, should have realized that what I was doing wouldn't remain quiet.

"You're very powerful. Why are you here?" His glance takes in me, the cheap room, the dangerous life outside. There's a plea in his voice.

"She deserves it," Colfax spits out.

"She doesn't deserve it." My mystery man shakes his head and focuses on an area just to my left.

"You heard that?" I ask.

His warm brown eyes meet mine. "Of course. Your twin said it. She's sitting right next to you."

No one else has ever heard Colfax. My pulse spikes.

"What's she saying now?" I ask him. Then I ask the voice what it thinks of me.

"Unlovable, no good bitch. No one loves you. No one could love you."

He repeats every word back to me, and asks me to get a mirror. I dig through my purse and hand him my compact. He opens it and places his palm on top for a minute or two, his eyes narrowed in concentration. Then he holds it so the mirror faces me.

"What do you see?"

I gasp. There's a ghost right next to me. Her pale face is inches away from mine, and she looks exactly like me.

"How long have you heard this voice?"

"For years." I'm unable to tear my eyes away from my twin.

He takes my hand. The warmth and the touch distract me, and I'm able to focus on him again.

"Look at her in the mirror and repeat after me: 'I hear you. That's unhelpful.'"

I feel stupid, but then her clear ghost eyes meet mine in the mirror and I shudder at the malice I see in them. "I hear you. That is unhelpful."

"Again," he urges.

"I hear you. That's unhelpful." And then I repeat it, again and again, until she disappears. Tears flow down my cheeks and he snaps the mirror shut.

"Anytime she appears, repeat this process. Eventually, you'll stop seeing her. After that, you'll only hear from her occasionally."

"I don't know how to thank you." I clutch the compact to my chest.

He smiles. "When you're ready, come find me at the Sparrow Center. We have some important work for you."

"Okay."

I call a cab for him, and help him downstairs when he's ready. It's only as I'm shutting the vehicle door that he tells me his name. It's a solid, normal name, but it means everything to me.

I have the room for the rest of the night, so I go back upstairs and lock the door behind me. Tears are washing my cheeks before I even reach the bed.

For the first time in years, I have hope. Hope that maybe I am worth something after all.

L. D. Silver

About the Author:

L. D. Silver is a writer, avid reader and movie fan. She was a finalist in the 2012 Colorado Gold Contest for her work titled "In a World of Orphans". She writes fantasy and horror, with a focus on zombies, magic and the occasional robot. She's lived in Colorado for nine years.

Colfax Kitsune
By Emily Singer

Emily reached deep into her bag of "tricks" for her Colfax story:

I've been fascinated with the Trickster archetype for a long time, and I've always wanted to write something where the trickster character didn't turn into a devilish antagonist—getting back to the roots of the trickster in ancient mythology, so to speak. The kitsune is one the best-known trickster characters from world myth, and I thought it would be fun to transplant one of them (and some other trickster characters—Piccolo is a Native American trickster god) into modern Denver.

Colfax Kitsune

Yuri crouched on the rooftop beside the motel, squinting through a pair of binoculars at the people passing on the street below. She knew Piccolo was here; she could feel his power pulsing, pounding, growing. Rhythmic, tinged with lust. Spiced with music. All contained in that one male body, wrapped up somewhere in that seedy motel.

Piccolo had abandoned her immediately after the successful completion of their last mission. After a day and a half of searching, she finally knew why the bastard had been so eager to leave. His favorite little tramp must have offered him a hell of a deal to keep him occupied for so long.

She should have gone without him as soon as she got their new orders. Instead, she had wasted four hours worrying, then spent the night prowling through Capitol Hill. Now she crouched on a rooftop near Colfax and Moline, spying on the freakishly dull mortals just because she hated going on these things alone.

Her last two solo missions had ended in disaster: one with a dead human and the other with Yuri herself nearly dead. Thinking about either of them still gave her shivers.

"Finally," she muttered as red-brown skin and a dark suit passed through her binoculars. She twisted and found the narrow-shouldered man before he disappeared into the crowd. No doubt about it; that was Piccolo.

Just as she was about to head down to the street, he looked up and winked at her.

Cursing under her breath, Yuri tossed the binoculars away. They hit the cement rooftop with a lens-shattering crash, but she didn't care. She'd swipe another pair if she needed them.

She slipped down the fire escape without a sound and scurried to the mouth of the alley, where Piccolo leaned against the brick wall, his ankles crossed. Even before she reached him, she could smell the pungent odor of sex surrounding him. By the time she stood beside him, the musky, sweet smell nearly overwhelmed her, making her wide nose wrinkle in revulsion.

"You couldn't shower before you came out?" she asked.

Piccolo laughed, a sound like a timpani in the rain that always hurt Yuri's sensitive ears, even though they looked completely human. He tugged on the neon green ribbon tied around her ponytail. "It's not my fault your nose is so sharp. Showered twice, just for you. Now, you want to tell me why you were spying on me up there, or do I have to guess?"

"Guessing is much more fun, don't you think?" she asked dryly as she stepped out of his reach.

He pouted dramatically and Yuri fought memories of what it had been like to feel those full lips trailing the curves of her body, his hand tugging gently on her concealed fox tails. Not everyone got a chance to fool around with a literal god of sex, and, despite their best efforts to keep things mostly platonic, the experience sometimes made it hard to concentrate on the task at hand.

Which, of course, was probably his goal at the moment.

She shoved the distracting memories aside and dug a folded piece of paper out from under her bra strap. "A group of miniature sphinxes came through from the Flipside yesterday afternoon.

All but one are back where they belong. We need to find that last one and get it through the wall before its magic starts acting up."

"And before the hole in the wall closes." Piccolo refused to take the paper, instead digging a smart phone out of his pocket and beginning to tap on it as if the conversation was over. "The hole's contained, but it's already started repairing itself. You should have about three hours, best guess."

Yuri stared at him. "What do you mean 'you'? You're coming with me."

He didn't look up from the glowing screen. "Nope. This one's all you, sexy."

Terror worked its way through her veins like a silk scarf through a frosted pipe—cold and smooth. Her fingers trembled as she tucked the note back into her bra. If he had been teasing her, he would have watched for her reaction. The fact that his attention was fully centered on the phone meant he wasn't waiting for an amusing response. He truly wanted her to track down a sphinx, find a weak place in the wall between worlds, and throw the creature back all on her own.

"I'd start in City Park, if I were you," Piccolo muttered, apparently oblivious to Yuri's panic. "Looks like someone's advertising a chance to see a 'magic talking cat'."

Yuri glowered at him, her hands still shaking. "I'm not walking to City Park on my own."

"Don't have to. Got you a cab. Should be here any minute." He finally looked up and grinned at her, white teeth flashing.

"*On my own.*" She emphasized each word with a forceful poke to his upper arm. The panic had already begun to give way to anger, sizzling in her blood.

Piccolo sighed and finally tucked the phone away in his breast pocket. "You can't sit in the shadow of gods forever, little kitsune. I know you're afraid because of what happened last time, but I believe in you." He paused, then sighed and gently took her chin, urging her head up. "Yuri, look at me."

She reluctantly tore her gaze from the bustling street and back to his placid face. For a moment, she wondered what would happen if she just turned tail and ran. Left Piccolo high and dry, forgot about this stupid sphinx altogether. She knew the answer, of course, and driving half of Denver's population mad wasn't something she wanted to take the blame for.

"If you want to be part of this team, you have to learn to work on your own. I'm not always going to be here to drag you out at the last minute." He wrapped an arm around her and pulled her into an awkward, sideways hug.

Her shoulder dug into the bottom of his ribcage. She couldn't tell if it was more uncomfortable for him or her, but she didn't want his awkward comfort. She squirmed out of his hold. "I know you've got other stuff to do, Piccolo. I just—"

"Just use your head and kick ass," he interrupted as a dirty, yellow taxi pulled up to the curb. With a grin and a wink, he opened the cab's rear door. "Off you go."

She stared at him for a long minute. The car's idling engine filled her ears and a light breeze blew the acrid smell of exhaust into her sensitive nose. She wanted to drag Piccolo into the cab with her—and she knew tricks that would have had a mortal man on the seat in seconds—but she knew he wouldn't budge. "Are you sure you can't come with me?"

"I know you can manage." He jerked his chin toward the

open door. "Quit wasting time."

Still trying to stop her nervous shaking, Yuri reluctantly slid into the back of the cab. It smelled like spearmint gum and sweat. The leather was hot under her thighs where her miniskirt ended. The door slammed and she jumped. She rolled down the window to swear at Piccolo, but a group of giggling girls strolled between him and the car. He was gone by the time they passed.

She left the window down the whole drive in an attempt to avoid making small talk with the gum-chewing cabbie.

#

By the time she reached City Park, Yuri's hands had stopped trembling. Her insides still squirmed at the thought that no one would be able to help her if things went terribly wrong, but at least she looked calm and collected.

The cab dropped her off on the western side of the park, in a roundabout just off 17th Avenue. She paid for the ride with a bundle of rice charmed to look like bills and climbed out of the cab. Standing beside the fountain in the center of the asphalt circle, she opened her mouth to take a whiff of the park air. The chemicals in the fountain water burned the back of her tongue, making it hard to smell anything beyond chlorine and algae poison.

She wrinkled her nose and trotted across the roundabout to the rest of the park. A group of humans gathered around a portable grill nearby, shouting and laughing over a loud radio. A few late-day joggers made their way around the wide bike path. Normally, Yuri would be intrigued by their summer antics, but she forced herself to focus.

She could feel another magical presence nearby, tugging at

the power inside her, but she couldn't pinpoint it yet. Piccolo had a knack for finding the exact location of whatever they were looking for. Another reason she wished he was there with her now.

Moving farther away from the fountain, she took another deep breath. This time, she caught a whiff of something that smelled distinctly magical—that musty, ancient smell that only came from power that didn't belong on this side of the wall.

Yuri zeroed in on that aroma and followed it to a bench shaded from the late afternoon sun by a tall elm tree. A ragged homeless man lay sprawled on the bench, one arm bent beneath his head and the other stroking a large cat resting on his chest. The cat lay stretched out, its head at the man's collarbone and the tip of its tail near the man's knees.

It was the cat that smelled like the Flipside. The creature lifted its head and blinked at Yuri with intelligent eyes. It rippled with a spell of illusion, no doubt to hide its human face, but the magic felt hasty.

"You forgot whiskers," Yuri said. Her voice wavered with the remains of her panic, but she forced herself to act brave.

The homeless man turned his head to frown at her. "If you're here because I said I had a talkin' cat, she don't talk to just anyone."

"Oh, she'll talk to me." Yuri flashed her sharp teeth and both the man and sphinx drew back in surprise. She loved watching people when she caught them off guard. She could get a glimpse of their true nature, and could use it to manipulate them if she wanted. Piccolo often told her it wasn't subtle enough for him, but he wasn't here to frown this time. "How much do you want for her? Name a price. Anything and you got it."

"She ain't for sale." He stroked the sphinx's tawny fur. It clung to his fingers, standing straight up from the animal's back. "She found me and I ain't givin' her up."

Yuri fought the urge to roll her eyes. Humans always thought they could own everything. Oh, sure, she would pay him—in the same way she had paid the cabbie—but she knew well enough that the sphinx was its own creature, not hers. "I've got two thousand bucks I can give you. Cash."

He hesitated, but shook his head. His eyes flashed with greed and terror, a combination that confused Yuri as much as worried her. One of his hands twitched as if he moved to draw an invisible weapon.

Before she could say anything else, the sphinx stretched and sat up, balancing on the man's stomach. After a moment of studying Yuri with its wide, golden eyes, it spoke. Its high voice and haughty tone grated on Yuri's nerves. "He won't accept, Small Ears. I'm not going back, and you're better off wasting someone else's time. Don't you have rabbits to chase or something?"

"Nope. I have a snotty little sphinx to take home." Yuri's mind raced. If she couldn't pay the guy to let her take the sphinx, she could easily put a spell on him. But her unique, Earthside power was at a severe disadvantage against pure Flipside magic. If she tried anything as small as a simple charm, the sphinx might be able to turn the spell back onto her. Using magic was out of the question. Which left persuasion, trickery, or pure speed.

"I told you: I'm not going." The sphinx lifted one paw and licked it, though its nose wrinkled like it wasn't used to the motion. "I'm sick of the desert, and this place has fish. I love fish."

Yuri considered asking if it also enjoyed driving mortals mad, but she swallowed the question and darted forward instead. Screw talking. Grab it and run. She closed the distance between them in the span of two rapid heartbeats. One hand closed around the scruff of the sphinx's neck and the other grabbed it around the belly.

"Hey!" The homeless man moved too fast, grabbing for Yuri's wrists. His fingers closed around her left arm before she could yank the sphinx away. "That's my cat!"

The sphinx yowled and squirmed, swiping with its claws. The needle-sharp talons tore into Yuri's right arm. Blood welled up along the cuts.

Yuri froze, cold panic crashing through her for the second time. One arm ached where the man held her and the other stung from the bleeding scratches. The sound of the man's breathing was harsh and erratic in her ears. The smell of the sphinx's magic—rotting fish, sun-bleached dust, and lotus flowers—made her eyes water.

Very slowly, she uncurled her fingers from the sphinx's fur. Grab-and-run had failed. She'd have to find another way to get the sphinx away from the man.

As soon as the sphinx's claws pulled out of her arm, Yuri jerked out of the man's hold and clapped her free arm over the gashes. They weren't deep, but they throbbed.

"I told you, you can't have her." The man glowered, a possessive hand on the sphinx's back. His next words sounded like a garbled incantation rather than anything Yuri recognized as actual words.

She tensed, ready to spring away from a giant fireball or whatever else the unknown spell might conjure.

Nothing happened.

The sphinx laughed, high and nasal. Its tail twitched. "You don't know much about language, do you, Small Ears?"

"What's that supposed to mean?" Yuri hated her voice for shaking so much. She didn't want anyone to know how panicked she felt, least of all an annoying sphinx that insisted on calling her names.

The man spat and the sphinx laughed again. "Whatever he said, it didn't mean anything. Not in any language on any world. And I should know—I know all of them."

Yuri swallowed hard and forced herself not to take a step backward. Her stinging arm and fear-frozen insides made it hard to think. Why would the man say something in a language that didn't exist? Why would he turn down her offer of two thousand dollars for this mangy animal? She would have thought he was drunk, except that she didn't smell alcohol. Another idea made her bite her lip.

"Your magic's already eaten his mind," she whispered. "Or at least part of it."

The sphinx didn't answer except to smile at her. With the catlike illusion still in place, the expression looked stretched and macabre.

Yuri tried not to shiver. With the man's mind already prey to Flipside magic, Yuri had to somehow convince the sphinx to come with her. She cleared her throat and rocked back on her heels. "Um. If you come with me, Sphinx, I'll tell you a riddle you've never heard before."

"I doubt that. And I know the herring one, so don't try." It sniffed and drew its paw over one ear. "Foxes never have good riddles."

Damn. A breeze plucked at the ribbon around her ponytail, tickling the back of her neck. Yuri allowed herself a small, slow smile. If bribery didn't work, maybe distraction would. After all, a sphinx shared quite a lot of personality traits with normal cats.

She reached up and untied the green ribbon. "Hey. You like chasing things, stinky?"

The sphinx straightened. "What did you call me?"

"You heard me." She waved the ribbon at the sphinx, glad she had chosen the long one that morning. This had to work. She couldn't let herself think about what would happen if it didn't.

"That's not fair," the sphinx whined. Its eyes widened, pupils dilating. First one paw then the other twitched and flexed sharp claws into the man's shirt. "You can't trick me like some cat."

Yuri tried not to let relief show in her smile. "Looks like I can. Come and get it."

The sphinx yowled as it launched itself off its human perch and leapt toward the waving ribbon. The bum began cheering for his 'cat' like it was playing some sort of major league game.

Yuri continued swishing the strip of silk back and forth until the sphinx was within reach. Then she let the creature pounce and clamp sharp teeth onto its prey. While it was distracted, Yuri leapt. She grabbed its scruff and hoisted it up. With a bit of struggle, she managed to pin the sphinx's hindquarters between her elbow and ribcage and grab its front paws with the hand under its belly.

The man's cheers stopped abruptly.

As hard the sphinx squirmed, it couldn't find leverage to free itself. After a moment, it seemed to settle for vehement cursing in a wide variety of languages.

"You can't take my cat," the man on the bench whimpered. He looked at Yuri, complete loss written across his face. "Please don't take her. She's all I have."

She met his gaze and shook her head. "Trust me. You're better off without it."

The sphinx cursed and spat and yowled all the way back to Colfax.

#

An hour later, Yuri stalked along the sidewalk with the sphinx tucked under her arm. Passing humans stared, but no one tried to stop her. Maybe it was the angry determination in her eyes. Maybe humans were just too wrapped up in their own heads. She didn't care either way.

She had the sphinx, but her job wasn't over yet. She still had to find the hole in the wall between the worlds before it disappeared, and she hadn't even caught a whiff of it after an hour of searching. Gaps in the wall typically only lasted one or two days, and she had already wasted the better part of that time searching for Piccolo and the sphinx.

"Do you remember where you came through?" she asked for the tenth time.

The sphinx tried to squirm its paws away from her fingers and growled when she tightened her hold.

She jostled the sphinx until it went limp again. Wandering around like this was a waste of time. She had a little under an hour left to find a hole in the wall and toss the sphinx through before the humans around them started going murderously insane. "You know what'll happen if you stay here, right? Your magic will eat away at reality and drive all the mortals bonkers."

"Compared to gods and kitsune, my magic is dust," the sphinx spat. It hung limp beneath Yuri's arm now, though its tail continued to switch back and forth. "And yet you all live on this side of the wall."

"We've all been here since before the wall was built. Humans are used to a tiny bit of magic, just us remnants of a time when Earth and the Flipside were more connected. Any more magic shows up and—poof! The whole world starts to fall apart."

"You? Here since before the wall was built?" The sphinx laughed its high, nasal laugh and Yuri gritted her teeth. "You're still a kitten!"

For a moment, Yuri considered throwing the sphinx into the street just to make it shut up. She hated to be reminded of how young she was, or that her birth on the mortal side of the wall had warped reality. And she definitely wasn't going to tell this obnoxious cat that the human world had accepted her power after decades of struggle, and only with the help of gods like Piccolo.

"Just tell me where the hole is," she demanded, her fingers tightening on the scruff of the sphinx's neck. "Tell me where you came through and I won't toss you under the next truck. Deal?"

The sphinx laughed again. "Not at all!"

"Listen, harebrain." She stopped walking and yanked the sphinx's scruff until its head tilted back to look at her. "My job is to get you back through that wall before it fixes itself and before you start causing trouble for me and my friends. I'm going to do that. And you're going to help me."

The sphinx smirked. "I really don't think I am."

This whole assignment sucked. Still, it could be worse, she supposed. At least the cuts from the sphinx's claws had stopped bleeding, and there didn't seem to be any real danger for Yuri at the moment. Though there might be if she didn't manage to get the sphinx back where it belonged. She didn't like the idea of several thousand crazy people drawn to any sources of magic in their vicinity.

With a heavy sigh, she loosened her grip on the sphinx's scruff once more and kept walking. The wall between Earth and the Flipside ran straight along Colfax between City Park and the Anschutz Medical Campus—the hole where the sphinx came through was likely along that stretch. But that was six miles long and she was running out of time.

Two blocks down, people were gathering in a knot at the edge of the sidewalk. Someone pointed at something on the opposite side of the street. Yuri couldn't see what they were looking at from where she stood, but a gaggle of mortals was as good a sign as any at this point.

The hum of magic started to tickle her ears when she was a block and a half away. By the time she was half a block away, the scent of the Flipside overwhelmed the burning smell of car exhaust. At least the smell of wet grass, hazelnut, and skunk was more pleasant than human vehicles.

She stopped on the edge of the crowd and attempted to see what the humans were looking at. It still looked like a blank brick wall, but there had to be something magical close by. She could smell it so clearly. She just couldn't *see* anything.

Emily Singer

With a deep breath, she steeled herself to dive into the jostling crowd, then thought better of it. Jumping in without all the details was what nearly got her killed the last time. Piccolo was always telling her to gather information before she acted. This time, she was going to remember it.

"What's going on?" she asked the woman who stood beside her.

The woman pointed to the blank wall across Colfax. "We saw a mural over there. At least, we thought it was just a drawing. Then it moved, so we thought it must be a video of some kind, but we can't find a projector, and it's only visible from the right angle. It's incredible, really."

That sounded like a hole in the wall to Yuri, especially with so much power buzzing in her ears and assaulting her nose.

"You're not really going to go in there, are you?" the sphinx asked, its voice even higher than normal. "You're going to get us killed!"

"I'm going to get you home, you little jerk." All the same, Yuri didn't truly want to dive into a crowd of humans on the verge of brawling for a spot at "the exact right angle" to see the hole. She was smaller than most of them and didn't have the power to charm or trick more than two or three people at a time—both things she tried to ignore on a daily basis. It was easier to forget her troubles until she ran into things like this.

She took another deep breath and dove into the writhing group of people. Someone elbowed her in the eye right away. She swallowed a curse and kept pushing her way through. For once, her smallness might have helped a bit, but the squirming sphinx in her arms overcame any advantage of size she might have had on her own.

By the time she finally reached the front of the crowd, she could feel bruises forming all over her body, and her left eye was beginning to swell shut.

The sight of the hole in the wall swept all the pain away. She had never seen something so beautiful, like a masterful chalk drawing on the brick, all intense colors and wide, artistic strokes. The "painted" scene showed a beautifully stark desert, sandy hills rolling into the distance. An eagle circled above crumbling ruins and a snake slithered from the shadow of one dune to the next.

As Yuri watched, the edges of the image shimmered and shifted. The hole was already closing, sooner than Piccolo had anticipated and faster than Yuri would like. She adjusted her grip on the whimpering sphinx and lifted her foot to step into the street.

A traffic light at the end of the block turned green and cars started trundling past, inches from Yuri's face. The sudden noise and stiff wind from their passing made her wince.

"No, no, no." Between cars, she could see the edges of the hole curling in on itself like a piece of burning paper. She had to get across the street before it closed. But how could she without waiting for the long light to turn red again or using her magic to blow out the light altogether?

You're a fox, she reminded herself with a deep breath. *Run.*

She wasn't going to fail another attempt at a solo assignment. She wouldn't give herself that option.

"Don't throw me back," the sphinx whimpered, trembling in her arms.

Yuri snorted in reply and forced herself to focus on the run, on dodging cars, and finishing this job. The humans on either side shuffled away from her. She was vaguely aware of a few of them giving her strange looks.

They didn't matter. All that mattered now was getting across Colfax and shoving the sphinx through the opening in the wall before it finished repairing itself.

Space between cars. There.

She leapt into the street in the split second between vehicles. Her legs pumped and her heart thumped so fast it felt like one endless beat.

Someone screamed. A car horn blared, deafening.

She leapt into the next lane and felt another car zoom past behind her.

The sphinx whimpered under her arm.

She ignored it, angling to her right as she raced for the center island, hoping to give herself a few more seconds before the next car.

Another horn nearly made her stumble. She fought to keep her balance and made it into the last lane before the island. This one was clearer, allowing her a straight shot to the concrete strip.

She jumped onto the island and took a second to catch her breath. Halfway there. The hole in the wall still looked wide enough for her to climb through, but barely. Time was running out and there were more cars headed west, crowding the three lanes between Yuri and her goal. Damn.

Without giving herself time to contemplate how idiotic this was, she threw herself back into traffic.

Brakes screeched. Horns shrieked. Yuri felt certain her ears would start bleeding if the noise didn't stop.

She jumped and ran and dodged, always trying to reach the sidewalk but sometimes running sideways or backwards to avoid getting hit.

By the time she finally reached the other side of the street, she could barely breathe and the hole was maybe two feet across. Chest and legs aching, she struggled to catch her breath as she lifted the sphinx up to meet its gaze.

It swiped at her, claws raking across her cheek just below her bruised eye.

She yelped and dropped it. Stinging pain made her eyes water, but she shoved it aside.

The sphinx turned and tried to scamper away, the magic of its illusion spell rippling and failing.

Growling curses in a mix of Japanese and English, Yuri grabbed the sphinx's tail and yanked. She didn't care that it screamed, or that she felt the tail dislocate in her hand, or that the stupid creature's illusion had completely disappeared, exposing that eerie human face on the cat body. All she cared about was finishing this damn job.

She yanked the yowling sphinx back to her and lifted it by the scruff of its neck. "Don't even think about coming back, stinky. Not until this wall comes down. The humans are under our protection. Got it?"

The creature glowered and bared razor-sharp teeth.

"Good enough." She tossed the creature through the hole in the wall.

The image rippled and shimmered as it swallowed the sphinx. Just before the hole closed altogether, Yuri saw the sphinx glance over its shoulder, looking both furious and betrayed, then slink away.

The thunder of cars stopped behind her and Yuri sat back on her heels, staring at the empty brick wall. She took several deep breaths. Her hands started to shake. Blood dripped down her cheek, hot and wet.

She had done it. All on her own, more or less. Piccolo *had* told her where to look for the sphinx at the beginning, but everything else was *her*.

"You did good, sexy."

Yuri's head jerked around at the dusky, musical voice. She glowered up at Piccolo and jabbed a trembling finger at him. "You could have done it ten times faster."

He shrugged and offered her a Starbucks cup. "Sure. But that's no fun, is it? You did it all on your own, and that's worth something, right? Hell, you can do this without me now."

"What, are you disowning me now?" She reluctantly took the cup and sniffed at the strong coffee. He had remembered the cream. How sweet.

"Nah. You're just going to be doing more solo runs." He took a casual sip of his own coffee and studied her with dark eyes. "Think you can handle it?"

She frowned down at the white plastic lid as she thought. The sphinx wasn't remotely the most dangerous thing she had dealt with in the last few years, but she had managed it on her own. Maybe she could survive without a partner, as long as she kept her head screwed on right.

That wasn't going to stop her from a bit of revenge.

She pulled herself to her feet, transferred her coffee to her left hand, and slugged Piccolo across the jaw with her right. The blow made her knuckles sting, but seeing his surprise was well worth it. "Yeah. I think I can handle it. Asshole."

"Good." He rubbed his chin, then draped his arm over her shoulders.

Yuri sighed and leaned against him, glad for the support now that the adrenaline had begun to wear off. All she wanted to do was sleep for a day. Maybe, if she was lucky, he might actually let her.

Emily Singer

About the Author:

Emily Singer began writing when she realized she didn't love math enough to become a paleontologist. When she's not writing or reading, she's likely at the comic shop, or studying world mythology. Then again, she might just be watching more Doctor Who, Castle, and Firefly than is probably healthy. She's also a co-host for the art and literature podcast, Beyond the Trope, where she talks mainly about nerdy things and uses perhaps a little too much sarcasm.

You can find Emily's podcast at www.beyondthetrope.com and you can connect directly with Emily online at www.emilykaysinger.com and via Twitter at @emilyksinger.

Phantom Brew
By Laura Kjosen

Laura wove a slice of celebrity history into the fabric of her story:

I was struck by the *Playboy Magazine* quote in the anthology's prompt describing Colfax "as the longest, wickedest street in America." A place so rich in history seemed a natural setting for a ghost story, and one of the most famous people to tread the sidewalks of Colfax was the author Jack Kerouac, who mentions Colfax Avenue in his iconic novel, *On the Road*. In *On the Road*, Kerouac writes, "...my whole life was a haunted life, the life of a ghost..." I wondered what it would be like if Kerouac's ghost was hanging out on Colfax today, and would his spirit have a reason to communicate with the living?

Colfax has a shady reputation, but it also is an area of Denver that continually has reinvented itself, and I wanted to write a story that had history and ancient magical arts colliding with some modern element, which in this case is the introduction of legalized, but controversial, retail marijuana to the eclectic mix of businesses on Colfax. I channeled that idea of moving on from dark events of the past and starting anew into the character of Tori.

Phantom Brew

Autumn Leaves had to push through a crowd of gawkers to get to the door of her shop, Tea Leaves on Colfax. Two cop cars and an ambulance, their red lights pulsing an eerie beat in the fog of a March morning in Denver, were parked at jaunty angles in front of the recently opened retail marijuana shop next door. A gruff officer stopped Autumn, and she explained she owned the teahouse and needed to open her shop.

"Oh," he grunted and shoved some onlookers aside. "Let this lady through!"

As she was unlocking the door, he took out an electronic tablet, poked the screen, and asked, "Could I have your name please?"

"Um, Autumn Leaves." The cop looked at her with raised brows. She pointed at the sign painted on the teahouse's front window that said "Tea Leaves."

The cop tried to stifle a laugh and emitted another grunt. "Yeah, cute...is that your legal name?"

"Yes."

"Okay. I'll be back in a bit to ask you some questions."

"Why? What happened over there?"

"Someone ransacked the marijuana business next to you. Really tore the place up. An employee found the owner knocked out on the floor when he came in this morning. A shelf fell on him. Ambulance is taking him to the ER."

"Oh, that's terrible! Is Jack going to be okay?"

The cop shrugged. "The paramedics are taking him to Denver Health if you want to inquire about his condition later. I'm not a doctor, but as he's a young guy, I expect he'll be okay. I'll be back in a few minutes." He nodded and strolled over to where two paramedics were rolling a stretcher toward the waiting ambulance. Autumn caught a glimpse of a pale face with a close-cut, livid red beard. Jack Gresham, a guy who had fought hard to legalize marijuana and one of the first to open a pot shop within just blocks of the state capitol building, was lying still as a corpse on the stretcher, his bald, bruised head cradled in a padded brace.

Autumn shivered in the cool fog. It was supposed to snow today, one of those heavy, wet snows the city experienced in March, but such fog was unusual, the white mist snaking across the wide expanse of Colfax Avenue like ghostly tentacles.

Colfax had its own energy; people were drawn to it. She had felt it when she moved to the city; it's why she chose it as the location for her teahouse. Oh, sure, she sold tea, but the divinations she did for certain clients who came for more than tea were more clear and powerful here than any other place she had practiced. But today, something in the energy of the place seemed a little off, and it wasn't just the excitement of the crime committed next door. Autumn huddled in her coat, pushed open the shop's door and then relocked it behind her, shutting out the noise from the street. She turned up the heat on the thermostat and went to the back to her office.

Goddess, more trouble from next door. I hope Jack is okay. I don't wish him harm, but really, strange vibes have been present since he opened. She shrugged off her coat and sank into the comfortable cushion of her wing chair. *And Tori is coming today. That girl doesn't need any more traumas in her life.*

Autumn turned on her computer. While it was booting, she went to the front, flicked on the lights, flipped over her open sign and unlocked the door with a sigh. She was spooning tea into a pot to brew when the Denver PD cop opened the door, setting the bell tinkling.

He cleared his throat. "Right, Ms., um, Leaves, could I take a few minutes of your time to ask some quick questions?"

Autumn didn't like it, but she knew it would be a good idea to cooperate.

She stood behind the counter displaying canisters of tea, putting a barrier between her and the cop. She realized this was a defensive posture, but she was a small woman, and the cop was one of the huge, muscly, aggressive types whose demeanor made her uncomfortable.

"What time did you close last night?"

Autumn pointed to the hours sign on the door. "Six, like always."

"Were you here after closing?"

"Yes, for about an hour, doing some accounting and inventory. They were still open next door when I left, but I didn't hear or see anything that looked like trouble, if that's what you're wondering."

The corner of the cop's mouth crooked. "Yes, I was going to ask that. One of the employees of the marijuana business said you had an argument with the owner, Jack Gresham, a couple weeks after they opened. What was that about?"

Oh, that's where this is going is it? Autumn straightened her spine. "It wasn't an argument. It was a discussion. I don't have anything against Jack."

"Did you ever witness Jack arguing with anyone else, or know of anyone who might want harm him or his business?"

"You mean besides the stoned guys who thought he was ripping them off and came out of there yelling?"

"Has that happened often?"

"A few times. I didn't pay much attention to what they looked like, and I don't know if any of them came back. "

"Were Jack's customers disruptive to your business?"

Autumn summoned her bitch voice. "If you are even remotely suggesting that I had anything to do with wrecking Jack's shop or hurting him, I won't comment further until my attorney is present."

The cop shrugged. "We'll be in touch if we have further questions. I need your contact information and ID please."

Autumn went back to the office and fished her wallet out of her purse. She handed the cop her license and watched him type in her address and driver's license number. She forced her voice into a friendly, cooperative tone as she gave him her cell number.

"Thank you for your time," the cop handed her a business card. "This is a number where you can contact me if you think of anything else." His mouth quirked in a brief smile—she supposed that's as friendly as he got, but at least he was polite.

As he was closing the shop's door, gray fingers emerged from the fog and twined around the cop's ankle. He stumbled and looked down at the sidewalk searching for what had tripped him up. He shook his head in confusion as nothing was there.

Autumn watched the fingers of mist roil and morph into an arm and then the torso of a man, who floated back across Colfax to melt into the fog.

I knew something was different today. Now, what is he doing here, and did he bring friends?

She wondered if the appearance of the specter had anything to do with the attack on Jack and his shop, but to suggest so to— she looked at the card in her hand—Sgt. Tom Brennan would be foolish. He would take her for a nutcase, which could also raise his suspicions. She would have to keep an eye out, though. She had sensed ghosts before, but never seen one in corporeal form. Paranormal activity wasn't her specialty. Reading the tarot, and, of course, reading tealeaves, yes, but dealing with visitors from beyond the veil? Not her thing.

She busied herself with brewing tea for her customers to sample and straightening the stock. Eventually, the street cleared of emergency vehicles, and snow started to fall, coating the sidewalks with a delicate white shroud.

About midmorning a bright red Ford pickup with a busted muffler rumbled to a stop in a parking spot within view of the shop's front window. Michael, her nephew, got out of the cab and came around to the passenger side to open the door for his sister, Tori. Michael kept one hand on his black cowboy hat as the wind was picking up.

He must still be in that country band. Shelly will be thinking it was a waste to send him to college up in Laramie when he spends most of his time playing a guitar in bars. Goddess, Tori looks thin, too thin.

Autumn hadn't seen her niece since that day four months ago when she had driven like a demon to a clinic in Lawrence,

Kansas, after a late-night phone call from a despondent Tori. She had held her niece's hand while a sympathetic female doctor performed the D&C. Her sister, Shelly, Tori's mother, had been furious, but not so furious that she kept away. She had driven her daughter from the college town to home on their farm near Goodland, Autumn following. Her brother-in-law had kicked Autumn out when he discovered her collusion in what Tori had done.

"Why did you sit there and let her go through with murder? You should have talked her out of it!" Steve's evangelism had morphed over the years from being just a bit overbearing to downright zealous. Stupid Shelly had told him everything, and he went ballistic, throwing pans in the kitchen, telling his own daughter she was damned, then throwing himself on the front lawn pleading with God to forgive him for being a bad father.

"What bothers you so, Steve?" Autumn had shouted at him when he paused to take a breath in his tirade against his daughter. "That the idiot Tori was dating got her pregnant, or that she realized what a toad he was when he took off to Texas, and she decided, rather intelligently I might add, that she was not ready to be a single mother and that pregnancy would interfere with getting her degree?"

She had expected him to argue with her, but it was scarier when he didn't.

"Get out," he had said. "Now. Don't ever show your witch face in this house again. If you weren't Shelly's sister, I'd shoot you right now and do the world a favor."

Autumn had given Tori a long hug, whispering in her ear that if she ever needed to get away...

And here she was, a tall, willowy girl with long, stick-straight hair the color of molten dark chocolate, holding her brother's hand as they huddled into their coats against the snow and wind. She yanked open the shop's door and ushered them inside, enclosing them in hugs.

Michael wouldn't stay for tea. He wanted to get north to Laramie before the snowstorm intensified.

"I don't want to hit a white-out on I-25, but I'll take some of those cookies with me." He smiled, and Autumn had to admit it was a dashing smile. He had Shelly's blue eyes and his father's square jaw, but, thankfully, not her brother-in-law's fanaticism. He was a handsome, light-hearted, talented kid, and she loved him.

"Yes, yes, be safe. Text me or Tori when you get there, okay?"

"Yes, ma'am." He grinned and tipped his black hat as he left, already fishing a cookie out of the bag Autumn had given him.

"Wish he would stay once and a while." Autumn looked at Tori, who was watching her brother pull away.

"Mmm hmm. Aunt Autumn, why is the ghost of Jack Kerouac hanging out on the roof of that pot shop next door? Is it like a joke because of the name—'Jack's Joint'?"

"No, the shop is owned by a man named Jack, who is, hopefully, still very much alive. Wait a minute—you can see Jack Kerouac's ghost?"

Tori took her aunt's hand and led her outside into the swirling snow. She pointed at the roof over the doorway of Jack's shop.

"Can you see him?"

Autumn squinted through the snowflakes pelting her face. Yes, she could make out a shadow of something, a figure of mist like she had seen on the street earlier.

"Well, I always knew this street had magical energy. It's why I put my shop here, but I didn't realize we were haunted. Everyone knows Kerouac passed through here—Colfax is mentioned in his book—but why is he here now? I can't see him clearly, but I know he's there. How does he appear to you?"

"Like he's drawn in neon red pen, pretty detailed. I can see features. That's how I know it's him. We read *On the Road* in lit last semester. I recognize him from the picture that was on the back cover of the book."

"That shop was ransacked last night and the owner hurt. Let's go inside for a minute." Autumn shooed her niece back into the teahouse. She poured them both cups of the steaming tea she had brewed earlier.

"Now," she said, leaning on the counter and gazing at Tori as the girl folded her lean body into a café chair, "how long have you been able to see ghosts?"

Tori kept her eyes fastened on her teacup and frowned. "Since my parents made me go to a funeral for the…the remains. They bought a little plot in the cemetery and everything. They pestered the hell out of the clinic and made me sign some forms, so the clinic would send…whatever they removed."

She twisted the cup around and around. "The pastor wouldn't come, but Dad and Mom made me stand out there while Dad prayed over this little grave. I was crying the whole time, but I guess it was the right thing to do. The ghosts came while I was kneeling there crying. I looked up, and they appeared a few feet away. I guessed they were the other people who were buried there. They didn't speak to me, but they seemed like they were sorry for me."

Tori let go of the cup. Her hands shook as she moved them to her lap. She raised her teary eyes to Autumn's. "I was pretty freaked out. I started shaking like mad, and Mom said that's enough, and made Dad leave off so we could go home. I didn't say anything to Dad about seeing the ghosts—he would have hauled me off to a mental hospital–but I told my mom that night. That's when she said it might be best if I came to stay with you."

Autumn came around the counter and folded her niece into a hug. The girl's damp hair brushed her cheek, and Autumn could feel Tori's bony ribs beneath her hands. Her brother-in-law was a fool. Who knows what the heck he actually buried and prayed over?

Autumn released Tori and looked in the girl's gray eyes. "Have you ever seen ghosts like this before? You never said…"

"Well, sometimes, when I was doing chores around the farm and stuff, it, well, it seemed like someone was following me or watching me, but I never saw anything—not like at the cemetery."

"Hmmm. Yes, it's the trauma. Times of great emotional upheaval, you know, can trigger the ability. For me, it was when your grandmother died, when Shelly and I were teenagers. I was scared, I tell you, when I went back to school after the funeral and discovered I could look at a classmate and see his future flash before my eyes."

She wandered over to a shelf to straighten some cans of tea. "It was so random back then. I thought I was going crazy. Then I started taking classes at the community college. The most fortunate day of my life was when I met Dr. Stephens. She was my history professor, and she was open about being Wiccan. I got up the nerve to confide in her. She knew I didn't have an illness but a gift—a gift I needed to harness and learn to control."

Autumn slumped into a chair at one of the tables in the small café area of the shop. "I didn't use my skill to benefit Jack, though, dammit. When I met him I saw him getting hurt sometime in the future, but I've learned not to tell people that without their asking."

She sighed. "When he started getting some rude customers, I was concerned that maybe one of them would get violent. I went over to talk to him. I told him I didn't want the totally stoned ones hanging out in front of my store, that it was bad for his business and mine. I was hoping he would take the hint, maybe have the police patrol more. Apparently, he didn't. But I can't very well tell the police I foresaw anything. Or that we're seeing ghosts. They suspect me already."

"What do you mean they suspect you?" Tori straightened to her full height. She was tall like her dad. "What kind of bullshit is that?"

Autumn appreciated the look of indignation on her face. "Oh, one of the guys next door made it out that Jack and I had an argument, but it wasn't like that."

"So what, now the cops think you hired some thugs to wreck this Jack's store?"

"I don't know what they think, but I wish I had a clue who did it. I don't like the idea of someone prowling the street trashing businesses. We made so much progress in lowering the crime in the area and now this."

Tori took a seat in the chair opposite her aunt. "What about their security cameras?"

Autumn pinched the bridge of her nose. "I don't know. I assume the police are looking at whatever the cameras recorded. They didn't ask to see mine, but I only have the one in the office anyway. I don't want to make my clients feel uncomfortable by recording their visits."

Tori nodded and shifted in her seat. "At least your skill is something useful. You can help people. I don't know how seeing ghosts helps anyone. It's creepy. It's a punishment…for what I did."

Autumn's hands trembled as she watched Tori blink back tears. "Oh, Tori. Don't think that, hon. It's only a punishment if you see it that way. I prefer to think of it as a gift. And I think we can put it to use. You said you didn't communicate with the ghosts in the cemetery, but do you think you could try to talk to Jack?" She motioned towards the ceiling, indicating the ghost perched on the roof. "Maybe our writer-ghost knows something about what happened next door."

Tori shrugged. "I don't know how."

"Well, paranormal communication is not my specialty, but we can wing it."

"You mean, just go out there and talk?"

"Why not?"

Tori turned to look out the front window. Even in the midst of a snowstorm, Colfax was a busy street.

"What are people going to think if they see me talking to a roof?"

Autumn was about to say 'who cares,' but then remembered that Tori was only an eighteen-year-old college freshman. She was still a teenager and hypersensitive to how others viewed her. Autumn had long ceased to care if people thought her strange, but Tori's gifts were new to her, and her instinct was to blend in, not seem weird—instinctual self-preservation for generations of practitioners of arcane arts.

Then again, this was Colfax, a street where crazy behavior from its diverse population was part of the vibe.

"We'll be standing in front of a pot shop. At most people will think you're high." Autumn laughed. "But if you don't want to, I understand. I don't want to make you uncomfortable."

Tori kept her gaze out the window, watching the snow, while Autumn waited, sipping her tea.

Finally, Tori turned back to face her aunt. "Let's put our coats on."

They waited for a guy with dreadlocks, jamming to whatever music was pumping through his headphones, to pass by.

"He's still there." Autumn could sense the ghost's energy nearby.

"Yup. Okay, here goes."

Tori took a few steps toward the curb to get a better look at the roof above Jack's shop. She clenched and unclenched her hands, glanced at Autumn, and called to the ghost.

"Um, Jack. Jack Kerouac! Um, hi. I'm Tori. Can I talk to you?"

Tori turned back to Autumn. "He's looking at me, but I don't hear anything. Maybe he can't talk?"

"Jack! Can you talk?"

Some lanky teenagers shoveling snow off the sidewalk in front of a skateboard shop across the street started laughing. Tori's head whipped around. She blushed pink and ran back inside Tea Leaves.

Autumn ran after her.

"Okay, people think I'm like schizophrenic. Maybe I am going crazy! Mom sent me here because she thought you could help me, but now I'm on a street with ghosts. I'm being punished, I know I am." Tori slumped at a table, put her head on her arms and sobbed.

Autumn stood over her and rubbed her hair and her back. "I know what your parents believe, my dear, but I don't believe in a vengeful god. You did what you had to do, what you thought was right for yourself and your future. Now you just need to find a way to forgive yourself for making a mistake with that boy and move on. I'll do anything I can to help you do that."

"I don't think I can. I'm a bad person!" Tori lunged to her feet and stalked into the tiny bathroom back by the office.

"Great," Autumn muttered as the bell above the door tinkled and a customer arrived. The middle-aged blond man was her first tarot reading of the day.

Tori kept out of sight during the reading although Autumn heard the faucet running in the bathroom, and she saw the girl crack open the door and peek out once.

When the client was gone, Tori appeared. "I'm sorry, Aunt Autumn. I know I'm supposed to work and help you out and all. Give me something to do."

Autumn set Tori to work unpacking some deliveries of tea and stocking the shelves.

"Good way to learn the inventory." She winked and smiled at her niece. Tori didn't smile or say another word, but she worked hard. Because of the snow, it was a slow day, so Autumn closed at noon and took Tori to lunch at the Mad Greens down the block.

"See any shadows out there?" Autumn studied Tori's pale face as she looked out the café's window.

The girl shook her head. "It's kind of random, I guess. That's what creepy about it. One minute everything's normal. The next, I see some dead person's face." She shivered and huddled in her parka.

Autumn nodded. "That's how it was for me as a teenager too. It will get better."

Tori only shrugged. Her cell phone lying on the table vibrated. She snatched it up. "Michael's in Laramie."

"Oh, good."

"Yeah," Tori mumbled and stared off into the snow.

The storm tapered off in the afternoon, and more customers wandered in to Tea Leaves. Autumn showed Tori how to work the cash register. The girl was content to stay behind the counter and ring up purchases. She frowned and turned away when Autumn led the next divination client back to the curtain-concealed nook where she did readings. Tori's eyes followed the woman as she left the shop, smiling, 20 minutes later.

"You saw something good for her, huh? She looked happy. Do you ever tell people anything bad?"

Autumn sighed and looked Tori in the eye. "Yes. They come here for insight. They deserve the truth of what I see."

"Did you see what would happen to me?"

"No, I didn't. My kind of gift requires proximity. I always knew you were special, though. I felt you would have a gift, too." Autumn smiled at her niece, she thought in an encouraging way, but Tori slid past her.

"It's not a gift to me." She slammed into the bathroom again.

#

At the end of the day, Autumn bought pizza and took Tori home to her apartment on 17th Avenue across from City Park.

Tori stood at the balcony looking at the snow-covered park. "It's a pretty view."

"Yes, this is the best place I've lived in Denver. When I first came, I had to live in the shop. This is quieter. We can talk about school if you want. There are some great city colleges where you could resume your degree."

"Maybe tomorrow. I'm kind of tired, Aunt Autumn."

Tori slumped into the den where Autumn had a placed a day bed. Autumn shook her head in frustration, but admonished herself to be patient. The girl had been through a lot. Asking her to try to communicate with a ghost today had been a bad idea. Still, she felt sure Jack Kerouac's ghost knew something about the vandalism at Jack's Joint.

She booted her laptop and emailed an acquaintance, Elijah Watts, who was part of a paranormal investigation society in Denver. She didn't mention Kerouac's ghost specifically, but told Elijah about the destruction of Jack's shop, the appearance of a ghost, and her desire to communicate with this ghost if possible. She didn't mention Tori. By the time she finished answering some other mail and surfing the web a bit, Elijah had emailed back.

"I'm in Cali, bummer! I'll be back in two weeks. Will definitely have to come to Colfax and check this activity out for myself." Elijah then described a procedure of inviting the ghost into confidence. Autumn would try it herself tomorrow. Tori was too fragile right now.

The next morning the sun was so bright against the snow, Tori and Autumn had to wear to sunglasses plus baseball caps to shade their eyes as they got off the bus near Tea Leaves.

"Typical Denver," Autumn told her, "one day snow, the next sun, and it's 70 degrees. We shovel snow in shorts around here. You sleep okay?"

It was a rhetorical question. Autumn had seen the dark circles under Tori's eyes this morning at breakfast.

Tori grunted, barely nodding her head, her sleep-deprived eyes hidden behind the sunglasses.

One of Jack's employees, a tall guy with a shaved head and bushy black beard, was unlocking the door to Jack's Joint.

"Good morning, Dylan," Autumn called as she fumbled with the keys to Tea Leaves. "How is Jack?"

Dylan sneered down at her; she was half his height. "He's got a goddam concussion. Hope you're happy."

Autumn took a couple steps towards Dylan. "Happy? Of course I'm not happy that Jack was injured. Why would you think that?"

"Whatever." Dylan shoved open the door to the pot shop, stepped inside and slammed it behind him.

"What a jerk," Tori said from behind her. "Is he the one who thinks you had it in for Jack just because you didn't want angry stoners in front of your shop?"

"Probably." Autumn sighed. "Is the ghost there?"

Tori flinched, but cast her eyes upward. "Yep. I can't see him as well in the bright sun, though."

"Good. Let's get you settled to deal with customers, and then

I'm going to try my friend Elijah's advice about making contact with our ghost."

Tori had no response to this proposal. She just waited for Autumn to open the door.

Once she had Tori stationed at the counter, Autumn hooked a Bluetooth headset over her right ear and went outside to sit on a bench in front of the shop. Customers sometimes liked to sip their tea while sitting there in the warm sun, but today she was hoping the ghost of Jack Kerouac would find it inviting. The Bluetooth headset had nothing to do with communicating with the ghost; it was a prop so people passing by wouldn't think she was nuts. She wasn't sure she could talk to the ghost with just her mind, as Elijah suggested. She might have to use her mouth, too. This way it would look like she was taking a phone call.

Strange how we think nothing at all of people walking along seeming to talk to themselves as long as they have one of these things wrapped around an ear, she thought as she settled on the bench, adjusting the headset.

Clairaudience, Elijah had called it, an inner voice different from one's own—the way an advanced spirit would communicate. She had to be still, clear her mind of extraneous stimuli as much as possible, be open. Autumn knew how to meditate. She employed those techniques now. The breathing. She lifted her face to the sun, relaxed. She waited, concentrating on welcoming Jack Kerouac into her mind.

But she heard nothing. Soon sweat began to trickle between her breasts, and her bottom was sore from sitting in one position on the bench. She kept at it a bit longer, determined, but still nothing.

Customers walked past her into the shop. Noticing the Bluetooth, they just waved, thinking she was listening to someone on a phone call. They came and went. She had a divination appointment at 11 AM. She sighed in frustration and got up to go prepare.

Tori raised her brows, questioning, as she walked in.

"Nothing. I may have to wait until Elijah gets back from California. I could let him try, but who knows if the ghost will still be around, or what might happen by then. Damn, this just isn't my talent. Elijah talks to all manner of creatures, horses, squirrels, and ghosts, I'm sure, in his paranormal investigations. I'm rather envious of his skill right now."

Autumn started toward the bathroom to splash water on her face. It had been warm out in the sun.

"Aunt Autumn?"

Autumn looked over her shoulder at Tori. "What?"

"You said he could talk to horses, this man Elijah?"

"Yes. Up here." Autumn pointed to her temple. "Last summer during the floods I went with him to a fairgrounds where rescue crews had brought horses they saved from the flood waters. The poor things were panicked and restless. I haven't seen this kind of magic performed very often, but it was amazing to watch Elijah walk around, put a hand on a horse's neck, and without saying a word aloud calm it. That movie horse whisperer has nothing on Elijah. Why?"

It came out as a whisper Autumn barely heard: "I can do it too."

"What?"

"Talk to horses and other animals. And I hear them, sort of, like in my head. I know if they're upset, or content, or hungry. That's why I did so well in 4-H with my goats and earned my college money. I just thought I was good with animals, but now…"

Autumn smiled. Her sister had been sending her pictures of Tori at 4H shows for years and talked of all her ribbons, and the college money earned from selling her goats. Autumn had seen the girl had a gift, but she wasn't sure until now that Tori had the clairvoyant ability, not like Autumn's, but like Elijah's.

"Hmm. Well," she said, smiling, "I will have to introduce you to Elijah. He's a college student, like you."

"Oh." Tori blushed. "I assumed he was, you know, older."

"Because I am?" Autumn laughed.

Tori looked flustered and shoved her hands in her jeans pockets.

"No, I mean, just older than me."

"Elijah is a couple years older than you, but already an interesting young man. The magical community is small. We all get to know each other eventually, despite our other differences, like age. Elijah came in to buy tea one day, fennel, sage. He asked for a reading. The minute I held his hand, I knew what he was. We've been friends ever since."

Tori nodded.

"He's quite good looking, I think."

Tori's face darkened. "I'm not looking to be set up, so don't. Please. I shouldn't be with boys…for a while."

Tori slid around the counter, pushed the door open and plopped down on the bench out front, arms crossed defensively over her chest.

Autumn resisted the urge to go mother her. Tori would have

to find a way to deal with her demons. Instead, she went to the bathroom, bathed her face, touched some patchouli oil to her wrists and settled behind the curtain to await her client.

The session took longer than she expected. The client, an elderly woman she had seen before, kept asking for specific details, and she had to keep explaining the cards didn't reveal situations like a television show did. When she showed the woman out of the shop, Tori was still sitting on the bench, her bent elbows resting on her knees, her chin resting on her clasped hands. She looked as if she was listening.

Autumn held her breath, and then released it in a whoosh as Tori finally stood and, stumbling a bit from stiffness, flung open the door of the shop and looked around wildly before her eyes lighted on her aunt.

"He saw... he told me... what went on in the shop next door. That's why he's been hanging out, kinda guarding it because he likes that it has his name on it. He says it was a poltergeist."

Autumn's knees trembled beneath her long skirt, and she flung out her hand to grip the display counter. "Oh, shit."

#

Autumn and Tori huddled around the computer in the office to write an email to Elijah.

"Tell him Jack says the poltergeist is a guy he used to see around Colfax, you know, in his day. The cops were always chasing this guy because he got violent when he was drunk. He says the poltergeist is pissed off that the street has gone legit. You know, it has some nice restaurants and stores, and people buy pot from a shop now and pay 'the establishment' high taxes on it. He didn't like that Jack—the living one—was chasing off the rowdies either."

Autumn snorted. "A poltergeist knows about taxes on pot?"

"Apparently."

"Hmm. Sounds like Jack did start to do something about his customers who were making trouble. That might have been what made the poltergeist target him. They love chaos."

Autumn typed the email and hit send. "I hope Elijah knows someone in his circle who can take care of this."

"You mean like a 'ghost buster'? Seriously?" Tori looked at her aunt, brows raised, her skepticism clear.

"Well, yes. Now, c'mon we have work to do."

Autumn and Tori were cleaning the few small café tables in the shop when a police car went flying by and screeched to a halt up the block.

Autumn ran outside to see what was going on. A few doors down, the large metal sign above the storefront of an upscale resale shop was lying, mangled, in the street. The pant legs of a man stuck out from under the sign.

Autumn gasped and clenched her hands into fists to keep them from shaking. "Oh, no."

Tori came out to join her, and they watched as paramedics and police officers lifted the sign off the person underneath. The middle-aged man was dressed in a dark blue suit and was probably one of the mortgage brokers, lawyers, or insurance agents who had offices nearby. Autumn didn't recognize him as one of her lunchtime customers, though.

She looked around for a ghostly hand or torso, but could see nothing. "Do you see anything?" she murmured to Tori.

Tori looked about. "Just Jack Kerouac's ghost floating above the entrance to Jack's Joint."

As the paramedics loaded the man into an ambulance, Autumn looked at Tori, who sighed and nodded. She left the girl outside to talk to the ghost next door.

Tori returned with a grim expression on her face. "Jack says it was the poltergeist. He tried to reason with him. He told him, yeah, it sucked that the street had changed, but pointed out all the cops that the poltergeist was attracting. He tried to get the poltergeist to leave, but this is the area where Ray—the guy who is now the poltergeist–used to hide out from the cops. He doesn't want to leave."

"Of course he doesn't. He's having too much fun causing chaos. Please stay in front and deal with any customers. I need to do some research." Autumn hustled to her office as Tori nervously drummed her fingers on the counter.

Later, Tori watched frowning, her thin arms wrapped around her middle, as Autumn put a layer of salt along the windows and doors to Tea Leaves. She was annoyed that she couldn't get up on the roof to sprinkle salt there, too.

"Is that actually going to work?" Tori asked as they closed up for the night.

"I have no idea. Not my specialty, but it's worth a try." Autumn pressed her lips together and double-checked the locks on the shop's door.

She was restless that night, tossing in bed, only dozing. In the middle of the night, she heard the clicking of keys on her laptop. She crept to her bedroom door and peered out into the living room. Tori, in tank top and pajama pants, was at the small table by the window, hunched over Autumn's laptop, intent on reading something on the screen. Autumn crept back into her bedroom and sat on the bed.

I hope it's not that imbecile boy who took off for Texas. Please let her be smart enough to not contact him. Autumn went back to bed uneasy.

She kept on eye on Tori the next day as the girl shyly served tea and muffins to customers, as she swept out the shop and dusted shelves. She had dark smudges under her eyes. She ate little at lunch and spoke only when asked a direct question. Autumn hated to pry, but she had to ask. So as they were getting ready to close that evening, she pulled Tori into a hug.

"Hon, I don't want to intrude, but who were you…" BAM! The shop door blew open so hard it smacked against the wall and set the bell flying off its bracket. It smashed into canisters of tea on a shelf on the other side of the room. Autumn instinctively pulled Tori behind the counter where they crouched as tables and chairs overturned, and tea canisters rained off the shelves. Autumn was dialing 911 on her cell when Tori stood up, shaking, but with a determined look on her pale face.

Autumn stared as her niece looked fixedly at a spot near the back shelves where a china teapot was hovering in the air. Tori didn't say a word, but her hands were animated, and then she flung out her left arm and pointed toward the open door of the shop.

The teapot sailed past Tori's head and smashed against the wall behind the counter, showering Autumn with china shrapnel. Autumn ducked her head in time, but yelped as the shards bit into her hands, which were covering her head.

When she got the nerve to raise her eyes over the counter, Tori was holding an expensive jade teapot in her left hand, the lid clutched in her right.

Tori was speaking, but the poltergeist was smashing saucers and cups, so Autumn only caught snatches of Tori's words above the noise—*"vinctus...quae...hydria."* Goddess, Autumn thought, *she's trying to trap him in the pot.*

Police sirens wailed outside, probably responding to Autumn's 911. She'd dropped her phone on the floor and could hear the faint voice of an operator.

"What the...?" A man shouted from the direction of the door. Elijah stood at the entrance to the shop, but he had to fall to his knees, ducking, as a teacup sailed above his head.

Tori's voice screamed in Latin. A gust of cold wind howled through the shop towards her, but Tori stood strong and clamped the lid on the jade pot.

"*Occludo.*" She set the pot on the counter in front of Autumn. Elijah rose to his feet, and they all stared at the pot holding their collective breath.

"I guess salt doesn't work against poltergeists, Aunt Autumn," Tori whispered, and their giggles broke the tension. They turned toward the sound of boots crunching on broken china as Sgt. Brennan strode into the shop.

"Wow." The officer's mouth hung open as he surveyed the damage. "Okay, what happened here? Anyone injured?" He waved in another officer and ordered him to start taking photos.

"No we're not hurt. We were out back." Autumn's mind rifled through explanations other than 'poltergeist,' anything that would be more plausible to Sgt. Brennan. "We were taking the trash out to the dumpster and talking a bit by the backdoor when we heard things smashing in here. We ran back in screaming as loud as we could. The vandals must have heard us and ran. We came into the front to find this mess."

Brennan's eyes lit up. "Did you see anyone running down the street? Phelps! Let's get some guys to search, find some witnesses."

The officer named Phelps ran outside, talking into his radio.

Autumn glanced at Tori and Elijah. Elijah's dark curls were damp with sweat around his forehead, and he was gazing with admiration at Tori, murmuring, "I caught the next flight to Denver after I got Autumn's email. I'm so glad I was here to witness that. I was going to try a blasting rod, but you were totally awesome."

Tori blushed, but for the first time since she had arrived, she was smiling broadly.

She boldly grabbed Elijah's hand. "C'mon, there's someone I want you to meet." She looked meaningfully at Autumn as she led Elijah toward the door of the shop.

Autumn nodded and distracted Brennan by asking him about a report for insurance purposes. *Elijah will be thrilled to meet Jack Kerouac,* she thought, as Brennan peppered her with questions about the damaged property.

Elijah and Tori didn't come back, and Brennan kept her busy for another half hour answering questions.

"Sorry you were hit too. We'll do our best to find these guys and stop the trouble around here."

Autumn smiled and thanked him as she picked up the jade pot.

"At least they didn't get that one, huh?"

"No, and I'm glad. This one is very valuable, Sergeant. I should have it in the safe. I'll put it there now."

"Good idea." He waved and closed the battered shop door behind him.

Autumn carried the jade pot to the back office. It felt cold in her hands. She unlocked the safe, moved some papers aside and placed the jade teapot inside.

"That's a phantom brew no one should ever drink. Ah, well, no more trouble now that the tempest is in the teapot." She laughed to herself. She felt so proud of her niece.

That's why Tori was on the computer last night—she was researching how to trap the poltergeist. She must have been so scared, but she did it. She found her gift.

Autumn closed the safe and turned the lock, whispering, "*Finis.*"

About the Author:

Laura Kjosen began writing stories on the pages of journals when she was teenager. When she wasn't writing, she was reading. Her favorite hangout was the local library. As an adult, she worked as a reporter for a daily newspaper. Then she wrote technical articles and press releases for a public relations firm. Now she teaches literature and writing at a community college in Colorado—and writes stories inspired by the fantastic worlds and characters she relished as a young reader. Her short fiction has appeared in online and print publications.

Take Me to Your Leader, Jackie Smack
By Warren Hammond

Warren stayed much closer to home for his Colfax story than he usually does in his other works:

I live on Colfax Avenue, so I was very excited to seize this opportunity to set a story in my literal back yard. As you might imagine, the alley behind my home attracts an abundance of colorful characters ranging from the unsavory to the tragic, and this story is my attempt to paint a simple day-in-the-life of two people who could be sitting on the pavement outside my window right now.

Take Me to Your Leader, Jackie Smack

"I hate aliens."

Jackie nodded, his mouth hanging open. "Aliens. Yep. Who doesn't?"

Darrell's gaze darkened. "You bein' smart, boy? You think I'm jokin'? Aliens is real. I seen 'em. They's real. You best believe it."

He couldn't tell if Darrell was joshing him. The old man sure sounded serious, but Jackie knew he was the gullible type. He had a hard time reading people. Back before he quit school, lots of kids would trick him into believing all kinds of stuff. His mother used to say he must've been born on the day God was having a clearance sale on smarts.

Darrell leaned in close, close enough that Jackie caught a blast of Thunderbird-soused BO. "Aliens, boy. I seen 'em."

Swallowing, Jackie thought it might be best if he split. But, the old bum had done him a nice favor, letting him shack up in his alley for a night. And he'd shared his can of ravioli, too. He didn't have to do that. He coulda just said you're on your own when it comes to food, but he'd been plenty generous with that ravioli. Downright hospitable. It'd be mighty un-Christian of him to just leave without chatting awhile.

But Jackie was a rambler now. And he didn't think a rambler was supposed to stay in one place. A rambler went where the wind took him. From his home in Waco to Albuquerque, where everything was brown. From Albuquerque to Phoenix, where hot got its name. From Phoenix to Denver, where the air was thin and the blunts were fat as sausages.

A rambler. No connections. No responsibilities. Free to do whatever he wanted, whenever he wanted. Independent-like. Leaning against a dumpster, wearing the same clothes he'd been wearing for a couple weeks now, with nothing to do since the sun rose but listen to Darrell and stare at a piss-stained concrete wall, Jackie suspected a rambler's life wasn't as glamorous as he'd imagined. But this was his life now, and he'd best make peace with it. Times like these he was prone to getting down about losing his Domino's job and getting his ass evicted six months back. But he had to remember to look at the positive. He'd freed himself of all those responsibilities. Now he could mainline whenever he wanted. And that wasn't a little thing.

"Mind if I shoot up?"

"Do whatever you got to, boy. I ain't the judgin' type."

Jackie broke out his kit: the cut-off bottom of a pop can, zebra-stripe Bic, hypo, and a baggie of smack. He made quick work of cooking down and filling the syringe. He had good veins for poking. Stood out like worms on a sidewalk after a thunderstorm.

The juice entered his arm, and the gears that normally scraped and ground inside his head started to hum with greased efficiency.

"What do the aliens look like?" he asked.

"They look just like the ones you see on TV. They got them almond-shaped eyes, and they got these big-ass heads, so big it's hard to believe those scrawny little bodies can hold them heads up. You see what I'm sayin'? You'd think their heads would just flop over and hang there like a sack o' onions, but they must be stronger than they look. You know what they is? Wiry. That's what. Wiry."

Jackie nodded. He'd wondered the same thing himself about how they kept those heads standing upright. Course in his case he'd passed it off as some of that movie bullshit. Those movie people were always makin' up stuff that couldn't happen in real life. Like that movie he saw with all these badass dudes, one who's a great swordfighter, and another who can't miss with a bow and arrow, and they got this old Gandalf dude with them, who's got all these amazing magic powers. But when the shit is on the line, who do they all look to? The midget, that's who. The *midget*. Like that could ever happen.

"When did you see the aliens?"

"I seen 'em every Tuesday for a few weeks now. They come for me."

"They come here? To this alley."

"Here or wherever I am. Don't matter if I move around. They always find me."

Wow. This very alley. How lucky was it that Jackie had found this alley when he did? Real aliens. Man, would he love to see that. He found himself liking the idea more and more as his high notched higher and higher. He decided that smack and aliens went well together. Like pizza and beer. Or nachos and cherry Slurpees. He looked to the sky to see if the aliens were coming right this second. Nope. When they did though, he'd jump up to shake hands and say, "How's it hangin'?"

"Every Tuesday they come," said Darrell.

"What's their skin feel like?"

"Why you askin' that?"

"Well, if they came right now, and I was to shake hands with one of 'em, I'm wondering what I'd be getting into. What if their hands are all slimy, or scaly like a snake? I wouldn't want to give no offense if I was to pull my hand away. It's best I know what to expect."

"What makes you think they'd be comin' right now?" Darrel sounded nervous.

"It's Tuesday ain't it?"

"You shittin' me, boy?"

"No. It's Tuesday. I know because yesterday was Monday."

Darrell looked as stunned as somebody who'd just had his head dunked in a toilet—pasty skin, trembling lips, beads of water dotting his forehead. Jackie knew how he felt—plain swirlies, lemon swirlies, chocolate swirlies. He'd tried all the flavors. Jackie caught a warm whiff of something. Looking at his newfound friend's lap, he could see a wet stain spreading out from the crotch.

"Why are you so scared?"

Darrell took a long time answering. It wasn't until Jackie pulled off the cap of Darrell's bottle of T-bird and told him to take a few shots that the old man seemed to come out of it. "They hurt me," he whispered.

These alien dudes weren't sounding so fun anymore. "Hurt you how?"

"They experiment on me. They take me to they's ship, and they poke me with needles, and they put me inside they's machines and do tests on me."

"Do they probe your anus?"

Darrell nodded.

Jackie shook his head. He didn't like the thought of that one bit. What was it about aliens and anuses? "How do they take you to their ship? Do they beam you up?"

"No. They take me in a smaller ship that's got these colored lights on top."

"Can't you just tell them you don't want to go?"

"They make me go. I'll die if I don't. That's what they tell me." Darrell's eyes got watery. "I don't want to go. Don't let them take me."

Jackie wanted to help. He didn't see why Darrell should have to go when he didn't want to. Couldn't the aliens just ask for volunteers? Maybe if they paid a little, like when he'd gone to that college where some professor showed him dirty videos and asked him all kinds of questions about the parts he liked best. Now that was the way to run an experiment. That professor had a line going out the door, he did.

"I'll do what I can," Jackie said. "The problem is, these aliens probably have all kinds of weapons, and I ain't no good at fighting."

"But you'll help?"

"I'll do what I can. I ain't promising that it'll help though."

A tear broke loose from the corner of Darrell's eye. It rolled down a ways, then got caught in wrinkle and channeled out to the side of his face. "You're a good boy."

"I sure try to be," mumbled Jackie, beginning to think about how to stop aliens.

"I have a son, you know. I ain't seen him since he was real young, but I sure hope he turned out like you."

That was some mighty fine praise, he had to admit, but this

was no time to pat himself on the back. How do you stop aliens? He could try to tackle one, but Darrell said they were stronger than they looked. And even if he did get one of them down, then what was he going to do about the others? It was a tough problem to solve. That was for damn sure.

He thought on it for a long time, and then it came to him. Water. Aliens were afraid of water. He'd seen it in a movie about these aliens who drew pictures in the cornfields.

He shared his idea with Darrell, who thought it was worth a go. Together, they dove dumpsters, seeking anything that could hold water. After a half hour, they'd amassed quite a collection: coffee cans, a dented trash pail, carefully uncrumpled fast food cups, an old saucepan.

Loading it all in Darrell's shopping cart, they walked down Colfax to a high school with a fountain out front. Dunking item after item into the fountain, they filled them all full of water. Carefully, they arranged as many items as they could in a single layer on the bottom of the cart before wheeling back to the alley to drop them off. After round-tripping back to the fountain for the second load, Jackie told Darrell to take a seat against the wall. Next, he placed the items side-by-side until he'd surrounded Darrel with a semi-circle of water-filled containers.

It was like a moat.

Jackie worried that some of the containers weren't full. They'd spilled a lot as they'd bumped the shopping cart along the sidewalk. He told himself it didn't matter. The aliens were either afraid of water or they weren't. The amount shouldn't matter.

He sat against the opposite wall. "You don't need to worry," he said. "This is going to work."

"I hope you's right," said Darrell. "They'll be here soon."

Jackie silently watched his new friend rake his fingers through his hair, little tufts of gray coming loose as he did. Shit, he'd never seen anybody so scared. He'd seen cats do that, shed clumps of fur when they got really startled, but he'd never seen a person so frightened that he lost his hair, not once.

Until today.

A rusted-up ambulance pulled into the alley. "They're here," said Darrell.

Jackie looked up at the sky. "Where?"

A man and a woman got out of the ambulance. They walked up to Darrell. Darrell was crying, sobbing big wet tears. "Don't let them take me," he said to Jackie.

Jackie looked to the sky again. "Where are they? I don't see any aliens."

"Hi, Darrell," said the woman. "It's me, Linda, from Community Outreach. We've been driving these alleys for twenty minutes trying to find you. It would be so much easier if you would just stay in the shelter, you know."

"I don't like it there," said Darrell. "People steal from me."

"We're going to take you to the hospital. It's time for your chemo."

"I don't want to go," he blubbered.

"I know. But you have cancer, remember? The doctors need to fix you up."

"I don't want to."

Jackie was confused. "I don't see any aliens, Darrell. Where are the aliens?"

Darrell snatched up a pan and threw it at the woman. Water

splashed her face, her hair, her shirt.

"Goddammit!" she yelled. "What are you doing?"

"Get in the ambulance, Linda," insisted the man she'd come with. "I'll take care of this."

"Jesus Christ," she said, shaking her head before doing what she was told. A trail of water drops marked her path back to the ambulance.

The man squatted down to Darrell's level. "That wasn't a very nice thing to do to a lady, was it?"

Darrell pouted.

"It's time to go to the hospital, Darrell. Now I expect you to come with us, and I expect you to apologize to Linda, understand?"

Darrell stood up, his head hanging low, meek-like.

Jackie was annoyed. "Wait, Darrell, where are the aliens?"

Darrell didn't wait.

He watched Darrell get in the back of the ambulance. He could see Linda through the windshield, in the passenger seat, rubbing her hair with a wad of paper towels. The man came back to hand Jackie a card. "You ever want help, you stop in and see us, okay?"

"Okay," mumbled Jackie, unable to hide his disappointment. "Thanks."

"No problem. You come by that address or call that number, and we'll get you some help."

"Will do."

The man walked away and soon the ambulance began to back out of the alley.

Jackie watched it go. A glimmer of something tickled at the

back of his mind. Something about the ambulance and its colored lights. He frowned as the glimmer faded, and he decided it must've all been a trick.

I'll be damned. All this time, Darrell had been joshing. Jackie had to admit, Darrell had fooled him pretty good. Aliens. People were always playing tricks on him.

He smiled, because he knew that was the right thing to do when you'd been had. But, boy, did he wish that, just this once, he'd get the joke.

About the Author:

Warren Hammond is known for his gritty, futuristic KOP novels. By taking the best of classic detective noir, and reinventing it on a destitute colony world, Warren has created these uniquely dark tales of murder, corruption and redemption. The third novel in the trilogy, KOP Killer, won the 2013 Colorado Book Award for best crime/mystery novel. Warren's latest, The Tides of Maritinia, will be published by HarperCollins in 2014. Always eager to see new places, Warren has traveled extensively. Whether it's camping in the wildlife reserves of Botswana, or trekking in the Himalayas, he's always up for a new adventure.

You can find Warren online at http://warrenhammond.net and at http://facebook.com/warren.hammond. He's also on Twitter at @whammondauthor.

Ghostly Attraction
By TJ Valour

TJ decided to try a new corner of speculative fiction for her story:

Dealing with Colfax's underbelly and the colorful characters that thrive there was a must for me. I knew I wanted to write about ghosts since I hadn't ever tackled them before, and a quaint Colfax mansion was the perfect setting.

The haunted house in my story is a compilation of several historic homes pulled out of James Bretz's *Mansions of Denver: The Vintage Years*. My protagonists took form while I was listening to a Nickelback song and surfing the Tattered Cover's website. A bit piecemeal and a tad spastic, but there it is, my creative process in a nutshell. Enjoy!

Ghostly Attraction

The sidewalk was bleeding. Again. Dina swore and forced her gaze up as the blood oozed out from between the cracks. She watched as the sign for 16th Avenue began to crumple in on itself in a soundless deformation. The group of women walking toward her didn't notice. Their cheery conversations carried on without pause. She quickened her steps, only another block to Colfax—she could make that, no problem.

The bookstore would be safe. It always had been. Ever since she'd come to Denver, the aura of the place had drawn her in. Dina shook her head. The bookstore couldn't have an *aura*. It was a building. She only went there because the owner was hot. Well, attractive in a nerdy, educated sort of way.

Dina frowned. She needed to come up with something believable for Derek to let her in at this time of night. *Hi, a ghost has hijacked my brain. Can I come in?* wasn't going to fly. He didn't strike her as the kind of guy that would be open to solicitations either, though she had been dreaming of seducing him for months.

The ghost's unreality burrowed its way deeper into her cerebral cortex. Dina's frozen fingers tightened into a fist. She'd been dealing with ghosts and their manifestations since she was five, but a ghost trying to take over her brain was something very different. Dina squeezed her eyes shut, using every ounce of will to try to force the trespassing presence out of her mind. Its icy fingers gouged the malleable flesh behind her eyes as it held on.

She cried out, her hands lifting to grab the sides of her head. Pain wracked her body until her legs gave out.

The sharp sting of her knees hitting the sidewalk was a welcome feeling. It was a real thing, as tangible as the city's dirt that no doubt now clung to her skin. The crushing agony in her head left and with a gasp, air flooded back into her starved lungs. Gingerly, she raised her head. The world listed violently to the side before righting itself.

A white car pulled up next to her and stopped. Dina forced herself to her feet. Daring a glance at the vehicle, she groaned. The blue Denver Police emblem stuck to the door was a familiar sight.

"You all right there, Dina?" the cop asked from within.

Dina nodded and carefully approached the car. She steadied herself with a hand on the cruiser's roof and leaned down to see in the passenger window. Greg Anderson. At least it was Greg and not a gung-ho rookie. He wouldn't harass her, much. "Hey, Sergeant, you heading in for dinner?"

"Yep. Taking it while it's quiet." His gaze held hers. "You sure you're okay, sweetheart? I saw you fall."

The flesh on his face melted away, revealing a maggot-filled skull with endless pits for eyes. Awesome. The ghost wasn't done with her after all. Dina smiled at him and willed her words to come out normally. "I'm fine." She gestured to her high-heeled Louboutin boots. "Some days these things are easier to walk in than others."

"Right." The cop's tone cooled as if he sensed her lie. "Where you headed tonight?"

She nodded toward Colfax. "Just to the bookstore. I'm meeting the owner to discuss a rare book." Dina's smile almost faltered as maggots dripped out of Greg's mouth to pool in the center console, but she was a professional and a fine actress, even if Hollywood hadn't thought so. The writhing mass of larva spilled over his take-out cup and onto the passenger seat, inching closer to her.

"Is that what we're calling it these days?" Greg asked. His fingers were now nothing more than bleached bones, and they tapped a steady rhythm on the steering wheel.

"Sergeant." Dina placed her hand over her heart. "I'm as legit as they come."

"Uh-huh. And I'm the tooth fairy." His skeleton face and hands morphed into sculpted yellow dust, and the particles hung suspended inside the car for several seconds before dissipating. Greg returned to normal from one heartbeat to the next. "Be safe out there, Dina."

"Always am." She waved as his window rolled back up. He pulled away and turned into the precinct parking lot. Dina kept her steps slow but elongated her stride. The hallucinations were getting stronger. She needed to get inside that store and to Derek.

Several men were smoking in the back lot of the purple and gray building that housed Romantix and the X Bar. Their cigarette smoke turned from pink to blue as she passed.

The majority of the transient population had already settled down for the night, but a few stragglers loitered in front of the check-cash store. Dina couldn't tell if they were planning on breaking in or if it was just another late night drug deal.

A gust of wind funneled down Colfax Avenue, blowing her

long black hair out of her eyes. Directly across the street, flickering neon words advertised "Used Books." All she had to do was cross Colfax and she'd be fine.

The hairs on the back of Dina's neck stood on end. She punched the crosswalk button. Her breath turned to frost, and each inhale felt like shards of glass coated her throat.

Not again.

She stabbed the button a second time and dared to glance over her shoulder. Dina blinked, and the dark shapes materialized. They clung to the shadows of the parking lot across from the police station, absorbing the meager light radiating from the street lamps. Bile churned in her stomach as the sweet smell of baby powder washed over her. Those weren't hallucinations. The other ghosts from the mansion had followed her too.

The light changed and she escaped across Colfax. Her heels stuck to the crosswalk as if it had just been painted. It hadn't been, and Dina knew if she looked down the asphalt would be hemorrhaging blood worse than a homicide victim. Halfway across the intersection, she took another look behind her. The doorway of the adult novelty store was empty, but her gaze lingered on the mouth of its parking lot where the ghosts had been. Nothing. Fear knotted in her gut.

The angled glass of the bookstore's front display windows funneled patrons into the narrow space leading to the entrance. The books stood, small and silent sentries mocking her, protected as they were behind the tempered glass. Ghosts couldn't mess with their heads.

Using both fists, she hammered on the worn wood door until her hands ached.

Ghostly Attraction

"Come on. Come on," Dina muttered between breaths.

Deathly silence greeted her attempts to rouse the man she knew lived in the apartment above the store. Derek would help her. If he just let her in, she'd be okay. She could regroup and figure out what had gone wrong.

"Please be here..." The hollow echoes of her knocking were the only sounds she could hear. The ghost had done something. There was no street noise, even though Dina knew cars passed and people were around. Whatever it was, it acted as a buffer between her and reality. If the ghost's barrier was preventing Derek from hearing her, she was so screwed.

Her fists, slick with sweat even though she was freezing, left rounded imprints on the wood like scorch marks from a flame. This hadn't been her first time manipulating a spirit, just the first time it didn't work. Dina hadn't known they would come after her—hadn't known they could. All the ghosts she had encountered previously were bound to their location and definitely hadn't been able to do any of this brain infusion crap. It had to be the hit of smack she'd done. Dina had always been able to see them, but she had read online that drugs helped intensify the sight. God, she was an idiot.

Putting her back against the bookstore's door, Dina kicked backward with the heel of her boot in order to continue her onslaught. Her heart beat a staccato rhythm in her chest, but she tried to force her breathing to slow. She could handle this. Derek would come any second now, open the door, and invite her in. She could sober up safely with him, surrounded by his books.

Two days was plenty of time to do a bit of research and release the ghosts from Richard's house. Rich had been Dina's client for years, and what he was asking wasn't hard. She had cleared energy from a building before. She did it every time she moved. Whatever was different about his house, she could circumvent it. Richard would be happy, and she'd get a big bonus.

Dina gritted her teeth and pulled her resolve around her like a cloak. Before she could take another breath, an invisible power slammed against her, shoving her flush against the unforgiving door. Her head ricocheted off the solid wood, and she saw stars. Dina's chest slowly began to compress under the pressure until every bit of air had been squeezed out of her lungs. Panic didn't even have a chance to set in. Her foot bounced weakly off the door one final time. Darkness prowled along the edges of her vision before it pulled her under.

#

Derek caught himself just before his face hit the coffee table. He looked slowly around his apartment and tried to sort out his jumbled thoughts.

"What the hell?" Nothing was out of the ordinary—everything was upright and in its place. Something had shoved him out of his trance though, and he would damn well figure out what it was. He uncrossed his legs and stood, preparing to go check the shop when something crashed into the main door downstairs. The aftershock rattled the windows of the building, and it wasn't like Denver often had earthquakes.

Derek took the stairs at a run and strengthened his mental shields. The protection wards around the bookstore should have repelled any otherworldly being, but something had smashed into them. Hard.

Spontaneous events coupled with human interference caused

some of the strongest psychic intrusions. The supernatural world liked to keep you on your toes, but something of this magnitude was unusual. Nothing had been mentioned in the Department's field agent bulletin either, and the only BOLO had been for the northern Colorado outpost.

Derek reached the front door. Wood wasn't a good conductor of energy, but the door was so cold it stung his fingers. A spirit shouldn't have been able to fixate on him here. Inside the wards he was invisible. Plus, if a vindictive spirit from his past had escaped the Beyond, it would have been in the bulletin.

He looked through the peephole and froze. There was more than just a pissed off spirit out there. He unlocked and threw open the door. His power word hissed through his lips, and as it reached the presence that hovered over Dina there was a loud pop. The apparition disappeared. The ambient noise from Colfax returned and brought with it the warmth of the real world. Dina lay perfectly still as if asleep, but her skin was like ice. Derek picked her up and had her inside in seconds.

He cradled her against his naked chest as he carried her up the stairs to his apartment and laid her down on the couch. Derek stared down at the woman in front of him and ran his hand through his hair.

She couldn't know about him, what he did, and who he worked for. He was going to have to find out exactly what happened, what brought her to his store, and play it off. Explain as little as possible and send her on her merry way.

Dina was petite, but carried herself with enough confidence that you didn't notice her size. You saw what she wanted you to see, and more often than not it was her perfect curves. Derek had no doubt that her breasts were on prominent display in whatever top she had worn today, which was why her jacket would be staying on. He didn't need more distractions—just having her in his space was short-circuiting his brain.

Nothing good could come of having her here like this.

Derek shook his head and checked her pulse when she still hadn't stirred. It was strong, but she was still out. He looked at the small purse that hung on a chain around her wrist. He frowned. As far as he knew, personal escorts didn't have a pimp, or a handler, or whatever, but if she didn't wake up soon, he would need to find someone to call. He should probably put on a shirt too.

A small whimper escaped Dina's perfect lips, and he crouched in front of her.

"Shhh. You're okay. You're fine now." Derek watched her face for any sign that she was waking. Her delicate features contorted, and she tensed as if fighting something he couldn't see. His hand moved toward her cheek, and he wanted nothing more than to touch her, soothe her in some way, but instead he dropped his arm and stood up. "Wake up, Dina."

A tremor shook her slender frame, and she crumpled inward until she was hugging her knees. Derek swore and squatted down next to her again. He was going to regret this. His thumb brushed along her cheek. "You're okay, Dina. Wake up."

As soon as Derek felt her stir, he jerked away, quickly moving to the far end of the couch. Her long eyelashes fluttered open to reveal midnight blue eyes. Dina looked around his living room. His loft was average: wood floors, tastefully practical furniture, and the pictures on his walls looked like they were from recreational travel—not spirit hunting assignments.

Her gaze stopped on him and her eyes widened. She slowly took in his body and the heat in her stare went straight to his head. For the last six months, his increased daily workouts had been for her.

The bitter bite of reality slammed into him. His thoughts cleared, and he snagged a shirt from his laundry basket. He wanted Dina to look at him that way so desperately that he had imagined she actually had. Pure and simple. She didn't date—you paid if you wanted to spend time with her.

There was no place for someone like Dina in his life anyway. To do his job was to be alone. End of story.

"Why are you here, Dina?" Derek's voice sounded like sandpaper in his ears. If that made him sound like a cold bastard, it was probably for the better. He pushed a glass of water across the table toward her and crossed his arms over his chest. Whatever he felt toward her didn't matter. His only concern was damage control, not on how much he enjoyed having her in his home where he could keep her safe. His jaw clenched.

Damage control. Right.

She blinked and slowly sat up. Her hand trembled as she reached for the water, but she masked it by quickly grabbing the glass and bringing it to her lips. He watched the movement of her throat as she swallowed. Dina's gaze fixated on the ashtray containing the remnants of his joint and the burning incense on the kitchen island.

Dina looked back at him. "What were you doing before I showed up?"

"Talking to my mother." His mother had been dead for over a

decade, but she was one of his spirit guides. Regular communication strengthened their psychic bond.

Dina nodded and then her forehead wrinkled. "What did you ask me?"

"Why did I find you passed out on my doorstep in the middle of the night?" He had to know what she'd seen and what she remembered, and then get her out of here as soon as possible. Someone like her shouldn't know about the Beyond.

She picked at one of her perfectly manicured nails. "I'm not sure…I haven't partied in a long time, so I must have just overdone it."

"What did you take?" Derek smoked but had never used anything hard. Obviously, she was far from an angel, but it surprised him that Dina would.

"Some China." She didn't look up at him but rubbed her hands up and down her arms as if she was still cold.

Derek grabbed a throw blanket off the recliner and handed it to her. "How much?"

Dina didn't answer. She looked at him with a bruised expression before her lips thinned. "I'm not going to OD if that's what you're concerned about."

"Good." He could look at her and tell she wasn't going to overdose, but if that's the only reason she thought he cared… fine. "But you didn't answer my first question."

"I came because it's safe here." Quiet words he had to strain to hear. He opened his mouth to reply, but she continued, "Something about you makes me feel safe—it always has."

Derek wished that she were right, that she was here because of him. He pointed to the character etched into the doorframe of his apartment. "It's not me—it's this building. That symbol means peace." The rune blocked all outside psychic energy so people who served as mediums or Channels, people like him, could have somewhere to go and recharge without unsolicited interference. This part of Denver had history, the ground, the buildings, everything around them, and the more colorful the history the greater the psychic imprint.

Dina stared at the rune. He wanted to know what she saw, if she had any touch of the sight...no. He wouldn't go there. The opiates in her system were the only thing that had brought her here. Sudden spikes in energy levels, like those brought on by drug use, drew earthbound spirits like moths to a flame. Great news for him—he wouldn't have a vindictive spirit waiting for him next time he left the bookstore.

"Have you seen them?" Dina asked, as she set her empty glass back on the coffee table.

Derek stilled. "Seen who?"

Midnight eyes bore into him, and he could see the fire in them. "The ghosts."

Well, hell. Most psychotropic drugs, especially taken in quantity, created a temporary psychic-like sight. Usually, the other side effects kept the user in the euphoric dreamlike state, not knowing that the phantoms they saw were often real beings.

Dina trusted him enough to be honest, but he wasn't going to be able to return the favor.

"What did you see?" he asked instead. He couldn't tell her that he did see them and that his real job was disposing of spirits when they started affecting the real world.

Dina looked back at the symbol above the door. "They were

in my head…making me see things. I didn't think they could follow me, but they stayed with me until I got here."

Derek drank in her profile. She tucked a strand of her hair back behind her pierced ear and pursed her lips. His subconscious wanted to linger on her lips and what they might taste like. Instead, he moved to sit in the chair across from her. "I read somewhere that drugs make it easier for spirits to manipulate and influence you. Is that what happened, Dina?" Saying her name sounded just as right as it always did.

She crossed her legs in front of her and wove her fingers together on her knee. Her toned legs disappeared into black boots that immediately made him think thoughts he shouldn't. Dina was doing a very good job of controlling his attention. Even as that thought left his head, she slowly began to unbutton her coat, revealing inch after inch of creamy pale skin.

"Knock off the seduction act, Dina. I'm not interested." Derek was surprised at how firm his voice sounded because nothing was further than the truth. "Now, tell me what happened."

Dina didn't look at him, but she didn't continue undressing either.

When she finally spoke, her words were cautious. "Ginger had a client cancel, so we were all partying and took a hit to keep the party going, you know? I started feeling sick, so I left and that was when I started seeing things." She finally made eye contact with him. "The sidewalk was bleeding."

The Department had strict rules. He could only bring up his sight if the other person had exhibited clear signs that they were a well-versed psychic user, or were experienced in physical psychic applications. Derek wanted her to have the sight—to be like him–but nothing she had said fit the guidelines. "Where were you?"

Dina glanced away, and swept her fingers over the arm of the couch brushing away dirt that didn't exist. "Around. Have you ever seen a ghost, Derek?"

His expressionless mask nearly failed when she said his name. It rolled off her tongue easily, as if it was common for her to say it. "I've never done hard drugs, Dina, and never will. The hallucinations you saw were probably nothing more than a bad trip." It was an exercise in self-control for Derek to stand up and walk away as if her experience didn't matter. He grabbed his cell off the kitchen counter. "Is there someone I can call to come get you?"

Her shoulders straightened. She probably hadn't been expecting him to throw her out. "Would you mind if I just crashed here for the night?"

Derek should have said no and called her a cab, but he didn't. His resolve crumbled almost instantly. "Fine. I'll get you a pillow." He pointed down the hall. "The bathroom is in there if you need it."

It was going to be a long night, knowing she was in his living room and not being able to touch her. Derek swore under his breath as he closed his bedroom door. He should have offered Dina his bed.

#

The next morning, Dina was sleeping soundly when Derek got up to open the store. Mondays were always a slow starting day for the business. He wasn't like the box stores; there was no coffee shop attached to his place, so the morning commuters bypassed him to hit up the neighborhood 7-11 or Starbucks.

Chester, one of his regular customers, was talking about the buyout of an e-reader company when he heard Dina come down the stairs. Luckily, Chester stood with his back to the stairs so the conversation didn't lag, but Derek's attention was completely focused on Dina. She smiled at him and then disappeared into the new age section. There were several plush chairs back there and he could clearly picture her curled up in one. The first time he met her had been back there. She had been reading a book about France. Her excitement about traveling, her smile—everything about her was intoxicating, so he asked her out. Dina had sheepishly looked around and told him what she did for a living. At the time, she had at least had the decency to look slightly upset.

Chester trailed off mid-sentence and Derek followed his gaze outside. A red Porsche had pulled up and parked in a handicapped spot directly outside his store. The driver got out of the car, and its lights flashed once as he locked it. Derek scowled. The man was exactly what he expected, middle-aged with an expensive suit and a strut that told the world of his money, just in case you missed the other clues.

Both he and Chester watched as the man looked around as if making sure he was in the right place before walking purposely toward the bookstore. The door chimed as the Porsche driver entered. His suit fit well and his shoes probably cost more than Derek's entire wardrobe, but otherwise he looked totally ordinary—nothing unique about him at all.

Porsche guy scanned the store, and his gaze didn't linger on either Derek or Chester. Derek caught movement out of the corner of his eye and watched as the man's face lit up in a grin. Dina. Of course, he was here for her. He was exactly the kind of man who would employ her. Derek's hand fisted under the counter.

"How are you, baby?" The stranger's deep voice echoed around the store.

Dina appeared from behind the bookshelves and gave Derek a small smile as she embraced the other male. "I'm great, Rich. Thanks for coming."

Idiot guy's name would be Rich. Dina had a stack of books tucked under her arm. She had never been one to buy much—a cozy mystery or romance here or there, nothing heavy, but the tomes in her hand were thick, reference books of some kind.

As Dina approached the counter Chester wandered away to look at magazines. She moved like a dancer, graceful, hypnotic. Derek frowned as Rich stalked behind her. His gold-ringed hand lingered on her hip and then drifted lower to caress the curves of her behind.

Dina placed the books on the counter, and Derek saw the other man's eyes wander over the titles.

A bark of harsh laughter broke through the quiet. "You don't need that shit, baby. You're better than that." Rich tugged her against his body and looked at Derek for the first time. Apparently, he wasn't concerned by what he saw. Part of Derek's job was to blend in, look normal, be average. The glasses he wore were only a prop, he could see just fine, but paired with his medium build and nothing-special clothing, he looked the part he played—a harmless bookstore owner. At that moment, Derek would have given anything to be able to grab the other guy by the throat and slam his face into the checkout counter.

Rich smirked and looked down at the woman between them. "Come on, let's do breakfast." An emotion far hotter than hunger bloomed in his eyes. "I'm starved."

"But I…" She never got to finish. Rich planted a kiss full on her lips. She didn't pull away, and it was several seconds before Derek cleared his throat.

Dina didn't meet his eyes as she and Rich walked out of the store.

Derek wanted to break something. Instead, he calmly picked up Dina's books and moved to put them back. He took one step and stiffened. Without breathing, he flipped through the stack of titles and his heart sank. Every one of them was on ghosts, spirit manipulation, the Beyond, or how to control clairvoyant sight.

He swore and ran to the front door, but they were gone. Maybe if he hadn't been such a jerk last night she would have come clean about what she was doing. Derek scanned the titles again as he put them away. Whatever Dina was mixed up in, Rich had known about it, and she was in way over her head.

Now she was out there with only tidbits of information doing only God knows what.

He'd track her down and make her tell him what was going on. Then he would help her. Derek's job as an Agent for the Department was to safeguard Americans from paranormal threats. The fact that it was Dina just increased his exigency.

#

Dina was probably the most abstinent personal escort in history. Richard had ended up being called into an urgent meeting, so instead of "breakfast" at his apartment she had gone home. Rich was a full-blown sitophilic and into sploshing. He usually paid Dina to come over, get naked, and rub food over her body so he could eat it. Occasionally he would throw cream pies at her, but they never had sex. He preferred to do the deed himself—apparently if they didn't have intercourse Richard wasn't cheating on his wife.

The few hours of sleep she had managed to get helped, but she still felt off, like some part of her brain had been scrambled. Whatever meager confidence she'd rebuilt in the early morning hours, laying on Derek's sofa, had dissipated the more she had read in his books. She was no trained medium. Half of what they mentioned she hadn't been familiar with, but at least she was better prepared than she had been yesterday.

Richard had come back for her in the afternoon, and it was more of the usual, except baked beans this time. She was a prop, a luxury that allowed him to have his cake and eat it too. Richard didn't care about her in particular. She was a means to an end and nothing more. That thought disturbed her more than it should. Her work had never bothered her, but then again someone like Derek had never cared for her before. If she closed her eyes, she could see his face—the hot emotion that had swum in his eyes when Richard kissed her, and then the remote coldness that had taken its place from one blink to the next.

The problem was Dina had liked the heat she had seen in Derek's eyes, and wanted to be able to do something about it. It was her luck that the one guy she wanted straight up told her he wasn't interested. She couldn't be *with* Derek anyway, she was with Richard.

Dina felt the sting of her nails as they bit into her palm and turned her attention on the man next to her. Richard's long fingers could have belonged to a piano player and had probably never done a hard day's work in their lifetime. Those same fingers squeezed her thigh as the Porsche came to a rolling stop in front of the mansion.

Richard's blue-eyed gaze fixated on her breasts, but he eventually dragged his focus up to her face. The hand that had been on her leg moved back to the wheel. "You know I appreciate you working this out for me, right?"

Dina nodded. Her foot touched the bag of supplies she had brought with her.

"Good. If you could save on the drama, and get it taken care of tonight that would be great. I need to have my crews in here first thing on Wednesday, and it would be nice if I could do a walk-through with the contractor tomorrow."

"Rich…I…"

He silenced her with a finger over her lips. "Don't screw this up. I need those superstitious assholes back in here and working by Wednesday or I lose millions." Richard traced his finger over her bottom lip before dropping his hand to her throat and then lower to the rise of her breast. "If you do this for me, I see an apartment in Paris in your future."

His phone rang and he didn't hesitate to answer. He dismissed her with a slight wave of his hand. Dina stared at him for a moment longer. He knew she had always wanted to see Paris. She undid her seatbelt and stepped out into the evening. The chill creeping into her bones had nothing to do with the sun dipping behind the mountains, and everything to do with what she was about to attempt. She shut the car door with a quiet snick, and Richard's ostentatious car drove away a second later.

Ghostly Attraction

Steeling herself, she turned toward the house. It was the kind of house she'd dreamed about living in as little girl. Richard had told her it was a Queen Anne style. Its red brick exterior was accented with fish scale shingles and a steeply pitched black roof. The front door was off the wrap-around porch, and a round tower stood sentry opposite several monumental chimneys. Once Richard restored it, it would be a dream, but right now, it was her nightmare. She needed to get this over with.

From what she could remember of last night's fiasco there were several distinct ghosts, or spirits according to Derek's books. She needed to get them to leave. They were disrupting the energy inside to the point that the construction workers noticed. Terrified of what they were feeling, even if they couldn't see anything, they had refused to work. Dina had seen and interacted with ghosts all her life, and never once had she gotten pushback from them. She asked them to leave, told them to go to the light, and that was that. But here, this damned house was happily haunted, and the ghosts were perfectly content on this side of the Beyond.

Dina took a deep breath and put the key in the lock. The door opened with a groan, but she stepped through into the reception hall. The dank darkness of the house instantly converged on her. A broad staircase curved in front of her to the upper rooms, but the top of the landing and the two hallways leading off the foyer were bathed in shadow. Residual sunshine filtered through the partially rotted drapes and helped focus her attention. She could do this. Dina closed the front door and sealed her fate.

She arranged the candles she'd brought in the pattern she had seen in the book and carefully lit each one in turn. Sitting cross-legged in the middle of them, Dina closed her eyes and took several deep breaths. Slowly, cautiously, she opened her senses, and tried to picture and taste the energy of the house. At first it was calm and clear, but that was what tricked her yesterday. Dina remained still and pictured her own mind, secure and strong inside her skull. Whatever had jacked with her yesterday would have another thing coming if they thought they could take her twice.

Focusing her reflection back outward, she felt it. The growing heaviness, as if the air itself was squeezing her. Discord and restless energy was next. They assaulted her senses in waves, each one stronger than the last.

She started to shake. Every breath of the fetid air felt like she was breathing sawdust. Knowing that the dust particles weren't real didn't make them any less palpable as they coated her lungs. Dina clenched her teeth and tried to follow the directions she had memorized. Visualizing a golden light coming down from above, she bathed in it and tried to feel its warmth and healing. Dina imagined she was pulling it within herself, letting it build. Now she just had to stay calm, hold on to it, and let it flow out from her to cleanse the house and ward off the spirits.

Her breathing echoed around her, raspy and uneven. Her heart hammered in her chest, but with a long exhale, she envisioned the light within her spreading out, filling the room and the house.

It worked…for a few seconds. The air was fresh again, and sawdust free, but the farther she spread her light, the weaker it got. Dina's radiating energy faltered just beyond the foyer.

Then the skittering started. Dina knew that sound. Insects—

lots of them, moving over plastered walls and hardwood. Fear shot up her spine, and her bowed head snapped up as her eyes opened. The shadows of the room moved. They detached from the corners to swarm toward her. Thousands of bugs crawled and took to the air. She squeezed her eyes shut, but that didn't stop them from attacking her face. Dina would have screamed but then she would have swallowed them. She tried to stand. Their exoskeletons exploded under the soles of her boots like Pop-Rocks. Her hands swatted and clawed at her exposed skin, but the second she scraped them off, more took their place. They probed around her nose and in her ears. Her lungs burned from her stinted breaths as she blindly lurched forward.

She fell, but the sharp pain of hitting the floor never came. The insects vanished, and Dina sucked a full breath into her starving lungs and opened her eyes. Pitch black surrounded her. Gasping, she sat back and tried to gather her wits.

If she could figure out which way the floorboards were facing, she could orient herself. Presumably, she was still in the main room, and she couldn't be far from the door. Reaching tentatively out, she felt nothing. Her knees were bent underneath her body, but there was no floor, no hardwood—it was just emptiness. It made no difference if her eyes were open or closed, what she saw remained the same. She was suspended in a void of black.

Dina choked on a sob. No one would notice or even care if she died. It would be an inconvenience to Richard to have to remove and explain her corpse, assuming there would be anything left of her to be found. Her lungs expanded and contracted, but slowly as if they were full of tar. She could taste the metallic energy of her blood and wondered if she was dying. She didn't want to die.

She hadn't thanked Derek.

An unseen hammer cracked against the walls of security and strength she had imagined around her innermost mind. The walls bowed and splintered. Sharp pain exploded inside her brain, but her silent screams were absorbed by the nothingness that entombed her.

Cackling laughter surrounded her. It echoed in her head as if it was coming from everywhere at once. Dina blinked and her sight returned in a nauseating wave. Her fingers, outstretched in front of her, twitched and then lay still. Wetness dripped onto her face, but she couldn't wipe it away. The warm fluid was too viscous to be water or tears. It was red as it ran into her eyes. The coppery-tasting liquid filled her nose and covered her mouth. She was drowning in it.

The last thing Dina saw as blood continued to rain down was the small frame of a child leaning over her, bathed in the deathly gloom of the mansion. Cold pressure cuddled against her chest as if the little girl's spirit was trying to lend Dina strength, but then there was nothing.

#

Derek hated crowds, and the club scene had never been his thing. He was sitting at the second floor bar, a smaller, less flashy version than the one on the main floor and rooftop. Behind him was a patent leather couch that fit into the corner and wrapped its way around the wall before it disappeared deeper into the club. Dina and her friends always sat there. Except tonight, it was empty.

It was just a few minutes past 1 o'clock when Ginger Cox, a so-called "Danish princess" per her ad online, finally came up the stairs. Every male head in the room turned and watched her walk over to the bar. She was true to her photos, blonde hair, long legs, mile high stilettos, and a barely-there outfit. A redhead followed and received the same treatment from the crowd.

Once they were sipping drinks and sitting in their booth, Derek made his move. He approached the table, smiled, and gestured to the seat across from them in the alcove. "Do you mind?" he asked, making eye contact with Ginger.

A coy smile flitted over her ruby red lips. "Go ahead, sugar." Ginger didn't extend her hand but leaned toward him. Her ample cleavage threatened to spill out of her top. "What can we do for you tonight?"

Derek kept his gaze on the woman's face as he slid into the chair across from her. "I'm looking for Dina."

The two women exchanged a quick glance. Ginger looked him up and down as she sat back into the booth. "You're bookstore Derek."

He nodded slowly. Neither of the women across from him had ever been in his store. "I own the bookstore at Colfax and Washington."

"She's talked about you." Ginger drummed her long nails against the silver table in front of them.

That Dina would have mentioned him was a surprise. The hope inside him grew before he could smash it down and lock it away.

"Well, Derek, I don't know where she is, but she's probably with Rich…" When the redhead nodded in agreement, Ginger continued, "Dina's on call with him, so she's his whenever he wants."

"He won't do in-calls." Derek's confusion must have been visible on his face because the redhead clarified. "Richard is too proud to be seen at her apartment, so everything is done at his place."

By some miracle, he kept his face impassive.

Ginger leaned forward and lowered her voice. "Is this business or personal for you?"

Both. He had a job to do. But the very masculine core of him wanted Dina for himself, and he wasn't going to let her go once he had her. "It's personal."

A smirk bloomed on Ginger's lips. "You're not her type. No offense, but you just need to let her go...Unless you have some sort of freaky fetish you're into?" She raised an eyebrow.

Thrown off by her last statement, Derek shook his head. Fetishes...was that what Dina specialized in? Maybe he didn't know her as well as he imagined.

"This thing she has with Rich is really good—it's what we all want. So whatever has that look in your eye, let it go. Girls like us—like Dina—aren't for men like you."

Like hell. He wouldn't be giving up that easy. "Right, well if you see her, tell her to call me. It's very important." He handed them each a business card and stood.

Ginger rose and followed him toward the stairs. Her hand on his shoulder made him pause. "His full name is Richard Jensen, and he works in real estate," was all she said, and then she was gone, disappearing back into the throng of people.

Walking out of the club and heading back toward Colfax was a blur. Ginger's comments circled in his head like vultures. They picked apart his already frayed thoughts. No matter what was or wasn't between him and Dina, he needed to find her. Something had happened. Rubbing his knuckles over his heart, he could sense it. The knowing.

Derek pulled out his cell phone and placed in a coded call to Dispatch. "I need a full work up on Richard Jensen: 40s, white male, blonde hair, blue eyes. He works in real estate." He paused while Dispatch confirmed the information. "Send anything you get to my phone."

He ended the call and looked around, momentarily disoriented. He always walked home on 15th street, but he was on 14th tonight. The Convention Center was lit up, and its floodlights made the dramatic architectural overhang look like a white pyramid against the black of the night sky. If only it would point the way to wherever Dina was.

No matter the time of year, he usually enjoyed walking by City Park, the amphitheater and Capitol, but not tonight. Every second that went by unease and dread wormed its way deeper into his chest. The park was far from empty. Most of the larger trees had occupants under their branches, people either bedding down for the night or those just looking to get out of the glow of the streetlights.

The traffic light changed at Lincoln and Derek made his way across. A couple hurried by in the other direction but didn't glance his way. He should have driven. Then he would already be back at home and could be tracking down Richard Jensen. Out of habit, his gaze wandered to the barely concealed shadow underneath a large tree adjacent to the looming Capitol. He nearly stumbled.

Dina. He ran to her side and carefully turned her over. Her

eyes were wide open but unseeing. She stared straight ahead as he brushed the dirt off her face. The slow rise and fall of her chest worked to calm him, but he needed to get her home. A thin trail of blood led from both of her ears, and clear fluid was drying under her nose. He had seen countless rookie Channels with the same injuries. The dried blood caked under her nails was presumably her own, judging by the still-bleeding scratches on both of her arms—classic ghostlighting trauma. Derek swore. If he hadn't pushed her away, she never would have been hurt.

#

Derek had just placed the cup of soup and water on the table when Dina came out of his bathroom. Steam billowed out from around her like a caress. She stole his breath away.

She was wearing his t-shirt and boxers, and Derek tried to commit the image to memory. Dina smiled tentatively as she approached. Just the way she moved her body promised the sweetest kind of pleasure.

He shook his head. She had just gone through hell, and he had a job to do. "I hope you like chicken noodle." He gestured to the bowl of soup. Taking a seat opposite her, he saw Dina nod, and then open her mouth and close it as if she wanted to say something but decided against it.

Dina sipped her water and then ate a small spoonful of soup. Their eyes met.

His brainpower stalled at the raw emotion he saw, and he said the first thing that came to mind. "You don't advertise online."

Her eyes widened in surprise. "What?"

"You're not on any of the websites for, you know…" He glanced down at the table then back up at her. "Escorting."

A small smile warmed her face. "You looked me up?"

"I needed to find you—make sure you were okay."

She drank some water. "For the last year I've been exclusively with Richard, so I haven't needed to advertise."

An image of Dina dressed in a rubber latex cat suit filled Derek's head, and he swallowed, looking away from her.

She ate another bite of soup. "Thank you for coming for me." Her gaze caught and held his again. "For caring about what happened to me."

Derek nodded, unsure of what to say. He sure as hell wasn't going to tell her that he was in love with her, so he went for another truth. "I'm what you would call a medium—in my business we refer to ourselves as Channels." Dina's spoon stopped, suspended in front of her mouth. "I work for an agency whose purpose is to protect humans from paranormal threats. We monitor and dispose of spirits who put people's lives in danger."

She slowly lowered her spoon. "But you own this store?"

"Yes, because we need safe zones." He waved in the direction of the doorway's ward symbol. "It's a block against all outside supernatural influences, so it gives us the peace we need to rebuild our mental shields after an assignment."

Dina was quiet and stirred her soup absently for several seconds. "You didn't believe me yesterday."

"When you said you were tripping it was an easier explanation. My agency has very strict guidelines on who we can approach—they have to exhibit clear signs of having the sight or we have to witness their abilities. Unfortunately, when drugs get involved it's not easy to differentiate." Derek got up and started to pace.

Dina traced the wood grain of the table with her fingertip. "I've seen ghosts ever since I could remember." She swallowed. "It was something I learned very quickly to not mention. Ever. It came out by accident when I was…with my client. Then later he asked me to look into one of his new properties, which was supposedly haunted. The construction crew refused to work after only two days because bad things happened to them. Not just tools missing, but accidents and injuries…"

"So you thought you could handle it alone, with no training?" Derek stopped and braced his hands on the back of his vacated seat.

Pools of the deepest blue threatened to drown him in their depths. "I've never had a problem before. The ghosts, or spirits, whatever, just went. I told them to leave, and they did." Dina shrugged. Derek swore under his breath and resumed his pacing. "I told Rich I'd do this for him and now that I've made it into a bigger mess, I want to fix it." She sipped the last of her soup and placed the bowl back on the table. "I need to. There's a child stuck in there. She should be with her family."

"I'll help you any way I can, but you have to trust me and do what I tell you."

Dina nodded and sat up straighter. "Okay. What do I do?"

Derek took a deep breath and released it as he sat back down across from her. Never in a million years had he expected to have this conversation. "Well, at least one of the spirits you've encountered is using ghostlighting as an offensive tactic." Dina's forehead wrinkled. "It's a mental attack that destroys your perception of reality. You see things that aren't real."

"The hallucinations."

"Exactly. Most spirits use this form of assault as more of an annoyance, like when you swear you tripped over something, but there wasn't anything there." She nodded. "They obscure objects from view: the bottom step, your keys, whatever. We see that sort of thing more often than not with poltergeists." Derek leaned forward. "What you've experienced is more advanced and coming from either a malevolent presence or a very defensive one."

"There's more than one. I can't tell you exactly how many, but it's an older male who hijacked my brain." Dina frowned and rubbed her temples. "I think he is well aware of what he's doing. He and the others are concealing the little girl's presence." She spun a ring she wore on her middle finger in circles. "What agency do you work for?" Dina asked, looking up from her ring.

Derek pulled at the suddenly tight collar of his shirt. "The Department of Homeland Security. We're an unpublished branch."

"Like SD-6 from *Alias*?"

He smiled. "Yeah. Something like that." He crossed his arms over his chest and watched as Dina's eyes followed the movement. She told him he looked good in this shirt months ago, so he'd worn it once a week since then. "So start at the beginning and tell me everything you remember."

Her memories of both encounters were so vivid he felt as if he'd been there with her. If he had been Dina wouldn't have been hurt, wouldn't have had to experience the terror of ghostlighting. Her voice waivered when she got to the child spirit, and there was something far deeper than just the experience at the house motivating her, but he wouldn't ask. Not now.

When she finished Dina's hands were clenched in her lap. Derek hated himself for discounting her and punching a hole in her trust. He would do whatever it took to make it up to her. He pulled down *The Psychic Investigators Casebook* from the bookshelf and placed it in front of her.

"If you're going to keep dabbling with the Beyond you'll want to read this." Derek stood behind her with his arms on either side of her chair. Mere inches separated them, and her warmth soaked into his skin. He flipped through the first few chapters and left the book open on chapter five, which dealt with the ghosts of children.

"From what you've said, we're dealing with more than just earthbound spirits. I have a buddy that works for the Assessor's office. We'll go down tomorrow and look through the property's records. Then we'll have a better idea of what we're up against."

Dina's finger traced over the page he left open in front of her. "Can I borrow this?" she asked.

"You can have it."

#

Derek's car was exactly what Dina expected, clean and economical. Even though it was only a half mile to the mansion, he had wanted to drive. He didn't want to have to walk back if their energy was drained after the release.

It was the first time she had seen him in anything other than his khakis and collared shirts. The black long sleeve t-shirt and dark cargo pants fit him—well, the other side of him. The man sitting next to her was Derek the covert agent who saved the world from paranormal threats.

He had opened her door for her too, and it hadn't been awkward or forced, just something he apparently did when he took women in his car. His respect for her, even knowing what she was, was a nice surprise. The entire day he had treated her as an equal, and anything she hadn't known he had explained without condescension.

A prominent physician had built Richard's mansion in 1890. It had changed hands and eventually became a restaurant in 1940. When the restaurant failed, another doctor had bought the property and turned it into a medical clinic. Derek hadn't seemed concerned about the possible lingering imprint caused by the clinic; he had only smiled, shrugged and said he'd handle it.

Dina had tried to contact Richard about what was going on, but her calls had gone straight to voicemail. Just listening to his recorded voice before she left her message had seemed oddly distant, like something from another life. She wouldn't miss him if she decided to do something else with her life. He'd only ever been a business arrangement.

Derek parked just south of the property and turned to face her. His features appeared stronger, harsher today. "I want you to know that whatever happens in here will be fine. I'll take care of it. If it gets to be too much, you say the word and I'll get you out, okay?"

She couldn't read his eyes, so she just nodded. She believed him.

Derek shut off the car and stared through the windshield. "Your boyfriend is here."

Dina followed his gaze and frowned. Richard's Porsche was sitting in front of the property. "He's a *client*." She opened her door. "Let me handle this."

Derek's phone chimed and he quickly silenced it, but she closed the door before he could say anything. Dina heard a window roll down, but Derek stayed in the car.

Richard was leaning against the side of his Porsche, and he watched her approach. The scowl on his face deepened with every step she took. When she stopped in front of him, his eyes narrowed as his gaze dropped down her body.

"What the hell are you wearing?" he asked, as if the very idea that she would wear jeans and a hoodie was unacceptable.

She shrugged. "I wasn't planning on seeing you tonight. Did you get my message?"

Richard ignored her question and glared at Derek's car. "How much is he paying you?"

"He's not, Richard. It's not like that." Dina looked back, picturing Derek's face in the dark interior. She found herself picking her words carefully. "He's just helping me out..."

"You spent the night with him, didn't you?" There was possessiveness in Rich's expression that she had never seen before. "I paid for exclusive rights."

Dina rolled her eyes. "Who I hang out with in my free time is none of your business and isn't stipulated in our contract. He's helping me get rid of *your* ghosts, Rich. Let it go."

Richard's spine straightened, and he glanced around the block. "Don't say that word, Dina. Don't you dare." He grabbed her arm and pulled her closer to him. With every one of his breaths, the stench of stale alcohol grew. "I don't pay you to talk, and I don't appreciate you screwing around on my dime."

"He's a friend, Richard." Dina pulled away, but he didn't release her. His fingers bit into her bicep like a vice.

"No dickhead is going to be *just friends* with a piece of ass like you. If you think you're *just friends* you're kidding yourself."

"Are you drunk?" Dina tried to see his face, but Rich's free arm came around her and hauled her against his chest. She could feel the press of his erection against her abdomen. "Richard, what's going on?" He had never acted like this before.

Richard fisted his hand in her hair and jerked her head toward him until they were nose to nose. "Everything in your fake life is going to crumble, you'll be alone and naked, lying in a pile of your own puke." He barked out a bitter laugh. "You'll die on Colfax, bitch, and no one will even care. You're just another worthless soul on that godforsaken street."

Fierce anger burned through Dina like fire. She shoved against Richard's chest until she finally succeeded in untangling herself and slapped him across the face.

"What the hell, Richard?"

"His wife filed for divorce." Derek words made her jump. She hadn't heard him get out of his car. "Her lawyers found out about you, so she's taking everything."

Richard threw himself at Derek with a guttural sound. Derek didn't even blink. His punch slammed Richard's head backward with a crack. The momentum of the hit knocked Rich against his car where he limply slid down the passenger door.

Dina stared at Richard, aware of Derek standing silent and strong behind her. She watched a drop of blood drip from Richard's split lip and fall onto his pristine white shirt. Richard would recover, move on, and build a new family. But she couldn't go back. She was so sick and tired of being lonely.

She looked down at her tennis shoes. "You know, that's my

greatest fear."

"What is?"

"Being alone." Dina turned and looked at the man behind her. "Dying alone." Every day she was so alone, even though people surrounded her. Nothing was personal. No one cared beyond the interaction, and the second it was over they forgot her—everyone except Derek.

He cocked his head to the side and studied her for several seconds before speaking. "I don't think that's something you have to worry about."

Derek looked at the house then back at her. "Do you want me to take care of this?"

She shook her head. "No. I want to help. I promised myself I would." She would get the little girl back to her family.

He didn't say anything, just turned toward the front door and offered her his arm. Dina took a deep breath and put her arm through his. Daylight scoured the outside of the mansion, and for the first time it just looked like a sad house in need of restoration.

Before she could push open the door, Derek released her arm. "There's something I want to say."

She turned so she could see his face. His gorgeous brown eyes searched hers, but his expression was so solemn it made her heart ache. "Um." He shoved a hand roughly through his dark hair. "Look, I like you, Dina, and I don't want anything to happen to you. So be careful, okay?"

Dina's heart stuttered in her chest. "I remember you very distinctly saying that you weren't interested in me."

His mouth quirked up in a lopsided grin that melted her

insides. "I lied."

It was the first time in her life she was truly speechless. She grinned like an idiot.

Stepping over the threshold was almost as exhilarating as Derek's announcement. She was here to help, and she now had the support she needed to do it right. They were going to do this together. She grabbed Derek's hand and took a step forward. He gave her fingers a little squeeze and didn't let go as they walked from room to room until they ended up back on the main floor. The dining room was apparently the heart of the house, and now that she was more aware she could feel the potency of the energy there.

Derek released her hand and walked over to a window in the corner. He opened it wide so the sunshine and fresh air could spill into the room. He nodded at her. "Now, let's do this."

Dina arranged her candles, moving them centimeters at a time until they were perfect. "Sit by me?"

"Sure." Derek moved and sat opposite her in the middle of the floor, surrounded by her lit candles.

She scooted closer to him until they were almost touching, but stopped short, unsure. Just being close to Derek was far more intimate than being with Richard had ever been.

Derek reached out and took hold of her hands. "Focus on this. Us. We're here together." He closed his eyes. His strength seemed to flow into her from their entwined hands, and it gave her more courage. He took a deep breath and released it slowly. "Feel the house. Its past, present, and focus on its future. Got it?"

"Yes." She could tap into an inanimate object's energy. Sure. No problem.

"Okay. Do what we talked about. I'll deal with the other spirits." Derek's voice took on a cadence that soothed her, so when she focused she was almost immediately sucked into the spirit realm. The realm itself was more of an overlay on top of the natural world, but to interact within it you had to take down your mental barriers. At least that was how she was going to do it. Derek's version was far more complicated since he was going to be dealing with all of the malicious energy in the house.

Derek's warmth washed over her, and underneath it, his presence, his spirit. But this time, when the air condensed against her skin, she was expecting it. The restless chill of energy crept up her back, but its frozen fingers didn't settle into her spine.

Cracks appeared in the floor all around her, and insects poured out like water, thousands upon thousands. With a deep groan, the floor closed up and the bugs vanished.

Dina looked around. It was just her, standing in the room. Except a transparent bubble enclosed her, covering her and about three feet in every direction. Black smoke hit her defensive shell and curled up as it bounced off. Derek was protecting her.

"Hello? Are you here?" Dina asked. She made her way up the stairs to the landing where Derek had said the little girl's presence was the strongest. She focused on sending thoughts of compassion toward the girl's essence. Derek had said she could just speak to the girl in her mind, but she thought Derek might be able to hear her too if she spoke aloud. She didn't want him to worry.

The little girl materialized, and as soon as she did, Dina's bubble expanded to include her. She looked to be about ten. Her hair was softly curled and hung to her shoulders. The sailor-style dress she wore had a large silk bow in the front that matched the one in her hair. Nothing was in color; it was as if a black and white image had come to life.

The spirit looked around and frowned. "You're back, but where are the others? The nasties? Can they not get in here?" The spirit touched Derek's shield and the bubble shimmered a brilliant red. She jerked her ghostly finger back as if burned. Her pale eyes widened, and she turned back to Dina. "There is much power in this."

Dina nodded. "That's my friend Derek—he's helping me help you."

"Help me?" The words were slow coming off the spirit's tongue, as if she wasn't sure of their taste.

"Yes. I can take you to see your family again," Dina said. She bent at the waist, her hands on her knees so she could be at eye level with the child.

The girl turned away, and buried her small face in her hands. "No, you can't."

Dina's heart broke, and she reached out to touch the girl. When her fingers fell on her small bony shoulder, it was real and so fragile. A shudder shook the child's body.

"It's okay, sweetheart. Let me help you," Dina whispered, and continued to focus her love and compassion toward the lost soul in front of her.

The spirit remained turned away, but her body relaxed under Dina's hand. "You know what I want?"

"What?" Dina rubbed soothing circles on the girl's back.

The air inside the bubble shifted, growing heavy and cold. A faint hint of baby powder brushed her senses. Dina dropped her hand, and looked around in alarm. Derek's protection was still in place and holding, so it wasn't coming from the outside. She glanced back at the child.

The primly dressed girl was gone. Color had bled into her features. Her neatly curled brown hair had come free of its ribbon and morphed into a snarled mess. The sailor dress was navy and white, but soaked in red. It dripped from the bottom hem, leaving macabre confetti around the floor at the child's feet.

Dina swallowed and took a step backward. The girl smiled. It lit her eyes with an evil glow that froze the blood in Dina's veins. A perfume of rusted iron filled the air. It overpowered the baby powder.

"Would you like to play?" The girl's question was spoken in a singsong tone that made Dina want to run.

"What did you do?" Dina asked with only the barest tremble in her voice.

In a movement that was too smooth, the child brought a crimson-drenched hand up to her mouth and delicately licked each of her fingers as if they were the sweetest tasting lollipop. Dina's heart pounded against her ribs with bruising force.

"My sisters were very naughty, always talking in church and never sharing their toys." The girl took a step toward Dina. "They never got in trouble though, but I did. It was always my fault." The smile shifted from deranged to something so angelic it made Dina want to throw up. "It was quiet when they stopped screaming."

"You don't have to be this way," Dina said just to say something, anything to buy herself more time to think. Dealing with a psycho murdering ten-year-old wasn't something she had prepared for.

The spirit took another step toward her. "I like it. It's so much fun." She lunged.

Instincts Dina didn't know she had flared to life. Sidestepping, Dina grabbed the back of the girl's neck and used her forward momentum to drive her into Derek's force field.

As soon as the spirit contacted its surface, a piercing scream erupted from her lips. She struggled and thrashed, her hands clawing behind her as her legs kicked out at Dina. The surface of the shield shuddered but held, flashing a deathly black and violent red. Dina didn't let go. It took all of her strength to keep the girl in place. The girl's shrieks faded into a desperate gurgling. Her panicked onslaught turned into a weak flailing of her limbs until she went utterly still.

Dina sagged under the weight of what she had done. "Oh God." She jerked away from the child spirit, and its body crumpled to the floor like a broken doll.

A gentle voice spoke from behind her. "Be at peace, Dina." She whirled around.

Standing next to her on the landing was a woman dressed in faded jeans and a loose-fitting top straight out of the seventies. Her face was angular but striking. She wasn't beautiful in a typical sense but attractive nonetheless. Her brown eyes were kind but strong like Derek's.

"I'm here to help you." Her warmth immediately consumed the piercing cold that surrounded Dina.

Dina took a shaky step away from the child. The woman moved to kneel down at the girl's side, an expression of sorrow contorted her features before grim determination took its place.

Leaning over, she ran her hands over the other spirit's form. The woman began to chant in a language Dina didn't understand.

Laying a hand on the child's bloody dress, she closed her eyes, and after just a few seconds the girl dissolved in a mist of light. The woman looked up and met Dina's eyes.

Dina opened her mouth, but the words wouldn't come. The woman gave her a small smile and rose. "She is where she belongs now. We have done all we could do."

Finally, Dina's lips moved. "Who are you?"

The woman's face lit up. "I'm a spirit guide. We exist to aid Channels." She glanced at the protective bubble that still surrounded them, and her smile grew impossibly wider. "Now, you must go back to my son. He's worried."

Dina nodded and counted to ten. She released her connection to the spirit world and opened her eyes. She was sitting cross-legged on the floor of the dining room. She blinked and allowed her eyes to adjust to the dimness. Night had fallen.

"You were out for almost four hours," Derek said. Concern creased his forehead. "Are you okay?"

Dina did inventory, tentatively straightening out her legs and rolling her shoulders. "I'm stiff but fine."

"And the girl?" he asked standing up, offering Dina his hand.

She took it and stood up. "She's gone." Derek held her hand a beat too long before releasing it.

"Good." His eyes roamed over her carefully as if not trusting that she was okay. "I was worried about you."

"Derek I..." Dina didn't know how to ask. "A guide showed up to help me."

His eyes widened in surprise, but he nodded and turned

away from her. "That's what they're for." She watched him as he started gathering up the candles.

"Who are they?"

He shrugged, and carefully placed items in the bag. "Sometimes they're loved ones that watch over you, and other times they come for a particular purpose. When we need them they step in to guard and protect us." Derek looked over his shoulder at her. "Why?"

"Just wondering. I've never seen one—didn't know they existed."

He zipped up the bag and then looked her in the eye. "My mother is one of mine. I have a few others, but she's always been there for me."

Dina nodded and started to say something, but Derek turned and walked away. She followed behind him as he locked up the house and gave her back the key. His shoulders were stiff, and he walked with a purpose as they headed toward the street. Richard's Porsche was gone.

"Where would you like me to take you?" he asked in a deadpan voice as they approached his car.

She could feel the wall Derek was trying to put between them. Dina would smash it apart with her bare hands if she had to. He looked so grim. He probably thought they were done and that she would leave him now that the house was cleansed. He was in for a rude awakening if he thought he was getting rid of her that easily. In all of her relationships, she had never once been introduced to someone's family. She had met Derek's mother after only three days.

He opened her door for her, and stashed the bag of candles in the floorboard of his car before turning to face her. His eyes were wary, but when Dina took a step forward and threw her arms around his neck, he caught her. Her lips brushed his ear. "I want to go wherever you're going."

When her lips touched his, it took him only a second to react. His grip around her tightened, and he pulled her closer. The heat from his body was a brand seared into her soul. His mouth softened against hers, and his lips were reverent as they stroked over her own. The tactile sensation of a simple kiss had never meant so much to her. This was right. She was exactly where she was supposed to be.

About the Author:

TJ Valour's invisible pet dinosaur landed her in the principal's office in second grade, and it was downhill from there. To protect her mental health she allows some of her crazy to bleed out onto the page. Having played on both sides of the law, TJ utilizes her experience in criminal justice when crafting fantastical urban stories. When she is not battling demons of deviance, she lives happily in Denver, Colorado with her husband and snaggle-toothed dog.

You can find TJ online at www.facebook.com/AuthorTJValour and on Twitter: @WolvesCanEatMe.

Charlie's Point of View
By Linda Berry

No Colfax anthology is complete without at least some reference to a fixture of retailing along that street that is of utmost importance to authors and readers alike. Linda's inspiration for this story is best shared after you read it, so it's included at the end. But as for how she came up with the idea:

I wanted to celebrate something besides the noir side of Colfax, and there sits The Tattered Cover! I tried to capture some of the rich texture of what takes place along the street.

Charlie's Point of View

Some people call me the man with the newspaper and hang around like they're waiting for me to finish reading and move so they can have my chair. Some call me Charlie and act like we're old friends, hunting all over the store until they can find me and say hello.

People are funny.

I've seen people who look like they couldn't afford a cup of coffee, let alone a book, come in day after day and get comfortable in one of those old arm chairs back in a corner where they hope nobody will notice, and keep at it, a few pages a day, day after day, until they read right through the book they're interested in. Maybe even some people with money in their pockets do that. Isn't that stealing?

This building used to be a theater. Did you know that? Maybe that's why I think of the big front window here as a stage. There's always a drama of some kind going on, believe you me, between the school across the street and the people coming and going from City Park, or just loafing along Colfax. The design etched into the window makes it hard to see through, so I have to make up some of the details. You never really know anybody else's story, though, so I don't mind. What I imagine might be more interesting than the truth. Not all the stories here are between the covers of books. A good story is a good story wherever it comes from, and this place is full of them.

For instance, there's this one woman who probably isn't as old as she looks who trudges by, going west in the morning, looking tired; trudging back east in the late afternoon looking almost dead. Maybe she's going to and from that bus stop down on Josephine. I figure her for a hard worker trying to keep her life together against a lot of bad breaks. Maybe she cleans house for somebody better off than she is, and she's supporting a no-good husband or a kid with a drug problem. Beat-down as she looks, faded and ragged and droopy like her clothes, there is something in her life that makes her keep going on. I like her.

Not all the drama is outside the store, either.

One day a couple of kids came in looking for the same hard-to-find book. And when I say hard to find, I mean *hard to find*. The staff here can find just about anything, but not fast enough for these two. We had just one copy and they both needed it right now! You know kids. They mess around and wait until deadline is right on them and then expect the universe to take care of them. They must have been looking for something more than just a book, too, because they worked out their problem by sitting side by side over there in the coffee shop and reading it together, talking about it and arguing and laughing. They left together. I've seen them several times since then. Now they come in together, usually holding hands. Must have been *some* book!

It's nice to think of books bringing people together in such a literal way, wouldn't you say?

That too sentimental, not dramatic enough for you? How about this? Happened across the street and involved some of those school kids. I know you can't tell a book by its cover, so I try to look past the tattoos and bizarre haircuts and clothes they ought to be ashamed of, and see the kids underneath. That school has a good arts program, so maybe some of the oddball stuff is their way of showing how creative they are. The students are called The Angels, probably supposed to give them something to live up to. A little unrealistic, if you ask me, which nobody did, but it strikes a better note than calling them the Vampires, which I hear are really popular these days.

The day it happened, I was just sitting here as usual, hiding behind my newspaper. I noticed a couple of women, what you'd probably call bag ladies, get into a situation. They looked just like you'd expect: Layers of clothes so old they might have been pulled out of a dumpster. Messy hair. Pokey, crouching, watchful gait, like they half expect somebody to jump out of a bush and attack. This isn't the worst stretch of Colfax, by any means, but people still need to be alert for trouble. Not that either one of these women looked like she had anything anybody would want. But one man's—or woman's—trash is another one's treasure, I've heard. You never know.

One of them was coming down Colfax from Josephine, pushing a wobbly old grocery cart, loaded with shopping bags, and a little dog up there in the basket. The other one had been poking around the columns with the statues there at the Esplanade, like she was looking for something. She was just sort of ambling and shambling, not paying attention, and she stumbled into the grocery cart.

Well, that set the cart woman off, waving her arms. Even from here I could tell she was yelling. It was such an over-reaction, like these two had been sworn enemies from childhood, that I started wondering if she was unbalanced and off her medication, or maybe if what looked like trash bags really did have something valuable inside, like drugs. Anyway, next thing I know, she hauled off and rammed the cart into the second woman, rammed her and kept on ramming her until she fell down right there in the street. The little dog either jumped or was thrown out of the cart and started running around, yapping his head off.

Excitement? Let me tell you! The woman in the street didn't get right back up, so one of those tattooed, wild-haired kids stood over her and started directing traffic around her, and a girl—I think it was a girl—bent down to see about her. I was thinking this was pretty good behavior for people who look like they do. Angels, maybe. All the while, the cart woman kept on having a fit, running this way and that way and waving her arms. She might have been trying to find her dog but all that commotion was probably scaring it off.

Meanwhile, somebody—some busybody maybe—must have called nine-one-one, because I started hearing sirens. First thing you know there were police cars and a fire truck and an ambulance screeching up. Maybe they stay on alert because of the school, but all I know is it didn't take them long to get here. So there's drama for you. Suspense. Was the fallen woman hurt, or worse? Would the cart-and-dog woman be arrested for assault, or murder? Would the dog run into traffic?

Now, here's where it got interesting.

Since I'm up here with what you could call a bird's eye view, I'm just about the only real witness to what happened, and what happened was that those two bag women disappeared. Right in front of my eyes. While she was doing all that arm waving and screaming, the cart-and-dog lady was peeling off some of those layers of clothes and a wig. She crammed them down into one of the bags in her cart. The girl who was helping the fallen woman was helping her out of her disguise, too, and that stuff went into the girl's backpack. They all have backpacks these days.

In half a minute, both those bag ladies turned into more-or-less normal-looking boys, whatever normal-looking means these days. They blended in with the other kids standing around looking bored like kids do, and a girl I hadn't noticed before scooped up the little dog and went off toward City Park with it. All those emergency responders stood there scratching their heads and wondering why they were there. They spent a while trying to talk to people who saw what had happened, but finally gave up. Besides, there obviously was nobody who needed help. Finally they went off, still scratching their heads. At least they got a good story for their trouble, something interesting to tell when somebody asked them how their day went.

The whole thing was so smooth—choreographed, you might say—that I finally decided it was some kind of guerrilla theater, where it's supposed to look like something real is happening but it's just a play. It could have been an exercise for a drama class that got out of hand. If that's what it was, I hope those Angels got good grades. Theater is supposed to be convincing, and this sure was.

Not every day is as exciting as that, but you just never know when a story will break out. All the world's a stage, and all those people making their entrances and exits are just players. Like you. Like me. Somebody smarter than I am said that first. I think it means we each have a role to play in this life and we need to get out there and play it.

Instead of just sitting here watching.

Linda Berry

You may recognize Charlie as the life-sized fiberglass and plaster sculpture that perpetually reads a newspaper at one or another of the Tattered Cover bookstores. He was modeled after Charlie Shugarts, who embraced the idea to the extent that he sometimes sat nearby in the same pose, confusing and delighting customers.

About the Author:

Linda Berry's published work includes short fiction for children and adults, some poetry, a newspaper entertainment column, preschool curriculum, and a few plays, in addition to her six Trudy Roundtree cozy mystery novels, which are set in Georgia and celebrate her southern roots and exploit a cousin whose career was law enforcement in that neck of the woods. She's a member of Colorado Dramatists, the Denver Woman's Press Club, as well as RMFW. She lives in Aurora, and she and her husband organize their lives around travel and theater.

About Rocky Mountain Fiction Writers

Rocky Mountain Fiction Writers (RMFW) is a non-profit, volunteer-run organization dedicated to supporting, encouraging, and educating writers seeking publication in commercial fiction. To that end, the organization strives to:

- Provide an environment of support and encouragement among members
- Stimulate interest in and appreciation for the art of writing
- Act as a dissemination point for information concerning commercial fiction writing
- Bring together authors, editors, agents, and other related professionals for the mutual benefit of all

RMFW hosts the Colorado Gold Writers Conference each September and sponsors an annual writers Contest for unpublished authors. We also sponsor critique groups, publish a newsletter, host monthly events on the craft and business of writing, and periodically publish an anthology of short fiction showcasing the talents of our members.

For more information, please visit www.rmfw.org.

CPSIA information can be obtained
at www.ICGtesting.com
Printed in the USA
LVHW031539080223
739012LV00001B/83